THE TRIALS OF

APOLLO

THE DARK PROPHECY

THE TRIALS OF

APOLLO

◀ 2 ▶

THE DARK PROPHECY

1

Lester (Apollo)
Still human; thanks for asking
Gods, I hate my life

WHEN OUR DRAGON declared war on Indiana, I knew it was going to be a bad day.

We'd been traveling west for six weeks, and Festus had never shown such hostility toward a state. New Jersey he ignored. Pennsylvania he seemed to enjoy, despite our battle with the Cyclopes of Pittsburgh. Ohio he tolerated, even after our encounter with Potina, the Roman goddess of childhood drinks, who pursued us in the form of a giant red pitcher emblazoned with a smiley face.

Yet for some reason, Festus decided he did not like Indiana. He landed on the cupola of the Indiana Statehouse, flapped his metallic wings, and blew a cone of fire that incinerated the state flag right off the flagpole.

"Whoa, buddy!" Leo Valdez pulled the dragon's reins. "We've talked about this. No blowtorching public monuments!"

Behind him on the dragon's spine, Calypso gripped Festus's scales for balance. "Could we *please* get to the ground? *Gently* this time?"

For a formerly immortal sorceress who once controlled

air spirits, Calypso was not a fan of flying. Cold wind blew her chestnut hair into my face, making me blink and spit.

That's right, dear reader.

I, the most important passenger, the youth who had once been the glorious god Apollo, was forced to sit in the back of the dragon. Oh, the indignities I had suffered since Zeus stripped me of my divine powers! It wasn't enough that I was now a sixteen-year-old mortal with the ghastly alias Lester Papadopoulos. It wasn't enough that I had to toil upon the earth doing (ugh) heroic quests until I could find a way back into my father's good graces, or that I had a case of acne which simply *would not* respond to over-the-counter zit medicine. Despite my New York State junior driver's license, Leo Valdez didn't trust me to operate his aerial bronze steed!

Festus's claws scrabbled for a hold on the green copper dome, which was much too small for a dragon his size. I had a flashback to the time I installed a life-size statue of the muse Calliope on my sun chariot and the extra weight of the hood ornament made me nosedive into China and create the Gobi Desert.

Leo glanced back, his face streaked with soot. "Apollo, you sense anything?"

"Why is it *my* job to sense things? Just because I used to be a god of prophecy—"

"You're the one who's been having visions," Calypso reminded me. "You said your friend Meg would be here."

Just hearing Meg's name gave me a twinge of pain. "That doesn't mean I can pinpoint her location with my mind! Zeus has revoked my access to GPS!"

"GPS?" Calypso asked.

"Godly positioning systems."

"That's not a real thing!"

"Guys, cool it." Leo patted the dragon's neck. "Apollo, just try, will you? Does this look like the city you dreamed about or not?"

I scanned the horizon.

Indiana was flat country—highways crisscrossing scrubby brown plains, shadows of winter clouds floating above urban sprawl. Around us rose a meager cluster of downtown high-rises—stacks of stone and glass like layered wedges of black and white licorice. (Not the yummy kind of licorice, either; the nasty variety that sits for eons in your stepmother's candy bowl on the coffee table. And, no, Hera, why would I be talking about you?)

After falling to earth in New York City, I found Indianapolis desolate and uninspiring, as if one proper New York neighborhood—Midtown, perhaps—had been stretched out to encompass the entire area of Manhattan, then relieved of two-thirds of its population and vigorously power-washed.

I could think of no reason why an evil triumvirate of ancient Roman emperors would take interest in such a location. Nor could I imagine why Meg McCaffrey would be sent here to capture me. Yet my visions had been clear. I had seen this skyline. I had heard my old enemy Nero give orders to Meg: Go west. Capture Apollo before he can find the next Oracle. If you cannot bring him to me alive, kill him.

The truly sad thing about this? Meg was one of my better friends. She also happened to be my demigod master, thanks to Zeus's twisted sense of humor. As long as I remained mortal, Meg could order me to do anything, even kill myself. . . . No. Better not to think of such possibilities.

I shifted in my metal seat. After so many weeks of travel, I was tired and saddle sore. I wanted to find a safe place to rest. *This* was not such a city. Something about the landscape below made me as restless as Festus.

Alas, I was sure this was where we were meant to be. Despite the danger, if I had a chance of seeing Meg McCaffrey again, of prying her away from her villainous stepfather's grasp, I had to try.

"This is the spot," I said. "Before this dome collapses under us, I suggest we get to the ground."

Calypso grumbled in ancient Minoan, "I already *said* that."

"Well, excuse me, sorceress!" I replied in the same language. "Perhaps if *you* had helpful visions, I'd listen to you more often!"

Calypso called me a few names that reminded me how colorful the Minoan language had been before it went extinct.

"Hey, you two," Leo said. "No ancient dialects. Spanish or English, please. Or Machine."

Festus creaked in agreement.

"It's okay, boy," Leo said. "I'm sure they didn't mean to exclude us. Now let's fly down to street level, huh?"

Festus's ruby eyes glowed. His metal teeth spun like drill bits. I imagined him thinking, *Illinois is sounding pretty good right about now.*

But he flapped his wings and leaped from the dome. We

hurtled downward, landing in front of the statehouse with enough force to crack the sidewalk. My eyeballs jiggled like water balloons.

Festus whipped his head from side to side, steam curling from his nostrils.

I saw no immediate threats. Cars drove leisurely down West Washington Street. Pedestrians strolled by: a middle-aged woman in a flowery dress, a heavyset policeman carrying a paper coffee cup labeled CAFÉ PATACHOU, a clean-cut man in a blue seersucker suit.

The man in blue waved politely as he passed. "Morning."

" 'Sup, dude," Leo called.

Calypso tilted her head. "Why was he so friendly? Does he not *see* that we're sitting atop a fifty-ton metal dragon?"

Leo grinned. "It's the Mist, babe—messes with mortal eyes. Makes monsters look like stray dogs. Makes swords look like umbrellas. Makes me look even more handsome than usual!"

Calypso jabbed her thumbs into Leo's kidneys.

"Ow!" he complained.

"I know what the Mist is, *Leonidas*—"

"Hey, I told you never to call me that."

"—but the Mist must be very strong here if it can hide a monster of Festus's size at such close range. Apollo, don't you find that a little odd?"

I studied the passing pedestrians.

True, I had seen places where the Mist was particularly heavy. At Troy, the sky above the battlefield had been so thick with gods you couldn't turn your chariot without running into another deity, yet the Trojans and Greeks saw only hints of our presence. At Three Mile Island in 1979, the mortals somehow failed to realize that their partial nuclear meltdown was caused by an epic chainsaw fight between Ares and Hephaestus. (As I recall, Hephaestus had insulted Ares's bell-bottom jeans.)

Still, I did not think heavy Mist was the problem here. Something about these locals bothered me. Their faces were too placid. Their dazed smiles reminded me of ancient Athenians just before the Dionysus Festival—everyone in a good mood, distracted, thinking about the drunken riots and debauchery to come.

"We should get out of the public eye," I suggested. "Perhaps—"

Festus stumbled, shaking like a wet dog. From inside his chest came a noise like a loose bicycle chain.

"Aw, not again," Leo said. "Everybody off!"

Calypso and I quickly dismounted.

Leo ran in front of Festus and held out his arms in a classic dragon-wrangler's stance. "Hey, buddy, it's fine! I'm just going to switch you off for a while, okay? A little down-time to—"

Festus projectile-vomited a column of flames that engulfed Leo. Fortunately, Valdez was fireproof. His clothes were not. From what Leo had told me, he could generally prevent his outfits from burning up simply by concentrating. If he were caught by surprise, however, it didn't always work.

When the flames dissipated, Leo stood before us wearing nothing but his asbestos boxer shorts, his magical tool belt, and a pair of smoking, partially melted sneakers.

"Dang it!" he complained. "Festus, it's cold out here!"

The dragon stumbled. Leo lunged and flipped the lever behind the dragon's left foreleg. Festus began to collapse. His wings, limbs, neck, and tail contracted into his body, his bronze plates overlapping and folding inward. In a matter of seconds, our robotic friend had been reduced to a large bronze suitcase.

That should have been physically impossible, of course, but like any decent god, demigod, or engineer, Leo Valdez refused to be stopped by the laws of physics.

He scowled at his new piece of luggage. "Man . . . I *thought* I fixed his gyro-capacitor. Guess we're stuck here until I can find a machine shop."

Calypso grimaced. Her pink ski jacket glistened with condensation from our flight through the clouds. "And if we find such a shop, how long will it take to repair Festus?"

Leo shrugged. "Twelve hours? Fifteen?" He pushed a button on the side of the suitcase. A handle popped up. "Also, if we see a men's clothing store, that might be good."

I imagined walking into a T.J. Maxx, Leo in boxer shorts and melted sneakers, rolling a bronze suitcase behind him. I did not relish the idea.

Then, from the direction of the sidewalk, a voice called, "Hello!"

The woman in the flowery dress had returned. At least she *looked* like the same woman. Either that or lots of ladies in Indianapolis wore purple-and-yellow honeysuckle-pattern dresses and had 1950s bouffant hairstyles.

She smiled vacantly. "Beautiful morning!"

It was in fact a miserable morning—cold and cloudy

with a smell of impending snow—but I felt it would be rude to ignore her completely.

I gave her a little parade wave—the sort of gesture I used to give my worshippers when they came to grovel at my altar. To me, the message was clear enough: *I see you, puny mortal; now run along. The gods are talking.*

The woman did not take the hint. She strolled forward and planted herself in front of us. She wasn't particularly large, but something about her proportions seemed off. Her shoulders were too wide for her head. Her chest and belly protruded in a lumpy mass, as if she'd stuffed a sack of mangos down the front of her dress. With her spindly arms and legs, she reminded me of some sort of giant beetle. If she ever tipped over, I doubted she could easily get back up.

"Oh, my!" She gripped her purse with both hands. "Aren't you children *cute!*"

Her lipstick and eye shadow were both a violent shade of purple. I wondered if she was getting enough oxygen to her brain.

"Madam," I said, "we are not children." I could have added that I was over four thousand years old, and Calypso was even older, but I decided not to get into that. "Now, if you'll excuse us, we have a suitcase to repair and my friend is in dire need of a pair of pants."

I tried to step around her. She blocked my path.

"You can't go yet, dear! We haven't welcomed you to Indiana!" From her purse, she drew a smartphone. The screen glowed as if a call were already in progress.

"It's him, all right," she said into the phone. "Everybody, come on over. Apollo is here!"

My lungs shriveled in my chest.

In the old days, I would have expected to be recognized as soon as I arrived in a town. *Of course* the locals would rush to welcome me. They would sing and dance and throw flowers. They would immediately begin constructing a new temple.

But as Lester Papadopoulos, I did not warrant such treatment. I looked nothing like my former glorious self. The idea that the Indianans might recognize me despite my tangled hair, acne, and flab was both insulting and terrifying. What if they erected a statue of me in my present form—a giant golden Lester in the center of their city? The other gods would never let me hear the end of it!

"Madam," I said, "I'm afraid you have mistaken me—"

"Don't be modest!" The woman tossed her phone and purse aside. She grabbed my forearm with the strength of a weightlifter. "Our master will be delighted to have you in custody. And please call me Nanette."

Calypso charged. Either she wished to defend me (unlikely), or she was not a fan of the name Nanette. She punched the woman in the face.

This by itself did not surprise me. Having lost her immortal powers, Calypso was in the process of trying to master other skills. So far, she'd failed at swords, polearms, shurikens, whips, and improvisational comedy. (I sympathized with her frustration.) Today, she'd decided to try fisticuffs.

What surprised me was the loud CRACK her fist made against Nanette's face—the sound of finger bones breaking.

"Ow!" Calypso stumbled away, clutching her hand.

Nanette's head slid backward. She released me to try to grab her own face, but it was too late. Her head toppled off her shoulders. It clanged against the pavement and rolled sideways, the eyes still blinking, the purple lips twitching. Its base was smooth stainless steel. Attached to it were ragged strips of duct tape stuck with hair and bobby pins.

"Holy Hephaestus!" Leo ran to Calypso's side. "Lady, you broke my girlfriend's hand with your face. What *are* you, an automaton?"

"No, dear," said decapitated Nanette. Her muffled voice didn't come from the stainless-steel head on the sidewalk. It emanated from somewhere inside her dress. Just above her collar, where her neck used to be, an outcropping of fine blond hair was tangled with bobby pins. "And I must say, hitting me wasn't very polite."

Belatedly, I realized the metal head had been a disguise. Just as satyrs covered their hooves with human shoes, this creature passed for mortal by pretending to have a human face. Its voice came from its gut area, which meant . . .

My knees trembled.

"A *blemmyae*," I said.

Nanette chuckled. Her bulging midsection writhed under the honeysuckle cloth. She ripped open her blouse—something a polite Midwesterner would never think of doing—and revealed her true face.

Where a woman's brassiere would have been, two enormous bulging eyes blinked at me. From her sternum protruded a large shiny nose. Across her abdomen curled a hideous mouth—glistening orange lips, teeth like a spread of blank white playing cards.

"Yes, dear," the face said. "And I'm arresting you in the name of the Triumvirate!"

Up and down Washington Street, pleasant-looking pedestrians turned and began marching in our direction.

2

Headless guys and gals
Not loving the Midwest vibe
Oh, look—a cheese ghost

GEE, APOLLO, you may be thinking, *why didn't you sim-*
ply pull out your bow and shoot her? Or charm her with a song
from your combat ukulele?

True, I had both those items slung across my back along
with my quiver. Sadly, even the best demigod weapons
require something called *maintenance.* My children Kayla
and Austin had explained this to me before I left Camp
Half-Blood. I couldn't just pull my bow and quiver out of
thin air as I used to when I was a god. I could no longer
wish my ukulele into my hands and expect it to be perfectly
in tune.

My weapons and my musical instrument were carefully
wrapped in blankets. Otherwise flying through the wet winter skies would've warped the bow, ruined the arrows, and
played Hades with the strings of my ukulele. To get them
out now would require several minutes that I did not have.

Also, I doubted they would do me much good against
blemmyae.

I hadn't dealt with their kind since the time of Julius

Caesar, and I would've been happy to go another two thousand years without seeing one.

How could a god of poetry and music be effective against a species whose ears were wedged under their armpits? Nor did the blemmyae fear or respect archery. They were sturdy melee fighters with thick skin. They were even resistant to most forms of disease, which meant they never called on me for medical help nor feared my plague arrows. Worst of all, they were humorless and unimaginative. They had no interest in the future, so they saw no use for Oracles or prophecies.

In short, you could not *create* a race less sympathetic to an attractive, multitalented god like me. (And believe me, Ares had tried. Those eighteenth-century Hessian mercenaries he cooked up? Ugh. George Washington and I had the *worst* time with them.)

"Leo," I said, "activate the dragon."

"I just put him into sleep cycle."

"Hurry!"

Leo fumbled with the suitcase's buttons. Nothing happened. "I told you, man. Even if Festus weren't malfunctioning, he's *really* hard to wake up once he's asleep."

Wonderful, I thought. Calypso hunched over her broken hand, muttering Minoan obscenities. Leo shivered in his underwear. And I . . . well, I was *Lester*. On top of all that, instead of facing our enemies with a large fire-breathing automaton, we would now have to face them with a barely portable piece of metal luggage.

I wheeled on the blemmyae. "BEGONE, foul Nanette!"

I tried to muster my old *godly wrath* voice. "Lay hands upon my divine person again and you shall be DESTROYED!"

Back when I was a god, that threat would have been enough to make entire armies wet their camouflage pants. Nanette just blinked her cow-brown eyes.

"Don't fuss, now," she said. Her lips were grotesquely hypnotic, like watching a surgical incision being used as a puppet. "Besides, dearie, you're not a god anymore."

Why did people have to keep reminding me of that?

More locals converged on our position. Two police officers trotted down the steps of the statehouse. At the corner of Senate Avenue, a trio of sanitation workers abandoned their garbage truck and lumbered over wielding large metal trash cans. From the other direction, a half dozen men in business suits tromped across the capitol lawn.

Leo cursed. "Is everybody in this town a metalhead? And I don't mean the *good* kind of metalhead."

"Relax, sweetie," Nanette said. "Surrender and we won't have to hurt you much. That's the emperor's job!"

Despite her broken hand, Calypso apparently didn't feel like surrendering. With a defiant yell she charged Nanette again, this time launching a karate kick toward the blemmyae's giant nose.

"Don't!" I blurted out, too late.

As I mentioned, blemmyae are sturdy beings. They're difficult to hurt and even more difficult to kill. Calypso's foot connected with its target, and her ankle bent with a nasty *pop*. She collapsed, gurgling in pain.

"Cal!" Leo ran to her side. "Back off, chest-face!"

"Language, dear," Nanette chided. "Now I'm afraid I'll have to stomp on you."

She raised one patent leather pump, but Leo was faster. He summoned a globe of fire and threw it like a baseball, hitting Nanette right between her huge chest-level eyes. Flames washed over her, setting her eyebrows and flowery dress ablaze.

As Nanette screamed and stumbled, Leo yelled, "Apollo, help me!"

I realized I'd been standing there, frozen in shock—which would've been fine if I'd been watching the scene unfold from the safety of my throne on Mount Olympus. Alas, I was very much down here in the trenches with the lesser beings. I helped get Calypso to her feet (her one good foot, at least). We slung her arms over our shoulders (with lots of screaming from Calypso when I accidentally grabbed her broken hand) and began hobbling away.

Thirty feet across the lawn, Leo suddenly stopped. "I forgot Festus!"

"Leave him," I snapped.

"What?"

"We can't manage him and Calypso! We'll come back later. The blemmyae might just ignore him."

"But if they figure out how to open him," Leo fretted, "if they hurt him—"

"MARRRGGGGH!" Behind us, Nanette ripped off the shreds of her burning dress. From the waist down, shaggy blond fur covered her body, not unlike a satyr. Her eyebrows smoldered, but otherwise her face looked unhurt. She spat ashes from her mouth and glared in our direction. "That was *not* nice! GET THEM!"

The businessmen were almost on top of us, eliminating any hope that we could make it back to Festus without getting caught.

We chose the only heroic option available: we ran.

I hadn't felt so encumbered since my three-legged death race with Meg McCaffrey back at Camp Half-Blood. Calypso tried to help, kicking along like a pogo stick between Leo and me, but whenever she jostled her broken foot or hand, she yelped and sagged against us.

"S-sorry, guys," she muttered, her face beaded with sweat. "Guess I'm not meant to be a melee fighter."

"Neither am I," I admitted. "Perhaps Leo can hold them off while—"

"Hey, don't look at me," Leo grumbled. "I'm just a repair guy who can throw the occasional fireball. Our fighter is stuck back there in suitcase mode."

"Hobble faster," I suggested.

We reached the street alive only because the blemmyae moved so slowly. I suppose I would, too, if I were balancing a fake metal head on my, er, head, but even without their disguises, the blemmyae were not as swift as they were strong. Their terrible depth perception made them walk with exaggerated caution, as if the ground were a multi-layered hologram. If only we could out-hobble them . . .

"Good morning!" A police officer appeared on our right, his firearm drawn. "Halt or I will shoot! Thank you!"

Leo pulled a stoppered glass bottle from his tool belt.

He tossed it at the officer's feet and green flames exploded around him. The officer dropped his gun. He began tearing off his burning uniform, revealing a chest-face with shaggy pectoral eyebrows and a belly beard in need of a shave.

"Phew," Leo said. "I was *hoping* he was a blemmyae. That was my only vial of Greek fire, guys. And I can't keep summoning fireballs unless I want to pass out, so—"

"We need to find cover," said Calypso.

Sensible advice, but *cover* did not seem to be an Indiana concept. The streets were wide and straight, the landscape flat, the crowds sparse, the sight lines endless.

We turned onto South Capitol. I glanced over my shoulder and saw the mob of smiling fake-headed locals gaining on us. A construction worker stopped to rip the fender off a Ford pickup, then rejoined the parade, his new chrome club slung over his shoulder.

Meanwhile, the regular mortals—at least, those who did not seem interested in killing us at the moment—went about their business, making phone calls, waiting at traffic lights, sipping coffee in nearby cafés, completely ignoring us. At one corner, sitting on a milk crate, a heavily blanketed homeless man asked me for change. I resisted the urge to tell him that change was coming up fast behind us, carrying assorted weapons.

My heart pounded. My legs shook. I hated having a mortal body. I experienced so many bothersome things, like fear, cold, nausea, and the impulse to whimper *Please don't kill me!* If only Calypso hadn't broken her ankle we might have moved faster, but we couldn't very well leave her behind. Not that I particularly liked Calypso, mind you, but I'd already convinced Leo to abandon his dragon. I didn't want to push my luck.

"There!" said the sorceress. She pointed with her chin to what looked like a service alley behind a hotel.

I shuddered, remembering my first day in New York as Lester Papadopoulos. "What if it's a dead end? The last time I found myself in a dead-end alley, things did not go well."

"Let's try," Leo said. "We might be able to hide in there, or . . . I dunno."

I *dunno* sounded like a sketchy plan B, but I had nothing better to offer.

Good news: the alley was not a dead end. I could clearly see an exit at the far end of the block. Bad news: the loading bays along the back of the hotel were locked, giving us nowhere to hide, and the opposite wall of the alley was lined with Dumpsters. Oh, Dumpsters! How I hated them!

Leo sighed. "I guess we could jump in—"

"No!" I snapped. "Never again!"

We struggled through the alley as fast as we could. I tried to calm my nerves by silently composing a sonnet about various ways a wrathful god could destroy Dumpsters. I became so engrossed I didn't notice what was in front of us until Calypso gasped.

Leo halted. "What the—? *Hijo.*"

The apparition glowed with a faint ginger light. He wore a traditional chiton, sandals, and a sheathed sword, like a Greek warrior in the prime of life . . . except for the fact that he had been decapitated. Unlike the blemmyae, however, this person obviously had once been human.

Ethereal blood trickled from his severed neck, splattering his luminous orange tunic.

"It's a cheese-colored ghost," Leo said.

The spirit raised one hand, beckoning us forward.

Not being born a mortal, I had no particular fear of the dead. You've seen one tormented soul, you've seen them all. But something about this ghost unsettled me. He stirred a distant memory, a feeling of guilt from thousands of years ago. . . .

Behind us, the voices of the blemmyae grew louder. I heard them calling out "Morning!" and "Excuse me!" and "Lovely day!" to their fellow Indianans.

"What do we do?" Calypso asked.

"Follow the ghost," I said.

"What?" Leo yelped.

"We follow the cheese-colored ghost. As you're always saying: *Vaya con queso.*"

"That was a joke, *ese.*"

The orange spirit beckoned again, then floated toward the end of the alley.

Behind us, a man's voice shouted, "There you are! Lovely weather, isn't it?"

I turned in time to see a truck fender spiraling toward us.

"Down!" I tackled Calypso and Leo, provoking more screams of agony from the sorceress. The truck fender sailed over our heads and slammed into a Dumpster, sending up a festive explosion of garbage confetti.

We struggled to our feet. Calypso was shivering, no longer complaining about the pain. I was fairly sure she was going into shock.

Leo pulled a staple gun from his tool belt. "You guys go ahead. I'll hold them off as long as I can."

"What are you going to do?" I demanded. "Sort and collate them?"

"I'm going to throw things at them!" Leo snapped. "Unless you've got a better idea?"

"B-both of you stop," Calypso stammered. "We d-don't leave anyone behind. Now walk. Left, right, left, right."

We emerged from the alley into a wide-open circular plaza. Oh, why couldn't Indianans build a proper city with narrow, twisting streets, plenty of dark corners, and perhaps some conveniently placed bombproof bunkers?

In the middle of a ring-shaped drive stood a fountain surrounded by dormant flower beds. To the north rose the twin towers of another hotel. To the south loomed an older, grander building of redbrick and granite—perhaps a Victorian-era train station. On one side of the edifice, a clock tower soared roughly two hundred feet into the sky. Above the main entrance, under a marble archway, a colossal rose window gleamed in a frame of green copper, like a stained-glass version of the dartboard we used for our weekly game night on Mount Olympus.

That thought made me heartsick with nostalgia. I would've given anything to be back home for game night, even if it meant listening to Athena gloat about her Scrabble scores.

I scanned the plaza. Our ghostly guide seemed to have disappeared.

Why had he brought us here? Should we try the hotel? The train station?

Those questions became moot when the blemmyae surrounded us.

The mob burst out of the alley behind us. A police car swerved into the roundabout next to the train station. A bulldozer pulled into the hotel's driveway, the operator waving and calling out cheerfully, "Hello! I'm going to bulldoze you!"

All exits from the plaza were quickly blocked.

A line of sweat freeze-dried against my neck. An annoying whine filled my ears, which I realized was my own subvocalized whimpering of *Please don't kill me, please don't kill me.*

I won't die here, I promised myself. *I'm much too important to bite it in Indiana.*

But my trembling legs and chattering teeth seemed to disagree.

"Who has an idea?" I asked my compatriots. "Please, any brilliant idea."

Calypso looked like her most brilliant idea at the moment was trying not to throw up. Leo hefted his staple gun, which didn't seem to frighten the blemmyae.

From the midst of the mob, our old friend Nanette emerged, her chest-face grinning. Her patent leather pumps clashed terribly with her blond leg fur. "Gosh darn it, dears, you've made me a bit miffed."

She grabbed the nearest street sign and single-handedly ripped it out of the ground. "Now, please hold still, won't you? I'm just going to smash your heads with this."

3

My last performance
Some old lady drops the mic
And kills everyone

I WAS ABOUT TO INITIATE Defense Plan Omega—falling to my knees and begging for mercy—when Leo saved me from that embarrassment.

"Bulldozer," he whispered.

"Is that a code word?" I asked.

"No. I'm going to sneak over to the bulldozer. You two distract the metalheads."

He shifted Calypso's weight to me.

"Are you crazy?" she hissed.

Leo shot her an urgent look, like *Trust me! Distract them!* Then he took a careful step sideways.

"Oh!" Nanette beamed. "Are you volunteering to die first, short demigod? You did hit me with fire, so that makes sense."

Whatever Leo had in mind, I imagined his plan would fail if he began arguing with Nanette about his height. (Leo was a bit sensitive about being called *short*.) Fortunately, I have a natural talent for focusing everyone's attention on me.

"I volunteer for death!" I shouted.

THE DARK PROPHECY 25

The policeman huffed impatiently. "We know all this. The emperor told us."

"Shh," said Nanette. "Be polite."

I put my hand over my heart. "We secured the Grove of Dodona, an ancient Oracle, and thwarted the plans of Nero! But alas, Meg McCaffrey fled from me. Her evil step-father had poisoned her mind!"

"Poison!" Calypso cried. "Like the breath of Lester Papadopoulos, most worthless of teens!"

I resisted the urge to push Calypso into the flower bed.

Meanwhile, Leo was making his way toward the bull-dozer under the guise of an interpretive dance routine, spinning and gasping and pantomiming my words. He looked like a hallucinating ballerina in boxer shorts, but the blemmyae politely got out of his way.

"Lo!" I shouted. "From the Oracle of Dodona we received a prophecy—a limerick most terrible!"

"Terrible!" Calypso chorused. "Like the skills of Lester, most worthless of teens."

"Vary your adjectives," I grumbled, then continued for my audience: "We traveled west in search of another Oracle, along the way fighting many fearsome foes! The Cyclopes we brought low!"

Leo jumped onto the running board of the bulldozer. He raised his staple gun dramatically, then stapled the bulldozer operator twice in the pectorals—right where his actual eyes would be. That could *not* have felt good—even for a tough species such as the blemmyae. The operator screamed and grabbed his chest. Leo kicked him out of the driver's seat.

The police officer yelled, "Hey!"

"Wait!" I implored them. "Our friend is only giving you a dramatic interpretation of how we beat the Cyclopes. That's totally allowed while telling a story!"

The crowd shifted uncertainly.

"These are very long last words," Nanette complained. "When will I get to smash your head in?"

"Soon," I promised. "Now, as I was saying . . . we traveled west!"

I hauled Calypso to her feet again with much whimpering on her part (and a little bit on mine).

"What are you doing?" she muttered.

"Work with me," I said. "Lo, frenemies! Behold how we traveled!"

The two of us staggered toward the bulldozer. Leo's hands flew over the controls. The engine roared to life.

"This isn't a story!" the police officer protested. "They're getting away!"

"No, not at all!" I pushed Calypso onto the bulldozer and climbed up after her. "You see, we traveled for many weeks like this. . . ."

Leo started backing up. *Beep. Beep. Beep.* The bulldozer's shovel began to rise.

"Imagine you are Camp Half-Blood," I shouted to the crowd, "and we are traveling away from you."

I realized my mistake. I had asked the blemmyae to imagine. They simply weren't capable of that.

"Stop them!" The police officer raised his gun. His first shot ricocheted off the dozer's metal scoop.

"Listen, my friends!" I implored. "Open your armpits!"

But we had exhausted their politeness. A trash can

sailed over our heads. A businessman picked up a decorative stone urn from the corner of the fountain and tossed it in our direction, annihilating the hotel's front window.

"Faster!" I told Leo.

"Trying, man," he muttered. "This thing wasn't built for speed."

The blemmyae closed in.

"Look out!" Calypso yelled.

Leo swerved just in time to deflect a wrought-iron bench off our dozer blade. Unfortunately, that opened us up to a different attack. Nanette threw her street sign like a harpoon. The metal pole pierced the bulldozer's chassis in a burst of steam and grease, and our getaway ride shuddered to a halt.

"Great," Calypso said. "Now what?"

This would have been an excellent time for my godly strength to return. I could have waded into battle, tossing my enemies aside like rag dolls. Instead, my bones seemed to liquefy and pool in my shoes. My hands shook so badly I doubted I could unwrap my bow even if I tried. Oh, that my glorious life should end this way—crushed by polite headless people in the American Midwest!

Nanette leaped onto the hood of our bulldozer, giving me a ghastly view straight up her nostrils. Leo tried to blast her with flames, but this time Nanette was prepared. She opened her mouth and swallowed the fireball, showing no sign of distress except for a small burp.

"Don't feel too bad, dears," she told us. "You never would have gained access to the blue cave. The emperor has it too well guarded! A shame you have to die, though. The naming celebration is in three days, and you and the girl were supposed to be the main attractions in his slave procession!"

I was too terrified to fully process her words. *The girl . . .* Did she mean Meg? Otherwise I heard only *blue—die— slave*, which at the moment seemed an accurate summary of my existence.

I knew it was hopeless, but I slipped my bow from my shoulder and began to unwrap it. Suddenly an arrow sprouted between Nanette's eyes. She went cross-eyed trying to see it, then tumbled backward and crumbled to dust.

I stared at my blanketed weapon. I was a fast archer, yes. But I was fairly sure I hadn't fired that shot.

A shrill whistle caught my attention. In the middle of the plaza, standing atop the fountain, a woman crouched in faded jeans and a silvery winter coat. A white birch bow gleamed in her hand. On her back, a quiver bristled with arrows. My heart leaped, thinking that my sister Artemis had come to help me at last! But no . . . this woman was at least sixty years old, her gray hair tied back in a bun. Artemis would never appear in such a form.

For reasons she had never shared with me, Artemis had an aversion to looking any older than, say, twenty. I'd told her countless times that beauty was ageless. All the Olympian fashion magazines will tell you that four thousand is the new one thousand, but she simply wouldn't listen.

The gray-haired woman shouted, "Hit the pavement!"

All around the plaza, manhole-size circles appeared in the asphalt. Each one scissored open like the iris of a camera and turrets sprang up—mechanical crossbows swiveling and sweeping red targeting lasers in every direction.

The blemmyae didn't try to take cover. Perhaps they didn't understand. Perhaps they were waiting for the gray-haired woman to say *please.*

I, however, didn't need to be an archery god to know what would happen next. I tackled my friends for the second time that day. (Which, in retrospect, I have to admit felt a wee bit satisfying.) We tumbled off the bulldozer as the crossbows fired in a flurry of sharp hisses.

When I dared to raise my head, nothing was left of the blemmyae but piles of dust and clothing.

The gray-haired woman jumped from the top of the fountain. Given her age, I was afraid she might break her ankles, but she landed gracefully and strolled toward us, her bow at her side.

Wrinkles were etched across her face. The skin under her chin had begun to sag. Liver spots dotted the backs of her hands. Nevertheless, she held herself with the regal confidence of a woman who had nothing left to prove to anyone. Her eyes flashed like moonlight on water. Something about those eyes was very familiar to me.

She studied me for a count of five, then shook her head in amazement. "So it's true. You're Apollo."

Her tone was not the general *Oh, wow, Apollo!* sort of attitude I was used to. She said my name as if she knew me personally.

"H-have we met?"

"You don't remember me," she said. "No, I don't suppose you would. Call me Emmie. And the ghost you saw—that was Agamethus. He led you to our doorstep."

The name Agamethus definitely sounded familiar, but

as usual, I couldn't place it. My human brain just kept giving that annoying *memory full* message, asking me to delete
a few centuries of experiences before I could continue.

Emmie glanced at Leo. "Why are you in your underwear?"

Leo sighed. "Been a long morning, *abuela*, but thanks
for the assist. Those crossbow turrets are the bomb-diggity."

"Thank you. . . . I think."

"Yeah, so maybe you could help us with Cal here?" Leo
continued. "She's not doing so well."

Emmie crouched next to Calypso, whose complexion
had turned the color of cement. The sorceress's eyes were
shut, her breathing ragged.

"She's badly hurt." Emmie frowned as she studied
Calypso's face. "You said her name was Cal?"

"Calypso," Leo said.

"Ah." Emmie's worry lines deepened. "That explains it.
She looks so much like Zoë."

A knife twisted inside me. "Zoë Nightshade?"

In her feverish state, Calypso muttered something I
couldn't make out . . . perhaps the name *Nightshade*.

For centuries, Zoë had been Artemis's lieutenant, the
leader of her Hunters. She'd died in battle just a few years
ago. I didn't know if Calypso and Zoë had ever met, but
they *were* half sisters—both daughters of the Titan Atlas.
I'd never considered how much they looked alike.

I regarded Emmie. "If you knew Zoë, then you must be
one of my sister's Hunters. But you can't be. You're . . ."

I stopped myself before I could say *old and dying*. Hunters neither aged nor died, unless they were killed in combat.
This woman was quite obviously mortal. I could sense her

fading life energy . . . so depressingly like mine; not at all like an immortal being's. It's hard to explain how I could tell, but it was perfectly clear to me—like hearing the difference between a perfect fifth and a diminished fifth.

In the distance, emergency sirens wailed. I realized we were having this conversation in the middle of a small disaster zone. Mortals, or more blemmyae, would soon be arriving.

Emmie snapped her fingers. All around the plaza, the crossbow turrets retracted. The portals closed as if they'd never existed.

"We need to get off the street," Emmie said. "Come, I'll take you into the Waystation."

4

No building should be
A secret from Apollo
Or drop bricks on him

WE DIDN'T HAVE TO GO FAR.

Carrying Calypso between us, Leo and I followed Emmie to the big ornate building at the plaza's south end. As I suspected, it was a railroad depot at some point. Carved in granite under the rose window were the words UNION STATION.

Emmie ignored the main entrance. She veered right and stopped in front of a wall. She ran her finger between the bricks, tracing the shape of a doorway. Mortar cracked and dissolved. A newly cut door swung inward, revealing a narrow chute like a chimney with metal rungs leading up.

"Nice trick," Leo said, "but Calypso's not exactly in wall-climbing condition."

Emmie knit her brow. "You're right." She faced the doorway. "Waystation, can we have a ramp, please?"

The metal rungs vanished. With a soft rumble, the chute's interior wall slanted backward, the bricks rearranging themselves into a gentle upward slope.

"Whoa," said Leo. "Did you just talk to the building?"

A smile tugged at the corner of Emmie's mouth. "The Waystation is more than a building."

Suddenly, I did not fancy the look of that ramp. "This is a living structure? Like the Labyrinth? And you expect us to go *inside?*"

Emmie's glance was definitely the look of a Hunter. Only my sister's followers would dare to give me such a malodorous stink-eye. "The Waystation is no work of Daedalus, Lord Apollo. It's perfectly safe . . . as long as you remain our guests."

Her tone suggested that my welcome was probationary. Behind us, the emergency sirens grew louder. Calypso inhaled raggedly. I decided we didn't have much choice. We followed Emmie into the building.

Lighting appeared along the walls—warm yellow candles flickering in bronze sconces. About twenty feet up the ramp, a door opened on our left. Inside, I glimpsed an infirmary that would've made my son Asclepius jealous: A fully stocked supply cabinet with medicine, surgical tools, and potion ingredients; a hospital bed with built-in monitors, GCI interface, and levitating bariatric slings. Racks of healing herbs dried against the wall next to the portable MRI machine. And in the back corner, a glassed-in habitat seethed with poisonous snakes.

"Oh, my," I said. "Your med bay is cutting-edge."

"Yes," Emmie agreed. "And Waystation is telling me I should treat your friend immediately."

Leo poked his head into the infirmary. "You mean this room just *appeared* here?"

"No," Emmie said. "Well, yes. It's always here, but . . . it's easier to find when we need it."

Leo nodded thoughtfully. "You think the Waystation could organize my sock drawer?"

A brick fell from the ceiling and clunked at Leo's feet.

"That's a *no*," Emmie interpreted. "Now, if I can have your friend, please."

"Uh . . ." Leo pointed to the glass habitat. "You got snakes in there. Just saying."

"I'll take good care of Calypso," Emmie promised.

She took Calypso from us, lifting the sorceress in her arms with no apparent difficulty. "You two go ahead. You'll find Jo at the top of the ramp."

"Jo?" I asked.

"You can't miss her," Emmie promised. "She'll explain the Waystation better than I could."

She carried the sorceress into the infirmary. The door shut behind her.

Leo frowned at me. "Snakes?"

"Oh, yes," I assured him. "There's a reason a snake on a rod symbolizes medicine. Venom was one of the earliest cures."

"Huh." Leo glanced at his feet. "You think I can keep this brick, at least?"

The corridor rumbled.

"I would leave it there," I suggested.

"Yeah, think I'll leave it there."

After a few more feet, another door opened on our right.

Inside, sunlight filtered through pink lace curtains onto the hardwood floor of a child's room. A cozy bed was piled with fluffy comforters, pillows, and stuffed animals. The eggshell-colored walls had been used as a canvas for crayon art—stick-figure people, trees, houses, frolicking animals that might have been dogs or horses or llamas. On the left-hand wall, opposite the bed, a crayon sun smiled down on a field of happy crayon flowers. In the center, a stick-figure girl stood between two larger parental stick figures—all three of them holding hands.

The wall art reminded me of Rachel Elizabeth Dare's cavern of prophecy at Camp Half-Blood. My Delphic Oracle had delighted in painting her cave with things she'd seen in her visions . . . before her oracular power ceased to work, that is. (Totally not my fault. You can blame that overgrown rat snake, Python.)

Most of the drawings in this bedroom seemed typical for a child of about seven or eight. But in the farthest corner of the back wall, the young artist had decided to inflict a nightmarish plague upon her crayon world. A scribbly black storm was brewing. Frowning stick figures threatened the llamas with triangular knives. Dark curlicues blotted out a primary-colored rainbow. Scratched over the field of green grass was a huge inky sphere like a black pond . . . or the entrance of a cave.

Leo stepped back. "I dunno, man. Don't think we should go in."

I wondered why the Waystation had decided to show us this room. Who lived here? Or more accurately . . . who *had* lived here? Despite the cheerful pink curtains and the pile of stuffed animals on the carefully made bed, the bedroom felt abandoned, preserved like a museum exhibit.

"Let's keep going," I agreed.

Finally, at the top of the ramp, we emerged into a cathedral-like hall. Overhead curved a barreled ceiling of wood carvings, with glowing stained-glass panels in the center creating green and gold geometric designs. At the far end of the room, the rose window I'd seen outside cast dartboard-line shadows across the painted cement floor. To our left and right, there were raised walkways with wrought-iron railings, and elegant Victorian lampposts lined the walls. Behind the railings, rows of doorways led into other rooms. Half a dozen ladders stretched up to the ornate molding at the base of the ceiling, where the ledges were stuffed with hay-like roosts for very large chickens. The whole place had a faint animal scent . . . though it reminded me more of a dog kennel than a henhouse.

In one corner of the main room gleamed a chef's kitchen big enough to host several celebrity cook-offs at once. Sets of sofas and comfy chairs were clustered here and there. At the center of the hall stood a massive dining table of rough-hewn redwood with seating for twenty.

Under the rose window, the contents of several different workshops seemed to have been disgorged at random: table saws, drills, lathes, kilns, forges, anvils, 3-D printers, sewing machines, cauldrons, and several other industrial appliances I couldn't name. (Don't judge me. I'm not Hephaestus.)

Hunched over a welding station, throwing sparks from her torch as she worked on a sheet of metal, was a muscular woman in a metal visor, leather apron, and gloves.

I'm not sure how she noticed us. Perhaps the Waystation chucked a brick at her back to get her attention. Whatever the case, she looked in our direction, shut off her torch, then lifted her visor.

"I'll be hexed!" She barked out a laugh. "Is that *Apollo?*"

She tugged off her safety gear and lumbered over. Like Emmie, the woman was in her sixties, but whereas Emmie had the physique of a former gymnast, this woman was built for brawling. Her broad shoulders and dark, well-sculpted arms stretched against the confines of a faded pink polo shirt. Wrenches and screwdrivers sagged from the pockets of her denim overalls. Against the umber skin of her scalp, her buzz-cut gray hair shimmered like frost.

She thrust out her hand. "You probably don't remember me, Lord Apollo. I'm Jo. Or Josie. Or Josephine. Whichever."

With each version of her name, she squeezed my hand tighter. I would not have challenged her to an arm-wrestling contest (though with her meaty fingers I doubt she could play guitar as well as I do, so *ha*). Her square-jawed face would've been quite intimidating except for her cheerful, twinkling eyes. Her mouth twitched as if she were exerting a great effort not to bust out laughing.

"Yes," I squeaked, extracting my hand. "I mean, no. I'm afraid I don't remember. May I introduce Leo?"

"Leo!" She crushed his hand with enthusiasm. "I'm Jo."

All these people whose names ended in *o*—*Jo, Leo, Calypso, Apollo*—suddenly made me feel like my brand was being diluted. I thanked the gods we were not in Ohio and our dragon was not named Festo.

"I think I'll call you Josephine," I decided. "It's a lovely name."

Josephine shrugged. "Fine by me. Where's your friend Calypso?"

"Wait," Leo said. "How'd you know about Calypso?"

Josephine tapped her left temple. "Waystation tells me stuff."

"Oooh." Leo's eyes widened. "That's cool."

I wasn't so sure. Normally, when someone said that a building was talking to them, I got away from them as quickly as possible. Sadly, I believed Josephine. I also had the feeling we would be needing her hospitality.

"Calypso's in the infirmary," I offered. "Broke her hand. And foot."

"Ah." The sparkle dimmed in Josephine's eyes. "Yeah, you met the neighbors."

"You mean the blemmyae." I imagined the *neighbors* stopping by to borrow a socket wrench, or take an order for Girl Scout cookies, or murder someone. "Do you often have problems with them?"

"Didn't use to." Josephine sighed. "By themselves, blemmyae are pretty harmless, as long as you're polite to them. They don't have enough imagination to organize an assault. But since last year—"

"Let me guess," I said. "Indianapolis has a new emperor?"

A ripple of anger washed across Josephine's face, giving me a glimpse of what it would be like to get on her bad side. (Hint: It involved pain.)

"Best we don't talk about the emperor until Emmie and your friend join us," she said. "Without Emmie around to keep me calm . . . I get worked up."

I nodded. Not getting Josephine worked up sounded like an excellent plan. "But we're safe here?"

Leo held out his palm as if checking for brick raindrops. "That was my question too. I mean . . . we kind of led an angry mob to your doorstep."

Josephine waved aside our concern. "Don't worry. The emperor's forces have been searching for us for months. The Waystation isn't easy to find unless we invite you in."

"Huh." Leo tapped the floor with his foot. "So, did you design this place? 'Cause it's pretty awesome."

Josephine chuckled. "I wish. A demigod architect with *way* more talent than me did that. Built the Waystation back in the 1880s, early days of the transcontinental railroad. It was meant as a refuge for demigods, satyrs, Hunters—pretty much anyone who needed one here in the middle of the country. Emmie and I are just lucky enough to be the present caretakers."

"I've never even heard of this place," I said grumpily.

"We . . . ah, keep a low profile. Lady Artemis's orders. Need-to-know basis."

As a god, I was the very definition of *need-to-know*, but it was typical of Artemis to keep something like this to herself. She was *such* a doomsday prepper, always hiding things from the other gods, like stashes of supplies, emergency bunkers, and small nation-states. "I assume this place isn't a train station anymore. What do mortals think it is?"

Josephine grinned. "Waystation, transparent floor, please."

Beneath our feet, the stained cement disappeared. I

leaped back as if standing on a hot skillet, but the floor was not actually gone. It had simply turned see-through. Around us, the rugs, furniture, and workshop equipment seemed to hover two stories over the actual ground floor of the hall, where twenty or thirty banquet tables had been set up for some sort of event.

"Our living space occupies the top of the grand hall," Josephine said. "That area below us was once the main concourse for the station. Now the mortals rent it out for weddings and parties and whatnot. If they look up—"

"Adaptive camouflage," Leo guessed. "They see an image of the ceiling, but they don't see you. Nice!"

Josephine nodded, obviously pleased. "Most of the time, it's quiet around here, though it gets noisy on weekends. If I have to hear 'Thinking Out Loud' from one more wedding cover band, I may have to drop an anvil."

She pointed to the floor, which immediately turned back to opaque cement. "Now if you guys don't mind, I need to finish a section of a project I'm working on. Don't want the metal plates to cool without proper welding. After that—"

"You're a child of Hephaestus, aren't you?" Leo said.

"Hecate, actually."

Leo blinked. "No way! But that sweet workshop area you got—"

"Magical construction is my specialty," said Josephine. "My dad, my *mortal* dad, was a mechanic."

"Nice!" Leo said. "My mom was a mechanic! Hey, if I could use your machine tools, I left this dragon at the state-house and—"

"Ahem," I interrupted. As much as I wanted Festus

back, I did not think a nearly indestructible, impossible-to-open suitcase was in any immediate danger. I was also afraid that if Leo and Josephine started chatting, they would soon be bonding over the wonders of serrated flange bolts and I would die of boredom. "Josephine, you were about to say *after that . . . ?*"

"Right," Josephine agreed. "Give me a few minutes. Then I can show you to some guest rooms and, uh, maybe get Leo here some clothing. These days, we've got plenty of vacancies, unfortunately."

I wondered why that was unfortunate. Then I remembered the little girl's empty room we'd passed. Something told me it might be best not to ask about that.

"We appreciate your help," I told Josephine. "But I still don't understand. You say Artemis knows about this place. You and Emmie are—or were—Hunters?"

Josephine's neck muscles tightened against the collar of her pink polo. "We were."

I frowned. I'd always thought of my sister's followers as a sort of all-maiden mafia. Once you were in, you never left—unless you left in a lovely silver coffin. "But—"

"Long story," Josephine cut me off. "I probably should let Hemithea tell it."

"*Hemithea?*" The name hit me like one of the Waystation's bricks. My face felt as if it were slipping down to the center of my chest, blemmyae-style. Suddenly I realized why Emmie had looked familiar. No wonder I'd felt such a sense of unease. "Emmie. Short for Hemithea. *The* Hemithea?"

Josephine glanced from side to side. "You really didn't

know?" She jabbed a finger over her shoulder. "So . . . I'm gonna get back to that welding now. There's food and drinks in the kitchen. Make yourselves at home."

She beat a hasty retreat back to her workshop.

"Dang," Leo muttered. "She's *awesome*."

"Humph."

Leo arched his eyebrows. "Were you and Hemithea an item back in the day or something? When you heard her name, you looked like somebody kicked you in the crotch."

"Leo Valdez, in four thousand years, no one has *ever* dared to kick me in the crotch. If you mean I looked slightly shocked, that's because I knew Hemithea when she was a young princess in ancient Greece. We were never an *item*. However, I'm the one who made her immortal."

Leo's eyes drifted toward the workshop, where Josephine had begun to weld again. "I thought all Hunters became immortal once they took the pledge to Artemis."

"You misunderstand," I said. "I made Hemithea immortal *before* she became a Hunter. In fact, I turned her into a god."

5

Tell you a story?
Or I could just, like, pass out
And twitch on the couch

THIS WAS LEO'S CUE to sit at my feet and listen, enraptured, as I told him the story.

Instead, he waved vaguely toward the workshop. "Yeah, okay. I'm gonna check out the forges."

He left me by myself.

Demigods today. I blame social media for their short attention spans. When you can't even take the time to listen to a god hold forth, that's just sad.

Unfortunately, the story insisted on being remembered. Voices, faces, and emotions from three thousand years ago flooded my mind, taking control of my senses with such force that I almost crumpled.

Over the past few weeks, during our travels west, these waking visions had been happening with alarming frequency. Perhaps they were the result of my faulty human neurons trying to process godly memories. Perhaps Zeus was punishing me with vivid flashbacks of my most spectacular failures. Or perhaps my time as a mortal was simply driving me crazy.

Whatever the case, I barely managed to reach the nearest couch before collapsing.

I was dimly aware of Leo and Josephine standing at the welding station, Josephine in her welder's gear and Leo in his boxer shorts, chatting about whatever project Josephine was working on. They didn't seem to notice my distress.

Then the memories swallowed me.

I found myself hovering above the ancient Mediterranean. Sparkling blue water stretched to the horizon. A warm, salty wind buoyed me up. Directly below, the white cliffs of Naxos rose from the surf like the baleen ridge of a whale's mouth.

From a town about three hundred yards inland, two teenage girls ran for their lives—making their way toward the edge of the cliff with an armed mob close behind them. The girls' white dresses billowed, and their long dark hair whipped in the wind. Despite their bare feet, the rocky terrain did not slow them down. Bronzed and lithe, they were clearly used to racing outdoors, but they were running toward a dead end.

At the head of the mob, a portly man in red robes screamed and waved the handle of a broken ceramic jar. A gold crown glinted on his brow. Streaks of wine had crusted in his gray beard.

His name came to me: Staphylus, king of Naxos. A demigod son of Dionysus, Staphylus had inherited all of his father's worst traits and none of his party-dude chill. Now in a drunken rage, he was yelling something about his daughters breaking his finest amphora of wine, and so, naturally, they had to die.

"I'll kill you both!" he screamed. "I will tear you apart!"

I mean . . . if the girls had broken a Stradivarius violin or gold-plated harmonica, I might have understood his rage. But a jar of wine?

The girls ran on, crying to the gods for help.

Normally, this sort of thing would not have been my problem. People cried to the gods for help all the time. They almost never offered anything interesting in return. I probably would have just hovered over the scene, thinking *Oh, dear, what a shame. Ouch. That must have hurt!* and then gone about my normal business.

This particular day, however, I was not flying over Naxos merely by chance. I was on my way to see the drop-dead gorgeous Rhoeo—the king's eldest daughter—with whom I happened to be in love.

Neither of the girls below was Rhoeo. I recognized them as her younger sisters Parthenos and Hemithea. Nevertheless, I doubted Rhoeo would appreciate it if I failed to help her sisters on my way to our big date. *Hey, babe. I just saw your sisters get chased off a cliff and plummet to their deaths. You want to catch a movie or something?*

But if I helped her sisters, against the wishes of their homicidal father and in front of a crowd of witnesses—that would require divine intervention. There would be forms to fill out, and the Three Fates would demand everything in triplicate.

While I was deliberating, Parthenos and Hemithea charged toward the precipice. They must have realized they had nowhere to go, but they didn't even slow down.

"Help us, Apollo!" Hemithea cried. "Our fate rests with you!"

Then, holding hands, the two sisters leaped into the void.

Such a show of faith—it took my breath away!

I couldn't very well let them go *SPLAT* after they'd entrusted me with their lives. Now, Hermes? Sure, he might have let them die. He would've found that hilarious. Hermes is a twisted little scamp. But Apollo? No. I had to honor such courage and panache!

Parthenos and Hemithea never hit the surface of the water. I stretched out my hands and zapped the girls with a mighty zap—imparting some of my own divine life force into them. Oh, how you should envy those girls! Shimmering and disappearing with a golden flash, filled with tingly warmth and newfound power, they floated upward in a cloud of Tinker Bell–quality glitter.

It is no small thing to make someone a god. The general rule is that power trickles down, so any god can theoretically make a new god of lesser power than him or herself. But this requires sacrificing some of one's own divinity, a small amount of what makes you *you*—so gods don't grant such a favor often. When we do, we usually create only the most *minor* of gods, as I did with Parthenos and Hemithea: just the basic immortality package with few bells and whistles. (Although I threw in the extended warranty, because I'm a nice guy.)

Beaming with gratitude, Parthenos and Hemithea flew up to meet me.

"Thank you, Lord Apollo!" Parthenos said. "Did Artemis send you?"

My smile faltered. "Artemis?"

"She must have!" Hemithea said. "As we fell, I prayed, 'Help us, Artemis!'"

"No," I said. "You cried out, 'Help us, Apollo!'"

The girls looked at each other.

"Er . . . no, my lord," said Hemithea.

I was *sure* she had said my name. In retrospect, however, I wondered if I had been assuming rather than listening. The three of us stared at one another. That moment when you turn two girls immortal and then find out they didn't call on you to do so . . . Awkward.

"Well, it doesn't matter!" Hemithea said cheerfully. "We owe you a great debt, and now we are free to follow our hearts' desires!"

I was hoping she would say *To serve Apollo for all eternity and bring him a warm lemon-scented towel before every meal!*

Instead, Parthenos said, "Yes, we will join the Hunters of Artemis! Thank you, Apollo!"

They used their new powers to vaporize, leaving me alone with an angry mob of Naxoans screaming and shaking their fists at the sea.

The worst thing? The girls' sister Rhoeo broke up with me like a week later.

Over the centuries, I saw Hemithea and Parthenos from time to time in Artemis's retinue. Mostly we avoided each other. Making them minor gods was one of those benevolent mistakes I didn't want to write any songs about.

My vision changed, shifting as subtly as the light through the Waystation's rose window.

I found myself in a vast apartment of gold and white marble. Beyond the glass walls and the wraparound terrace, afternoon shadows flooded the skyscraper canyons of Manhattan.

I had been here before. No matter where my visions took me, I always seemed to end up back in this nightmarish scene.

Reclining on a gilded chaise lounge, the emperor Nero looked horrifically resplendent in a purple suit, a blue pastel shirt, and pointy alligator-leather shoes. On his sizable paunch he balanced a plate of strawberries, popping them one at a time into his mouth with his little finger raised to show off the hundred-karat diamond on his pinky ring.

"Meg . . ." He shook his head sadly. "Dear Meg. You should be more excited! This is your chance for redemption, my dear. You won't disappoint me, will you?"

His voice was soft and gentle, like a heavy snowfall—the sort that builds up and brings down power lines, collapses roofs, kills entire families.

Standing before the emperor, Meg McCaffrey looked like a wilting plant. Her dark pageboy hair hung listlessly around her face. She slumped in her green T-shirt dress, her knees bent in her yellow leggings, one red high-top kicking listlessly at the marble floor. Her face was lowered, but I could see that her cat-eye glasses had been broken since our last encounter. Scotch tape covered the rhinestone tips at either joint.

Under the weight of Nero's gaze, she seemed so small and vulnerable. I wanted to rush to her side. I wanted to smash that plate of strawberries into Nero's chinless, neck-bearded excuse for a face. Alas, I could only watch, knowing that this scene had already happened. I had seen it unfold several times in my visions over the last few weeks.

Meg didn't speak, but Nero nodded as if she'd answered his question.

"Go west," he told her. "Capture Apollo before he can find the next Oracle. If you cannot bring him to me alive, kill him."

He crooked his diamond-weighted pinky finger. From the line of imperial bodyguards behind him, one stepped forward. Like all Germani, the man was enormous. His muscular arms bulged against his leather cuirass. His brown hair grew wild and long. His rugged face would have been scary even without the serpent tattoo that coiled around his neck and up his right cheek.

"This is Vortigern," said Nero. "He will keep you . . . safe."

The emperor tasted the word *safe* as if it had many possible meanings, none of them good. "You will also travel with another member of the Imperial Household just in case, ah, *difficulties* arise."

Nero curled his pinky again. From the shadows near the stairs appeared a teenage boy who looked very much like the sort of boy who enjoyed appearing from shadows. His dark hair hung over his eyes. He wore baggy black pants, a black muscle shirt (despite his lack of muscles), and enough gold jewelry around his neck to make him a proper festival idol. At his belt hung three sheathed daggers, two on the right and one on the left. The predatory gleam in his eyes made me suspect those blades were not just for show.

In all, the boy reminded me somewhat of Nico di Angelo, the son of Hades, if Nico were slightly older, more vicious, and had been raised by jackals.

"Ah, good, Marcus," Nero said. "Show Meg your destination, will you?"

Marcus smiled thinly. He held up his palm, and a glowing image appeared above his fingertips: a bird's-eye view of a city I now recognized as Indianapolis.

Nero popped another strawberry in his mouth. He chewed it slowly, letting the juice dribble down his weak chin. I decided that if I ever returned to Camp Half-Blood, I would have to convince Chiron to change their cash crop to blueberries.

"Meg, my dear," Nero said, "I *want* you to succeed. *Please* don't fail. If the Beast becomes cross with you again . . ." He shrugged helplessly. His voice ached with sincerity and concern. "I just don't know how I could protect you. Find Apollo. Subject him to your will. I know you can do this. And, my dear, *do* be careful in the court of our friend the New Hercules. He is not as much a gentleman as I. Don't get caught up in his obsession with destroying the House of Nets. That's a mere sideshow. Succeed quickly and come back to me." Nero spread his arms. "Then we can be one happy family again."

The boy Marcus opened his mouth, perhaps to make a snide comment, but when he spoke it was Leo Valdez's voice, shattering the vision. "Apollo!"

I gasped. I was back in the Waystation, sprawled across the couch. Standing over me, frowning with concern, were our hosts, Josephine and Emmie, along with Leo and Calypso.

"I—I had a dream." I pointed weakly at Emmie. "And you were there. And . . . the rest of you, not so much, but—"

"A dream?" Leo shook his head. He was now dressed in a pair of grimy overalls. "Man, your eyes were wide open. You were lying there all twitching and stuff. I've seen you have some visions before, but not like that."

I realized my arms were shaking. I grabbed my right hand with my left, but that only made it worse. "I—I heard some new details, or things I didn't remember from before. About Meg. And the emperors. And—"

Josephine patted my head as if I were a cocker spaniel. "You sure you're okay there, Sunny? You don't look so hot."

There was a time when I would have deep-fried anyone who called me Sunny. After I took over the reins of the sun chariot from the old Titan god Helios, Ares had called me Sunny for centuries. It was one of the few jokes he understood (at least one of the few *clean* jokes).

"I'm fine," I snapped. "Wh-what's going on? Calypso, you're already healed?"

"You've been out for hours, actually." She raised her recently broken hand, which now looked as good as new, and wriggled her fingers. "But yes. Emmie is a healer to rival Apollo."

"You had to say that," I grumbled. "You mean I've been lying here for hours and nobody noticed?"

Leo shrugged. "We were kinda busy talking shop. We

probably wouldn't have noticed you as soon as we did except, uh, somebody here wants to talk to you."

"Mmm," Calypso agreed, a worried look in her eyes. "He's been very insistent about it."

She pointed toward the rose window.

At first, I thought I was seeing orange spots. Then I realized an apparition was floating toward me. Our friend Agamethus, the headless ghost, had returned.

6

Oh, Magic 8 Ball
Epic fail at prophecies
Leo's ear's on fire

THE GHOST DRIFTED toward us. His mood was difficult to discern, since he had no face, but he seemed agitated.
He pointed at me, then made a series of hand gestures I
didn't understand—shaking his fists, lacing his fingers, cup-
ping one hand as if holding a sphere. He stopped on the
opposite side of the coffee table.

"'Sup, Cheese?" Leo asked.

Josephine snorted. *"Cheese?"*

"Yeah, he's orange," Leo said. "Why is that? Also, why
is he headless?"

"Leo," Calypso chided. "Don't be rude."

"Hey, it's a fair question."

Emmie studied the ghost's hand gestures. "I've never
seen him this worked up. He glows orange because . . .
Well, actually I have no idea. As for why he is headless—"

"His brother cut off his head," I supplied. The memory
surfaced from the dark stew of my mortal brain, though I
did not recall the details. "Agamethus was the brother of
Trophonius, the spirit of the Dark Oracle. He . . ." There

was something else, something that filled me with guilt, but I couldn't remember.

The others stared at me.

"His brother did *what?*" Calypso asked.

"How did you know that?" Emmie demanded.

I had no answer. I was not sure myself where the information had come from. But the ghost pointed at me as if to say, *This dude knows what's up,* or possibly, more disturbingly, *It's your fault.* Then he again made the gesture of holding a sphere.

"He wants the Magic 8 Ball," Josephine interpreted. "I'll be right back."

She jogged over to her workshop.

"The Magic 8 Ball?" Leo grinned at Emmie. The name tag on his borrowed overalls read GEORGIE. "She's kidding, right?"

"She's dead serious," Emmie said. "Er . . . so to speak. We might as well sit."

Calypso and Emmie took the armchairs. Leo hopped onto the couch next to me, bouncing up and down with such enthusiasm I had an annoying pang of nostalgia for Meg McCaffrey. As we waited for Josephine, I tried to dredge my memory for more specifics about this ghost Agamethus. Why would his brother Trophonius have decapitated him, and why did *I* feel so guilty about it? But I had no success— just a vague sense of unease, and the feeling that despite his lack of eyes, Agamethus was glaring at me.

Finally, Josie trotted back over. In one hand, she gripped a black plastic sphere the size of a honeydew melon. On one side, painted in the middle of a white circle, was the number 8.

"I love those things!" Leo said. "Haven't seen one in years."

I scowled at the sphere, wondering if it was some sort of bomb. That would explain Leo's excitement. "What does it do?"

"Are you kidding?" asked Leo. "It's a Magic 8 Ball, man. You ask it questions about the future."

"Impossible," I said. "I am the god of prophecy. I know *every* form of divination, and I have never heard of a Magic 8 Ball."

Calypso leaned forward. "I'm not familiar with this form of sorcery, either. How does it work?"

Josephine beamed. "Well, it's supposed to be just a toy. You shake it, turn it over, and an answer floats up in this little plastic window on the bottom. I made some modifications. Sometimes the Magic 8 Ball picks up on Agamethus's thoughts and conveys them in writing."

"Sometimes?" Leo asked.

Josephine shrugged. "Like, thirty percent of the time. Best I could manage."

I still had no idea what she was talking about. The Magic 8 Ball struck me as a very shady form of divination—more like a Hermes game of chance than an Oracle worthy of me.

"Wouldn't it be faster if Agamethus simply wrote down what he wanted to say?" I asked.

Emmie shot me a warning look. "Agamethus is illiterate. He's a little sensitive about that."

The ghost turned toward me. His aura darkened to the color of a blood orange.

"Ah . . ." I said. "And those hand gestures he was making?"

"It's no form of sign language that we can figure out," Jo said. "We've been trying for seven years, ever since Agamethus joined us. The Magic 8 Ball's the best form of communication we've got. Here, buddy."

She tossed him the magical sphere. Since Agamethus was ethereal, I expected the ball to sail right through him and shatter on the floor. Instead, Agamethus caught it easily.

"Okay!" Josephine said. "So, Agamethus, what do you want to tell us?"

The ghost shook the Magic 8 Ball vigorously and then threw it to me. I was not prepared for the sphere to be full of liquid, which, as any water-bottle-flipper can tell you, makes an object much more difficult to control. It hit my chest and dropped into my lap. I barely caught it before it wobbled off the couch.

"Master of dexterity," Calypso muttered. "Turn it over. Weren't you listening?"

"Oh, be quiet." I wished Calypso could only communicate 30 percent of the time. I rotated the ball bottom-up.

As Josephine had described, a layer of clear plastic was set in the base of the sphere, providing a window to the liquid inside. A large white multisided die floated into view. (I knew this thing smacked of Hermes's wretched gambling games!) One side of it pressed against the window, revealing a sentence written in block letters.

"'Apollo must bring her home,'" I read aloud.

I looked up. Emmie's and Josephine's faces had become twin masks of shock. Calypso and Leo exchanged a wary glance.

Leo started to say, "Uh, what—?"

Simultaneously, Emmie and Josephine unleashed a torrent of questions: "Is she alive? Is she safe? Where is she? Tell me!"

Emmie shot to her feet. She began to pace, sobbing in great dry heaves, while Josephine advanced on me, her fists clenched, her gaze as sharp as the pointed flame of her welding torch.

"I don't know!" I tossed Josephine the ball as if it were a hot baklava. "Don't kill me!"

She caught the Magic 8 Ball, then seemed to check herself. She took a heavy breath. "Sorry, Apollo. Sorry. I . . ." She turned to Agamethus. "Here. Answer us. Tell us."

She threw him the ball.

Agamethus seemed to regard the magical sphere with his nonexistent eyes. His shoulders slumped as if he did not relish his job. He shook the ball once again and tossed it back to me.

"Why *me*?" I protested.

"Read it!" Emmie snapped.

I turned it over. A new message appeared out of the liquid.

" 'Reply hazy,' " I read aloud. " 'Try again later.' "

Emmie wailed in despair. She sank into her seat and buried her face in her hands. Josephine rushed to her side.

Leo frowned at the ghost. "Yo, Cheese, just shake it again, man."

"It's no use," Josephine said. "When the Magic 8 Ball says *try again later*, that's exactly what it means. We'll have to wait."

She sat on the arm of Emmie's chair and cradled Emmie's head against her. "It's all right," Josie murmured. "We'll find her. We'll get her back."

Hesitantly, Calypso stretched out her palm, as if she weren't sure how to help. "I'm so sorry. Who—who is missing?"

With a quivering lip, Josephine pointed to Leo.

Leo blinked. "Uh, I'm still here—"

"Not you," Josephine said. "The name tag. Those overalls—they were hers."

Leo patted the stitched name on his chest. "Georgie?"

Emmie nodded, her eyes puffy and red. "Georgina. Our adopted daughter."

I was glad I was sitting down. Suddenly, so many things made sense that they overwhelmed me like another vision: the two aging Hunters who were not Hunters, the child's empty bedroom, the crayon drawings done by a little girl. Josephine had mentioned that Agamethus arrived in their lives approximately seven years ago.

"You two left the Hunters," I said. "For each other."

Josephine gazed into the distance, as if the building's walls were as transparent as the Magic 8 Ball's base. "We didn't exactly plan it. We left in . . . what, 1986?"

"Eighty-seven," Emmie said. "We've been aging together ever since. Very happily." She wiped away a tear, not looking terribly happy at the moment.

Calypso flexed her recently broken hand. "I don't know much about Lady Artemis, or her rules for followers—"

"That's fine," Leo interrupted.

Calypso glared at him. "But don't they forswear the company of *men*? If you two fell in love—"

"No," I said bitterly. "All romance is off-limits. My sister is quite unreasonable in that regard. The mission of the Hunters is to live without romantic distractions of any kind."

Thinking about my sister and her anti-romantic ideas irritated me. How could two siblings be *so* different? But I was also irritated with Hemithea. She had not only given up being a Hunter; in doing so she had also given up the divinity I had granted her.

Just like a human! We give you immortality and godly power, then you trade it in for love and a loft in downtown Indianapolis. The nerve!

Emmie wouldn't meet my eyes.

She sighed wistfully. "We delighted in being Hunters, both of us. They were our family. But . . ." She shrugged.

"We loved each other more," Josephine supplied.

I got the feeling they finished each other's sentences a lot, their thoughts were in such comfortable harmony. That did not help my irritation levels.

"You must have parted with Artemis on good terms," I said. "She let you live."

Josephine nodded. "The Lady's Hunters often stop here at the Waystation . . . though we have not seen Artemis herself in decades. Then, seven years ago, we were blessed with Georgina. She . . . she was brought to our door by Agamethus."

The orange ghost bowed.

"He brought her from where?" I wondered.

Emmie spread her hands. "We've never been able to get that information from him. It's the one question the Magic 8 Ball never answers."

Leo must have been thinking deeply—a tuft of fire broke out at the top of his left ear. "Hold up. Agamethus isn't your kid's dad, is he? Also . . . you're telling me I'm wearing the overalls of a seven-year-old girl, and they *fit*?"

That got a broken laugh from Josephine. "I suppose they do. And no, Leo, Agamethus is not Georgina's father. Our ghostly friend has been dead since ancient times. Like Apollo said, he was the brother of Trophonius, the spirit of the Oracle. Agamethus appeared here with baby Georgie. Then he led us to the Oracle. That was the first we knew of its existence."

"So you have its location," I said.

"Of course," Emmie murmured. "For all the good it does us."

Too many questions crowded in my head. I wanted to divide myself into a dozen different manifestations so I could pursue every answer at once, but alas, mortals don't split easily. "But the girl and the Oracle must be connected somehow."

Emmie closed her eyes. I could tell she was trying hard to suppress a sob. "We didn't realize how closely they were connected. Not until Georgie was taken from us."

"The emperor," I guessed.

Josephine nodded.

I hadn't even met this second member of the Triumvirate yet, and I already hated him. I had lost Meg McCaffrey to Nero. I did not like the idea of another young girl being taken by another evil emperor.

"In my vision," I recalled, "I heard Nero call this emperor *the New Hercules*. Who is he? What did he do with Georgina?"

Emmie rose unsteadily to her feet. "I—I need to do something productive with my hands. It's the only way I've stayed sane the past two weeks. Why don't you all help us make lunch? Then we'll talk about the monster who controls our city."

7

I chopped those onions
With my own ex-godly hands
You'd better eat them

BEING PRODUCTIVE.

Ugh.

It's such a human concept. It implies you have limited time (LOL) and have to work hard to make something happen (double LOL). I mean, perhaps if you were laboring away for years writing an opera about the glories of Apollo, I could understand the appeal of being productive. But how can you get a sense of satisfaction and serenity from preparing food? That I did *not* understand.

Even at Camp Half-Blood I wasn't asked to make my own meals. True, the hot dogs were questionable, and I never found out what sort of bugs were in bug juice, but at least I'd been served by a cadre of beautiful nymphs.

Now I was compelled to wash lettuce, dice tomatoes, and chop onions.

"Where does this food *come* from?" I asked, blinking tears from my eyes.

I'm no Demeter, but even I could tell this produce was fresh from the earth, probably because of the amount of dirt I had to wash off.

The thought of Demeter made me think of Meg, which might've caused me to weep even if I hadn't already been afflicted by onion fumes.

Calypso dumped a basket of muddy carrots in front of me. "Emmie's got a garden on the roof. Greenhouses. Year-round growing. You should see the herbs—basil, thyme, rosemary. It's *amazing*."

Emmie smiled. "Thank you, dear. You definitely know your gardening."

I sighed. Now *those* two were bonding. Soon I would be stuck between Emmie and Calypso discussing kale-growing techniques and Leo and Josephine waxing poetic about carburetors. I couldn't win.

Speak of the daimon: Leo burst through the door next to the pantry, holding aloft a wheel of cheese like a victor's laurel crown.

"BEHOLD THE CHEDDAR!" he announced. "ALL HAIL THE CHEESE CONQUERORS!"

Josephine, chuckling good-naturedly, lumbered in behind him with a metal pail. "The cows seemed to like Leo."

"Hey, *abuelita*," Leo said. "All da cows love Leo." He grinned at me. "And these cows are red, man. Like . . . *bright red*."

That definitely made me want to weep. Red cows were my favorite. For centuries I had a herd of sacred scarlet cattle before cow-collecting went out of fashion.

Josephine must have seen the miserable look on my face.

"We just use their milk," she said hastily. "We don't butcher them."

"I should hope not!" I cried. "Killing red cattle would be sacrilege!"

Josephine didn't look properly terrified by the idea. "Yeah, but mostly it's because Emmie made me give up meat twenty years ago."

"It's much better for you," Emmie chided. "You're not immortal anymore, and you need to take care of yourself."

"But cheeseburgers," Jo muttered.

Leo plunked the cheese wheel in front of me. "Cut me a wedge of this, my good man. Chop-chop!"

I scowled at him. "Don't test me, Valdez. When I am a god again, I will make a constellation out of you. I will call it the Small Exploding Latino."

"I like it!" He patted my shoulder, causing my knife to jiggle.

Did no one fear the wrath of the gods anymore?

While Emmie baked loaves of bread—which I must admit smelled incredible—I tossed a salad with carrots, cucumbers, mushrooms, tomatoes, and all manner of roof-grown plant material. Calypso used fresh lemons and cane sugar to make lemonade, while humming tracks from Beyoncé's album of the same name. (During our travels west, I had taken it upon myself to catch Calypso up on the last three millennia of popular music.)

Leo cut the cheese. (You can interpret that any way you want.) The cheddar wheel turned out to be bright red all the way through and quite tasty. Josephine made dessert, which she said was her specialty. Today this meant fresh berries and homemade sponge cake in sweet red cream, with a meringue topping lightly toasted with a welding torch.

As for the ghost Agamethus, he hovered in one corner of the kitchen, holding his Magic 8 Ball dejectedly as if it were a third-place prize from a three-person competition.

Finally, we sat down to lunch. I hadn't realized how hungry I was. It had been quite a while since breakfast, and Festus's in-flight meal service left much to be desired.

I shoveled my food in while Leo and Calypso told our hosts about our travels west. Between bites of fresh bread with bright red butter, I added commentary as needed, since of course I had the superior storytelling skills.

We explained how my ancient foe Python had retaken the original site of Delphi, cutting off access to the most powerful Oracle. We explained how the Triumvirate had sabotaged all forms of communication used by demigods—Iris-messages, magical scrolls, ventriloquist puppets, even the arcane magic of e-mail. With the help of Python, the three evil emperors now intended to control or destroy *all* the Oracles from ancient times, thus putting the very future of the world in a stranglehold.

"We freed the Grove of Dodona," I summed up. "But that Oracle simply sent us here to secure the next source of prophecy: the Cave of Trophonius."

Calypso pointed to my quiver, which lay against the nearest sofa. "Apollo, show them your talking arrow."

Emmie's eyes gleamed with the keen interest of an archer. "Talking arrow?"

I shuddered. The arrow I had retrieved from the whispering trees of Dodona had so far done me little good. Only I could hear its voice, and whenever I asked its advice, it spouted nonsense in Elizabethan English, which infected my speech patterns and left me talking like a bad Shakespearean actor for hours. This amused Calypso to no end.

"I will not show them my talking arrow," I said. "I will, however, share the limerick."

"No!" said Calypso and Leo in unison. They dropped their forks and covered their ears.

I recited:

> *"There once was a god named Apollo*
> *Who plunged in a cave blue and hollow*
> *Upon a three-seater*
> *The bronze fire-eater*
> *Was forced death and madness to swallow."*

Around the table, an uncomfortable silence fell.

Josephine glowered. "Never before has any voice dared to utter a limerick in this house, Apollo."

"And let us hope no one will ever do so again," I agreed. "But such was the prophecy of Dodona that brought us here."

Emmie's expression tightened, removing any lingering doubts that this was the same Hemithea I had immortalized so many centuries ago. I recognized the intensity in her eyes—the same determination that had sent her over a cliff, trusting her fate to the gods.

" 'A cave blue and hollow' . . ." she said. "That's the Oracle of Trophonius, all right. It's located in the Bluespring Caverns, about eighty miles south of town."

Leo grinned as he chewed, his mouth an avalanche of earth-toned food particles. "Easiest quest ever, then. We get

Festus back, then we look up this place on Google Maps and fly down there."

"Doubtful," Josephine said. "The emperor has the surrounding countryside heavily guarded. You couldn't fly a dragon anywhere near Bluespring without getting shot out of the sky. Even if you could, the cave entrances are all *way* too small for a dragon to plunge into."

Leo pouted. "But the limerick—"

"May be deceptive," I said. "It is, after all, a limerick."

Calypso sat forward. She had wrapped a napkin around her formerly broken hand—perhaps because it still ached, perhaps because she was nervous. It reminded me of torch wadding—not a happy association after my last encounter with the mad emperor Nero.

"What about the last line?" she asked. "*Apollo will be forced death and madness to swallow.*"

Josephine stared at her empty plate. Emmie gave her hand a quick squeeze.

"The Oracle of Trophonius is dangerous," Emmie said. "Even when we had free access to it, before the emperor moved in, we would only consult the spirit in extreme emergencies." She turned to me. "You must remember. You were the god of prophecy."

Despite the excellent lemonade, my throat felt parched. I didn't like being reminded of what I used to be. I also didn't like the gigantic holes in my memory, filled with nothing but vague dread.

"I—I remember the cave was dangerous, yes," I said. "I don't recall why."

"You don't recall." Emmie's voice took on a dangerous edge.

"I normally concentrated on the godly side of things," I said. "The quality of the sacrifices. What sort of incense the petitioners burned. How pleasing the hymns of praise were. I never asked what kind of trials the petitioners went through."

"You never asked."

I didn't like Emmie echoing my words. I had a feeling she would make an even worse Greek chorus than Calypso.

"I did some reading at Camp Half-Blood," I said defensively. "There wasn't much about Trophonius. Chiron couldn't help, either. He'd completely forgotten about the Oracle. Supposedly, Trophonius's prophecies were dark and scary. Sometimes they drove people insane. Perhaps his cave was a sort of haunted house? With, uh, dangling skeletons, priestesses jumping out and saying *BOO?*"

Emmie's sour expression told me that my guess was off the mark.

"I also read something about petitioners drinking from two special springs," I persisted. "I thought *swallowing death and madness* might be a symbolic reference to that. You know, poetic license."

"No," Josephine muttered. "It's not poetic license. That cave literally drove our daughter mad."

A cold draft swept across my neck, as if the Waystation itself had let out a forlorn sigh. I thought about the apocalypse I'd seen crayoned on the wall of the child's now-abandoned bedroom.

"What happened?" I asked, though I wasn't sure I wanted to know—especially if it might be a portent of what I would soon face.

Emmie tore a piece of bread crust. She let the pieces fall. "Once the emperor came to Indianapolis . . . this *New Hercules* . . ."

Calypso started to ask a question, but Emmie raised a hand. "Please, dear, don't ask me to name him. Not here. Not now. As I'm sure you know, many gods and monsters hear you when you speak their names. *He* is worse than most."

A pang of sympathy pulled at the corner of Calypso's mouth. "Please, go on."

"At first," Emmie said, "we didn't understand what was happening. Our friends and companions began to disappear." She gestured around her at the vast living area. "We used to have a dozen or so living here at any given time. Now . . . we're all that's left."

Josephine leaned back in her chair. In the light of the rose window, her hair gleamed the same steel gray as the wrenches in her coverall pockets. "The emperor was looking for us. He knew about the Waystation. He wanted to destroy us. But like I said, this isn't an easy place to find unless we invite you in. So, instead, his forces waited until our people were outside. They took our friends a few at a time."

"Took them?" I asked. "As in *alive*?"

"Oh, yeah." Josephine's grim tone made it sound as if death would've been preferable. "The emperor loves prisoners. He captured our guests, our griffins."

A berry slipped out of Leo's fingers. "Griffins? Uh . . . Hazel and Frank told me about griffins. They fought some in Alaska. Said they were like rabid hyenas with wings."

Josephine smirked. "The small ones, the wild ones, can be, yeah. But we raise the best here. At least . . . we did. Our last mating pair disappeared about a month ago. Heloise and Abelard. We let them out to hunt—they have to do that to stay healthy. They never returned. For Georgina, that was the final insult."

A bad feeling began to nag at me. Something beyond the obvious *we're talking about creepy things that might get me killed*. The griffin nests in the niches above us. A distant memory about my sister's followers. A comment Nero had made in my vision: that the New Hercules was obsessed with destroying the House of Nets, as if that were another name for the Waystation . . . I felt like someone's shadow was falling over the dining table, someone I should know, perhaps someone I should be running away from.

Calypso unwrapped the napkin from her hand. "Your daughter," she asked. "What happened to her?"

Neither Josephine nor Emmie responded. Agamethus bowed slightly, his bloody tunic glowing in various shades of nacho topping.

"It's obvious," I said into the silence. "The girl went to the Cave of Trophonius."

Emmie looked past me to Agamethus, her eyes as sharp as arrow points. "Georgina got it into her head that the only way to save the Waystation and find the captives was to consult the Oracle. She'd always been drawn to the place. She didn't fear it the way most people did. One night she slipped away. *Agamethus* helped her. We don't know exactly how they got there—"

The ghost shook his Magic 8 Ball. He tossed it to Emmie, who frowned at the answer on the bottom.

" '*It was ordained,*' " she read. "I don't know what you mean, you old, dead fool, but she was just a *child*. Without the throne, you *knew* what would happen to her!"

"The throne?" Calypso asked.

Another memory bobbed to the surface of my eight-ball brain.

"Oh, gods," I said. "The throne."

Before I could say more, the entire hall shuddered. Plates and cups rattled on the dining table. Agamethus vanished in a flash of nacho orange. At the top of the barreled ceiling, the green and brown stained-glass panels darkened as if a cloud had blacked out the sun.

Josephine rose. "Waystation, what's happening on the roof?"

As far as I could tell, the building didn't respond. No bricks shot out of the wall. No doors banged open and shut in Morse code.

Emmie set the Magic 8 Ball on the table. "The rest of you, stay here. Jo and I will check it out."

Calypso frowned. "But—"

"That's an order," Emmie said. "I'm not losing any more guests."

"It can't be Com—" Josephine stopped herself. "It can't be him. Maybe Heloise and Abelard are back?"

"Maybe." Emmie didn't sound convinced. "But just in case . . ."

The two women moved quickly to a metal supply cabinet in the kitchen. Emmie grabbed her bow and quiver. Josephine pulled out an old-fashioned machine gun with a circular drum magazine between the two handles.

Leo nearly choked on his dessert. "Is that a *tommy gun?*"

Josephine patted the weapon affectionately. "This is Little Bertha. A reminder of my sordid past life. I'm sure there's nothing to worry about. You all sit tight."

With that comforting advice, our heavily armed hosts marched off to check the roof.

8

Lovebirds arguing
Trouble in Elysium?
I'll just scrub these plates

THE ORDER TO *sit tight* seemed clear enough to me.

Leo and Calypso, however, decided that the least we could do was clean up the lunch dishes. (See my previous comment re: the dumbness of productivity.) I scrubbed. Calypso rinsed. Leo dried, which wasn't even work for him, since all he had to do was heat his hands a little.

"So," Calypso said, "what's this throne Emmie mentioned?"

I scowled at my foamy stack of bread pans. "The Throne of Memory. It's a chair carved by the goddess Mnemosyne herself."

Leo leered at me over the top of a steaming salad plate. "You forgot the Throne of Memory? Isn't that a mortal sin or something?"

"The only mortal sin," I said, "would be failing to incinerate you as soon as I become a god again."

"You could try," Leo said. "But then how would you learn those secret scales on the Valdezinator?"

I accidentally sprayed myself in the face. "What secret scales?"

"Both of you, stop," Calypso ordered. "Apollo, why is this Throne of Memory important?"

I wiped the water off my face. Talking about the Throne of Memory had jogged loose a few more pieces of information from my mind, but I didn't like what I'd remembered.

"Before a petitioner went into the Cave of Trophonius," I said, "he or she was supposed to drink from two magical springs: Forgetfulness and Memory."

Leo picked up another plate. Steam curled from the porcelain. "Wouldn't the two springs, like, cancel each other out?"

I shook my head. "Assuming the experience didn't kill you, it would prepare your mind for the Oracle. You would then descend into the cave and experience . . . untold horrors."

"Such as?" Calypso asked.

"I just said they were *untold*. I do know that Trophonius would fill your mind with bits of nightmarish verse that, if assembled properly, became a prophecy. Once you stumbled out of the cave—assuming you lived and weren't driven permanently insane—the priests would sit you down on the Throne of Memory. The verses would come spilling out of your mouth. A priest would write them down, and *voilà!* There's your prophecy. With any luck, your mind would return to normal."

Leo whistled. "That is one *messed-up* Oracle. I like the singing trees better."

I suppressed a shudder. Leo hadn't been with me in the Grove of Dodona. He didn't appreciate just how terrible those clashing voices were. But he had a point. There was a reason few people remembered the Cave of Trophonius. It wasn't a place that got rave write-ups in the yearly "Hot Oracles to Visit Now" articles.

Calypso took a bread pan from me and began to rinse it. She seemed to know what she was doing, though her hands were so lovely I couldn't imagine she often did her own dishes. I would have to ask her which moisturizer she used.

"What if the petitioner couldn't use the throne?" she asked.

Leo snickered. *"Use the throne."*

Calypso glared at him.

"Sorry." Leo tried to look serious, which for him was always a losing battle.

"If the petitioner couldn't use the throne," I said, "there would be no way to extract the bits of verse from his or her mind. The petitioner would be stuck with those horrors from the cave—forever."

Calypso rinsed the pan. "Georgina . . . that poor child. What do you think happened to her?"

I didn't want to think about *that*. The possibilities made my skin crawl. "Somehow she must have made it into the cave. She survived the Oracle. She made it back here, but . . . not in good shape." I recalled the frowny-faced knife-wielding stick figures on her bedroom wall. "My guess is that the emperor subsequently seized control of the Throne of Memory. Without that, Georgina would never be able to recover fully. Perhaps she left again and went looking for it . . . and was captured."

Leo muttered a curse in Spanish. "I keep thinking about my little bro Harley back at camp. If somebody tried to hurt him . . ." He shook his head. "Who is this emperor and how soon can we stomp him?"

I scrubbed the last of the pans. At least this was one epic quest I had successfully completed. I stared at the bubbles fizzing on my hands.

"I have a pretty good idea who the emperor is," I admitted. "Josephine started to say his name. But Emmie is right—it's best not to speak it aloud. *The New Hercules* . . ." I swallowed. In my stomach, salad and bread seemed to be holding a mud-wrestling contest. "He was not a nice person."

In fact, if I had the right emperor, this quest could be personally awkward. I hoped I was wrong. Perhaps I could stay at the Waystation and direct operations while Calypso and Leo did the actual fighting. That seemed only fair, since I'd had to scrub the dishes.

Leo put away the dinner plates. His eyes scanned side to side as if reading invisible equations.

"This project Josephine is working on," he said. "She's building some kind of tracking device. I didn't ask, but . . . she must be trying to find Georgina."

"Of course." Calypso's voice took on a sharper edge. "Can you imagine losing your child?"

Leo's ears reddened. "Yeah. But I was thinking, if we can get back to Festus, I could run some numbers, maybe reprogram his Archimedes sphere—"

Calypso threw in the towel, quite literally. It landed in the sink with a damp *flop*. "Leo, you can't reduce everything to a program."

He blinked. "I'm not. I just—"

"You're trying to fix it," Calypso said. "As if every problem is a machine. Jo and Emmie are in serious pain. Emmie told me they're thinking about abandoning the Waystation, giving themselves up to the emperor if it'll save their daughter. They don't need gadgets or jokes or fixes. Try *listening*."

Leo held out his hands. For once, he didn't seem to know what to do with them. "Look, babe—"

"Don't *babe* me," she snapped. "Don't—"

"APOLLO?" Josephine's voice boomed from the main hall. She didn't sound panicked exactly, but definitely tense—somewhat like the atmosphere in the kitchen.

I stepped away from the happy couple. Calypso's outburst had taken me by surprise, but as I thought about it, I recalled half a dozen other spats between her and Leo as we had traveled west. I simply hadn't thought much about them because . . . well, the fights weren't about me. Also, compared to godly lovers' quarrels, Leo and Calypso's were nothing.

I pointed over my shoulder. "I think I'll just, uh . . ."

I left the kitchen.

In the middle of the main hall, Emmie and Josephine stood with their weapons at their sides. I couldn't quite read their expressions—expectant, on edge, the way Zeus's cupbearer Ganymede looked whenever he gave Zeus a new wine to try.

"Apollo." Emmie pointed over my head, where griffin nests lined the edge of the ceiling. "You have a visitor."

In order to see who Emmie was pointing at, I had to

step forward onto the rug and turn around. In retrospect, I shouldn't have done that. As soon as I placed my foot on the rug, I thought, Wait, was this rug here before?

Which was followed closely by the thought: Why does this rug look like a tightly woven net?

Followed by: This is a net.

Followed by: YIKES!

The net enmeshed me and rocketed me into the air. I regained the power of flight. For a microsecond, I imagined I was being recalled to Olympus—ascending in glory to sit at the right hand of my father. (Well, three thrones down on Zeus's right, anyway.)

Then gravity took hold. I bounced like a yo-yo. One moment I was eye-level with Leo and Calypso, who were gaping at me from the kitchen entrance. The next moment I was even with the griffins' nests, staring into the face of a goddess I knew all too well.

You're probably thinking: *It was Artemis. This net trap was just a little sibling prank. Surely no loving sister would let her brother suffer so much for so long. She has finally come to rescue our hero, Apollo!*

No. It was not Artemis.

The young woman sat on the molding ledge, playfully swinging her legs. I recognized her elaborately laced sandals, her dress made from layers of mesh in forest-colored camouflage. Her braided auburn hair made a ponytail so long it wrapped around her neck like a scarf or a noose. Her fierce dark eyes reminded me of a panther watching its prey from the shadows of the underbrush—a panther with a twisted sense of humor.

A goddess, yes. But not the one I had hoped for.

"You," I snarled. It was difficult to sound menacing while bobbing up and down in a net.

"Hello, Apollo." Britomartis, the goddess of nets, smiled coyly. "I hear you're human now. This is going to be fun."

9

Of course it's a trap
With her, it always is one
Trappy McTrapface

BRITOMARTIS JUMPED from the ledge and landed in a kneeling position, her skirts spread around her in a pool of netting.

(She loves those dramatic entrances. She is *such* an anime-character wannabe.)

The goddess rose. She pulled out her hunting knife. "Apollo, if you value your anatomy, hold still."

I had no time to protest that I couldn't exactly hold still while suspended in a swaying net. She slashed her knife across my groin. The net broke and spilled me to the floor, thankfully with my anatomy intact.

My landing was not graceful. Fortunately, Leo and Calypso rushed to my aid. They each took an arm and helped me up. I was reassured to see that despite their recent spat, they could still unite on important matters like my welfare.

Leo reached into his tool belt, perhaps searching for a weapon. Instead he produced a tin of breath mints. I doubted that would do us much good.

"Who is this lady?" he asked me.

"Britomartis," I said. "The Lady of Nets."

Leo looked dubious. "Does that include basketball and the Internet?"

"Just hunting and fishing nets," I said. "She is one of my sister's minions."

"*Minion?*" Britomartis wrinkled her nose. "I am no minion."

Behind us, Josephine coughed. "Uh, sorry, Apollo. The Lady insisted on getting your attention this way."

The goddess's face brightened. "Well, I had to see if he would step in my trap. And he did. As usual. Hemithea, Josephine . . . give us the room, please."

Our hosts glanced at each other, probably wondering which of them would have to clean up the bodies after Britomartis was through with us. Then they retreated through a doorway at the back of the hall.

Calypso sized up the net goddess. "Britomartis, eh? Never heard of you. You must be minor."

Britomartis smiled thinly. "Oh, but I've heard of *you*, Calypso. Exiled to Ogygia after the Titan War. Waiting for whatever *man* might wash up on your shores to break your heart and leave you alone again. That must have gotten terribly old." She turned to Leo. "This is your rescuer, eh? A bit short and scruffy for a knight in shining armor."

"Hey, lady." Leo shook his tin of breath mints. "I've blown up way more powerful goddesses than you before."

"And he's not my *rescuer*," Calypso added.

"Yeah!" Leo frowned. "Wait, I kind of was, actually."

"Nor is he a knight," Calypso mused. "Although he is short and scruffy."

A puff of smoke rose from Leo's collar. "Anyway"—he faced Britomartis—"where do you get off ordering Jo and Emmie around like this is your house?"

I grabbed his breath mints before Britomartis could transform them into nitroglycerin. "Leo, I'm afraid this *is* her house."

The goddess gave me that coquettish smile I hated so much—the one that made me feel as if hot nectar were bubbling in my stomach. "Why, Apollo, you made a correct deduction! How did you manage it?"

Whenever I was faced with Britomartis, I made myself just a bit taller than she. Alas, now I could not change my height at will. The best I could do was push up on the balls of my feet.

"Nero called this place the House of Nets," I said. "I should've realized the Waystation was your idea. Whenever my sister wanted to design some elaborate contraption— something twisted and dangerous—she always turned to you."

The goddess curtsied, swirling her net skirts. "You flatter me. Now come, my friends! Let's sit and talk!"

She gestured to the nearest cluster of sofas.

Leo approached the furniture cautiously. For all his faults, he was not stupid. Calypso was about to sink into an armchair when Leo caught her wrist. "Hold up."

From his tool belt he pulled a folding yardstick. He extended it and poked the chair's seat cushion. A bear trap snapped shut, ripping through stuffing and fabric like an upholstery sharknado.

Calypso glared at Britomartis. "Are you *kidding*?"

THE DARK PROPHECY   83

"Oops!" Britomartis said gleefully.

Leo pointed to one of the sofas, though I could see nothing amiss. "There's a trip wire along the back of those cushions, too. Does that . . . Does that trigger a Bouncing Betty?"

Britomartis laughed. "You're good! Yes, indeed. That is a modified pressure-activated S-mine."

"Lady, if that went off, it would bounce three feet in the air, explode, and kill all of us with shrapnel."

"Exactly!" Britomartis said with delight. "Leo Valdez, you'll do nicely."

Leo glowered at her. He pulled some wire cutters from his belt, walked over to the sofa, and deactivated the mine.

I took a breath for the first time in several seconds. "I think I'll sit . . . over here." I pointed to the opposite sofa. "Is that safe?"

Leo grunted. "Yeah. Looks okay."

Once we were all comfortably settled in, with no one mangled or killed, Britomartis lounged across the formerly bear-trapped armchair and smiled. "Well, isn't this nice?"

"No," the three of us chorused.

Britomartis toyed with her braid, possibly looking for trip wires she might have forgotten about. "You asked me why I sent Jo and Emmie away. I love them dearly, but I don't think they'd appreciate the quest I'm about to give you."

"Quest?" Calypso arched her eyebrows. "I'm pretty sure I'm an older divinity than you, Bouncing Betty. What right do you have to give *me* a quest?"

Britomartis flashed that flirty smile. "Aren't you cute.

Hon, I was around when the ancient Greeks were living in caves. I started out as a *Cretan* goddess. When the rest of my pantheon died out, Artemis befriended me. I joined her Hunters and here I am, thousands of years later, still weaving my nets and setting my traps."

"Yes," I grumbled. "Here you are."

The goddess spread her arms. Lead weights and fishing hooks dangled from her embroidered sleeves. "Dear Apollo, you really do make a darling Lester Papadopoulos. Come here."

"Don't tease me," I begged.

"I'm not! Now that you're a harmless mortal, I've decided to finally give you that kiss."

I knew she was lying. I knew that her dress would entangle me and hurt me. I recognized the malicious gleam in her rust-red eyes.

She had led me astray so many times over the millennia.

I flirted shamelessly with *all* my sister's followers. But Britomartis was the only one who ever flirted back, even though she was just as much an avowed maiden as any Hunter. She *delighted* in tormenting me. And how many times had she pranked me by offering to set me up with other people? Gah! Artemis had never been known for her sense of humor, but her sidekick Britomartis more than made up for that. She was insufferable. Beautiful, but insufferable.

I admit I was tempted. Weak mortal flesh! Even weaker than divine flesh!

I shook my head. "You're tricking me. I won't do it."

She looked offended. "When have I ever tricked you?"

"Thebes!" I cried. "You promised to meet me in the

forest for a romantic picnic. Instead I was trampled by a giant wild boar!"

"That was a misunderstanding."

"What about the Ingrid Bergman incident?"

"Oh, she really did want to meet you. How was I to know someone had dug a Burmese tiger pit outside her trailer?"

"And the date with Rock Hudson?"

Britomartis shrugged. "Well, I never actually *said* he was waiting for you in the middle of that minefield. I just let you assume. You have to admit, though, the two of you would've made a cute couple."

I whimpered and pulled my curly mortal hair. Britomartis knew me too well. I was a fool for being in a cute couple.

Leo looked back and forth between us as if he'd stumbled across a heated game of Greek fire toss. (It was big in Byzantium. Don't ask.)

"Rock Hudson," he said. "In a minefield."

Britomartis beamed. "Apollo was *so* adorable, skipping through the daisies until he exploded."

"In case you've forgotten," I muttered, "I am no longer immortal. So, please, no Burmese tiger pits."

"I wouldn't dream of it!" said the goddess. "No, this quest isn't designed to kill you. It *might* kill you, but it's not designed to. I just want my griffins back."

Calypso frowned. "*Your* griffins?"

"Yes," the goddess said. "They are winged lion-eagle hybrids with—"

"I know what a griffin is," Calypso said. "I know Jo and Emmie breed them here. But why are they *yours?*"

I coughed. "Calypso, griffins are the goddess's sacred animals. She is their mother."

Britomartis rolled her eyes. "Only in a figurative sense. I don't sit on their eggs and hatch them."

"You convinced me to do that once," I recalled. "For a kiss I never got."

She laughed. "Yes, I'd forgotten about that! At any rate, the local emperor has captured my babies Heloise and Abelard. In fact, he's been capturing mythical animals from all over the Midwest to use in his diabolic games. They must be freed."

Leo studied the disassembled land mine pieces in his lap. "The kid. Georgina. That's why you don't want Jo and Emmie here. You're putting your griffins' safety ahead of their daughter's."

Britomartis shrugged. "Jo and Emmie's priorities have been compromised. They would not be able to hear this, but the griffins must come first. I have my reasons. Being a goddess, my needs take precedence."

Calypso sniffed with disgust. "You're as greedy and ter-ritorial as your *babies*."

"I'll pretend I didn't hear that," said the goddess. "I promised Artemis I would try to help you three, but don't test my patience. You'd look wonderful as a northern crested newt."

A mixture of hope and sadness welled in my chest. Artemis, my loving sister, had not abandoned me after all. Zeus may have forbidden the other Olympians from helping me, but at least Artemis had sent her lieutenant Britomartis. Of course, Britomartis's idea of "help" involved testing us with land mines and bear traps, but at this point I would take what I could get.

"And if we find these griffins?" I asked.

"Then I'll tell you how to infiltrate the emperor's lair," Britomartis promised. "Being the goddess of traps, I know all about secret entrances!"

I stared at her. "How is that a fair trade?"

"Because, you adorable Lester, you *need* to infiltrate the palace to rescue Georgina and the other prisoners. Without them, the Waystation is doomed, and so are your chances of stopping the Triumvirate. Also, the palace is where you'll find the Throne of Memory. If you can't retrieve that, your trip to the Cave of Trophonius will kill you. You'll never save the other Oracles. You'll never get back to Mount Olympus."

I turned to Leo. "I'm new to this heroic-quest business. Shouldn't there be a reward at the end? Not just more deadly quests?"

"Nope," Leo said. "This is pretty standard."

Oh, the injustice! A minor goddess forcing *me*, one of the twelve Olympians, to retrieve animals for her! I silently vowed that if I ever regained my godhood, I would never again send a poor mortal on a quest. Unless it was really important. And unless I was sure the mortal could handle it. And unless I was pressed for time . . . or I just really didn't feel like doing it myself. I would be *much* kinder and more generous than this net goddess was being to me.

"What would you have us do?" I asked Britomartis. "Wouldn't these griffins be held at the emperor's palace? Couldn't we do some one-stop shopping?"

"Oh, no," Britomartis said. "The really important

animals, the rare and valuable ones . . . the emperor keeps those in a special facility with the proper resources to care for them. The Indianapolis Zoo."

I shuddered. I find zoos to be depressing places, full of sad caged animals, screaming children, and bad food.

"The griffins will be well guarded," I guessed.

"Absolutely!" Britomartis sounded a bit too excited about the prospect. "So please try to release the griffins *before* you get injured or killed. Also, you must hurry—"

"Here comes the time limit." Leo looked at me knowingly. "There's always a time limit."

"In three days," Britomartis continued, "the emperor plans to use all the animals and prisoners in one massive celebration."

"A naming ceremony," I recalled. "Nanette, the blemmyae who almost killed us, she mentioned something about that."

"Indeed." Britomartis grimaced. "This emperor . . . he *loves* naming things after himself. At the ceremony, he plans to rechristen Indianapolis."

That in itself did not strike me as a tragedy. Indianapolis was a rather difficult name to love. However, if this emperor was who I thought he was, his idea of a celebration involved slaughtering people and animals by the thousands. He really was not the sort of person you wanted organizing your child's birthday party.

"The blemmyae mentioned something else," I said. "The emperor wanted to sacrifice two special prisoners. Me and *the girl*."

Calypso clasped her hands like the jaws of the bear trap. "Georgina."

"Exactly!" Britomartis again sounded a bit too cheerful. "The girl is safe enough for now. Imprisoned and insane, yes, but alive. You concentrate on freeing my griffins. Go to the zoo at first light. The emperor's guards will be ending their night shift then. They'll be tired and inattentive."

I gazed at the land mine pieces in Leo's hands. Death by explosion was starting to sound like a kinder fate than Britomartis's quest.

"At least I won't be alone," I muttered.

"Actually," said the goddess, "Leo Valdez must remain here."

Leo flinched. "Say what?"

"You've proven yourself skilled with traps!" the goddess explained. "Emmie and Josephine need your help. The Waystation has defied discovery by the emperor so far, but that won't last much longer. He can't tolerate any opposition. He *will* find this sanctuary. And he means to destroy it. You, Leo Valdez, can help shore up the defenses."

"But—"

"Cheer up!" Britomartis faced Calypso. "*You* can go with Apollo, my dear. Two former immortals on a quest for me! Yes, I like that idea a lot."

Calypso paled. "But . . . No. I don't—"

"She can't," I added.

The sorceress nodded emphatically. "We don't get along, so—"

"It's settled, then!" The goddess rose from her chair. "I'll meet you back here when you have my griffins. Don't fail me, mortals!" She clapped her hands with glee. "Oh, I've always wanted to say that!"

She twirled and disappeared in a flash like a fishing lure, leaving nothing behind but a few treble hooks snagged in the carpet.

10

Scrubbing toilets now
At least there's a great reward
Leftover tofu

AFTER BEAR TRAPS and pressure-activated explosives, I didn't think the afternoon could get any worse. Of course, it did.

Once we told Emmie and Josephine what had happened with Britomartis, our hosts sank into despair. They didn't seem reassured that the griffin quest might lead to Georgina's rescue, or that their little girl would remain alive until the spectacular kill-fest the emperor had planned in three days.

Emmie and Jo were so resentful—not just of Britomartis but also of *us*—that they assigned us more chores. Oh, sure, they *claimed* that all guests had to help out. The Waystation was a communal living space, not a hotel, blah, blah, blah.

I knew better. There was no way scrubbing toilets in the Waystation's twenty-six known bathrooms was anything but a punishment.

At least I didn't have to change the hay in the griffins' lofts. By the time Leo was done with that, he looked like the victim of mugging by scarecrow. As for Calypso, she got to plant mung beans all afternoon with Emmie. I ask you, how is that fair?

By dinnertime, I was starving. I hoped for another fresh meal, preferably one prepared *for* me, but Josephine waved listlessly toward the kitchen. "I think there's some leftover tofu enchiladas in the fridge. Agamethus will show you to your rooms."

She and Emmie left us to fend for ourselves.

The glowing orange ghost escorted Calypso to her room first. Agamethus let it be known, via the Magic 8 Ball and lots of gesticulation, that girls and boys always slept in entirely different wings.

I found this ridiculous, but like so many things about my sister and her Hunters, it was beyond logic.

Calypso didn't complain. Before leaving, she turned to us hesitantly and said, "See you in the morning," as if this was a *huge* concession. As if by talking to Leo and me at all, she was going above and beyond the courtesy we deserved. Honestly, I didn't see how anyone could act so haughty after an afternoon planting legumes.

A few minutes later, armed with leftovers from the fridge, Leo and I followed Agamethus to our guest room.

That's right. We had to *share*, which I took as another sign of our hosts' displeasure.

Before leaving us, Agamethus tossed me his Magic 8 Ball.

I frowned. "I didn't ask you a question."

He pointed emphatically at the magic orb.

I turned it over and read APOLLO MUST BRING HER HOME.

I wished the ghost had a face so I might interpret it. "You already told me that."

I tossed the ball back to him, hoping for further explanation. Agamethus hovered expectantly, as if waiting for me to realize something. Then, shoulders slumped, he turned and floated away.

I was in no mood for reheated tofu enchiladas. I gave mine to Leo, who sat cross-legged on his bed and inhaled his food. He still wore Georgina's coveralls with a light frosting of hay. He seemed to have decided that being able to fit in a seven-year-old girl's work clothes was a mark of honor.

I lay back on my bed. I stared at the arched brickwork on the ceiling, wondering if and when it would collapse on my head. "I miss my cot at Camp Half-Blood."

"This place ain't so bad," Leo said. "When I was between foster homes, I slept under the Main Street Bridge in Houston for like a month."

I glanced over. He did look quite comfortable in his nest of hay and blankets.

"You *will* change clothes before turning in?" I asked.

He shrugged. "I'll shower in the morning. If I get itchy in the middle of the night, I'll just burst into flames."

"I'm not in the mood for joking. Not after Britomartis."

"Who's joking? Don't worry. I'm sure Jo has this place rigged with fire-suppression equipment."

The thought of waking up burning and covered in extinguisher foam did not appeal to me, but it would be about par for the course.

Leo tapped his fork against his plate. "These tofu enchiladas are *sabrosas*. Gotta get the recipe from Josephine. My homegirl Piper would love them."

"How can you be so calm?" I demanded. "I am going

on a dangerous quest tomorrow with your girlfriend!"

Normally, telling a mortal man that I was going somewhere with his girlfriend would've been enough to break his heart.

Leo concentrated on his tofu. "You guys will do fine."

"But Calypso has no powers! How will she help me?"

"It ain't about powers, *ese*. You watch. Calypso will still save your sorry butt tomorrow."

I didn't like that idea. I didn't want my sorry butt dependent on a former sorceress who had failed at street fighting and improvisational comedy, especially given her recent mood.

"And if she's still angry in the morning?" I asked. "What's going on between you two?"

Leo's fork hovered over his last enchilada. "It's just . . . Six months we were traveling, trying to get to New York. Constant danger. Never staying in the same place longer than a night. Then another month and a half getting to Indianapolis."

I considered that. I tried to imagine suffering through four times as many trials as I'd already experienced. "I suppose that would put pressure on a new relationship."

Leo nodded glumly. "Calypso lived on her island for thousands of years, man. She's all about gardening, weaving tapestries, making her surroundings beautiful. You can't do any of that when you don't have a home. Then there's the fact that I—I took her away."

"You rescued her," I said. "The gods were in no hurry to free her from her prison. She might have been on that island for a thousand more years."

Leo chewed his last bite. He swallowed as if the tofu had turned to clay (which, in my opinion, would not have been a dramatic change).

"Sometimes she's happy about it," he said. "Other times, without her powers, without her immortality . . . it's like . . ." He shook his head. "I was going to compare our relationship to a machine. She would hate that."

"I don't mind machines."

He set his plate on the nightstand. "An engine is only built to handle so much stress, you know? Run it too fast for too long, it starts to overheat."

This I understood. Even my sun chariot got a bit tetchy when I drove it all day in Maserati form. "You need time for maintenance. You haven't had a chance to find out who you are as a couple without all the danger and constant movement."

Leo smiled, though his eyes were devoid of their usual impish gleam. "Yeah. Except danger and constant movement—that's pretty much my life. I don't—I don't know how to fix that. If it's even fixable."

He picked a few pieces of straw off his borrowed coveralls. "Enough of that. Better sleep while you can, Sunny. I'm gonna crash."

"Don't call me Sunny," I complained.

But it was too late. When Leo shuts down, he does so with the efficiency of a diesel generator. He flopped down sideways and immediately began to snore.

I was not so lucky. I lay in bed for a long while, counting golden carnivorous sheep in my mind, until at last I drifted into uneasy sleep.

11

Four beheaded dudes
Are too much for one nightmare
Why me? Sob. Sob. Sob.

NATURALLY, I had terrible dreams.

I found myself standing at the foot of a mighty fortress on a moonless night. Before me, rough-hewn walls soared hundreds of feet upward, flecks of feldspar glittering like stars.

At first, I heard nothing but the whistling cries of owls in the woods behind me—a sound that always reminded me of nighttime in ancient Greece. Then, at the base of the stronghold, stone ground against stone. A small hatch appeared where none had been before. A young man crawled out, lugging a heavy sack behind him.

"Come on!" he hissed to someone still in the tunnel.

The man struggled to his feet, the contents of his sack clinking and clanking. Either he was taking out the recycling (unlikely) or he had just stolen a great deal of treasure.

He turned in my direction, and a jolt of recognition made me want to scream like an owl.

It was Trophonius. My son.

You know that feeling when you *suspect* you might have fathered someone thousands of years ago, but you're not really sure? Then you see that child as a grown man, and looking into his eyes, you know beyond a doubt that he is yours? Yes, I'm sure many of you can relate.

I didn't recall who his mother was . . . the wife of King Erginus, perhaps? She had been quite a beauty. Trophonius's lustrous dark hair reminded me of hers. But his muscular physique and handsome face—that strong chin, that perfect nose, those rosy lips—yes, Trophonius clearly got his knockout good looks from me.

His eyes gleamed with confidence as if to say, *That's right. I just crawled out of a tunnel, and I still look gorgeous.*

From the hatch, the head of another young man emerged. He must have had broader shoulders, because he was having trouble squeezing through.

Trophonius laughed under his breath. "I told you not to eat so much, brother."

Despite his struggle, the other man looked up and grinned. He didn't resemble Trophonius at all. His hair was blond and curly, his face as guileless, goofy, and ugly as a friendly donkey's.

I realized this was Agamethus—Trophonius's half brother. He was no son of mine. The poor boy had the misfortune of being the actual offspring of King Erginus and his wife.

"I can't believe it worked," said Agamethus, wriggling his left arm free.

"Of *course* it worked," said Trophonius. "We're famous architects. We built the temple at Delphi. Why wouldn't King Hyrieus trust us to build his treasury?"

"Complete with a secret thieves' tunnel!"

"Well, he'll never know about that," Trophonius said. "The paranoid old fool will assume his servants stole all his treasure. Now hurry up, Wide Load."

Agamethus was too busy laughing to free himself. He stretched out his arm. "Help me."

Trophonius rolled his eyes. He slung his sack of treasure to the ground—and thereby sprang the trap.

I knew what would happen next. I remembered the tale now that I saw it unfolding, but it was still hard to watch. King Hyrieus was paranoid, all right. Days before, he had scoured the treasury for any possible weaknesses. Upon find-ing the tunnel, he said nothing to his servants, his building crew, or his architects. He didn't move his treasure. He sim-ply laid a deadly trap and waited to find out exactly who planned to rob him. . . .

Trophonius set the bag of gold right on the trip wire, which only became active once a thief had exited the tun-nel. The king intended to catch his betrayers red-handed.

In the nearest tree, a mechanical bow fired a scream-ing flare skyward, cutting an arc of red flame across the dark. Inside the tunnel, a support beam snapped, crushing Agamethus's chest under a shower of stone.

Agamethus gasped, his free arm flailing. His eyes bulged as he coughed blood. Trophonius cried in horror. He ran to his brother's side and tried to pull him free, but this only made Agamethus scream.

"Leave me," said Agamethus.

"I won't." Tears streaked Trophonius's face. "This is my fault. This was my idea! I'll get help. I'll—I'll tell the guards—"

"They'll only kill you, too," Agamethus croaked. "Go. While you can. And, brother, the king knows my face." He gasped, his breath gurgling. "When he finds my body—"

"Don't talk that way!"

"He'll know you were with me," Agamethus continued, his eyes now clear and calm with the certainty of death. "He'll track you down. He'll declare war on our father. Make sure my body can't be identified."

Agamethus clawed weakly at the knife hanging from his brother's belt.

Trophonius wailed. He understood what his brother was asking. He heard the guards shouting in the distance. They would be here soon.

He raised his voice to the heavens. "Take me instead! Save him, Father, please!"

Trophonius's father, Apollo, chose to ignore his prayer.

I gave you fame, Apollo was thinking. *I let you design my temple at Delphi. Then you used your reputation and talents to become a thief. You brought this upon yourself.*

In despair, Trophonius drew his knife. He kissed his brother's forehead one last time, then laid the blade across Agamethus's neck.

My dream changed.

I stood in a long subterranean chamber like an alternate image of the Waystation's main hall. Overhead, a curved ceiling glittered with white subway tiles. Along either side of the room, where the rail pits would've been in a train depot, open canals of water flowed. Rows of television monitors lined the walls, flashing video clips of a bearded man with curly brown hair, perfect teeth, and brilliant blue eyes.

The videos reminded me of Times Square ads for a late-night talk show host. The man mugged for the camera, laughing, kissing the screen, pretending to be off-balance. In each shot, he wore a different outfit—an Italian business suit, a race-car driver's uniform, hunting fatigues—each cut from the skin of a lion.

A title bounced around the screen in garish colors: THE NEW HERCULES!

Yes. That's what he liked to call himself back in Roman times. He had that hero's shockingly good physique, but he wasn't the actual Hercules. I should know. I'd dealt with Hercules on many occasions. This emperor was more like someone's *idea* of Hercules—an airbrushed, overly muscular caricature.

In the middle of the hall, flanked by bodyguards and attendants, was the man himself, lounging on a white granite throne. Not many emperors can look imperial wearing only lion-skin swim trunks, but Commodus managed. One of his legs was thrown casually over the throne's armrest. His golden abs formed such a six-pack I imagined I could see the pop-top tabs. With an immensely bored expression, using only two fingers, he twirled a six-foot-long poleax that came very close to threatening his nearest advisor's anatomy.

I wanted to whimper. Not just because I still found Commodus attractive after so many centuries, not just because we had a, er, complicated history, but also because he reminded me what *I* used to be like. Oh, to be able to look in the mirror and see perfection again, not a pudgy awkward boy with a bad complexion!

I forced myself to focus on the other people in the room.

Kneeling before the emperor were two people I'd seen in my vision of Nero's penthouse—Marcus the blinged-out jackal boy, and Vortigern the barbarian.

Marcus was trying to explain something to the emperor. He waved his hands desperately. "We tried! Sire, listen!"

The emperor did not seem inclined to listen. His uninterested gaze drifted across the throne room to various amusements: a rack of torture tools, a row of arcade games, a set of weights, and a freestanding target board plastered with . . . oh, dear, the face of Lester Papadopoulos, bristling with embedded throwing knives.

In the shadows at the back of the room, strange animals moved restlessly in cages. I saw no griffins, but there were other fabled beasts I hadn't seen in centuries. Half a dozen winged Arabian serpents fluttered in an oversize canary cage. Inside a golden pen, a pair of bull-like creatures with huge horns snuffled at a feeding trough. European yales, perhaps? Goodness, those had been rare even back in ancient times.

Marcus kept yammering excuses until, on the emperor's left, a portly man in a crimson business suit snapped, "ENOUGH!"

The advisor made a wide arc around the emperor's spinning poleax. His face was so red and sweaty that, as a god of medicine, I wanted to warn him he was dangerously close to congestive heart failure. He advanced on the two supplicants.

"You are telling us," he snarled, "that you *lost* her. Two strong, capable servants of the Triumvirate lost a little girl. How could that happen?"

Marcus cupped his hands. "Lord Cleander, I don't know! We stopped at a convenience store outside of Dayton. She went to the restroom and—and she disappeared."

Marcus glanced at his companion for support. Vortigern grunted.

Cleander, the red-suited advisor, scowled. "Was there any sort of plant near this restroom?"

Marcus blinked. "Plant?"

"Yes, you fool. The *growing* kind."

"I . . . well, there was a clump of dandelions growing from a crack in the pavement by the door, but—"

"*What?*" yelled Cleander. "You let a daughter of Demeter near a *plant?*"

A *daughter of Demeter*. My heart felt like it had been launched upward in one of Britomartis's nets. At first I had wondered if these men were talking about Georgina, but they meant Meg McCaffrey. She had given her escorts the slip.

Marcus gaped like a fish. "Sir, it—it was a just a *weed!*"

"Which is all she needed to teleport away!" screamed Cleander. "You should have *realized* how powerful she is becoming. Gods only know where she is now!"

"Actually," said the emperor, sending a flash freeze through the room, "I'm a god. And I have no idea."

He stopped twirling his poleax. He scanned the throne room until his gaze fixed on a blemmyae servant arranging cakes and canapés on a tea cart. She was not in disguise— her chest-face was in full view, though below her belly-chin she wore a maid's black skirt with a white lace apron.

The emperor took aim. He casually chucked his poleax across the room, the blade burying itself between the maid's eyes. She staggered, managed to say, "Good shot, my lord," then crumbled to dust.

The advisors and bodyguards clapped politely.

Commodus waved away their praise. "I'm bored with these two." He gestured at Marcus and Vortigern. "They failed, yes?"

Cleander bowed. "Yes, my lord. Thanks to them, the daughter of Demeter is on the loose. If she reaches Indianapolis, she could cause us no end of trouble."

The emperor smiled. "Ah, but Cleander, you failed too, did you not?"

The red-suited man gulped. "Sire, I—I assure you—"

"It was *your* idea to allow Nero to send these idiots. You thought they'd be *helpful* in capturing Apollo. Now the girl has betrayed us. *And* Apollo is somewhere in *my* city, and you haven't apprehended him yet."

"Sire, the meddlesome women of the Waystation—"

"That's right!" the emperor said. "You haven't found them yet, either. And don't get me started on all your failures concerning the naming ceremony."

"B-but, sire! We will have thousands of animals for you to slaughter! Hundreds of captives—"

"BORING! I told you, I want something *creative*. Are you my praetorian prefect or not, Cleander?"

"Y-yes, sire."

"And so you're responsible for any failures."

"But—"

"And you're boring me," Commodus added, "which is punishable by death." He glanced to either side of the throne. "Who's next in the chain of command? Speak up."

A young man stepped forward. Not a Germanus bodyguard, but definitely a fighter. His hand rested easily on the pommel of a sword. His face was a patchwork of scars. His clothes were casual—just jeans, a red-and-white T-shirt that read CORNHUSKERS, and a red bandana tied across his curly dark hair—but he held himself with the easy confidence of a practiced killer.

"I am next, sire."

Commodus inclined his head. "Do it, then."

Cleander shrieked, "No!"

The Cornhusker moved with blinding speed. His sword flashed. In three fluid slices, three people fell dead, their heads severed from their bodies. On the bright side, Cleander no longer had to worry about congestive heart failure. Neither did Marcus nor Vortigern.

The emperor clapped with delight. "Oh, nice! That was *very* entertaining, Lityerses!"

"Thank you, sire." The Cornhusker flicked the blood from his blade.

"You are almost as skilled with the sword as I am!" the emperor said. "Have I ever told you how I decapitated a rhinoceros?"

"Yes, my lord, most impressive." Lityerses's voice was as bland as oatmeal. "Your permission to clear away these bodies?"

"Of course," the emperor said. "Now—you're Midas's boy, aren't you?"

Lityerses's face seemed to develop a few new scars when he scowled. "Yes, sire."

"But you can't do the golden-touch thing?"

"No, sire."

"Pity. You *do* kill people well, though. That's good. Your first orders: Find Meg McCaffrey. And Apollo. Bring them to me, alive if possible, and . . . hmm. There was something else."

"The naming ceremony, sire?"

"Yes!" The emperor grinned. "Yes, yes. I have some wonderful ideas to spice up the games, but since Apollo and the girl are running around loose, we should move forward our plan for the griffins. Go to the zoo right away. Bring the animals here for safekeeping. Manage all that for me, and I won't kill you. Fair?"

Lityerses's neck muscles tensed. "Of course, sire."

As the new praetorian prefect barked orders to the guards, telling them to drag away the decapitated bodies, someone spoke my name.

"Apollo. Wake up."

My eyes fluttered open. Calypso stood over me. The room was dark. Nearby, Leo was still snoring away in his bed.

"It's almost first light," said the sorceress. "We need to get going."

I tried to blink away the remnants of my dreams. Agamethus's Magic 8 Ball seemed to float to the surface of my mind. *Apollo must bring her home.*

I wondered if the ghost had meant Georgina, or another girl whom I very much wanted to find.

Calypso shook my shoulder. "Come on! You wake up very slowly for a sun god."

"W-what? Where?"

"The zoo," she said. "Unless you want to wait around here for morning chores."

12

I sing of taters!
Chili, sweet potato, blue!
Why? Ask my arrow

CALYPSO KNEW how to motivate me.

The thought of scrubbing toilets again was more terrifying than my dreams.

We walked the dark streets in the cold early morning, keeping an eye out for polite mobs of killer blemmyae, but no one bothered us. Along the way, I explained my nightmares to Calypso.

I spelled out the name C-O-M-M-O-D-U-S, in case saying it aloud might attract the god-emperor's attention. Calypso had never heard of him. Of course, she'd been stuck on her island for the last few millennia. I doubted she would recognize the names of many people who hadn't washed up on her shores. She barely knew who Hercules was. I found that refreshing. Hercules was *such* an attention hog.

"You know this emperor personally?" she asked.

I convinced myself I wasn't blushing. The wind was just stinging my face. "We met when he was younger. We had a surprising amount in common. Once he became emperor . . ." I sighed. "You know how it is. He got too much power and fame at a tender age. It messed with his head. Like Justin, Britney, Lindsay, Amanda, Amadeus—"

"I don't know any of those people."

"We need to spend more time on your pop culture lessons."

"No, please." Calypso struggled with the zipper of her coat.

Today she was wearing an assortment of borrowed clothing she must have picked out in total darkness: a battered silver parka, probably from Emmie's Hunters of Artemis days; a blue INDY 500 T-shirt; an ankle-length brown skirt over black leggings; and bright purple-and-green workout shoes. Meg McCaffrey would have approved of her fashion sense.

"What about the sword-wielding Cornhusker?" Calypso asked.

"Lityerses, son of King Midas. I don't know much about him, or why he is serving the emperor. We can only hope to get in and out of the zoo before he shows up. I don't relish the idea of meeting him in combat."

Calypso flexed her fingers, perhaps remembering what happened the last time she punched someone. "At least your friend Meg escaped her escorts," she noted. "That's good news."

"Perhaps." I wanted to believe Meg was rebelling against Nero. That she had finally seen the truth about her monstrous stepfather and would now rush to my side, ready to aid me in my quests and stop giving me vexing orders.

Unfortunately, I knew firsthand how hard it was to extricate oneself from an unhealthy relationship. Nero's hooks were buried deep in the girl's psyche. The idea of Meg on the run without a destination, terrified, pursued by the minions of two different emperors . . . that did not reassure me. I hoped she at least had her friend Peaches the grain spirit to rely on, but I had seen no sign of him in my visions.

"And Trophonius?" asked Calypso. "Do you often forget when someone is your child?"

"You wouldn't understand."

"We're looking for a dangerous Oracle that drives people insane. The spirit of this Oracle happens to be your son, who just might hold a grudge against you because you didn't answer his prayers, thus forcing him to cut off his own brother's head. Those facts would have been good to know."

"I've had a lot on my mind! It's a very small *mortal* mind."

"At least we agree on the size of your brain."

"Oh, stick a brick in it," I muttered. "I was hoping for advice on how to proceed. You're useless."

"My advice is to stop being such a *gloutos*."

The word meant *buttocks*, except that in ancient Greek it had a much ruder connotation. I tried to think of a withering reply, but the ancient Greek phrase for *I know you are, but what am I?* eluded me.

Calypso ruffled the fletching in my quiver. "If you want advice, why not ask your arrow? Perhaps he knows how to rescue griffins."

"Humph." I did not like Calypso's advice for seeking advice. I didn't see what a Shakespearean-talking arrow could contribute to our present quest. Then again, I had nothing to lose except my temper. If the arrow annoyed me too much, I could always fire him into some monster's gloutos.

I pulled out the Arrow of Dodona. Immediately, his sonorous voice spoke in my mind, the shaft resonating with each word.

LO, it said. THE MORTAL DOTH FINALLY SHOW SENSE.

"I've missed you, too," I said.

"It's talking?" Calypso asked.

"Unfortunately, yes. O, Arrow of Dodona, I have a question for you."

HITTEST ME WITH THY BEST SHOT.

I explained about my visions. I'm sure I looked ridiculous, talking to an arrow as we strolled along West Maryland Street. Outside the Indiana Convention Center, I tripped and nearly impaled myself through the eye, but Calypso didn't even bother to laugh. During our travels together she'd seen me humiliate myself in much more spectacular ways.

Talking proved a slower way of bringing a projectile up to speed than by simply launching it from a bow, but at last I succeeded.

FIE. The arrow shuddered in my hand. THOU HAST GIVEN ME NOT A QUESTION BUT A STORY.

I wondered if it was testing me—gauging just how far it could push me before I snapped it in two. I might have done so long ago except I feared I would then have *two* fragments of a talking arrow, which would give me bad advice in harmony.

"Very well," I said. "How can we find the griffins? Where is Meg McCaffrey? How can we defeat the local emperor, free his prisoners, and take back control of the Oracle of Trophonius?"

NOW HAST THOU ASKED TOO MANY QUESTIONS, the arrow intoned. MY WISDOM DOTH NOT SPEW FORTH ANSWERS AS IF 'TWERE GOOGLE.

Yes, the arrow was definitely tempting me to snap it.

"Let's start simply, then," I said. "How do we free the griffins?"

GOEST THOU TO THE ZOO.

"We're already doing that."

FINDEST THOU THE GRIFFINS' ENCLOSURE.

"Yes, but where? And don't tell me at the zoo. Where exactly in the Indianapolis Zoo are the griffins being kept?"

SEEKEST THOU THE CHOO-CHOO.

"The choo-choo."

IST THERE AN ECHO IN HERE?

"Fine! We look for a choo—a train. Once we locate the griffins, how do we free them?"

LO, THOU SHALT GAIN THE BEASTS' TRUST WITH TATER TOTS.

"Tater Tots?"

I waited for clarification, or even just another snarky comment. The arrow remained silent. With a snort of disgust, I returned it to my quiver.

"You know," Calypso said, "hearing only one side of that conversation was very confusing."

"'Twas not much better hearing both sides," I assured her. "Something about a train. And children made of potatoes."

"Tater Tots are food. Leo—" Her voice caught on his name. "Leo likes them."

My vast experience with women told me that Calypso was either feeling remorseful about her argument with Leo yesterday or she got emotional on the subject of Tater Tots. I wasn't inclined to find out which.

"Whatever ist the case, I knowest not—" I spat the Shakespearean English off my tongue. "I don't know what the arrow's advice means. Perhaps when we get to the zoo, it will make sense."

"Because that happens so often when we arrive in new places," Calypso said. "Suddenly everything makes sense."

"You have a point." I sighed. "But much like the point on my talking arrow, it does us no good. Shall we continue?"

We used the Washington Street Bridge to cross the White River, which was not at all white. It flowed wide, sluggish, and brown between cement retaining walls, the water breaking around islands of scrubby bushes like acne patches (with which I was now all too familiar). It reminded me strangely of the Tiber in Rome—another underwhelming, long-neglected river.

Yet world-altering history had been made along the banks of the Tiber. I shuddered to think what plans Commodus had for this city. And if the White River fed the canals I'd glimpsed in his throne room, his lair might be close. Which meant that his new prefect, Lityerses, might already be at the zoo. I decided to walk faster.

The Indianapolis Zoo was tucked away in a park just off West Washington. We crossed an empty parking lot, heading toward the turquoise marquee of the main entrance. A banner out front read WILDLY CUTE! For a moment I thought perhaps the zoo staff had heard I was coming and decided to welcome me. Then I realized the banner was just an advertisement for koala bears. As if koalas needed advertising.

Calypso frowned at the shuttered ticket booths. "Nobody here. The place is locked up tight."

"That *was* the idea," I reminded her. "The fewer mortals around, the better."

"But how do we get in?"

"If only someone could control wind spirits and carry us over the fence."

"If only some god could teleport us," she countered. "Or snap his fingers and bring the griffins to us."

I folded my arms. "I'm beginning to remember why we exiled you on that island for three thousand years."

"Three thousand five hundred and sixty-eight. It would have been longer if you'd had your way."

I hadn't meant to start this argument again, but Calypso made it so easy. "You were on a tropical island with pristine beaches, aerial servants, and a lavishly appointed cave."

"Which made Ogygia not a prison?"

I was tempted to blast her with godly power, except . . . well, I didn't have any. "You don't miss your island, then?"

She blinked as if I'd thrown sand in her face. "I—no. That's not the point. I was kept in exile. I had no one—"

"Oh, please. You want to know what *real* exile feels like?

This is my third time as a mortal. Stripped of my powers. Stripped of immortality. I can *die*, Calypso."

"Me too," she snapped.

"Yes, but you *chose* to go with Leo. You gave up your immortality for love! You're as bad as Hemithea!"

I hadn't realized how much anger was behind that last shot until I let it fly. My voice resounded across the parking lot. Somewhere in the zoo, a rudely awakened tropical bird squawked in protest.

Calypso's expression hardened. "Right."

"I only meant—"

"Save it." She gazed down the perimeter of the fence. "Shall we find a place to climb over?"

I tried to formulate a gallant apology that would also completely vindicate my position, but I decided to let the matter drop. My shout might have woken up more than the toucans. We needed to hurry.

We found a breaching point where the fence was slightly lower. Even in a skirt, Calypso proved the more agile climber. She made it over the top with no problem, while I snagged my shoe on barbed wire and found myself hanging upside down. It was complete luck that I did not fall into the tiger habitat.

"Shut up," I told Calypso when she pulled me free.

"I didn't say anything!"

The tiger glared at us from the other side of his enclosure glass as if to say, *Why are you bothering me if you haven't brought me breakfast?*

I'd always found tigers to be sensible creatures.

Calypso and I crept through the zoo, keeping a lookout

for mortals or imperial guards. Except for a zookeeper hosing down the lemur display, we saw no one.

We stopped in an area that seemed to be the park's main crossroads. To our left stood a carousel. To our right, orangutans lounged in the trees of a large netted compound. Strategically placed around the plaza were several gift shops and cafés, all closed. Signs pointed toward various attractions: OCEAN, PLAINS, JUNGLE, FLIGHTS OF FANCY.

"'Flights of fancy,'" I said. "Surely they would file griffins under fanciful flights."

Calypso scanned our surroundings. She had unnerving eyes—dark brown and intensely focused, not unlike Artemis's gaze when she took aim at a target. I suppose on Ogygia Calypso had had many years of practice staring at the horizon, waiting for someone or something interesting to appear.

"Your arrow mentioned a train," she said. "There's a sign for a train ride."

"Yes, but my arrow also said something about Tater Tots. I think it's getting a bit warped."

Calypso pointed. "There."

At the nearest outdoor café, next to a shuttered serving window, a lunch menu was posted on the wall. I scanned the selections.

"Four different kinds of Tater Tots?" I felt overwhelmed by culinary confusion. "Why would anyone need so many? Chili. Sweet potato. *Blue?* How can a Tot be—?" I froze.

For a nanosecond, I wasn't sure what had startled me. Then I realized my keen ears had picked up on a sound in the distance—a man's voice.

"What is it?" Calypso asked.

"*Shh.*" I listened more intently.

I hoped I might have been mistaken. Perhaps I'd simply heard some exotic bird with a gravelly croak, or the zoo-keeper cursing as he hosed out lemur poop. But no. Even in my diminished mortal state, my hearing was exceptional.

The voice spoke again, familiar and much closer. "You three, that way. You two, with me."

I touched Calypso's jacket sleeve. "It's Lityerses, the Cornhusker."

The sorceress muttered another Minoan curse, naming a part of Zeus's body that I did *not* want to think about. "We need to hide."

Unfortunately, Lityerses was approaching from the way we'd come. Judging from the sound of his voice, we had only seconds before he'd arrive. The crossroads offered any number of escape routes, but all of them would be within Lityerses's line of sight.

Only one place was close enough to offer cover.

"When in doubt," Calypso said, "Tater Tots."

She grabbed my hand and pulled me around the back of the café.

13

Fast-food restaurant
My life goal is realized
Any fries with that?

WHEN I WAS A GOD, I would've been pleased to have a beautiful woman pull me behind a building. But as Lester with Calypso, I was more likely to get killed than kissed.

We crouched next to a stack of milk crates by the kitchen entrance. The area smelled of cooking grease, pigeon droppings, and chlorine from the nearby children's splash park. Calypso rattled the locked door, then glared at me.

"Help!" she hissed.

"What am *I* supposed to do?"

"Well, now would be a good time to have a burst of godly strength!"

I should never have told her and Leo about that. Once, when facing Nero at Camp Half-Blood, my superhuman power had briefly returned, allowing me to overcome the emperor's Germani. I'd thrown one of them into the sky where, for all I knew, he was still in low earth orbit. But that moment had quickly passed. My strength hadn't returned since.

Regardless, Leo and Calypso seemed to think I could

summon godly bursts of awesomeness anytime I wanted, just because I was a former god. I found that unfair.

I gave the door a try. I yanked the handle and almost pulled my fingers out of their sockets.

"Ow," I muttered. "Mortals have gotten good at making doors. Now, back in the Bronze Age—"

Calypso shushed me.

Our enemies' voices were getting closer. I couldn't hear Lityerses, but two other men were conversing in a guttural language that sounded like ancient Gallic. I doubted they were zookeepers.

Calypso frantically pulled a bobby pin from her hair. Aha, so her lovely coiffed locks did not stay in place by magic! She pointed at me, then pointed around the corner. I thought she was telling me to flee and save myself. That would have been a sensible suggestion. Then I realized she was asking me to keep watch.

I didn't know what good that would do, but I peered over the rampart of milk crates and waited for Germani to come and kill us. I could hear them at the front of the café, rattling the shutter over the order window, then conversing briefly with lots of grunts and grumbling. Knowing the emperor's bodyguards, they were probably saying something like *Kill? Kill. Bash heads? Bash heads.*

I wondered why Lityerses had split his people into two groups. Surely they already knew where the griffins were being kept. Why, then, were they searching the park? Unless, of course, they were searching for intruders, specifically *us.* . . .

Calypso snapped her hairpin in two. She inserted the

metal pieces in the door lock and began to wriggle them, her eyes closed as if she were in deep concentration.

Ridiculous, I thought. That only works in movies and Homeric epics!

Click. The door swung inward. Calypso waved me inside. She yanked the pin shards out of the lock, then followed me across the threshold, gently closing the door behind us. She turned the dead bolt just before someone outside shook the handle.

A gruff voice muttered in Gallic, probably something like *No luck. Bash heads elsewhere.*

Footsteps receded.

I finally remembered to breathe.

I faced Calypso. "How did you pick the lock?"

She stared at the broken hairpin in her hand. "I—I thought about weaving."

"Weaving?"

"I can still *weave*. I spent thousands of years practicing at the loom. I thought maybe—I don't know—manipulating pins in a lock wouldn't be too different than weaving thread in a loom."

The two things sounded *very* different to me, but I couldn't argue with the results.

"So it wasn't magic, then?" I tried to contain my disappointment. Having a few wind spirits at our command would have been very helpful.

"No," she said. "You'll know when I get my magic back, because you'll find yourself being tossed across Indianapolis."

"That's something to look forward to."

I scanned the dark interior of the snack bar. Against

the back wall were the basics: a sink, a deep fryer, a stove top, two microwaves. Under the counter sat two horizontal freezers.

How did I know the basics of a fast-food kitchen, you ask? I had discovered the singer Pink while she was working at McDonalds. I found Queen Latifah at Burger King. I've spent a fair amount of time in such places. You can't discount *any* site where you might find talent.

I checked the first freezer. Inside, wreathed in cold mist, were carefully labeled boxes of ready-to-cook meals, but nothing that read TATER TOTS.

The second freezer was locked.

"Calypso," I said, "could you weave this open?"

"Who's useless now, eh?"

In the interest of getting my way, I decided not to answer. I stepped back as Calypso worked her non-magical skills. She popped this lock even faster than the first.

"Well done." I lifted the freezer lid. "Ah."

Hundreds of packages were wrapped in white butcher paper, each labeled in black marker.

Calypso squinted at the descriptions. "*Carnivorous horse mix? Combat ostrich cubes? And . . . griffin taters.*" She turned to me with a horrified look. "Surely they're not grinding animals into *food?*"

I remembered a long-ago banquet with the spiteful King Tantalus, who had served the gods a stew made from his own sons. With humans, anything was possible. But in this case, I didn't think the café was putting mythical wildlife on the menu.

"These items are under lock and key," I said. "I'm guessing they've been set aside as treats for the zoo's rarest animals. That's a mix of food *for* a carnivorous horse, not a mixture *of* carnivorous horse."

Calypso looked only slightly less nauseated. "What in the world is a combat ostrich?"

The question triggered an old memory. I was overwhelmed by a vision as powerful as the stench of an unwashed lemur cage.

I found myself lounging on a couch in the campaign tent of my friend Commodus. He was in the midst of a military campaign with his father, Marcus Aurelius, but nothing about the tent suggested the harsh life of the Roman legion. Overhead, a white silk canopy billowed in the gentle breeze. In one corner, a musician sat discreetly serenading us with his lyre. Under our feet spread the finest rugs from the eastern provinces—each one as expensive as an entire villa in Rome. Between our two couches, a table was spread with an afternoon snack of roast boar, pheasant, salmon, and fruit spilling from a solid gold cornucopia.

I was amusing myself by throwing grapes at Commodus's mouth. Of course, I never missed unless I wanted to, but it was fun to watch the fruit bounce off Commodus's nose.

"You are *terrible*," he teased me.

And you are perfect, I thought, but I merely smiled.

He was eighteen. In mortal form, I appeared to be a youth of the same age, but even with my godly enhancements I could hardly have been more handsome than the *princeps*. Despite his easy life, being born into the purple of the Imperial Household, Commodus was the very model of athletic perfection—his body lithe and muscular, his golden hair in ringlets around his Olympian face. His physical strength was already renowned, drawing comparisons to the legendary hero Hercules.

I threw another grape. He caught it in his hand and studied the little orb. "Oh, Apollo . . ." He knew my real identity, yes. We had been friends, *more* than friends, for almost a month at that point. "I get so weary of these campaigns. My father has been at war virtually his entire reign!"

"Such a hard life for you." I gestured at the opulence around us.

"Yes, but it's *ridiculous*. Tromping around Danubian forests, stamping out barbarian tribes that are really no threat to Rome. What's the point of being emperor if you're never in the capital having fun?"

I nibbled on a piece of boar meat. "Why not talk to your father? Ask for a furlough?"

Commodus snorted. "You know what he'll do—give me another lecture on duty and morality. He is so virtuous, so perfect, so esteemed."

He put those words in air circles (since air quotes had not yet been invented). I could certainly sympathize with his feelings. Marcus Aurelius was the sternest, most powerful father in the world aside from my own father, Zeus. Both loved to lecture. Both loved to remind their offspring how lucky they were, how privileged, how far short they fell of their fathers' expectations. And of course, both had gorgeous, talented, tragically underappreciated sons.

Commodus squished his grape and watched the juice

THE DARK PROPHECY   123

trickle down his fingers. "My father made me his junior co-emperor when I was *fifteen*, Apollo. It's stifling. All duty, all the time. Then he married me off to that horrid girl Bruttia Crispina. Who names their child *Bruttia?*"

I didn't mean to laugh at the expense of his distant wife . . . but part of me was pleased when he talked badly about her. I wanted all his attention for myself.

"Well, someday you'll be the sole emperor," I said. "Then *you* can make the rules."

"I'll make peace with the barbarians," he said immediately. "Then we'll go home and celebrate with games. The *best* games, all the time. I'll gather the most exotic animals in the world. I'll fight them personally in the Colosseum—tigers, elephants, ostriches."

I laughed at that. "Ostriches? Have you ever even *seen* an ostrich?"

"Oh, yes." He got a wistful look in his eyes. "Amazing creatures. If you trained them to fight, perhaps designed some sort of armor for them, they would be *incredible*."

"You're a handsome idiot." I threw another grape, which bounced off his forehead.

A brief flash of anger washed over his face. I knew my sweet Commodus could have an ugly temper. He was a little too fond of slaughter. But what did I care? I was a god. I could speak to him in ways no one else dared.

The tent flap opened. A centurion stepped inside and saluted crisply, but his face was stricken, gleaming with sweat. "Princeps . . ." His voice quavered. "It's your father. He . . . he is . . ."

He never spoke the word *dead*, but it seemed to float

into the tent all around us, sapping the heat from the air. The lyre player stopped on a major seventh chord.

Commodus looked at me, panic in his eyes.

"Go," I said, as calmly as I could, forcing down my misgivings. "You will always have my blessings. You will do fine."

But I already suspected what would happen: the young man I knew and loved was about to be consumed by the emperor he would become.

He rose and kissed me one last time. His breath smelled of grapes. Then he left the tent—walking, as the Romans would say, into the mouth of the wolf.

"Apollo." Calypso nudged my arm.

"Don't go!" I pleaded. Then my past life burned away.

The sorceress was frowning at me. "What do you mean *don't go*? Did you have another vision?"

I scanned the dark kitchen of the snack bar. "I—I'm fine. What's going on?"

Calypso pointed to the freezer. "Look at the prices."

I swallowed down the bitter taste of grapes and boar meat. In the freezer, on the corner of each white butcher-paper package, a price was written in pencil. By far the most expensive: griffin taters, $15,000 per serving.

"I'm not good at modern currency," I admitted, "but isn't that a bit pricey for a meal?"

"I was going to ask you the same thing," Calypso said. "I know the S symbol with the line through it means American dollars, but the amount . . . ?" She shrugged.

I found it unfair that I was adventuring with someone

as clueless as I was. A modern demigod could have easily told us, and they also would have had useful twenty-first-century skills. Leo Valdez could repair machines. Percy Jackson could drive a car. I would even have settled for Meg McCaffrey and her garbage-bag-throwing prowess, though I knew what Meg would say about our present predicament: *You guys are dumb.*

I pulled out a packet of griffin taters and unwrapped one corner. Inside, small frozen cubes of shredded potato gleamed with a golden metallic coating.

"Are Tater Tots usually sprayed with precious metal?" I asked.

Calypso picked one up. "I don't think so. But griffins like gold. My father told me that ages ago."

I shuddered. I recalled her father, General Atlas, unleashing a flock of griffins on me during the Titans' first war with the gods. Having your chariot swarmed by eagle-headed lions is not something you easily forget.

"So we take these taters to feed the griffins," I guessed. "With luck, this will help us win their trust." I pulled the Arrow of Dodona from my quiver. "Is that what you had in mind, Most Frustrating of Arrows?"

The arrow vibrated. *VERILY, THOU ART DENSER THAN A COMBAT OSTRICH CUBE.*

"What did he say?" Calypso asked.

"He said yes."

From the counter, Calypso grabbed a paper menu with a map of the zoo on it. She pointed to an orange loop circling the PLAINS area. "Here."

The loop was labeled TRAIN RIDE, the least creative name I could imagine. At the bottom, in a map key, was a more detailed explanation: TRAIN RIDE! A LOOK AT THE ZOO BEHIND THE ZOO!

"Well," I said, "at least they advertise the fact that they have a secret zoo behind the zoo. That was nice of them."

"I think it's time to ride the choo-choo," Calypso agreed.

From the front of the café came a crashing sound, like a Germanus had tripped over a trash can.

"Stop that!" barked Lityerses. "You, stay here and keep watch. If they show, capture them—don't kill them. You, come with me. We need those griffins."

I counted silently to five, then whispered to Calypso, "Are they gone?"

"Let me use my super vision to look through this wall and check," she said. "Oh, wait."

"You are a terrible person."

She pointed to the map. "If Lityerses left one guard at the crossroads, it will be difficult to get out of here and reach the train without him seeing us."

"Well," I said, "I suppose we could go back to the Waystation and tell Britomartis that we tried."

Calypso threw a frozen golden Tater Tot at me. "When you were a god, if some heroes had returned empty-handed from a quest and told you *Oh, sorry, Apollo. We tried*, would you be understanding?"

"Certainly not! I would incinerate them! I would . . . Oh. I see your point." I wrung my hands. "Then what do we do? I don't feel like being incinerated. It hurts."

"Perhaps there's a way." Calypso traced her finger across the map to a section labeled MEERKAT, REPTILE & SNAKE, which sounded like the worst law firm ever.

"I have an idea," she said. "Bring your Tots and follow me."

14

Yeah, we got the skills
Fake hexes and shooting feet
Teach you 'bout pancakes

I DID NOT WISH to follow Calypso, with or without my Tots.

Sadly, my only other option was to hide in the café until the emperor's men found me or the café manager arrived and impressed me into service as a short-order cook.

Calypso led the way, darting from hiding place to hiding place like the urban ninja she was. I spotted the lone Germanus on sentry duty, about fifty feet across the plaza, but he was busy studying the carousel. He pointed his polearm warily at the painted horses as if they might be carnivorous.

We made it to the far side of the crossroads without attracting his attention, but I was still nervous. For all we knew, Lityerses might have multiple groups sweeping the park. On a telephone pole near the souvenir shop, a security camera stared down at us. If the Triumvirate was as powerful as Nero claimed, they could easily control surveillance inside the Indianapolis Zoo. Perhaps that was why Lityerses was searching for us. He already knew we were here.

I thought about shooting the camera with an arrow, but

it was probably too late. Cameras loved me. No doubt my face was all over the security office monitors.

Calypso's plan was to circumvent the orangutans and cut through the reptile display, skirting the park perimeter until we reached the train depot. Instead, as we passed the entrance to the ape habitat, voices of an approaching Germanus patrol startled us. We dove into the orangutan center for cover.

All right . . . *I* got startled and dove for cover. Calypso hissed, "No, you idiot!" then followed me inside. Together we crouched behind a retaining wall as two Germani strolled past, chatting casually about head-bashing techniques.

I glanced to my right and stifled a yelp. On the other side of a glass wall, a large orangutan was staring at me, his amber eyes curious. He made some hand gestures—sign language? Agamethus might have known. Judging from the great ape's expression, he was not terribly delighted to see me. Alas, among the great apes, only humans are capable of proper awe for the gods. On the plus side for orangutans, they have *amazing* orange fur that no human could possibly rival.

Calypso nudged my leg. "We need to keep moving."

We scurried deeper into the display room. Our simian movements must have amused the orangutan. He made a deep barking noise.

"Shut up!" I stage-whispered back at him.

At the far exit, we huddled behind a curtain of camouflage netting. I cradled my taters and tried to steady my breathing.

Next to me, Calypso hummed under her breath—a

nervous habit of hers. I wished she would stop. Whenever she hummed a tune I knew, I had the urge to sing harmony very loudly, which would have given away our position.

At last, I whispered, "I think the coast is clear."

I stepped out and smacked straight into another Germanus. Honestly, how many barbarians did Commodus have? Was he buying them in bulk?

For a moment, all three of us were too surprised to speak or move. Then the barbarian made a rumbling sound in his chest as if about to shout for backup.

"Hold these!" I thrust my package of griffin food into his arms.

Reflexively, he took them. After all, a man giving up his Tots is a gesture of surrender in many cultures. He frowned at the package as I stepped back, slung my bow off my shoulder, fired, and planted an arrow in his left foot.

He howled, dropping the Tater Tots package. I scooped it up and ran, Calypso close behind me.

"Nicely done," she offered.

"Except for the fact that he probably alerted— Veer left!"

Another Germanus came barreling out of the reptile area. We scrambled around him and ran toward a sign that said SKYLINE.

In the distance loomed an aerial tram—wires strung from tower to tower above the treetops, a single green gondola hanging about fifty feet in the air. I wondered if we could use the ride to reach the secret zoo area, or at least gain a height advantage, but the gondola house entrance was fenced off and padlocked.

Before I could ask Calypso to work her hairpin hocus-pocus, the Germani cornered us. The one from the reptile area advanced, his polearm leveled at our chests. The one from the orangutan house came snarling and limping behind, my arrow still sticking out of his bloody leather boot.

I nocked another arrow, but there was no way I could bring them both down before they killed us. I'd seen Germani take six or seven arrows to the heart and still keep fighting.

Calypso muttered, "Apollo, when I curse you, pretend to faint."

"What?"

She wheeled on me and shouted, "You have failed me for the last time, slave!"

She made a series of hand gestures I recognized from ancient times—hexes and curses that no one had ever dared to make in my direction. I was tempted to slap her. Instead, I did as she asked: I gasped and collapsed.

Through my half-lidded eyes, I watched Calypso turn on our enemies.

"Now it is *your* turn, fools!" She began making the same rude gestures toward the Germani.

The first one stopped. His face paled. He glanced at me lying on the ground, then turned and fled, barreling past his friend.

The Germanus with the wounded foot hesitated. Judging from the hatred in his eyes, he wanted revenge for the missile weapon that had ruined his left boot.

Calypso, undaunted, waved her arms and began to incant. Her tone made it sound as if she were raising the worst daimons from Tartarus, though her words, in ancient Phoenician, were actually a recipe for making pancakes.

The wounded Germanus yelped and hobbled away, leaving a trail of smeared red prints behind him.

Calypso offered me a hand and pulled me up. "Let's move. I've only bought us a few seconds."

"How did you— Did your magic return?"

"I wish," she said. "I faked it. Half of magic is *acting* like it will work. The other half is picking a superstitious mark. They'll be back. With reinforcements."

I'll admit I was impressed. Her "hexing" had certainly unnerved me.

I made a quick gesture to ward off evil, just in case Calypso was better than she realized. Then we ran together along the perimeter fence.

At the next crossroads, Calypso said, "This way to the train."

"You're sure?"

She nodded. "I'm good at memorizing maps. Once, I made one of Ogygia; reproduced every square foot of that island. It was the only way I kept myself sane."

This sounded like a terrible way to keep oneself sane, but I let her lead the way. Behind us, more Germani were shouting, but they seemed to be heading toward the Skyline gates we'd just left. I allowed myself to hope that the train station might be clear.

HA-HA-HA. It was not.

On the tracks sat a miniature train—a bright green steam engine with a line of open passenger cars. Next to it on the station platform, under an ivy-covered canopy,

Lityerses stood with his feet planted, his unsheathed sword resting over his shoulder like a hobo's bindle. A battered leather cuirass was strapped over his Cornhuskers shirt. His dark curly hair hung in tendrils over his red bandana, making it look as if a large spider were crouched on his head, ready to spring.

"Welcome." The prefect's smile might have seemed friendly, except for the crosshatching of scars on his face. He touched something on his ear—a Bluetooth device, perhaps. "They're here at the station," he announced. "Converge on me, but *slow and calm*. I'm fine. I want these two alive."

He shrugged at us apologetically. "My men can be over-enthusiastic when it comes to killing. Especially after you've made them look like fools."

"It was our pleasure." I doubt I pulled off the self-assured, swashbuckling tone I was going for. My voice cracked. Sweat beaded on my face. I held my bow sideways like an electric guitar, which was not proper shooting stance, and in my other hand, instead of an arrow that might have been useful, I held a package of frozen Tater Tots.

It was probably just as well. In my dream, I'd seen how rapidly Lityerses could swing his sword. If I tried to fire on him, our heads would be rolling on the pavement before I drew back my bowstring.

"You're able to use a phone," I noticed. "Or a walkie-talkie, or whatever that is. I hate it when the bad guys get to talk to each other and we can't."

Lityerses's laugh was like a file across metal. "Yes. The Triumvirate likes to have certain advantages."

"I don't suppose you'd tell us how they manage it—blocking demigod communications?"

"You won't live long enough for that to matter. Now, drop your bow. As for your friend . . ." He sized up Calypso. "Keep your hands at your side. No sudden curses. I'd hate to chop off that pretty head of yours."

Calypso smiled sweetly. "I was just thinking the same thing about you. Drop your sword and I won't destroy you."

She was a good actor. I made a mental note to recommend her to my Mount Olympus invitation-only summer camp, *Method Acting with the Muses*—if we got out of this alive.

Lityerses chuckled. "That's good. I like you. But in about sixty seconds, a dozen Germani are going to swarm this depot. They will *not* ask as politely as I did." He took a step forward and swung his sword to his side.

I tried to think of a brilliant plan. Unfortunately, the only thing that came to mind was weeping in terror. Then, above Lityerses, the ivy rustled on the canopy.

The swordsman didn't seem to notice. I wondered if orangutans were playing up there, or perhaps some Olympian gods had gathered for a picnic to watch me die. Or maybe . . . The thought was too much to wish for, but in the interest of buying time, I dropped my bow.

"Apollo," Calypso hissed. "What are you doing?"

Lityerses answered for me. "He's being smart. Now, where's the third member of your little party?"

I blinked. "It—it's just the two of us."

Lityerses's facial scars rippled, white lines on tan skin, like the ridges of a sand dune. "Come now. You flew into the city on a dragon. Three passengers. I *very much* want to see Leo Valdez again. We have unfinished business."

"You know Leo?" Despite the danger we were in, I felt a small sense of relief. Finally, some villain wanted to kill Leo more than he wanted to kill me. That was progress!

Calypso didn't seem so happy. She stepped toward the swordsman with her fists clenched. "What do you want with Leo?"

Lityerses narrowed his eyes. "You're not the same girl who was with him before. Her name was Piper. You wouldn't happen to be Leo's girlfriend?"

Red blotches appeared on Calypso's cheeks and neck.

Lityerses brightened. "Oh, you are! That's wonderful! I can use you to hurt him."

Calypso snarled. "You *will not* hurt him."

Above Lityerses, the canopy roof shook again, as if a thousand rats were scurrying through the rafters. The vines seemed to be growing, the foliage turning thicker and darker.

"Calypso," I said, "step back."

"Why should I?" she demanded. "This Cornhusker just threatened—"

"Calypso!" I grabbed her wrist and yanked her from the shadow of the canopy just as it collapsed on top of Lityerses. The swordsman disappeared under hundreds of pounds of shingles, lumber, and ivy.

I surveyed the mass of quivering vines. I saw no orang-utans, no gods, no one who might have been responsible for the collapse.

"She *must* be here," I muttered.

"Who?" Calypso stared at me with wide eyes. "What just happened?"

I wanted to hope. I was afraid to hope. Whatever the case, we couldn't stay. Lityerses was shouting and struggling under the wreckage, which meant he wasn't dead. His Germani would be here any second.

"Let's get out of here." I pointed to the green locomotive. "I'm driving."

15

Drivin' the green train
I'm all like, Choo-choo! Choo-choo!
Can't catch me!— Oh, poop!

A SLOW-MOTION GETAWAY was not what I had in mind.

We both jumped onto the conductor's bench, which was barely wide enough for one, and jostled for space while punching pedals and turning random levers.

"I told you, *I'll* drive!" I yelled. "If I can drive the sun, I can drive this!"

"This isn't the sun!" Calypso elbowed me in the ribs. "It's a model train."

I found the ignition switch. The train lurched into motion. (Calypso will claim *she* found the ignition switch. This is a blatant lie.) I pushed Calypso off the bench and onto the ground. Since the train was only going half a mile an hour, she simply stood up, brushed off her skirt, and walked alongside me, glaring.

"*That's* top speed?" she demanded. "Push some more levers!"

Behind us, from somewhere under the wreckage of the canopy, came a mighty "BLARG!" Ivy shivered as Lityerses tried to bust his way out.

A half dozen Germani appeared at the far end of the platform. (Commodus was *definitely* buying his barbarians by the imperial family-size pack.) The bodyguards stared at the screaming mass of roof wreckage, then at us choo-chooing away. Rather than give chase, they began clearing the beams and vines to free their boss. Given the progress we were making, they probably assumed they'd have plenty of time to come after us.

Calypso hopped onto the running board. She pointed to the controls. "Try the blue pedal."

"The blue pedal is never the right one!"

She kicked it with her foot. We shot forward at three times our previous speed, which meant our enemies would now have to jog at a moderate pace to catch us.

The track curved as we continued to accelerate, our wheels squealing against the outer rail. The station disappeared behind a line of trees. On our left, the terrain opened up, revealing the majestic butts of African elephants who were picking through a pile of hay. Their zookeeper frowned as we trundled past. "Hey!" he yelled. "Hey!"

I waved. "Morning!"

Then we were gone. The cars shook dangerously as we picked up steam. My teeth clattered. My bladder sloshed. Up ahead, almost hidden behind a screen of bamboo, a fork in the track was marked by a sign in Latin: BONUM EFFERCIO.

"There!" I yelled. "*The Good Stuff!* We need to turn left!"

Calypso squinted at the console. "How?"

"There should be a switch," I said. "Something that operates the turnout."

Then I saw it—not on our console, but ahead of us on the side of the tracks—an old-fashioned hand lever. There was no time to stop the train, no time to run ahead and turn the switch by hand.

"Calypso, hold this!" I tossed her the Tots and unslung my bow. I nocked an arrow.

Once, such a shot would've been child's play for me. Now it was nearly impossible: shooting from a moving train, aiming for a point where the focused impact of an arrow would have the maximum chance of triggering the switch.

I thought of my daughter Kayla back at Camp Half-Blood. I imagined her calm voice as she coached me through the frustrations of mortal archery. I remembered the other campers' encouragement the day on the beach when I'd made a shot that brought down the Colossus of Nero.

I fired. The arrow slammed into the lever and forced it backward. The point blades shifted. We lurched onto the spur line.

"Down!" Calypso yelled.

We crashed through bamboo and careened into a tunnel just wide enough for the train. Unfortunately, we were going much too fast. The choo-choo tilted sideways, throwing sparks off the wall. By the time we shot out the other side of the tunnel, we were completely off-balance.

The train groaned and tilted—a sensation I knew well from those times the sun chariot had to veer to avoid a launching space shuttle or a Chinese celestial dragon. (Those things are *annoying*.)

"Out!" I tackled Calypso—yes, *again*—and leaped from the right side of the train as the line of cars spilled to the left, toppling off the tracks with a sound like a bronze-clad army being crushed by a giant fist. (I may have crushed a few armies that way back in the old days.)

The next thing I knew I was on all fours, my ear pressed against the ground as if listening for a herd of buffalo, though I had no idea why.

"Apollo." Calypso tugged at the sleeve of my coat. "Get up."

My throbbing head felt several times larger than usual, but I didn't seem to have broken any bones. Calypso's hair had come loose around her shoulders. Her silver parka was dusted with sand and bits of gravel. Otherwise she looked intact. Perhaps our formerly divine constitutions had saved us from damage. Either that or we were just lucky.

We had crashed in the middle of a circular arena. The train lay curled sideways across the gravel like a dead caterpillar, a few feet shy of where the tracks ended. The perimeter was ringed with animal enclosures—Plexiglas walls framed in stone. Above that rose three tiers of stadium seating. Over the top of the amphitheater stretched a canopy of camouflage netting like I'd seen at the orangutan habitat—though here I suspected the netting was meant to keep winged monsters from flying away.

Around the arena floor, chains with empty manacles were fastened to spikes in the ground. Near these stood racks of sinister-looking tools: cattle prods, noose poles, whips, harpoons.

A cold lump formed in my throat. I would've thought I'd swallowed a griffin tater, except the packet was still miraculously intact in Calypso's arms. "This is a training facility," I said. "I've seen places like it before. These animals are being readied for the games."

"*Readied?*" Calypso scowled at the weapon racks. "How, exactly?"

"They're enraged," I said. "Baited. Starved. Trained to kill anything that moves."

"Savagery." Calypso turned to the nearest pen. "What have they done to those poor ostriches?"

Through the Plexiglas, four of the birds stared at us, their heads jerking sideways in a series of fits. They were strange-looking animals to begin with, but these had been outfitted with rows of iron-studded collars along their necks, spiked war helmets in the Kaiser Wilhelm style, and razor wire wreathed like Christmas lights around their legs. The nearest bird snapped at me, revealing jagged steel teeth that had been fitted inside his beak.

"The emperor's combat ostriches." I felt like a roof was collapsing inside my chest. The plight of these animals depressed me . . . but so did thinking about Commodus. The games he had engaged in as a young emperor were disagreeable to start with, and they had transformed into something much worse. "He used to enjoy using them for target practice. With a single arrow, he could decapitate a bird running at a full gallop. Once that wasn't entertaining enough . . ." I gestured at the enhanced war birds.

Calypso's face turned jaundice yellow. "*All* these animals will be killed?"

I was too dispirited to answer. I had flashbacks to the Flavian Amphitheater during Commodus's rule—the glistening red sand of the stadium floor littered with the carcasses of thousands of exotic animals, all butchered for sport and spectacle.

We moved to the next enclosure. A large red bull paced restlessly, his horns and hooves gleaming bronze.

"That's an Aethiopian Bull," I said. "Their hides are impervious to all metal weapons—like the Nemean Lion, except, ah . . . much larger, and red."

Calypso drifted past several more cells—some Arabian winged serpents, a horse that I judged to be of the carnivorous, fire-breathing variety. (I once thought about using those for my sun chariot, but they were *so* high maintenance.)

The sorceress froze at the next window. "Apollo, over here."

Behind the glass were two griffins.

Emmie and Josephine had been correct. They were magnificent specimens.

Over the centuries, with their natural habitats shrinking, wild griffins had become scrawny creatures, smaller and scrappier than in ancient times. (Much like the endangered three-eyed stoat or the giant gassy badger.) Few griffins had ever been large enough to support the weight of a human rider.

The male and female in front of us, however, truly were the size of lions. Their light brown fur gleamed like copper chain mail. Their russet wings folded regally across their backs. Their aquiline heads bristled with gold and white plumage. In the old days, a Grecian king would have paid a trireme full of rubies for a breeding pair like this.

Thankfully, I saw no sign that the animals had been

abused. However, both were chained by their back legs. Griffins get *very* cantankerous when they're imprisoned or restrained in any way. As soon as the male, Abelard, saw us, he snapped and squawked, flapping his wings. He dug his claws in the sand and strained against his shackle, trying to reach us.

The female backed into the shadows, making a low gurgling noise like the growl of a threatened dog. She swayed from side to side, her belly low to the ground as if . . .

"Oh, no." I feared my weak mortal heart would burst. "No wonder Britomartis wanted these two back so badly."

Calypso seemed entranced by the animals. With some difficulty, she refocused on me. "What do you mean?"

"The female is *with egg*. She needs to nest immediately. If we don't get her back to the Waystation . . ."

Calypso's expression turned as sharp and steely as ostrich teeth. "Will Heloise be able to fly out of here?"

"I—I think so. My sister is more the expert on wild animals, but yes."

"Can a pregnant griffin carry a rider?"

"We don't have much choice except to try." I pointed at the netting above the arena. "That's the quickest way out, assuming we can unlock the griffins and remove the net. The problem is, Heloise and Abelard are *not* going to see us as friends. They're chained. They're caged. They're expecting a baby. They'll tear us apart if we get close."

Calypso crossed her arms. "What about music? Most animals like music."

I recalled the way I had used a song to mesmerize the *myrmekes* back at Camp Half-Blood. But I really didn't feel like singing about all my failures again, especially not in front of my companion.

I glanced back at the train tunnel. Still no sign of Lityerses or his men, but that didn't make me feel better. They should have been here by now. . . .

"We need to hurry," I said.

The first problem was the easiest: the Plexiglas wall. I reasoned there must be a switch somewhere for lowering the partitions to release the various animals. I climbed into the spectator tiers with the help of a stepladder named Calypso, and found just such a control panel next to the arena's only padded seat—clearly for the emperor himself when he wanted to check on his killer beasts in training.

Each lever was conveniently labeled with masking tape and marker. One said GRIFFINS.

I called down to Calypso, "Are you ready?"

She stood directly in front of the griffin enclosure, hands out as if preparing to catch a projectile egg. "What would constitute *ready* in a situation like this?"

I flipped the switch. With a heavy *ka-chunk*, the griffins' Plexiglas screen dropped away, disappearing into a slot across the threshold.

I rejoined Calypso, who was humming some sort of lullaby. The two griffins were not impressed. Heloise growled loudly, pressing herself against the back wall of the enclosure. Abelard pulled at his chain twice as hard, trying to reach us and bite off our faces.

Calypso handed me the packet of Tots. She pointed with her chin into the enclosure.

"You must be kidding," I said. "If I get close enough to feed them, they'll eat *me*."

She stopped her song. "Aren't you the god of ranged weapons? Throw the Tots!"

I raised my eyes toward the netted-off heavens—which, by the way, I considered a rude and completely unnecessary metaphor for my exile from Olympus. "Calypso, do you know nothing about these animals? To gain their trust, you must hand-feed them, putting your fingers inside the beak. This emphasizes that the food comes from you, as the mother bird."

"Huh." Calypso bit her lower lip. "I see the problem. You would make a terrible mother bird."

Abelard lunged and squawked at me. Everyone was a critic.

Calypso nodded as if she'd come to a decision. "It's going to take both of us. We'll sing a duet. You have a decent voice."

"I have a . . ." My mouth was paralyzed from shock. Telling *me*, the god of music, that I had a decent voice was like telling Shaquille O'Neal he played decent offense, or telling Annie Oakley she was a decent shot.

Then again, I was *not* Apollo. I was Lester Papadopoulos. Back at camp, despairing of my puny mortal abilities, I had sworn an oath on the River Styx not to use archery or music until I was once again a god. I had promptly broken that oath by singing to the myrmekes—for a good cause, mind you. Ever since, I had lived in terror, wondering when and how the spirit of the Styx would punish me. Perhaps, instead of a grand moment of retribution, it would be a slow death by a thousand insults. How often could a music god hear that he had a *decent voice* before he crumbled into a self-loathing pile of dust?

"Fine." I sighed. "Which duet should we sing? 'Islands in the Stream'?"

"Don't know it."

"'I Got You, Babe'?"

"No."

"Dear gods, I'm *sure* we covered the 1970s in your pop culture lessons."

"What about that song Zeus used to sing?"

I blinked. "Zeus . . . singing?" I found the concept mildly horrifying. My father thundered. He punished. He scolded. He glowered like a champion. But he did not sing.

Calypso's eyes got a little dreamy. "In the palace at Mount Othrys, when he was Kronos's cupbearer, Zeus used to entertain the court with songs."

I shifted uncomfortably. "I . . . hadn't been born yet."

I knew, of course, that Calypso was older than I, but I'd never really thought about what that meant. Back when the Titans ruled the cosmos, before the gods rebelled and Zeus became king, Calypso had no doubt been a carefree child, one of General Atlas's brood, running around the palace harassing the aerial servants. Ye gods. Calypso was old enough to be my babysitter!

"Surely you know the song." Calypso began to sing.

Electricity tingled at the base of my skull. I *did* know the song. An early memory surfaced of Zeus and Leto singing this melody when Zeus visited Artemis and me as children on Delos. My father and mother, destined to be forever apart because Zeus was a married god—they had happily sung this duet. Tears welled in my eyes. I took the lower part of the harmony.

It was a song older than empires—about two lovers separated and longing to be together.

Calypso edged toward the griffins. I followed behind her—not because I was scared to lead, mind you. Everyone knows that when advancing into danger, the soprano goes first. They are your infantry, while the altos and tenors are your cavalry, and the bass your artillery. I've tried to explain this to Ares a million times, but he has *no* clue about vocal arrangement.

Abelard ceased yanking at his chain. He prowled and preened, making deep clucking sounds like a roosting chicken. Calypso's voice was plaintive and full of melancholy. I realized that she empathized with these beasts—caged and chained, yearning for the open sky. Perhaps, I thought, just *perhaps* Calypso's exile on Ogygia had been worse than my present predicament. At least I had friends to share my suffering. I felt guilty that I hadn't voted to release her earlier from her island, but why would she forgive me if I apologized now? That was all Styx water under the gates of Erebos. There was no going back.

Calypso put her hand on Abelard's head. He could easily have snapped off her arm, but he crouched and turned into the caress like a cat. Calypso knelt, removed another hairpin, and began working on the griffin's manacle.

While she tinkered, I tried to keep Abelard's eyes on me. I sang as decently as I could, channeling my sorrow and sympathy into the verses, hoping Abelard would understand that I was a fellow soul in pain.

Calypso popped the lock. With a clank, the iron cuff fell from Abelard's back leg. Calypso moved toward Heloise—a much trickier proposition, approaching an expecting mother. Heloise growled suspiciously but did not attack.

We continued to sing, our voices in perfect pitch now, melding together the way the best harmonies do—creating something greater than the sum of two individual voices.

Calypso freed Heloise. She stepped back and stood shoulder to shoulder with me as we finished the last line of the song: *As long as gods shall live, so long shall I love you.*

The griffins stared at us. They seemed more intrigued now than angry.

"Tots," Calypso advised.

I shook half the packet into her palms.

I didn't relish the idea of losing my arms. They were useful appendages. Nevertheless, I proffered a handful of golden Tater Tots to Abelard. He scuttled forward and sniffed. When he opened his beak, I reached inside and pressed the Tots on his warm tongue. Like a true gentleman, he waited until I removed my hand before swallowing down the snack.

He ruffled his neck feathers, then turned to squawk at Heloise, *Yeah, good eatin'. Come on over!*

Calypso fed her Tots to Heloise. The female griffin butted her head against the sorceress in a sign of obvious affection.

For a moment, I felt relief. Elation. We had succeeded. Then behind us, someone clapped.

Standing at the threshold, bloody and battered but still very much alive, was Lityerses, all by himself.

"Well done," said the swordsman. "You found a perfect place to die."

16

Son of a Midas
You, sir, are a stupid-head
Here, have an ostrich

IN MY FOUR THOUSAND years of life, I had searched for many things—beautiful women, handsome men, the best composite bows, the perfect seaside palace, and a 1958 Gibson Flying V. But I had *never* searched for a perfect place to die.

"Calypso?" I said weakly.

"Yeah?"

"If we die here, I'd just like to say you aren't as bad as I originally thought."

"Thanks, but we're not going to die. That would deprive me of killing you later."

Lityerses chuckled. "Oh, you two. Bantering like you have a future. It must be hard for former immortals to accept that death is real. Me, I've died. Let me tell you, it's no fun."

I was tempted to sing to him the way I had with the griffins. Perhaps I could convince him I was a fellow sufferer. Something told me it wouldn't work. And alas, I was all out of Tater Tots.

"You're the son of King Midas," I said. "You came back to the mortal world when the Doors of Death were open?"

I didn't know much about that incident, but there'd been some massive Underworld jailbreak during the recent war with the giants. Hades had ranted nonstop about Gaea stealing all his dead people so they could work for her. Honestly, I couldn't blame the Earth Mother. Good cheap labor is *terribly* difficult to find.

The swordsman curled his lip. "We came through the Doors of Death, all right. Then my idiot father promptly got himself killed again, thanks to a run-in with Leo Valdez and his crew. I survived only because I was turned into a gold statue and covered with a rug."

Calypso backed toward the griffins. "That's . . . quite a story."

"Doesn't matter," snarled the swordsman. "The Triumvirate offered me work. They recognized the worth of Lityerses, Reaper of Men!"

"Impressive title," I managed.

He raised his sword. "I earned it, believe me. My friends call me Lit, but my enemies call me Death!"

"I'll call you Lit," I decided. "Though you don't strike me as very *lit*. You know, your father and I used to be great friends. Once, I even gave him ass's ears."

As soon as I said that, I realized it was perhaps not the best proof of my friendship.

Lit gave me a cruel smile. "Yes, I grew up hearing about that music contest you made my dad judge. Gave him donkey ears because he declared your opponent the winner?

Heh. My father hated you *so* much for that, I was almost tempted to like you. But I don't." He sliced through the air in a practice swipe. "It'll be a pleasure to kill you."

"Hold on!" I shrieked. "What about all that *take them alive* business?"

Lit shrugged. "I changed my mind. First, that roof collapsed on me. Then my bodyguards got swallowed by a stand of bamboo. I don't suppose you know anything about that?"

My pulse boomed like timpani in my ears. "No."

"Right." He regarded Calypso. "I think I'll keep *you* alive long enough to kill you in front of Valdez's face. That'll be fun. But this former god here . . ." Lit shrugged. "I'll just have to tell the emperor he resisted arrest."

This was it. After four millennia of glory, I was going to die in a griffin enclosure in Indianapolis. I confess I hadn't envisioned my death this way. I hadn't envisioned it at all, but if I *had* to go, I wanted a lot more explosions and blazing spotlights, a host of beautiful weeping gods and goddesses crying *No! Take us instead!*, and a lot less animal poop.

Surely Zeus would intercede. He couldn't allow my punishment on earth to include actual death! Or perhaps Artemis would slay Lit with an arrow of death. She could always tell Zeus it was a freak longbow malfunction. At the very least, I hoped the griffins would come to my aid, since I'd fed them and sung to them so sweetly.

None of that happened. Abelard hissed at Lityerses, but the griffin seemed reluctant to attack. Perhaps Lityerses had used those sinister training implements on him and his mate.

The swordsman rushed me with blinding speed. He

swung his blade horizontally—right toward my neck. My last thought was how much the cosmos would miss me. The last thing I smelled was the scent of baked apples.

Then, from somewhere above, a small humanoid form dropped between me and my attacker. With a clang and a burst of sparks, Lityerses's blade stopped cold in the crook of a golden X—the crossed blades of Meg McCaffrey.

I may have whimpered. I had never been so happy to see anyone in my life, and that *includes* Hyacinthus the time he wore that *amazing* tuxedo on our date night, so you know I mean it.

Meg pushed with her blades and sent Lityerses stumbling backward. Her dark pageboy hair was festooned with twigs and blades of grass. She wore her usual red hightops, her yellow leggings, and the green dress Sally Jackson had lent her the first day we met. I found this strangely heartwarming.

Lityerses sneered at her, but he did not look particularly surprised. "I wondered if threatening this idiot god would smoke you out of hiding. You've signed your death warrant."

Meg uncrossed her blades. She retorted in her typical poetic fashion. "Nope."

Calypso glanced at me. She mouthed the question, *THIS is Meg?*

This is Meg, I agreed, which encompassed a lot of explanation in a very short exchange.

Lityerses stepped sideways to block the exit. He was limping slightly, probably from his incident with the canopy. "*You* dropped that ivy-covered roof on me," he said. "You made the bamboo attack my men."

"Yep," Meg said. "You're stupid."

Lit hissed in annoyance. I understood this effect Meg had on people. Still, my heart was humming a perfect middle C of happiness. My young protector had returned! (Yes, yes, she was technically my master, but let's not mince words.) She had seen the error of her ways. She had rebelled against Nero. Now she would stay by my side and help me retain my godhood. Cosmic order had been restored!

Then she glanced back at me. Instead of beaming with joy, or hugging me, or apologizing, she said, "Get out of here."

The command jarred me to the bones. I stepped back as if pushed. I was filled with the sudden desire to flee. When we'd parted, Meg had told me I was released from her service. Now it was clear that our master-servant relationship could not be so easily broken. Zeus meant me to follow her commands until I died or became a god again. I wasn't sure he cared which.

"But, Meg," I pleaded. "You just arrived. We must—"

"Go," she said. "Take the griffins and get out. I'll hold off stupid-head."

Lit laughed. "I've heard you're a decent sword fighter, McCaffrey, but no child can match the Reaper of Men."

He spun his blade like Pete Townshend windmilling his guitar (a move I taught Pete, though I never approved of the way he smashed his guitar into the speakers afterward— such a waste!).

"Demeter is *my* mother, too," Lit said. "Her children make the best swordsmen. We understand the need to reap.

It's just the flipside of sowing, isn't it, little sister? Let's see what you know about reaping lives!"

He lunged. Meg countered his strike and drove him back. They circled each other, three swords whirling in a deadly dance like blender blades making an air smoothie.

Meanwhile, I was compelled to walk toward the griffins as Meg had ordered. I tried to do it slowly. I was reluctant to take my eyes off the battle, as if merely by watching Meg, I was somehow lending her strength. Once, when I was a god, that would've been possible, but now, what good could a spectating Lester do?

Calypso stood in front of Heloise, protecting the mother-to-be with her body.

I made it to Calypso's side. "You're lighter than I," I said. "You ride Heloise. Be careful of her gut. I'll take Abelard."

"What about Meg?" Calypso demanded. "We can't leave her."

Just yesterday, I had toyed with the idea of leaving Calypso behind to the blemmyae when she was wounded. I'd like to say that wasn't a serious thought, but it had been, however briefly. Now Calypso refused to leave Meg, whom she barely knew. It was almost enough to make me question whether I was a good person. (I stress the word *almost*.)

"You're right, of course." I glanced across the arena. In the opposite enclosure, the combat ostriches were peering through their Plexiglas, following the sword fight with professional interest. "We need to move this party."

I turned to address Abelard. "I apologize in advance. I'm terrible at riding griffins."

The griffin squawked as if to say, *Do what you gotta do, man*. He allowed me to climb aboard and tuck my legs behind the base of his wings.

Calypso followed my example, carefully straddling Heloise's spine.

The griffins, impatient to be gone, bounded past the sword fight and into the arena. Lityerses lunged as I passed him. He would have taken off my right arm, but Meg blocked his strike with one sword and swept at Lit's feet with the other, forcing him back again.

"Take those griffins and you'll only suffer more!" Lit warned. "All the emperor's prisoners will die slowly, especially the little girl."

My hands shook with anger, but I managed to nock an arrow in my bow. "Meg," I yelled, "come on!"

"I told you to leave!" she complained. "You're a bad slave."

On that, at least, we agreed.

Lityerses advanced on Meg again, slashing and stabbing. I was no expert on swordplay, but as good as Meg was, I feared she was outmatched. Lityerses had more strength, speed, and reach. He was twice Meg's size. He'd been practicing for countless more years. If Lityerses hadn't recently been injured from having a roof dropped on him, I suspected this fight might have been over already.

"Go on, Apollo!" Lit taunted. "Fire that arrow at me."

I had seen how fast he could move. No doubt he would pull an Athena and slash my arrow out of the sky before it hit him. So unfair! But shooting at him had never been my plan.

I leaned toward Abelard's head and said, "Fly!"

The griffin launched himself into the air as if my added weight was nothing. He circled around the stadium tiers, screeching for his mate to join him.

Heloise had more trouble. She lumbered halfway across the arena floor, flapping her wings and growling with discomfort before getting airborne. With Calypso clinging to her neck for dear life, Heloise began flying in a tight circle behind Abelard. There was nowhere for us to go—not with the net above us—but I had more immediate problems.

Meg stumbled, barely managing to parry Lit's strike. His next cut sliced across Meg's thigh, ripping her legging. The yellow fabric quickly turned orange from the flow of blood.

Lit grinned. "You're good, little sister, but you're getting tired. You don't have the stamina to face me."

"Abelard," I murmured, "we need to get the girl. Dive!"

The griffin complied with a bit too much enthusiasm. I almost missed my shot. I let my arrow fly not at Lityerses, but at the control box next to the emperor's seat, aiming for a lever I had noted earlier: the one that read OMNIA—*everything*.

WHANG! The arrow hit its mark. With a series of satisfying *ka-chunks*, the Plexiglas shields dropped from all the enclosures.

Lityerses was too busy to realize what had happened. Being dive-bombed by a griffin tends to focus one's attention. Lit backed away, allowing Abelard to snatch Meg McCaffrey in his paws and soar upward again.

Lit gaped at us in dismay. "Good trick, Apollo. But where will you go? You're—"

That's when he was run over by a herd of armored ostriches. The swordsman disappeared under a tidal wave of feathers, razor wire, and warty pink legs.

As Lityerses squawked like a goose, curling up to protect himself, the winged serpents, fire-breathing horses, and Aethiopian Bull came out to join the fun.

"Meg!" I stretched out my arm. While precariously gripped in Abelard's paws, she willed her swords to shrink back into golden rings. She caught my hand. Somehow I managed to pull her onto Abelard and seat her in front of me.

The flying serpents fluttered toward Heloise, who squawked defiantly and beat her mighty wings, climbing toward the netting. Abelard followed.

My heart hammered against my ribs. Surely we couldn't bust through the net. It would be designed to withstand brute force, beaks, and claws. I imagined us hitting the barrier and getting bounced back to the arena floor as if on a reverse trampoline. It seemed an undignified way to die.

A moment before we would have slammed into the net, Calypso thrust up her arms. She howled in rage and the net blasted upward, ripped from its moorings, and was tossed into the sky like a giant tissue in a gale-force wind.

Free and unhurt, we soared out of the arena. I stared at Calypso in amazement. She seemed as surprised as I was. Then she slumped and listed sideways. Heloise compensated, shifting her pitch to keep the sorceress on board. Calypso, looking only semiconscious, clung weakly to the griffin's fur.

As our two noble steeds rose into the sky, I glanced down at the arena. The monsters were engaged in a vicious free-for-all, but I saw no sign of Lityerses.

Meg twisted to face me, her mouth set in a ferocious scowl. "You were *supposed* to go!"

Then she wrapped her arms around me and hugged me so tightly I felt new fracture lines developing on my ribs. Meg sobbed, her face buried in my shirt, her whole body shaking.

As for me, I did not weep. No, I'm sure my eyes were quite dry. I did not bawl like a baby in the slightest. The most I will admit is this: with her tears moistening my shirt, her cat-eye glasses digging uncomfortably into my chest, her smell of baked apples, dirt, and sweat overwhelming my nostrils, I was quite content to be annoyed, once again, by Meg McCaffrey.

17

To the Waystation
Meg McCaffrey eats my bread
I cry godly tears

HELOISE AND ABELARD knew where to go. They circled the Waystation roof until a section of shingles slid open, allowing the griffins to spiral into the great hall.

They landed on the ledge, side by side in their nest, as Josephine and Leo scrambled up the ladders to join us.

Josephine threw her arms first around Heloise's neck, then Abelard's. "Oh, my sweethearts! You're alive!"

The griffins cooed and leaned against her in greeting.

Josephine beamed at Meg McCaffrey. "Welcome! I'm Jo."

Meg blinked, apparently not used to such an enthusiastic greeting.

Calypso half climbed, half tumbled from Heloise's back. She would have toppled off the ledge if Leo hadn't caught her.

"Whoa, *mamacita*," he said. "You okay?"

She blinked sleepily. "I'm fine. Don't fuss. And don't call me—"

She crumpled against Leo, who struggled to keep her upright.

He glared at me. "What did you do to her?"

"Not a thing!" I protested. "I believe Calypso managed some magic."

I explained what had happened at the zoo: our encounter with Lityerses, our escape, and how the arena's netting had suddenly shot into the sky like a squid from a water cannon (one of Poseidon's less successful prototype weapons).

Meg added unhelpfully, "It was crazy."

"Lityerses," Leo muttered. "I *hate* that guy. Is Cal going to be okay?"

Josephine checked Calypso's pulse, then pressed a hand against her forehead. Slumped against Leo's shoulder, the sorceress snored like a razorback sow.

"She's blown a circuit," Josephine announced.

"Blown a circuit?" Leo yelped. "I don't like blown circuits!"

"Just an expression, bud," said Josephine. "She's over-extended herself magically. We should get her to Emmie in the infirmary. Here."

Josephine scooped up Calypso. Ignoring the ladder, she jumped off the ledge and landed easily on the floor twenty feet below.

Leo scowled. "I could have done that."

He turned to Meg. No doubt he recognized her from my many tales of woe. After all, young girls in stoplight-colored clothing and rhinestone cat-eye glasses were not common.

"You're Meg McCaffrey," he decided.

"Yep."

"Cool. I'm Leo. And, uh . . ." He pointed at me. "I understand you can, like, control this guy?"

I cleared my throat. "We merely *cooperate*! I'm not controlled by anyone. Right, Meg?"

"Slap yourself," Meg commanded.

I slapped myself.

Leo grinned. "Oh, this is too good. I'm going to check on Calypso, but later we need to talk." He slid down the ladder railings, leaving me with a deep sense of foreboding.

The griffins settled into their nest, clucking contentedly to each other. I was no griffin midwife, but Heloise, thank the gods, seemed no worse for wear after her flight.

I faced Meg. My cheek stung where I'd slapped myself. My pride had been trampled like Lityerses under a herd of combat ostriches. Nevertheless, I felt remarkably happy to see my young friend.

"You rescued me." Then I added two words that never come easily to a god: "Thank you."

Meg gripped her elbows. On her middle fingers, her gold rings glinted with the crescent symbol of her mother, Demeter. I had bandaged her cut thigh as best I could while we were in flight, but she still looked shaky on her feet.

I thought she might cry again, but when she met my eyes, she wore her usual willful expression, as if she were about to call me Poop Face, or order me to play princess versus dragon with her. (I *never* got to be the princess.)

"I didn't do it for you," she said.

I tried to process that meaningless phrase. "Then why—"

"That guy." She waved her fingers over her face, indicating Lityerses's scars. "He was bad."

"Well, I can't argue with that."

"And the ones who drove me from New York." She made her *icky* expression. "Marcus. Vortigern. They said things, what they would do in Indianapolis." She shook her head. "Bad things."

I wondered if Meg knew that Marcus and Vortigern had been beheaded for letting her escape. I decided not to mention it. If Meg was really curious, she could check their Facebook status updates.

Next to us, the griffins snuggled in for a well-deserved rest. They tucked their heads under their wings and purred, which would have been cute if they didn't sound like chainsaws.

"Meg . . ." I faltered.

I felt as if a Plexiglas wall divided us, though I wasn't sure whom it was protecting from whom. I wanted to say so many things to her, but I wasn't sure how.

I summoned my courage. "I am going to try."

Meg studied me warily. "Try what?"

"To tell you . . . how I feel. To clear the air. Stop me if I say something wrong, but I think it's obvious we still need each other."

She didn't respond.

"I don't blame you for anything," I continued. "The fact that you left me alone in the Grove of Dodona, that you lied about your stepfather—"

"Stop."

I waited for her faithful servant Peaches the karpos to fall from the heavens and tear my scalp off. It didn't happen.

"What I mean," I tried again, "is that I am sorry for

everything you have been through. None of it was your fault. You should not blame yourself. That fiend Nero played with your emotions, twisted your thoughts—"

"Stop."

"Perhaps I could put my feelings into a song."

"Stop."

"Or I could tell you a story about a similar thing that once happened to me."

"Stop."

"A short riff on my ukulele?"

"Stop." This time, though, I detected the faintest hint of a smile tugging at the corner of Meg's mouth.

"Can we at least agree to work together?" I asked. "The emperor in this city is searching for us both. If we don't stop him, he will do many more bad things."

Meg raised her left shoulder to her ear. "Okay."

A gentle crackling sound came from the griffin's nest. Green shoots were sprouting from the dry hay, perhaps a sign of Meg's improving mood.

I remembered Cleander's words in my nightmare: *You should have realized how powerful she is becoming.* Meg had somehow tracked me to the zoo. She'd caused ivy to grow until it collapsed a roof. She'd made bamboo plants swallow a squad of Germani. She'd even teleported away from her escorts in Dayton using a clump of dandelions. Few children of Demeter had ever had such abilities.

Still, I was under no illusions that Meg and I could skip away from here arm in arm, our problems forgotten. Sooner or later, she would have to confront Nero again. Her loyalties would be tested, her fears played upon. I could not free her of her past, even with the best song or ukulele riff.

Meg rubbed her nose. "Is there any food?"

I hadn't realized how tense I'd been until I relaxed. If Meg was thinking of food, we were back on the path to normalcy.

"There is food." I lowered my voice. "Mind you, it's not as good as Sally Jackson's seven-layer dip, but Emmie's fresh-baked bread and homemade cheese are quite acceptable."

Behind me, a voice said drily, "So glad you approve."

I turned.

At the top of the ladder, Emmie was glaring griffin claws at me. "Lady Britomartis is downstairs. She wants to talk to you."

The goddess did not say thank you. She did not shower me with praise, offer me a kiss, or even give me a free magic net.

Britomartis simply waved to seats across the dinner table and said, "Sit."

She was dressed in a gauzy black dress over a fishnet bodysuit, a look that reminded me of Stevie Nicks, circa 1981. (We did a fabulous duet on "Stop Draggin' My Heart Around." I got *zero* credit on the album, though.) She propped her leather boots on the dining table as if she owned the place, which I guess she did, and twirled her auburn braid between her fingers.

I checked my seat, then Meg's, for any spring-activated explosive devices, but without Leo's expert eye, I couldn't be sure. My only hope: Britomartis looked distracted, perhaps *too* distracted for her usual fun and games. I sat. Happily, my gloutos did not explode.

A simple meal had been laid out: more salad, bread, and cheese. I hadn't realized it was lunchtime, but when I saw the food, my stomach growled. I reached for the loaf of bread. Emmie pulled it away and gave it to Meg.

Emmie smiled sweetly. "Apollo, I wouldn't want you to eat anything that's only *acceptable*. There's plenty of salad, though."

I stared miserably at the bowl of lettuce and cucumbers. Meg grabbed the entire bread loaf and ripped off a chunk, chewing it with gusto. Well . . . I say *chewing*. Meg stuffed so much into her mouth it was difficult to know if her teeth ever connected.

Britomartis laced her fingers in front of her. Even that simple gesture looked like an elaborate snare. "Emmie," she said, "how is the sorceress?"

"Resting comfortably, my lady," said Emmie. "Leo and Josephine are looking in on her— Ah, here they are now."

Josephine and Leo strode toward the dining table, Leo's arms spread like the Rio de Janeiro Christ statue. "You can all relax!" he announced. "Calypso is okay!"

The net goddess grunted as if disappointed.

A thought struck me. I frowned at Britomartis. "The net over the arena. Nets are *your* department. You helped blast it away, didn't you? Calypso couldn't have done that magic by herself."

Britomartis smirked. "I may have jump-started her power a bit. She'll be more useful to me if she can master her old abilities."

Leo dropped his arms. "But you could've killed her!"

The goddess shrugged. "Probably not, but it's hard to say. Tricky stuff, magic. You never know when or how it's going to come out." She spoke with distaste, as if magic were some poorly controlled bodily function.

Leo's ears began to smoke. He stepped toward the goddess.

Josephine grabbed his arm. "Let it go, bud. Between Emmie and me, we can take care of your girl."

Leo wagged a finger at Britomartis. "You're lucky these ladies are such bosses. Jo here, she told me that with enough time and training she could probably help Calypso get her magic back all the way."

Josephine shifted, her wrenches clinking in the pockets of her coveralls. "Leo—"

"Did you know she was a gangster?" He grinned at me. "Jo knew Al Capone! She had this secret identity and—"

"Leo!"

He flinched. "Which . . . isn't my place to talk about. Oh, look, food."

He took a seat and began cutting the cheese.

Britomartis pressed her hands against the table. "But enough about the sorceress. Apollo, I must admit you did moderately well retrieving my griffins."

"Moderately well?" I bit back a few nasty comments. I wondered if demigods ever felt the need to restrain themselves when facing ungrateful gods like this. No. Surely not. I was special and different. And I deserved better treatment.

"So glad you approve," I muttered.

Britomartis's smile was thin and cruel. I imagined nets

wrapping around my feet, constricting the flow of blood in my ankles. "As promised, I will now reward you. I'll give you information that will lead you directly to the palace of the emperor, where you'll either make us proud . . . or be executed in some horrible but creative fashion."

18

My dear Commodus,
Commode is named after you
Hail, Toilet Caesar

WHY DID PEOPLE keep ruining my meals?

First they served me food. Then they explained how I was likely to die in the near future. I longed to be back on Mount Olympus, where I could worry about more interesting things, like hot trends in techno-pop, bumper-car poetry slams, and laying waste to naughty communities with my arrows of vengeance. One thing I'd learned from being mortal: contemplating death is *much* more fun when you're contemplating someone else's.

Before Britomartis would give us our "reward," she insisted on a briefing from Josephine and Emmie, who had spent all day, with Leo's help, preparing the Waystation for a siege.

"This guy's good." Josephine punched Leo's arm affectionately. "The things he knows about Archimedes spheres . . . *really* impressive."

"Spheres?" Meg asked.

"Yeah," Leo said. "They're these round things."

"Shut up." Meg went back to inhaling carbohydrates.

"We reset all the crossbow turrets," Jo continued.

"Primed the catapults. Closed all exits and put Waystation on twenty-four-hour-surveillance mode. If anyone tries to get in, we'll know."

"They will try," Britomartis promised. "It's only a matter of time."

I raised my hand. "And, uh, Festus?"

I hoped the wistfulness in my voice was not too obvious. I didn't want the others to think I was ready to fly off on our bronze dragon and leave the Waystation to sort out its own problems. (Though I was ready to do exactly that.)

Emmie shook her head. "I scouted the statehouse grounds late last night, and again this morning. Nothing. The blemmyae must have taken your bronze suitcase to the palace."

Leo clicked his tongue. "I bet Lityerses has it. When I get my hands on that crust-sucking Cornhusker—"

"Which brings us to the point," I said. "How does Leo—I mean, how do *we* find the palace?"

Britomartis slid her feet off the table. She sat forward. "The main gates to the emperor's palace are under the Soldiers' and Sailors' Monument."

Josephine grunted. "Should've known."

"Why?" I asked. "What is that?"

Josephine rolled her eyes. "A *huge* decorated column thing in the middle of a plaza, a few blocks north of here. Just the kind of ostentatious, over-the-top edifice you'd expect the emperor to have for his entrance."

"It's the biggest monument in the city," Emmie added.

I tried to contain my bitterness. Soldiers and sailors were all very well, but if your city's biggest monument is not to Apollo, I'm sorry, you're doing something wrong. "I suppose the palace is heavily guarded?"

Britomartis laughed. "Even by my standards, the monument is a death trap. Machine gun turrets. Lasers. Monsters. Attempting the front door without an invitation would have dire consequences."

Meg swallowed a chunk of bread, somehow managing not to choke. "The emperor would let us in."

"Well, true," Britomartis agreed. "He'd love for you and Apollo to knock on his front door and give yourselves up. But I only mention the main entrance because you should *avoid* it at all costs. If you want to get inside the palace without being apprehended and tortured to death, there's another possibility."

Leo bit a cheese slice into the shape of a smile. He held it up to his mouth. "Leo is happy when he's not being tortured to death."

Meg snorted. A gob of bread shot out of her right nostril, but she didn't have the decency to look embarrassed. I could tell Leo and Meg were *not* going to be healthy influences on each other.

"Then, to get inside," said the goddess, "you must use the waterworks."

"The plumbing system," I guessed. "In my vision of the emperor's throne room, I saw open trenches of flowing water. You know how to access them?"

Britomartis winked at me. "You're not still afraid of water, I hope?"

"I have never been afraid of water!" My voice came out shriller than I intended.

"Hmm," Britomartis mused. "Then why did the Greeks always pray to you for a safe landing whenever they were in dangerous waters?"

"B-because my mother was stuck in a boat when she was trying to give birth to me and Artemis! I can appreciate wanting to be on solid ground!"

"And those rumors you can't swim? I remember at Triton's pool party—"

"I can *totally* swim! Just because I didn't want to play Marco Polo with you in the deep end with contact mines—"

"Hey, goddy people," Meg interrupted. "The water-works?"

"Right!" For once I was relieved at Meg's lack of patience. "Britomartis, how do we access the throne room?"

Britomartis narrowed her eyes at Meg. *"Goddy people?"* She seemed to be pondering how McCaffrey would look wrapped in a lead-weighted hook net and dropped into the Mariana Trench. "Well, Miss McCaffrey, to access the emperor's water system, you'll need to search the city's Canal Walk."

"What's that?" Meg asked.

Emmie patted her hand. "I can show you. It's an old canal that runs through downtown. They refurbished the area, built a bunch of new apartments and restaurants and whatnot."

Leo popped his cheese smile into his mouth. "I *love* whatnot."

Britomartis smiled. "That's fortunate, Leo Valdez. Because your skills will be required to find the entrance, disarm the traps, and whatnot."

"Hold up. *Find* the entrance? I thought you'd tell us where it was."

"I just did," said the goddess. "Somewhere along the canal. Look for a grate. You'll know it when you see it."

"Uh-huh. And it'll be booby-trapped."

"Of course! But not nearly as much as the fortress's main entrance. And Apollo will have to overcome his fear of water."

"I *don't* have a fear—"

"Shut up," Meg told me, causing my vocal cords to solidify like cold cement. She pointed a carrot at Leo. "If we find the grate, can you get us in?"

Leo's expression made him look as serious and dangerous as it was possible for a small elfin demigod to look in a little girl's coveralls (a clean pair, mind you, which he'd *intentionally* found and put on). "I'm a son of Hephaestus, *chica*. I can problem-solve. This guy Lityerses tried to kill me and my friends once before. Now he's threatened Calypso? Yeah, I'll get us inside that palace. Then I'm going find Lit and . . ."

"Light him up?" I suggested, surprised but pleased to find I could speak again so soon after being told to shut up. "So he's literally lit?"

Leo frowned. "I wasn't going to say that. Seemed too corny."

"When I say it," I assured him, "it's poetry."

"Well." Britomartis rose, fishhooks and weights clinking in her dress. "When Apollo starts talking poetry, that's my cue to leave."

"I wish I'd known that sooner," I said.

She blew me an air-kiss. "Your friend Calypso should

remain here. Josephine, see if you can help her regain control over her magic. She'll need it for the coming battle."

Josephine drummed her fingers on the table. "Been a long time since I've trained anyone in the ways of Hecate, but I'll do my best."

"Emmie," the goddess continued, "you watch after my griffins. Heloise could lay her egg at any moment."

Emmie's scalp turned crimson along her silver hairline. "What about Georgina? You've given us a way into the emperor's palace. Now you expect us to stay here rather than go free our girl?"

Britomartis raised a hand in caution, as if to say, *You're very close to the Burmese tiger pit, my dear.* "Trust Meg, Leo, and Apollo. This is their task: to find and free the captives, to retrieve the Throne of Mnemosyne—"

"And get Festus," Leo added.

"And especially Georgina," Jo added.

"We can pick up some groceries, too," Leo offered. "I noticed you're low on hot sauce."

Britomartis chose not to destroy him, though from her expression I could tell she came close. "Tomorrow at first light, search for the entrance."

"Why not earlier?" Meg asked.

The goddess smirked. "You're fearless. I respect that. But you must be rested and prepared to meet the emperor's forces. You need that leg wound tended to. I also suspect it's been many nights since you've had a proper sleep. Besides, the incident at the zoo has the emperor's security on high alert. Best to let the dust settle. If he catches you, Meg McCaffrey—"

"I know." She did not sound afraid. Her tone was that of a child who'd been reminded for the fifth time to clean her room. The only sign of Meg's anxiety: in her hand, her last piece of bread had begun to sprout green tendrils of wheat.

"In the meantime," Britomartis said, "I will try to locate the Hunters of Artemis. They were in the area on a quest not long ago. Perhaps they are still close enough to come help defend this place."

A hysterical giggle escaped my mouth. The idea of twenty or thirty other competent archers at my side, even if they were sworn maidens with no sense of humor, made me feel much safer. "That would be good."

"But if not," said the goddess, "you must be prepared to fight on your own."

"That would be typical." I sighed.

"And remember, the emperor's naming ceremony is the day after tomorrow."

"Thank you so much," I said. "I needed the reminder."

"Oh, don't look so glum, Apollo!" Britomartis gave me one last flirtatious, irritatingly cute smile. "If you come out alive, we'll catch a movie together. I promise."

Her gauzy black dress swirled around her in a tornado of netting. Then she was gone.

Meg turned to me. "Naming ceremony?"

"Yes." I stared at her furry green piece of bread, wondering if it was still edible. "The emperor is quite the megalomaniac. As he did in ancient times, he plans to rename this capital city after himself. Probably he'll rename the state, the inhabitants, and the months of the year too."

Meg snorted. "Commode City?"

Leo gave her a tentative smile. "What now?"

"His name is—"

"Don't, Meg," Josephine warned.

"—Commodus," Meg continued, then frowned. "Why am I not supposed to say his name?"

"He pays attention to such things," I explained. "There's no point in letting him know we are talking about—"

Meg took a deep breath and yelled, "COMMODUS, COMMODUS, COMMODUS! COMMODE CITY, COMMODIANA. COMMODE DAY, MONTH OF COMMODES! COMMODE MAN!"

The great hall shook as if the Waystation itself had taken offense. Emmie blanched. Up in their roost, the griffins clucked nervously.

Josephine grumbled, "You shouldn't have done that, hon."

Leo just shrugged. "Well, if Commode Man wasn't watching this channel before, I think he is now."

"That's dumb," Meg said. "Don't treat him like he's so powerful. My stepfather—" Her voice caught. "He—he said Commodus is the weakest of the three. We can take him."

Her words struck me in the gut like one of Artemis's blunted arrows. (And I can assure you, those hurt.)

We can take him.

The name of my old friend, shouted over and over.

I staggered to my feet, gagging, my tongue trying to dislodge itself from my throat.

"Whoa, Apollo." Leo rushed to my side. "You okay?"

"I—" Another dry retch. I staggered toward the nearest bathroom as a vision engulfed me . . . bringing me back to the day I committed murder.

19

Call me Narcissus
Today I'll be your trainer
I'll also kill you

I KNOW WHAT YOU are thinking. *But, Apollo! You are divine! You cannot commit murder. Any death you cause is the will of the gods and entirely beyond reproach. It would be an honor if you killed me!*

I like the way you think, good reader. It's true I had laid waste to whole cities with my fiery arrows. I had inflicted countless plagues upon humanity. Once Artemis and I slew a family of twelve because their mama said something bad about *our* mama. The nerve!

None of that did I consider murder.

But as I stumbled to the bathroom, ready to vomit into a toilet I had cleaned just yesterday, dreadful memories consumed me. I found myself in ancient Rome on a cold winter day when I truly *did* commit a terrible act.

A bitter wind swept through the palace halls. Fires guttered in the braziers. The faces of the praetorian guards betrayed no sign of discomfort, but as I passed them at every doorway, I could hear their armor clattering as they shivered.

No one challenged me as I strode toward the emperor's

private chambers. Why would they? I was Narcissus, Caesar's trusted personal trainer.

Tonight I wore my mortal disguise poorly. My stomach churned. Sweat trickled down the back of my neck. The shock of that day's games still overwhelmed my senses: the stench of carcasses on the arena floor; the bloodthirsty crowd shouting, "COMMODUS! COMMODUS!"; the emperor in resplendent golden armor and purple robes, tossing the severed heads of ostriches into the seats of the senators, gesturing toward the old men with the point of his sword: *You're next.*

The praetorian prefect Laetus had pulled me aside only an hour ago: *We failed at lunch. This is our last chance. We can take him, but only with your help.*

Marcia, Commodus's mistress, had wept as she tugged at my arm. *He will kill us all. He will destroy Rome. You know what must be done!*

They were right. I'd seen the list of names—the enemies real or imagined whom Commodus intended to execute tomorrow. Marcia and Laetus were at the top of the list, followed by senators, noblemen, and several priests in the temple of Apollo Sosianus. That sort of thing I couldn't overlook. Commodus would chop them down as carelessly as he did his ostriches and lions.

I pushed open the bronze doors of the emperor's chambers.

From the shadows, Commodus bellowed, "GO AWAY!"

A bronze pitcher sailed past my head, slamming into the wall with such force it cracked the mosaic tiles.

"Hello to you, too," I said. "I never did like that fresco."

The emperor blinked, trying to focus. "Ah . . . it's you, Narcissus. Come in, then. Hurry! Bar the doors!"

I did as he asked.

Commodus knelt on the floor, clinging to the side of a sofa for support. In the opulence of the bedchamber with its silk curtains, gilded furniture, and colorfully frescoed walls, the emperor looked out of place—like a beggar pulled from some Suburra alley. His eyes were wild. His beard glistened with spittle. Vomit and blood spattered his plain white tunic, which wasn't surprising considering his mistress and prefect had poisoned his wine at lunch.

But if you could look *past* that, Commodus hadn't changed much since he was eighteen, lounging in his campaign tent in the Danubian Forest. He was thirty-one now, but the years had barely touched him. To the horror of Rome's fashionistas, he had grown his hair out long and had a shaggy beard to resemble his idol, Hercules. Otherwise he was the picture of manly Roman perfection. One might almost have thought he was an immortal god, as he so often claimed to be.

"They tried to kill me," he snarled. "I *know* it was them! I won't die. I'll show them all!"

My heart ached to see him this way. Only yesterday, I'd been so hopeful.

We'd practiced fighting techniques all afternoon. Strong and confident, he'd wrestled me to the ground and would have broken my neck if I'd been a regular mortal. After he let me up, we'd spent the rest of the day laughing and talking as we used to in the old days. Not that he knew my true identity, but still . . . disguised as Narcissus, I was sure

I could restore the emperor's good humor, eventually rekindle the embers of the glorious young man I'd once known.

And yet this morning, he'd woken up more bloodthirsty and manic than ever.

I approached cautiously, as if he were a wounded animal. "You won't die from the poison. You're much too strong for that."

"Exactly!" He pulled himself up on the couch, his knuckles white with effort. "I'll feel better tomorrow, as soon as I behead those traitors!"

"Perhaps it would be better to rest for a few days," I suggested. "Take some time to recuperate and reflect."

"REFLECT?" He winced from the pain. "I don't need to *reflect*, Narcissus. I will kill them and hire new advisors. You, perhaps? You want the job?"

I did not know whether to laugh or cry. While Commodus concentrated on his beloved games, he turned the powers of state over to prefects and cronies . . . all of whom tended to have a very short life expectancy.

"I'm just a personal trainer," I said.

"Who cares? I will make you a nobleman! You will rule Commodiana!"

I flinched at the name. Outside the palace, no one accepted the emperor's rechristening of Rome. The citizens refused to call themselves Commodians. The legions were furious that they were now known as Commodianae. Commodus's crazy proclamations had been the final straw for his long-suffering advisors.

"Please, Caesar," I implored him. "A rest from the

executions and the games. Time to heal. Time to consider the consequences."

He bared his teeth, his lips specked with blood. "Don't *you* start too! You sound like my father. I'm done thinking about consequences!"

My spirits collapsed. I knew what would happen in the coming days. Commodus would survive the poisoning. He would order a ruthless purge of his enemies. The city would be decorated with heads on pikes. Crucifixions would line the Via Appia. My priests would die. Half the senate would perish. Rome itself, the bastion of the Olympian gods, would be shaken to its core. And Commodus would still be assassinated . . . just a few weeks or months later, in some other fashion.

I inclined my head in submission. "Of course, Caesar. May I draw you a bath?"

Commodus grunted assent. "I should get out of these filthy clothes."

As I often did for him after our workout sessions, I filled his great marble bath with steaming rose-scented water. I helped him out of his soiled tunic and eased him into the tub. For a moment, he relaxed and closed his eyes.

I recalled how he looked sleeping beside me when we were teens. I remembered his easy laugh as we raced through the woods, and the way his face scrunched up adorably when I bounced grapes off his nose.

I sponged away the spittle and blood from his beard. I gently washed his face. Then I closed my hands around his neck. "I'm sorry."

I pushed his head underwater and began to squeeze.

Commodus was strong. Even in his weakened state, he thrashed and fought. I had to channel my godly might to keep him submerged, and in doing so, I must have revealed my true nature to him.

He went still, his blue eyes wide with surprise and betrayal. He could not speak, but he mouthed the words: *You. Blessed. Me.*

The accusation forced a sob from my throat. The day his father died, I had promised Commodus: *You will always have my blessings.* Now I was ending his reign. I was interfering in mortal affairs—not just to save lives, or to save Rome, but because I could not stand to see my beautiful Commodus die by anyone else's hands.

His last breath bubbled through the whiskers of his beard. I hunched over him, crying, my hands around his throat, until the bathwater cooled.

Britomartis was wrong. I didn't fear water. I simply couldn't look at the surface of any pool without imagining Commodus's face, stung with betrayal, staring up at me.

The vision faded. My stomach heaved. I found myself hunched over a different water basin—a toilet in the Waystation.

I'm not sure how long I knelt there, shivering, retching, wishing I could get rid of my hideous mortal frame as easily as I lost my stomach contents. Finally, I became aware of an orange reflection in the toilet water. Agamethus stood behind me, holding his Magic 8 Ball.

I whimpered in protest. "Must you sneak up on me while I'm vomiting?"

The headless ghost proffered his magic sphere.

"Some toilet paper would be more helpful," I said.

Agamethus reached for the roll, but his ethereal fingers went right through the tissue. Odd that he could hold a Magic 8 Ball and not a roll of toilet paper. Perhaps our hosts had not sprung for the extra-soft two-ply ghost-friendly Charmin.

I took the ball. Without much conviction, I asked, "What do you want, Agamethus?"

The answer floated up through the dark liquid: WE CANNOT REMAIN.

I groaned. "Not another warning of doom. Who's *we*? Remain where?"

I shook the ball once more. It provided the answer OUTLOOK NOT SO GOOD.

I put the Magic 8 Ball back in Agamethus's hands, which was like pressing against the wind from a moving vehicle. "I can't play guessing games right now."

He did not have a face, but his posture seemed forlorn. The blood from his severed neck trickled sluggishly down his tunic. I imagined Trophonius's head transposed on his body—my son's agonized voice crying to the heavens, *Take me instead! Save him, Father, please!*

This blended with the face of Commodus, staring at me, wounded and betrayed as his carotid pulse hammered against my hands. *You. Blessed. Me.*

I sobbed and hugged the commode—the only thing in the universe that wasn't spinning. Was there *anyone* I hadn't betrayed and disappointed? Any relationship I hadn't destroyed?

After a miserable eternity in my private toilet-verse, a voice spoke behind me. "Hey."

I blinked away my tears. Agamethus was gone. In his place, leaning against the sink, was Josephine. She offered me a fresh roll of toilet paper.

I sniffled weakly. "Are you supposed to be in the men's room?"

She laughed. "Wouldn't be the first time, but our bathrooms are gender neutral here."

I wiped my face and clothes. I didn't accomplish much beyond toilet-papering myself.

Josephine helped me into a sitting position on the toilet. She assured me this was better than hugging it, though at the moment I saw little difference.

"What happened to you?" she asked.

Not having any concerns about my dignity, I told her.

Josephine pulled a cloth from her coverall pocket. She wet it at the sink and began cleaning the sides of my face, getting the places I'd missed. She treated me as if I were her seven-year-old Georgie, or one of her mechanical crossbow turrets—something precious but high maintenance. "I'm not going to judge you, Sunny. I've done a few bad things in my time."

I studied her square-jawed face, the metallic sheen of her gray hair against her dark skin. She seemed so gentle and affable, the same way I thought of Festus the dragon, yet at times I had to step back and remember, *Oh, right, this is a giant fire-breathing death machine.*

"Leo mentioned gangsters," I recalled. "Al Capone?"

Josephine smirked. "Yep, Al. And Diamond Joe. And

Papa Johnny. I knew 'em all. I was Al's—what would you call it?—liaison to the African American bootleggers."

Despite my dour mood, I couldn't help feeling a spark of fascination. The Jazz Age had been one of my favorites because . . . well, jazz. "For a woman in the 1920s, that's impressive."

"The thing is," Jo said, "they never knew I was a woman."

I had a sudden image of Josephine in black leather shoes with spats, a pinstripe suit, a diamond-studded tie pin, and a black fedora, her submachine gun, Little Bertha, propped against her shoulder. "I see."

"They called me Big Jo." She gazed at the wall. Perhaps it was just my state of mind, but I imagined her as Commodus, throwing a pitcher so hard it cracked the tiles. "That lifestyle . . . it was intoxicating, dangerous. It took me to a dark place, almost destroyed me. Then Artemis found me and offered me a way out."

I remembered Hemithea and her sister Parthenos launching themselves over a cliff, in a time when women's lives were more expendable than jars of wine. "My sister has saved many young women from horrible situations."

"Yes, she has." Jo smiled wistfully. "And then Emmie saved my life again."

"You two could still be immortal," I grumbled. "You could have youth, power, eternal life—"

"We could," Josephine agreed. "But then we wouldn't have had the past few decades of growing old together. We've had a good life here. We've saved a lot of demigods and other outcasts—raised them at the Waystation, let them go to school and have a more or less normal childhood, then sent them out into the world as adults with the skills they needed to survive."

I shook my head. "I don't understand. There's no comparison between that and immortality."

Josephine shrugged. "It's okay if you don't get it. But I want you to know, Emmie didn't give up your divine gift lightly. After sixty-odd years together with the Hunters, we discovered something. It's not how long you live that matters. It's what you live for."

I frowned. That was a very ungodly way of thinking—as if you could have immortality *or* meaning, but not both.

"Why are you telling me this?" I asked. "Are you trying to convince me that I should stay as . . . as this abomination?" I gestured at my pathetic mortal body.

"I'm not telling you what to do. But those folks out there—Leo, Calypso, Meg—they need you. They're counting on you. Emmie and I are, too, to get our daughter back. You don't have to be a god. Just do your best for your friends."

"Ugh."

Jo chuckled. "Once upon a time, that kind of talk would've made me throw up too. I thought friendship was a trap. Life was every woman for herself. But when I joined the Hunters, Lady Britomartis told me something. You know how she first became a goddess?"

I thought for a moment. "She was a young maiden, running to escape the king of Crete. To hide, she jumped in a fishing net in the harbor, didn't she? Instead of drowning, she was transformed."

"Right." Jo intertwined her fingers like a cat's cradle.

"Nets can be traps. But they can also be *safety* nets. You just have to know when to jump in."

I stared at her. I waited for a moment of revelation when everything would make sense and my spirits would be lifted.

"Sorry," I said at last. "I have no idea what that means."

"That's okay." She offered me a hand. "Let's get you out of here."

"Yes," I agreed. "I'd like a good long sleep before our trip tomorrow."

Jo grinned her affable killing-machine smile. "Oh, no. No sleep yet. You've got afternoon chores, my friend."

20

Pedaling in style
Leg irons are fashionable
Cue the screaming god

AT LEAST I DIDN'T have to clean toilets.

I spent the afternoon in the griffin roost, playing music for Heloise to keep her calm while she laid her egg. She enjoyed Adele and Joni Mitchell, which strained my human vocal cords considerably, but she had no use for my impersonation of Elvis Presley. Griffin musical tastes are a mystery.

Once, I spotted Calypso and Leo down in the great hall, walking with Emmie, the three of them deep in conversation. Several times I saw Agamethus float through the hall, wringing his hands. I tried not to think about his Magic 8 Ball message: WE CANNOT REMAIN, which was neither cheerful nor helpful when one was trying to provide egg-laying mood music.

About an hour into my second set, Jo resumed the manufacture of her tracking device in the workshop, which necessitated me finding tunes that went well with the sound of a welding torch. Fortunately, Heloise enjoyed Patti Smith.

The only person I *didn't* see during the afternoon was

Meg. I assumed she was on the roof, making the garden grow at five times its normal rate. Occasionally I glanced up, wondering when the roof might collapse and bury me in rutabagas.

By dinnertime, my fingers were blistered from playing my combat ukulele. My throat felt like Death Valley. However, Heloise was clucking contentedly on top of her newly laid egg.

I felt surprisingly better. Music and healing, after all, were not so different. I wondered if Jo had sent me to the roost for my own good as well as Heloise's. Those Waystation women were tricky.

That night I slept like the dead—the *actual* dead, not the restless, headless, glowing orange variety. By first light, armed with Emmie's directions to the Canal Walk, Meg, Leo, and I were ready to navigate the streets of Indianapolis.

Before we left, Josephine pulled me aside. "Wish I was going with you, Sunny. I'll do my best to train your friend Calypso this morning, see if she can regain control over her magic. While you're gone, I'll feel better if you wear this."

She handed me an iron shackle.

I studied her face, but she did not seem to be joking. "This is a griffin manacle," I said.

"No! I would never make a griffin wear a manacle."

"Yet you're giving *me* one. Don't prisoners wear these for house arrest?"

"That's not what it's for. This is the tracking device I've been working on."

She pressed a small indentation on the rim of the shackle. With a *click*, metallic wings extended from either side, buzzing at hummingbird frequency. The shackle almost leaped out of my hands.

"Oh, no," I protested. "*Don't* ask me to wear flying apparel. Hermes tricked me into wearing his shoes once. I took a nap in a hammock in Athens and woke up in Argentina. Never again."

Jo switched off the wings. "You don't have to fly. The idea was to make *two* ankle bracelets, but I didn't have time. I was going to send them off to"—she paused, clearly trying to control her emotions—"to find Georgina and bring her home. Since I can't do that, if you get in trouble, if you find her . . ." Jo pointed to a second indentation on the manacle. "This activates the homing beacon. It'll tell me where you are, and you'd better believe we'll send reinforcements."

I didn't know how Josephine would accomplish that. They didn't have much of a cavalry. I also did not want to wear a tracking device on general principle. It went against the very nature of being Apollo. I should *always* be the most obvious, most brilliant source of light in the world. If you had to search for me, something was wrong.

Then again, Josephine was giving me that look my mother, Leto, always pulled when she was afraid I'd forgotten to write her a new song for Mother's Day. (It's kind of a tradition. And yes, I am a wonderful son, thanks.)

"Very well." I fastened the shackle around my ankle. It fit snugly, but at least that way I could hide it under the hem of my jeans.

"Thank you." Jo pressed her forehead against mine. "Don't die." Then she turned and marched purposefully back to her workshop, no doubt anxious to create more restraining devices for me.

Half an hour later, I discovered something important: one should never wear an iron manacle while operating a pedal boat.

Our mode of transportation was Leo's idea. When we arrived at the banks of the canal, he discovered a boat-rental dock that was shut down for the season. He decided to liberate a teal plastic pedal boat, and insisted we call him the Dread Pirate Valdez. (Meg loved this. I refused.)

"This is the best way to spot that secret-entrance grate thing," he assured us as we pedaled along. "At water level, we can't miss it. Plus, we're traveling in style!"

We had very different ideas of traveling in style.

Leo and I sat in the front, operating the pedals. Under the iron manacle, my ankle felt like it was being slowly chewed off by a Doberman pinscher. My calves burned. I did not understand why mortals would pay money for this experience. If the boat were pulled by hippocampi, perhaps, but physical labor? Ugh.

Meanwhile, Meg faced the reverse direction in the backseat. She claimed she was "scouting our six" for the secret entrance to the sewers, but it looked an awful lot like she was relaxing.

"So what's with you and the emperor?" Leo asked me, his feet pedaling merrily along as if the exertion didn't bother him at all.

I wiped my brow. "I don't know what you mean."

"C'mon, man. At dinner, when Meg started shouting about commodes? You ran straight to the bathroom and spewed."

"I did not spew. It was more like *heaving*."

"Ever since, you've been awfully quiet."

He had a point. Being quiet was another un-Apollo-like trait. Usually I had so many interesting things to say and delightful songs to sing. I realized I should tell my companions about the emperor. They deserved to know what we were pedaling into. But forming the words was difficult.

"Commodus blames me for his death," I said.

"Why?" Meg asked.

"Probably because I killed him."

"Ah." Leo nodded sagely. "That would do it."

I managed to tell them the story. It wasn't easy. As I stared ahead of us, I imagined the body of Commodus floating just below the surface of the canal, ready to rise from the icy green depths and accuse me of treachery. *You. Blessed. Me.*

When I was done with the story, Leo and Meg remained silent. Neither of them screamed *Murderer!* Neither of them looked me in the eye, either.

"That's rough, man," Leo said at last. "But it sounds like Emperor Toilet needed to go."

Meg made a sound like a cat's sneeze. "It's *Commodus*. He's handsome, by the way."

I glanced back. "You've met him?"

Meg shrugged. At some point since yesterday, a rhinestone had fallen out of her glasses' frames, like a star winked out of existence. It bothered me that I'd noticed such a small detail.

"Once," she said. "In New York. He visited my step-father."

"Nero," I urged. "Call him Nero."

"Yeah." Red blotches appeared on her cheeks. "Commodus was handsome."

I rolled my eyes. "He's also vainglorious, puffed up, egotistical—"

"So he's like your competition, then?" Leo asked.

"Oh, shut up."

For a while, the only sound on the canal was the chugging of our pedal boat. It echoed off the ten-foot-high embankments and up the sides of brick warehouses that were in the process of conversion to condominiums and restaurants. The buildings' dark windows stared down at us, making me feel both claustrophobic and exposed.

"One thing I don't get," Leo said. "Why Commodus? I mean, if this Triumvirate is the three biggest and baddest emperors, the Roman supervillain dream team . . . Nero makes sense. But Commode Man? Why not some eviler, more famous guy, like Murderous Maximus or Attila the Hun?"

"Attila the Hun was not a Roman emperor," I said. "As for Murderous Maximus . . . well, that's actually a good name, but not a real emperor. As for why Commodus is part of the Triumvirate—"

"They think he's weak," Meg said.

She kept her gaze on our wake, as if she saw her own assortment of faces below the surface.

"You know this how?" I asked.

"My step—Nero told me. Him and the third one, the

emperor in the west, they wanted Commodus between them."

"The third emperor," I said. "You know who he is?"

Meg frowned. "I only saw him once. Nero never used his name. He just called him *my kinsman*. I think even Nero is afraid of him."

"Fantastic," I muttered. Any emperor who scared Nero was not someone I wanted to meet.

"So Nero and the dude in the west," Leo said, "they want Commodus to be a buffer between them. Monkey in the middle."

Meg rubbed her nose. "Yeah. Nero told me. . . . He said Commodus was like his Peaches. A vicious pet. But controllable."

Her voice wavered on the name of her karpos companion.

I was afraid Meg might order me to slap myself or jump in the canal, but I asked, "Where *is* Peaches?"

She stuck out her lower lip. "The Beast—"

"Nero," I corrected gently.

"Nero took him. He said—he said I didn't deserve a pet until I behaved."

Anger made me pedal faster, made me almost welcome the chafing pain on my ankle. I didn't know how Nero had managed to imprison the grain spirit, but I understood why he'd done it. Nero wanted Meg to depend entirely on him. She wasn't allowed to have her own possessions, her own friends. Everything in her life had to be tainted with Nero's poison.

If he got his hands on me, no doubt he would use me the same way. Whatever horrible tortures he had planned for Lester Papadopoulos, they wouldn't be as bad as the way he tortured Meg. He would make her feel responsible for my pain and death.

"We'll get Peaches back," I promised her.

"Yeah, chica," Leo agreed. "The Dread Pirate Valdez never abandons a crew member. Don't you worry about—"

"Guys." Meg's voice took on a sharp edge. "What's that?"

She pointed to starboard. A line of chevrons rippled on the green water—like an arrow had been shot horizontally across the surface.

"Did you see what it was?" Leo asked.

Meg nodded. "A—a fin, maybe? Do canals have fish?"

I didn't know the answer, but I didn't like the size of those ripples. My throat felt as if it were sprouting fresh wheat shoots.

Leo pointed off the bow. "There."

Right in front of us, about half an inch below the surface, green scales undulated, then submerged.

"That's not a fish," I said, hating myself for being so perceptive. "I think that's another part of the same creature."

"As over there?" Meg pointed again to starboard. The two disturbances had happened at least forty feet apart. "That would mean something bigger than the boat."

Leo scanned the water. "Apollo, any idea what that thing is?"

"Only a hunch," I said. "Let's hope I'm wrong. Pedal faster. We have to find that grate."

21

Get me a legion
And about six tons of rocks
Need to kill a snake

I DO NOT LIKE SERPENTS.

Ever since my famous battle with Python, I've had a phobia of scaly reptilian creatures. (Especially if you include my stepmother, Hera. BOOM!) I could barely tolerate the snakes on Hermes's caduceus, George and Martha. They were friendly enough, but they *constantly* pestered me to write a song for them about the joy of eating rats—a joy I did not share.

I told myself the creature in the Central Canal wasn't an aquatic serpent. The water was much too cold. The canal didn't offer enough tasty fish to eat.

On the other hand, I knew Commodus. He loved to collect exotic monsters. I could think of one particular river serpent he would love—one that might easily sustain itself by eating tasty pedal-boaters. . . .

Bad Apollo! I told myself. *Stay focused on your mission!*

We chugged along for another fifty feet or so, long enough for me to wonder if the threat had been imaginary. Perhaps the monster had been nothing more than an abandoned pet alligator. Did they have those in the Midwest? Very polite ones, perhaps?

Leo nudged me. "Look over there."

On the far embankment wall, peeking above the waterline, was the brick archway of an old sewer main, the entrance blocked by golden bars.

"How many sewers have you seen with gold grates on them?" Leo asked. "Betcha that one leads right to the emperor's palace."

I frowned. "That was much too easy."

"Hey." Meg poked me in the back of the neck. "Remember what Percy told us? Never say stuff like *We made it* or *That was easy.* You'll jinx us!"

"My entire existence is a jinx."

"Pedal faster."

Since that was a direct order from Meg, I had no choice. My legs already felt like they were turning into sacks of hot coals, but I picked up the pace. Leo steered our teal plastic pirate ship toward the sewer entrance.

We were ten feet away when we triggered the First Law of Percy Jackson. Our jinx rose from the water in the form of a glistening arc of serpentine flesh.

I may have screamed. Leo shouted a completely unhelpful warning: "Look out!"

The boat tilted sideways. More arcs of serpent flesh breached around us—undulating hills of green and brown ridged with serrated dorsal fins. Meg's twin blades flashed into existence. She tried to stand, but the pedal boat capsized, plunging us into a cold green explosion of bubbles and thrashing limbs.

My only consolation: the canal was not deep. My feet found the bottom and I was able to stand, gasping and shivering, the water up to my shoulders. Nearby, a three-foot-diameter coil of serpent flesh encircled our pedal boat and squeezed. The hull imploded, shattering teal plastic with a sound like firecrackers. One shard stung my face, narrowly missing my left eye.

Leo popped to the surface, his chin barely at water level. He waded toward the sewer grate, climbing over a hill of serpent flesh that got in his way. Meg, bless her heroic heart, slashed away at the monster's coils, but her blades just skidded off its slimy hide.

Then the creature's head rose from the canal, and I lost all hope that we would be home in time for tofu enchilada night.

The monster's triangular forehead was wide enough to provide parking for a compact car. Its eyes glowed as orange as Agamethus's ghost. When it opened its vast red maw, I remembered another reason I hate serpents. Their breath smells worse than Hephaestus's work shirts.

The creature snapped at Meg. Despite being neck-deep in water, she somehow sidestepped and thrust her left-handed blade straight into the serpent's eye.

The monster threw its head back and hissed. The canal boiled with snake flesh. I was swept off my feet and submerged once more.

When I came to the surface, Meg McCaffrey stood at my side, her chest heaving as she gasped for air, her glasses crooked and filmed with canal water. The serpent's head flailed from side to side as if trying to shake the blindness out of its wounded eye. Its jaw smacked against the nearest condominium building, shattering windows and webbing the brick wall with cracks. A banner along the roofline said LEASING SOON! I hoped that meant the building was empty.

Leo made it to the grate. He traced his fingers along the golden bars, perhaps looking for buttons or switches or traps. Meg and I were now thirty feet away from him, which seemed a great distance over the vast serpentine terrain.

"Hurry!" I called to him.

"Gee, thanks!" he yelled back. "I didn't think of that."

The canal churned as the serpent drew in its coils. Its head rose two stories above us. Its right eye had gone dark, but its glowing left iris and its hideous maw reminded me of those pumpkin things mortals make for Halloween—jack-o'-lanterns? A silly tradition. I always preferred running around in goatskins at Februalia. Much more dignified.

Meg stabbed at the creature's underbelly. Her golden blade only sparked against it.

"What *is* this thing?" she demanded.

"The Carthaginian Serpent," I said. "One of the most fearsome beasts ever to face Roman troops. In Africa, it almost drowned an entire legion under Marcus Atilius Regulus—"

"Don't care." Meg and the serpent eyed each other warily—as if a giant monster and a twelve-year-old girl were well-matched opponents. "How do I kill it?"

My mind raced. I didn't do well in panic situations, which meant most of the situations I had been in recently. "I—I think the legion finally crushed it with thousands of rocks."

"I don't have a legion," Meg said. "Or thousands of rocks."

The serpent hissed, spraying venom across the canal. I unslung my bow, but I ran into that pesky *maintenance* issue again. A wet bowstring and arrows were problematic, especially if I planned to hit a target as small as the serpent's other eye. Then there were the physics of firing a bow while shoulder-deep in water.

"Leo?" I called.

"Almost!" He banged a wrench against the grate. "Keep it distracted!"

I gulped. "Meg, perhaps if you could stab its other eye, or its mouth."

"While you do what, hide?"

I really hated how this young girl could get inside my brain. "Of course not! I'll just be, um—"

The serpent struck. Meg and I dove in opposite directions. The creature's head caused a tsunami between us, somersaulting me through the water. I swallowed a few gallons of the canal and came up spluttering, then gagged in horror when I saw Meg encircled in the snake's tail. The serpent lifted her out of the water, bringing her level with its remaining eye. Meg slashed wildly, but the monster kept her out of striking distance. It regarded her as if thinking, *What is this stoplight-colored thing?*

Then it began to squeeze.

Leo yelled, "I got it!"

Clang. The grate's golden bars swung inward.

Leo turned, grinning in pride, then saw Meg's predicament.

"Nuh-uh!" He raised his hand above the water and tried to summon fire. All he managed was a puff of steam. He threw a wrench that bounced harmlessly off the snake's side.

Meg yelped. The snake's tail constricted around her waist, turning her face tomato red. She hammered her swords uselessly against the monster's hide.

I stood paralyzed, unable to help, unable to think.

I knew the strength of such a serpent. I remembered being wrapped in Python's coils, my divine ribs cracking, my godly ichor being squeezed into my head and threatening to spurt out my ears.

"Meg!" I shouted. "Hold on!"

She glared down at me, her eyes bulging, her tongue swollen, as if thinking, *Like I have a choice?*

The serpent ignored me, no doubt too interested in watching Meg implode like the pedal boat. Behind the snake's head rose the damaged brick wall of a condominium. The sewer entrance stood just to the right of that.

I remembered the tale of the Roman legion that had once fought this thing by showering it with stones. If only that brick wall were part of the Waystation, and I could command it. . . .

The idea seized me like a coil of the monster.

"Leo!" I yelled. "Get in the tunnel!"

"But—"

"Do it!"

Something began to swell inside my chest. I hoped it was power and not my breakfast.

I filled my lungs and bellowed in the baritone voice I

usually reserved for Italian operas: "BEGONE, SNAKE! I AM APOLLO!"

The frequency was perfect.

The wall of the warehouse trembled and cracked. A three-story-tall curtain of bricks peeled away and collapsed onto the serpent's back, pushing its head underwater. Its coiled tail loosened. Meg dropped into the canal.

Ignoring the rain of bricks, I waded forward (quite bravely, I thought) and pulled Meg to the surface.

"Guys, hurry!" Leo yelled. "The grate's closing again!"

I dragged Meg toward the sewer (because that's what friends are for) as Leo did his best to wedge the grate open with a tire iron.

Thank goodness for scrawny mortal bodies! We squeezed through just as the bars locked into place behind us.

Outside, the serpent surged upward from its baptism of bricks. It hissed and banged its half-blind head against the grate, but we did not linger to chat. We forged on, into the darkness of the emperor's waterworks.

22

I wax poetic
On the beauty of sewers
Real short poem. Done

WADING SHOULDER-DEEP through freezing sewer water, I felt nostalgic for the Indianapolis Zoo. Oh, for the simple pleasures of hiding from murderous Germani, crashing miniature trains, and serenading angry griffins!

Gradually, the sound of the serpent banging on the grate faded behind us. We walked for so long, I feared we'd die of hypothermia before reaching our goal. Then I spotted a raised alcove built into the side of the tunnel—an old service platform, maybe. We climbed out of the frigid green muck for a break. Meg and I huddled together while Leo attempted to light himself on fire.

On his third try, his skin sputtered and hissed, finally bursting into flames.

"Gather round, children." His grin looked diabolical with orange fire washing across his face. "Nothing like a blazing-hot Leo to warm you up!"

I tried to call him an idiot, but my jaw was shivering so badly, all that came out was, "Id—id—id—id—id—"

Soon our little alcove was infused with the smell of reheated Meg and Apollo—baked apples, mildew, body odor, and just a hint of awesomeness. (I'll let you guess which scent was *my* contribution.) My fingers turned from blue back to pink. I could feel my legs well enough again to be bothered by the chafing from the iron shackle. I was even able to speak without stuttering like Josephine's tommy gun.

When Leo judged us sufficiently dry, he shut off his personal bonfire. "Hey, Apollo, that was nice work back there."

"Which part?" I said. "The drowning? The screaming?"

"Nah, man—how you collapsed that brick wall. You should do that more often."

I plucked a teal plastic shard from my coat. "As an annoying demigod once told me, *Gee, why didn't I think of that?* I've explained before—I can't control those bursts of power. Somehow, in that moment, I found my godly voice. Brick mortar resonates at a certain frequency. It's best manipulated by a baritone at one hundred twenty-five decibels—"

"You saved me," Meg interrupted. "I was going to die. Maybe that's why you got your voice back."

I was reluctant to admit it, but she might have been right. The last time I'd experienced a burst of godly power, in the woods of Camp Half-Blood, my children Kayla and Austin had been in imminent danger of burning alive. Concern for others was a logical trigger for my powers. I was, after all, selfless, caring, and an all-around nice guy. Nevertheless, I found it irritating that my *own* well-being wasn't sufficient to give me godly strength. My life was important too!

"Well," I said, "I'm glad you weren't crushed to death, Meg. Anything broken?"

She touched her rib cage. "Nah. I'm good."

Her stiff movement, her pale complexion, and the tightness around her eyes told me otherwise. She was in more pain than she would admit. However, until we got back to the Waystation infirmary, I couldn't do much for her. Even if I'd had proper medical supplies, wrapping the ribs of a girl who'd almost been crushed to death might do more harm than good.

Leo stared at the dark green water. He looked more pensive than usual, or perhaps it was just the fact that he wasn't on fire anymore.

"What are you thinking about?" I asked.

He glanced over—no snappy comeback, no playful grin. "Just . . . Leo and Calypso's Garage: Auto Repair and Mechanical Monsters."

"What?"

"Something Cal and I used to joke about."

It didn't sound like a very funny joke. Then again, mortal humor wasn't always up to my godly standards. I recalled Calypso and Leo deep in conversation with Emmie yesterday as they walked through the great hall.

"Something to do with what Emmie was telling you?" I ventured.

He shrugged. "Stuff for the future. Nothing to worry about."

As a former god of prophecy, I'd always found the future a wonderful source of worry. But I decided not to press the issue. Right now, the only future goal that mattered was getting me back to Mount Olympus so the world could once again bask in my divine glory. I had to think of the greater good.

"Well," I said, "now that we're warm and dry, I suppose it's time to get in the water again."

"Fun," Meg said. She jumped in first.

Leo led the way, keeping one burning hand above the water for light. Every so often, small objects floated up from the pockets of his tool belt and drifted past me—Velcro tabs, Styrofoam peanuts, multicolored twist ties.

Meg guarded our backs, her twin swords gleaming in the darkness. I appreciated her fighting skills, but I *did* wish we had some additional help. A demigod child of the sewer goddess Cloacina would have been welcome . . . which is the first time I'd ever had *that* depressing thought.

I trudged along in the middle, trying to avoid flashbacks of my long-ago, unintended trip through a sewage-treatment facility in Biloxi, Mississippi. (That day would've been a total disaster, except that it ended with an impromptu jam session with Lead Belly.)

The current became stronger, pushing against us. Up ahead, I detected the glow of electric lights, the sound of voices. Leo extinguished his hand fire. He turned to us and put his finger to his lips.

After another twenty feet, we arrived at a second set of golden bars. Beyond that, the sewer opened into a much larger space where the water ran at a crosscurrent, some of it diverting into our tunnel. The force of the outflow made it difficult to stand.

Leo pointed at the golden grate. "This runs on a clepsy-dra lock," he said just loud enough to be heard. "I think I can open it quietly, but keep watch for me just in case . . . I don't know . . . giant serpents."

"We have faith in you, Valdez." I had no idea what a clepsydra lock was, but I'd learned from dealing with Hephaestus that it was best to show optimism and polite interest. Otherwise the tinkerer took offense and stopped making shiny toys for me to play with.

Within moments, Leo had the grate open. No alarms sounded. No contact mines exploded in our faces.

We emerged in the throne room I'd seen in my vision.

Fortunately, we were neck-deep in one of the open channels of water that lined the sides of the chamber, so I doubted anyone could easily spot us. Along the wall behind us, videos of Commodus looped over and over on the giant television screens.

We trudged toward the opposite side of the channel.

If you have ever tried to walk while immersed in a swift stream, you know how difficult it is. Also, if you have tried it, then may I ask *why*? It was absolutely exhausting. With every step, I feared the current would sweep me off my feet and flush me into the bowels of Indianapolis. Somehow, though, we made it to the far side.

I peeked over the edge of the channel and was immediately sorry I did.

Commodus was *right there*. Thank the gods, we had crossed slightly *behind* his throne, so neither he nor his Germani guards saw me. My least favorite Cornhusker, Lityerses, knelt before the emperor, facing my direction, but his head was lowered. I ducked back below the edge before he could spot me. I gestured to my friends: *Quiet. Yikes. We're going to die.* Or something to that effect. They seemed to get the message. Shivering miserably, I pressed against the wall and listened to the conversation going on just above us.

"—part of the plan, sire," Lityerses was saying. "We know where the Waystation is now."

Commodus grunted. "Yes, yes. Old Union Station. But Cleander searched that place several times before and found nothing."

"The Waystation is there," Lityerses insisted. "The tracking devices I planted on the griffins worked perfectly. The place must be protected by some sort of magic, but it won't stand up to a fleet of blemmyae bulldozers."

My heart climbed above water level, which put it somewhere between my ears. I dared not look at my friends. I had failed once again. I had unwittingly betrayed the location of our safe haven.

Commodus sighed. "Fine. Yes. But I want Apollo captured and brought to me in chains! The naming ceremony is tomorrow. Our dress rehearsal is, like, *right now*. When can you have the Waystation destroyed?"

Lityerses hesitated. "We need to scout the defenses. And gather our forces. Two days?"

"TWO DAYS? I'm not asking you to cross the Alps! I want it to happen *now*!"

"Tomorrow, then, at the latest, sire," said Lityerses. "Definitely by tomorrow."

"Hmph. I'm beginning to wonder about you, son of Midas. If you don't deliver—"

An electronic alarm blared through the chamber. For a moment, I thought we'd been discovered. I may or may not have emptied my bladder in the channel. (Don't tell Leo. He was downstream.)

Then, from the other side of the room, a voice shouted in Latin, "Incursion at the front gates!"

Lityerses growled. "I will deal with this, sire. Never fear. Guards, with me!"

Heavy footsteps faded into the distance.

I glanced at Meg and Leo, who were both giving me the same silent question: *What the Hades?*

I had not ordered an incursion at the front gates. I hadn't even activated the iron manacle on my ankle. I didn't know who would be so foolish as to launch a frontal assault on this underground palace, but Britomartis *had* promised to look for the Hunters of Artemis. It occurred to me that this was the sort of diversionary tactic they might arrange if they were trying to distract Commodus's security forces from our presence. Could we be so lucky? Probably not. More likely, some magazine-subscription salesman had rung the emperor's doorbell and was about to get a very hostile reception.

I risked another peek over the edge of the canal. Commodus was alone now with just one guard.

Perhaps we could take him—three on two?

Except that we were all about to pass out from hypothermia, Meg probably had some broken ribs, and my own powers were unpredictable at best. On the opposing team, we had a trained barbarian killer and a semi-divine emperor with a well-deserved reputation for superhuman strength. I decided to stay put.

Commodus glanced at his bodyguard. "Alaric."

"Lord?"

"I think your time is approaching. I grow impatient with my prefect. How long has Lityerses had this job?"

"About a day, my lord."

"Seems like forever!" Commodus pounded his fist on his armrest. "As soon as he's dealt with this incursion, I want you to kill him."

"Yes, lord."

"I want you to wipe out the Waystation *tomorrow morning* at the *latest*. Can you do that?"

"Of course, lord."

"Good! We'll have the naming ceremony immediately afterward in the colosseum."

"Stadium, my lord."

"Same difference! And the Cave of Prophecy? Is it secure?"

My spine took a jolt of electricity so strong I wondered if Commodus kept electric eels in the channel.

"I have followed your orders, sire," Alaric said. "The beasts are in place. The entrance is well guarded. None shall gain access."

"Lovely!" Commodus jumped to his feet. "Now let's go try on our racing outfits for the dress rehearsal, shall we? I can't wait to remake this city in my own image!"

I waited until the sound of their footsteps receded. I peeked over and saw no one in the room.

"Now," I said.

We dragged ourselves out of the canal and stood dripping and shivering in front of the golden throne. I could still smell the scent of Commodus's favorite body oil—a mix of cardamom and cinnamon.

Meg paced for warmth, her swords glowing in her hands. "Tomorrow morning? We gotta warn Jo and Emmie."

"Yeah," Leo agreed. "But we stick to the plan. First we find the captives. And that Throne of Whatever-It-Is—"

"Memory," I said.

"Yeah, that. *Then* we get out of here and warn Jo and Emmie."

"It may not help," I fretted. "I've *seen* how Commodus remakes a city. There will be chaos and spectacle, fire and wholesale slaughter, and lots and *lots* of pictures of Commodus *everywhere*. Add to that an army of blemmyae bulldozers—"

"Apollo." Leo made a fiery *time-out* sign. "We're gonna use the Valdez method on this."

Meg frowned. "What's the Valdez method?"

"Don't overthink it," Leo said. "It'll just make you depressed. In fact, try not to think at all."

Meg considered this, then seemed to realize she was thinking, then looked sheepish. "'Kay."

Leo grinned. "See? Easy! Now let's go blow some stuff up."

23

So amaze! Such name!
Ssssssarah with five s's is
Still two syllablessssss

AT FIRST, the Valdez method worked fine.

We found nothing to blow up, but we also didn't have to overthink anything. This was because we embraced the McCaffrey method as well, which involved chia seeds.

Faced with a choice of which corridor to take from the throne room, Meg pulled a soggy package of seeds from her red high-top. (I did not ask why she kept seeds in her shoes.) She caused the chia to sprout in her cupped palm, and the tiny forest of green stalks pointed toward the left-hand corridor.

"That way," Meg announced.

"Awesome superpower," Leo said. "When we get out of here, I'ma hook you up with a mask and a cape. We'll call you Chia Girl."

I hoped he was kidding. Meg, however, looked delighted.

The chia sprouts led us down one corridor then another. For an underground lair in the Indianapolis sewer system, the palace was quite opulent. The floors were rough-hewn slate, the gray stone walls decorated with alternating tap-estries and television monitors showing—you guessed it—videos of Commodus. Most of the mahogany doors were labeled with engraved bronze plates: COMMODUS SAUNA, COMMODUS GUEST ROOMS 1–6, COMMODUS EMPLOYEE CAFETERIA, and, yes, COMMODUS COMMODES.

We saw no guards, no employees, no guests. The only person we encountered was a maid coming out of the COMMODUS IMPERIAL GUARD BARRACKS with a basket of dirty laundry.

When she saw us, her eyes widened in terror. (Probably because we looked dirtier and damper than anything she'd pulled from the Germani's hamper.) Before she could scream, I knelt before her and sang "You Don't See Me" by Josie and the Pussycats. The maid's eyes became misty and unfocused. She sniffled nostalgically, walked back into the barracks, and closed the door behind her.

Leo nodded. "Nice one, Apollo."

"It wasn't hard. That tune is wonderful for inducing short-term amnesia."

Meg sniffed. "Would've been kinder to hit her over the head."

"Oh, come now," I protested. "You *like* my singing."

Her ears reddened. I remembered how young McCaffrey had cried when I poured out my heart and soul in the giant ants' lair at Camp Half-Blood. I'd been rather proud of my performance, but I guess Meg did not feel like reliving it.

She punched me in the gut. "Come on."

"Ow."

The chia seeds led us deeper into the emperor's compound. Silence began to weigh on me. Imaginary insects crawled across my shoulder blades. Surely Commodus's men had dealt with the front-door incursion by now. They would be returning to their normal posts, perhaps checking security monitors for other intruders.

At last, we turned a corner and spotted a blemmyae keeping watch outside a metal vault door. The guard wore black dress pants and shiny black shoes, but he made no attempt to hide his chest-face. The hair across his shoulders/scalp was clipped in a military flattop. The wire of a security earpiece ran from beneath his armpit to his pants pocket. He did not appear to be armed, but that gave me no comfort. His meaty fists looked quite capable of crushing a pedal boat or a Lester Papadopoulos.

Leo grumbled under his breath, "Not these guys again." Then he forced a smile and strode toward the guard. "Hello! Lovely day! How are you?"

The guard turned in surprise. I imagined that proper procedure would have been to alert his superiors to the intrusion, but he'd been asked a question. It would've been rude to ignore it.

"I'm fine." The guard couldn't seem to decide between a friendly smile or an intimidating glower. His mouth spasmed, which made him look like he was doing an ab exercise. "I don't think you're supposed to be here."

"Really?" Leo kept marching forward. "Thank you!"

"You're welcome. Now if you'll please raise your hands."

"Like this?" Leo ignited his hands and torched the blemmyae's chest-face.

The guard stumbled, choking on flames, batting his huge eyelashes like burning palm fronds. He groped for the button on the microphone attached to his earpiece. "Post twelve," he croaked. "I've got—"

Meg's twin golden swords scissored across his midsection, reducing him to a pile of yellow dust with a partially melted earpiece.

A voice warbled from the tiny speaker. "Post twelve, please repeat."

I grabbed the device. I had *no* desire to wear something that had been in a blemmyae's armpit, but I held the speaker next to my ear and spoke into the mic. "False alarm. Everything is hunky-dorky. Thank you."

"You're welcome," said the voice in the speaker. "Daily passcode, please."

"Why, certainly! It's—"

I threw the microphone down and crushed it under my heel.

Meg stared at me. "Hunky-*dorky?*"

"It sounded like something a blemmyae would say."

"That's not even the right expression. It's hunky-*dory.*"

"A girl who says *goddy* is correcting my language."

"Guys," Leo said. "Keep a lookout while I take care of this door. There's gotta be something important in here."

I kept watch while he went to work on the vault lock. Meg, not being good at following directions, strolled back the way we'd come. She crouched and began picking up the chia sprouts she'd dropped when summoning her swords.

"Meg," I said.

"Yeah?"

"What are you doing?"

"Chia."

"I can see that, but . . ." I almost said, *They're only sprouts*.

Then I remembered one time I'd said something similar to Demeter. The goddess had cursed me so that every piece of clothing I put on immediately sprouted and bloomed. Nothing is quite as uncomfortable as having your cotton underwear burst into actual bolls of cotton, complete with stems, spurs, and seeds right where your . . . Well, I think you get the idea.

Meg gathered the last of her sprouts. With one of her swords, she cracked the slate floor. She carefully planted the chia in the fissure, then wrung out her still-wet skirt to water them.

I watched, fascinated, as the small patch of green thickened and flourished, forcing new cracks in the slate. Who knew chia could be so robust?

"They wouldn't last any longer in my hand." Meg stood, her expression defiant. "Everything alive deserves a chance to grow."

The mortal Lester part of me found this sentiment admirable. The Apollo part of me wasn't so sure. Over the centuries, I'd met many living beings that hadn't seemed worthy or even capable of growth. A few of those beings I'd killed myself. . . .

Still, I suspected Meg was saying something about herself. She had endured a horrid childhood—the death of her father, then the abuse of Nero, who'd twisted her mind into seeing him both as her kindly stepfather and the terrible Beast. Despite that, Meg had survived. I imagined she could empathize with small green things that had surprisingly strong roots.

"Yes!" Leo said. The vault lock clicked. The door swung inward. Leo turned and grinned. "Who's the best?"

"Me?" I asked, but my spirits quickly fell. "You didn't mean me, did you?"

Leo ignored me and stepped into the room.

I followed. Immediately, an intense, unpleasant moment of déjà vu struck me. Inside, a circular chamber was lined with glass partitions like the emperor's training facility at the zoo. But here, instead of animals, the cages held people.

I was so appalled I could hardly breathe.

In the nearest cell on my left, huddled in a corner, two painfully emaciated teenage boys glared at me. Their clothes were rags. Shadows filled the cavernous recesses of their clavicles and ribs.

In the next cell, a girl in gray camouflage paced like a jaguar. Her shoulder-length hair was stark white, though she looked no more than fifteen. Given her level of energy and outrage, I guessed she was a recent captive. She had no bow, but I pegged her as a Hunter of Artemis. When she saw me, she marched to the glass. She banged on it with her fists and shouted angrily, but her voice was too muffled for me to make out the words.

I counted six other cells, each one occupied. In the center of the room was a metal post with iron hooks and chains—the sort of place where one could fasten slaves for inspection before sale.

"*Madre de los dioses,*" Leo muttered.

I thought the Arrow of Dodona was trembling in my quiver. Then I realized it was just me, shaking with anger.

I have always despised slavery. Partly, this is because twice before Zeus made me mortal and forced me to work as a slave for human kings. The most poetic description I can offer about that experience? It sucked.

Even before that, my temple at Delphi had created a special way for slaves to gain their freedom. With the help of my priests, thousands bought their emancipation through a ritual called the *trust sale*, by which I, the god Apollo, became their new master and then set them free.

Much later, one of my biggest grudges against the Romans was that they turned my holy island of Delos into the region's biggest slave market. Can you *believe* the nerve? I sent an angry army led by Mithradates to correct that situation, slaughtering twenty thousand Romans in the process. But I mean, *come on*. They had it coming.

Suffice to say: Commodus's prison reminded me of everything I hated about the Good Old Days.

Meg strode to the cell that held the two emaciated boys. With the point of her sword, she cut a circle in the glass and kicked it in. The dislodged section wobbled on the floor like a giant transparent coin.

The boys tried to stand without success. Meg jumped into the cell to help them.

"Yeah," Leo muttered with approval. He pulled a hammer from his tool belt and marched to the cell of the captive Hunter. He gestured *get back*, then whacked the glass. The hammer bounced off, narrowly missing Leo's nose on the rebound.

The Hunter rolled her eyes.

"Okay, Mr. Sheet of Glass." Leo tossed aside the hammer. "You're gonna be like that? It's on!"

His hands blazed white-hot. He pressed his fingers against the glass, which began to warp and bubble. Within seconds, he melted a ragged hole at face level.

The silver-haired girl said, "Good. Step aside."

"Hold on, I'll make you a bigger exit," Leo promised.

"No need." The silver-haired girl backed up, launched herself through the hole, and gracefully somersaulted next to us, grabbing Leo's discarded hammer as she stood.

"More weapons," the girl demanded. "I need more weapons."

Yes, I thought, definitely a Hunter of Artemis.

Leo pulled out a selection of tools for the girl's consideration. "Um, I got a screwdriver, a hacksaw, and . . . I think this is a cheese cutter."

The girl wrinkled her nose. "What are you, a tinkerer?"

"That's Lord Tinkerer to you."

The girl swiped the tools. "I'll take them all." She scowled at me. "What about your bow?"

"You can't have my bow," I said. "I'm Apollo."

Her expression changed from shock to understanding to forced calm. I guessed the plight of Lester Papadopoulos was known among the Hunters.

"Right," the girl said. "The rest of the Hunters should be on their way. I was the nearest to Indianapolis. I decided to play advance scout. Obviously, that didn't work out so well for me."

"In fact," I said, "there was an incursion at the front

gates a few minutes ago. I suspect your comrades have arrived."

Her eyes darkened. "We need to leave, then. Quickly."

Meg helped the emaciated boys from their cell. Up close, they looked even more pathetic and fragile, which made me angrier.

"Prisoners should never be treated this way," I growled.

"Oh, they weren't denied food," the silver-haired girl said, admiration creeping into her voice. "They've been on a hunger strike. Courageous . . . for a couple of boys. I'm Hunter Kowalski, by the way."

I frowned. "A Hunter named Hunter?"

"Yeah, I have heard *that* a million times. Let's free the others."

I found no convenient switch box to lower the glass doors, but with Meg and Leo's help, we began slowly liberating the captives. Most seemed to be human or demigod (it was difficult to tell which) but one was a dracaena. She looked human enough from the waist up, but where her legs should have been, twin snake tails undulated.

"She's friendly," Hunter assured us. "We shared a cell last night until the guards separated us. Her name's Sssssarah, with five s's."

That was good enough for me. We let her out.

The next cell held a lone young man who looked like a professional wrestler. He wore only a red-and-white loincloth with matching beads around his neck, but he did not seem underdressed. Just as gods are often depicted nude because they are perfect beings, this prisoner had no reason to hide his body. With his dark, glossy skin, his shaved head, and his muscular arms and chest, he looked like a teak warrior brought to life through the craft of Hephaestus. (I made a mental note to ask Hephaestus about such a project later.) His eyes, also teak brown, were piercing and angry— beautiful in the way only dangerous things can be. Tattooed on his right shoulder was a symbol I did not recognize, some sort of a double-bladed ax.

Leo fired up his hands to melt the glass, but the dracaena Sssssarah hissed.

"Not that one," she warned. "Too dangerousssss."

Leo frowned. "Lady, we *need* dangerous friends."

"Yessss, but that one fought for money. He wassss employed by the emperor. He'sssss only here now because he did ssssomething to anger Commodussss."

I studied Tall, Dark & Handsome. (I know that's a cliché, but he really *was* all three.) I didn't intend to leave anyone behind, especially someone who wore a loincloth so well.

"We're going to free you," I shouted through the glass, not sure how much he could hear. "Please don't kill us. We are enemies of Commodus, the man who put you here."

TD&H's expression did not change: part anger, part disdain, part indifference—the same way Zeus looked every morning before his coffee-infused nectar.

"Leo," I said. "Do it."

Valdez melted the glass. TD&H stepped out slowly and gracefully, as if he had all the time in the world.

"Hello," I said. "I'm the immortal god Apollo. Who might you be?"

His voice rolled like thunder. "I am Jamie."

"A noble name," I decided, "worthy of kings."

"Apollo," Meg called. "Get over here."

She was staring into the last cell. *Of course* it would be the last cell.

Hunched in the corner, sitting on a familiar bronze suitcase, was a young girl in a lavender wool sweater and green jeans. On her lap sat a plate of prison slop, which she was using to finger-paint on the wall. Her tufts of brown hair looked like she'd cut them herself with gardening shears. She was large for her age—about Leo's size—but her baby-ish face told me she couldn't have been more than seven.

"Georgina," I said.

Leo scowled. "Why is she sitting on Festus? Why would they put him in there with her?"

I didn't have an answer, but I motioned for Meg to cut through the glass wall.

"Let me go first," I said.

I stepped through. "Georgie?"

The girl's eyes were like fractured prisms, swirling with unanchored thoughts and waking nightmares. I knew that look too well. Over the centuries I'd seen many mortal minds broken under the weight of prophecy.

"Apollo." She let out a burst of giggles as if her brain had developed a leak. "You and the dark. Some death, some death, some death."

24

Science can be fun
Squirt those toxic chemicals
Anywhere, really

GEORGINA GRABBED MY WRIST, sending an unpleasant chill up my forearm. "Some death."

On the list of things that freaked me out, seven-year-old girls who giggled about death were right at the top, along with reptiles and talking weapons.

I remembered the prophetic limerick that had brought us west—the warning that I would be *forced death and madness to swallow.* Clearly, Georgina had encountered such horrors in the Cave of Trophonius. I did not fancy following her example. For one thing, I had zero skill at painting with prison slop.

"Yes," I said agreeably. "We can talk more about death once we get you home. Emmie and Josephine sent me to get you."

"Home." Georgina spoke the word as if it were a difficult term from a foreign language.

Leo got impatient. He climbed into the cell and trotted over. "Hey, Georgie. I'm Leo. That's a nice suitcase. Can I see it?"

Georgina tilted her head. "My clothes."

"Oh, uh . . . yeah." Leo brushed the name tag on his borrowed coveralls. "Sorry about the sewage stains and the burning smell. I'll get 'em cleaned."

"The burning hot," Georgie said. "You. All of it."

"Right . . ." Leo smiled uncertainly. "Ladies often tell me I'm all the burning hot. But don't worry. I won't set you on fire or anything."

I offered Georgie my hand. "Here, child. We'll take you home."

She was content to let me help her. As soon as she was on her feet, Leo rushed to the bronze suitcase and began fussing over it.

"Oh, buddy, I'm so sorry," he murmured. "I should *never* have left you. I'll get you back to the Waystation for a good tune-up. Then you can have all the Tabasco sauce and motor oil you want."

The suitcase did not respond. Leo managed to activate its wheels and handle so he could lug it out of the cell.

Georgina remained docile until she saw Meg. Then, suddenly, she had a burst of strength worthy of me.

"No!" She yanked herself from my grip and plunged back into her cell. I tried to calm her, but she continued to howl and stare at Meg in horror. "NERO! NERO!"

Meg did her famous turn-to-cement expression, shutting down all emotion, extinguishing all light from her eyes.

Hunter Kowalski rushed in to help with Georgie. "Hey. Hey, hey, hey." She stroked the girl's ratty hair. "It's okay. We're friends."

"Nero!" Georgie shrieked again.

Hunter frowned at Meg. "What's she talking about?"

Meg stared down at her high-tops. "I can leave."

"We're *all* leaving," I insisted. "Georgie, this is Meg. She escaped from Nero, that's true. But she's on our side."

I decided not to add, *Except for that one time she betrayed me to her stepfather and almost got me killed.* I didn't want to complicate matters.

In Hunter's kind embrace, Georgie calmed down. Her wide eyes and trembling body reminded me of a terrified bird held in cupped hands. "You and death and fire." Suddenly she giggled. "The chair! The chair, the chair."

"Ah, taters," I cursed. "She's right. We still need the chair."

Tall, Dark & Jamie appeared on my left, a brooding presence not unlike a storm front. "What chair is this?"

"A throne," I said. "Magical. We need it to cure Georgie."

From the blank looks of the prisoners, I guessed I wasn't making much sense. I also realized I couldn't ask the entire group to go tromping through the palace in search of a piece of furniture, especially not the half-starved boys or the dracaena (who, not having feet, was incapable of tromping). Nor was Georgie likely to go anywhere with Meg—not without a great deal of shrieking.

"We'll have to split up," I decided. "Leo, you know the way back to the sewer tunnel. Take our new friends with you. Hopefully the guards will still be distracted. Meg and I will find the chair."

Leo glanced at his beloved dragon suitcase, then at Meg and me, then at the prisoners. "Just you and Meg?"

"Go," Meg said, careful to avoid Georgie's eyes. "We'll be okay."

"What if the guards *aren't* distracted?" Leo asked. "Or if we have to fight that snake thingie again?"

Jamie rumbled, "Snake thingie?"

"I ressssent your choice of wordssss," said Sssssarah.

Leo sighed. "I don't mean you. It's a . . . well, you'll see. Maybe you can talk to it and convince it to let us pass." He sized up Jamie. "Or if not, the monster's probably about the right size for you to make a belt out of."

Sssssarah hissed in disapproval.

Hunter Kowalski wrapped her arms protectively around Georgie. "We'll get everyone to safety," she promised. "Apollo, Meg, thank you. If you see the emperor, send him to Tartarus for me."

"Pleasure," I said.

In the hallway, alarms began to blare.

Leo led our new friends back the way we'd come. Hunter held Georgina's hand while Jamie and Sssssarah propped up the hunger-strike boys.

Once the group disappeared around the corner, Meg walked to her little patch of chia. She closed her eyes in concentration. Faster than you could say *ch-ch-ch-chia*, the sprouts went into overdrive, spreading across the corridor like a fast-motion sheet of green ice. Sprouts wove together from ceiling to floor, wall to wall, until the hallway was clogged with an impassable curtain of plants.

"Impressive," I said, though I was also thinking, *Well, we won't be exiting that way.*

Meg nodded. "It'll slow down anybody chasing our friends. Come on. The chair is down here."

"How do you know?"

Rather than answering, she dashed off. Since she was the one with all the cool powers, I decided to follow.

Alarms continued to blare, the noise stabbing my eardrums like hot skewers. Red lights swept the corridors, turning Meg's blades the color of blood.

We poked our heads inside the COMMODUS STOLEN ART GALLERY, the COMMODUS IMPERIAL CAFÉ, and the COMMODUS-CARE INFIRMARY. We saw no one and found no magical thrones.

Finally, Meg stopped at a steel door. At least I assumed it was a door. It had no handle, lock, or visible hinges—it was just a featureless rectangle of metal set in the wall.

"It's in here," she said.

"How can you tell?"

She gave me her *nyah-nyah-nyah* look—the kind of expression your mother used to warn you about: *If you make that face, it'll stick.* (I'd always taken this threat seriously, since divine mothers are fully capable of making it happen.)

"It's like the trees, dummy."

I blinked. "You mean, how you led us to the Grove of Dodona?"

"Yeah."

"You can sense the Throne of Mnemosyne . . . because it is made of magical wood?"

"Dunno. I guess."

That seemed like a stretch, even for a powerful daughter of Demeter. I didn't know how the Throne of Mnemosyne had been created. It certainly *might* have been carved from some special tree from a sacred forest. Gods loved that sort of thing. If so, Meg might have been able to sense the chair.

I wondered if she could find me a magical dining table once I got back to Olympus. I really needed one with foldout leaves for accommodating the Nine Muses at Thanksgiving.

Meg tried slicing the door the way she had with the glass walls in the prison. Her swords didn't even scratch the metal. She tried wedging her blades into the door frame. No luck.

She stepped back and frowned at me. "Open it."

"*Me?*" I felt sure she was picking on me because I was the only enslaved god she had. "I'm not Hermes! I'm not even Valdez!"

"Try."

As if that were a simple request! I attempted all the obvious methods. I shoved the door. I kicked it. I attempted to get my fingertips under the edges and pry it open. I spread my arms and yelled the standard magic words: MELLON! SHAZAM! SESAME STREET! None of these worked. At last I tried my infallible ace in the hole. I sang "Love Is an Open Door" from the *Frozen* soundtrack. Even this failed.

"Impossible!" I cried. "This door has no taste in music!"

"Be more goddy," Meg suggested.

If I could be more goddy, I wanted to scream, *I wouldn't be here!*

I ran down the list of things I used to be the god of: archery, poetry, flirting, sunlight, music, medicine, prophecy, flirting. None of these would open a literal stainless steel door.

Wait . . .

I thought back to the last room we'd peeked in—the Commoduscare Infirmary. "Medical supplies."

Meg peered at me from behind her filmy cat-eye lenses. "You're going to heal the door?"

"Not exactly. Come with me."

In the infirmary, I riffled through supply cabinets, filling a small cardboard box with potentially useful items: medical tape, oral syringes, scalpels, ammonia, distilled water, baking soda. Then, finally . . . "Aha!" In triumph, I held up a bottle labeled H_2SO_4. "Oil of vitriol!"

Meg edged away. "What is that?"

"You'll see." I grabbed some safety equipment: gloves, mask, goggles—the sort of stuff I would not have bothered with as a god. "Let's go, Chia Girl!"

"It sounded better when Leo said it," she complained, but she followed me out.

Back at the steel door, I suited up. I readied two syringes: one with vitriol, one with water. "Meg, stand back."

"I . . . Okay." She pinched her nose against the stench as I squirted oil of vitriol around the door. Vaporous tendrils curled from the seams. "What *is* that stuff?"

"Back in medieval times," I said, "we used oil of vitriol for its healing properties. No doubt that's why Commodus had some in his infirmary. Today we call it sulfuric acid."

Meg flinched. "Isn't that dangerous?"

"Very."

"And you *healed* with it?"

"It was the Middle Ages. We were crazy back then."

I held up the second syringe, the one filled with water. "Meg, what I'm about to do—never, ever try this on your own." I felt a bit silly giving this advice to a girl who regularly fought monsters with golden swords, but I had promised Bill Nye the Science Guy I would always promote safe laboratory practices.

"What's going to happen?" she asked.

I stepped back and squirted water into the door seams. Immediately the acid began to hiss and spit more aggressively than the Carthaginian Serpent. To speed the process along, I sang a song of heat and corrosion. I chose Frank Ocean, since his soulful power could burn its way through even the hardest substances.

The door groaned and creaked. At last it fell inward, leaving a steaming wreath of mist around the frame.

"Whoa," Meg said, which was probably the highest compliment she'd ever given me.

I pointed to the cardboard supply box near her feet. "Hand me that baking soda, would you?"

I sprinkled powder liberally around the doorway to neutralize the acid. I couldn't help smirking at my own ingenuity. I hoped Athena was watching, because WISDOM, BABY! And I did it with so much more style than Old Gray Eyes.

I bowed to Meg with a flourish. "After you, Chia Girl."

"You actually did something good," she noted.

"You just *had* to step on my moment."

Inside, we found a twenty-foot-square storage area holding just one item. The Throne of Mnemosyne hardly deserved the name *throne*. It was a straight-backed chair of sanded white birch, devoid of decoration except for the carved silhouette of a mountain on the seat back. Ugh, Mnemosyne! Give me a proper golden throne encrusted with ever-flaming rubies! Alas, not every deity knows how to flaunt it.

Still, the chair's simplicity made me nervous. I've found that many terrible and powerful items are quite underwhelming in appearance. Zeus's lightning bolts? They don't look menacing until my father throws them. The trident of Poseidon? Please. He *never* scrubs the seaweed and moss off that thing. And the wedding dress Helen of Troy wore to marry Menelaus? Oh, gods, it was *so* drab. I told her, "Girl, you have got to be kidding me. That neckline doesn't work for you at all!" Then Helen put it on, and *wow*.

"What's the mountain design?" Meg stirred me from my reverie. "Olympus?"

"Actually, no. I'm guessing that would be Mount Pierus, where the goddess Mnemosyne gave birth to the Nine Muses."

Meg scrunched up her face. "All nine of them at once? Sounds painful."

I'd never thought about that. Since Mnemosyne was the goddess of memory, with every detail of her eternal existence engraved on her brain, it did seem strange that she'd want a reminder of her labor and delivery experience carved on her throne.

"Whatever the case," I said, "we've tarried too long. Let's get the chair out of here."

I used my roll of medical tape to make shoulder straps, turning the chair into a makeshift backpack. Who said Leo was the only handy person on our team?

"Meg," I said, "while I'm doing this, fill those syringes with ammonia."

"Why?"

"Just for emergencies. Humor me."

Medical tape is wonderful stuff. Soon Meg and I both had bandoliers of ammonia syringes, and I had a chair on my back. The throne was a light piece of furniture, which was fortunate, since it was knocking around with my ukulele, my bow, and my quiver. I added a few scalpels to my bandolier, just for fun. Now all I needed was a bass drum and some juggling pins and I could be a one-man traveling show.

I hesitated in the corridor. In one direction, the hallway extended about a hundred feet before angling left. The alarms had stopped blaring, but from around that corner came an echoing roar like ocean surf or a cheering crowd. Multicolored lights flashed across the walls. Just looking in that direction made me nervous.

Our only other option would take us back to the Meg McCaffrey Memorial Wall of Chia.

"Fastest exit," I said. "We may have to retrace our steps."

Meg stood enthralled, her ear tilted toward the distant roar. "There's . . . something down there. We need to check it out."

"Please, no," I begged. "We've rescued the prisoners. We found Festus. We scored a lovely piece of furniture. That's a full day's work for *any* hero!"

Meg straightened. "Something important," she insisted.

She summoned her swords and strode toward the strange lights in the distance.

"I hate you," I muttered.

Then I shouldered my magical chair and jogged after her—around the corner and straight into a vast spotlighted arena.

25

Big birds are evil
They charge me with razor legs
I die and it hurts

I WAS NO STRANGER to stadium concerts.

In ancient times, I played a dozen sold-out shows at the amphitheater in Ephesus. Frenzied young women threw their *strophiae* at me. Young men swooned and fainted. In 1965, I sang with the Beatles at Shea Stadium, though Paul would *not* agree to turn up my microphone. On the recordings, you can't even hear my voice on "Everybody's Tryin' to Be My Baby."

However, none of my previous experiences prepared me for the emperor's arena.

Spotlights blinded me as we emerged from the corridor. The crowd cheered.

As my eyes adjusted, I saw that we stood at the fifty-yard line of a professional football stadium. The field was arranged in an odd fashion. Around the circumference ran a three-lane racetrack. Pincushioning the artificial turf, a dozen iron posts anchored the chains of various beasts. At one post, six combat ostriches paced like dangerous merry-go-round animals. At another, three male lions snarled and blinked at the spotlights. At a third, a sad-looking elephant swayed, no doubt unhappy that she'd been outfitted in spiked chain mail and an oversize Colts football helmet.

Reluctantly, I raised my eyes to the stands. In the sea of blue seats, the only occupied section was the end zone on the left, but the crowd was certainly enthusiastic. Germani banged their spears against their shields. The demigods of Commodus's Imperial Household jeered and yelled insults (which I will not repeat) about my divine person. Cynocephali—the tribe of wolf-headed men—howled and tore at their Indianapolis Colts souvenir jerseys. Rows of blemmyae clapped politely, looking perplexed at the rude behavior of their peers. And, predictably, an entire section of the stands was filled with wild centaurs. Honestly, you can't have a sporting event or bloodbath *anywhere* without them somehow getting wind of it. They blew their vuvuzelas, sounded air horns, and trampled all over one another, sloshing root beer from their double-cup drinking hats.

In the center of the crowd gleamed the emperor's box, bedecked in purple and gold banners that clashed horribly with the blue-and-steel Colts decor. Flanking the throne were a grim mix of Germani and mortal mercenaries with sniper rifles. What the mercenaries saw through the Mist, I couldn't guess, but they must have been specially trained to work in magical environments. They stood emotionless and alert, their fingers resting across their triggers. I didn't doubt that they would kill us at one word from Commodus, and we would be powerless to stop them.

Commodus himself rose from his throne. He wore white-and-purple robes and a golden laurel crown, as one would expect of an emperor, but under the folds of his toga

I caught a glimpse of a golden-brown racing suit. With his shaggy beard, Commodus looked more like a Gallic chieftain than a Roman, though no Gaul would have such perfect gleaming white teeth.

"At last!" His commanding voice boomed through the stadium, amplified by giant speakers that hung above the field. "Welcome, Apollo!"

The audience cheered and hooted. Lining the upper tiers, TV screens flashed digital fireworks and blazed the words WELCOME, APOLLO! High above, along the girders of the corrugated steel roof, bags of confetti burst, dumping a snowstorm of purple and gold that swirled around the championship banners.

Oh, the irony! This was *exactly* the sort of welcome I'd been longing for. Now I just wanted to slink back into the corridor and disappear. But, of course, the doorway we'd come through had disappeared, replaced with a cinder-block wall.

I crouched as inconspicuously as possible and pressed the indentation on my iron manacle. No wings sprang from the shackle, so I guessed I'd found the right button for the emergency signal. With luck, it would alert Jo and Emmie to our plight and location, though I still wasn't sure what they could do to help us. At least they'd know where to collect our bodies later.

Meg seemed to be withdrawing into herself, rolling down her mental shutters against the onslaught of noise and attention. For a brief terrible moment, I wondered if she might have betrayed me once again—leading me right into the clutches of the Triumvirate.

No. I refused to believe it. And yet . . . why *had* she insisted on coming this direction?

Commodus waited for the roar of the crowd to subside. Combat ostriches strained at their tethers. Lions roared. The elephant shook her head as if trying to remove her ridiculous Colts helmet.

"Meg," I said, trying to control my panic. "Why did you . . . Why are we . . . ?"

Her expression was as mystified as the demigods at Camp Half-Blood who'd been drawn to the Grove of Dodona by its mysterious voices.

"Something," she murmured. "Something is here."

That was a horrifying understatement. *Many* things were here. Most of them wanted to kill us.

The video screens flashed more fireworks, along with digital nonsense like DEFENSE! and MAKE SOME NOISE! and advertisements for energy drinks. My eyes felt as if they were bleeding.

Commodus grinned down at me. "I had to rush things, old friend! This is just the dress rehearsal, but since you're here, I scrambled to put together a few surprises. We'll restage the whole show tomorrow with a full audience, after I bulldoze the Waystation to the ground. Do try to stay alive today, but you're welcome to suffer as much as you want. And Meg . . ." His *tsk-tsk-tsk* echoed through the stadium. "Your stepfather is *so* disappointed in you. You're about to find out just how much."

Meg pointed one of her swords at the emperor's box. I waited for her to issue some withering retort, like *You're stupid*, but the sword seemed to be her entire message. This brought back an unsettling memory of Commodus himself in the Colosseum, tossing severed ostrich heads at the senators' seats and pointing: *You're next.* But Meg couldn't have known about that . . . could she?

Commodus's smile wavered. He held up a page of notes. "So, anyway, the run of show! First, the citizens of Indianapolis are marched in at gunpoint and seated. I'll say a few words, thank them for coming, and explain how their city is now named Commodianapolis."

The crowd howled and stomped. A lone air horn blasted.

"Yes, yes." Commodus waved away their enthusiasm. "Then I send an army of blemmyae into the city with champagne bottles to smash against all the buildings. My banners are unfurled along all the streets. Any bodies we retrieve from the Waystation are dangled on ropes from the girders up there"—he gestured at the peaked ceiling—"and then the fun starts!"

He threw his notes in the air. "I can't tell you how excited I am, Apollo! You understand, don't you, this was all preordained? The spirit of Trophonius was *very* specific."

My throat made the sound of a vuvuzela. "You consulted the Dark Oracle?"

I wasn't sure my words would carry that far, but the emperor laughed. "Well, of course, dear heart! Not me personally. I have minions to do that sort of thing. But Trophonius was quite clear: once I destroy the Waystation and sacrifice your life in the games, only then can I rechristen this city and rule the Midwest forever as god-emperor!"

Twin spotlights fixed on Commodus. He ripped off his toga, revealing a one-piece racing suit of Nemean Lion hide, the front and sleeves decorated with the decals of various corporate sponsors.

The crowd oohed and ahhed as the emperor turned a circle, showing off his outfit.

"You like?" he asked. "I've done a lot of research on my new hometown! My two fellow emperors call this place boring. But I will prove them wrong! I will stage the best Indy-Colt-500-Double-A Gladiatorial Championship ever!"

Personally, I thought Commodus's branding needed work, but the crowd went wild.

Everything seemed to happen at once. Country music blared from the speakers: possibly Jason Aldean, though with the distortion and reverb, even my keen ears could not be sure. At the opposite side of the track, a wall opened. Three Formula One race cars—red, yellow, and blue, like a children's toy set—rumbled onto the tarmac.

Around the field, chains disconnected from the animals' collars. In the stands, wild centaurs threw fruit and blew their vuvuzelas. From somewhere behind the emperor's box, cannons fired, launching a dozen gladiators over the goalposts toward the field. Some landed with graceful rolls and came up ready to fight. Others hit the artificial turf like heavily-armored spit wads and didn't move again.

The race cars revved and sped around the track, forcing Meg and me onto the field to avoid getting run over. Gladiators and animals began a free-for-all, no-claws-barred destructo-match to the Nashville beat. And then, for no logical reason, a huge sack opened under the Jumbotron monitor, spilling hundreds of basketballs onto the fifty-yard line.

Even by Commodus's standards, the spectacle was crass and too much of everything, but I doubted I would live long enough to write a bad review. Adrenaline raced through my system like a 220-volt current. Meg yelled and charged the nearest ostrich. Since I had nothing better to do, I raced after her, the Throne of Mnemosyne and thirty pounds of other gear bouncing on my back.

All six ostriches bore down on us. That may not sound as terrifying as the Carthaginian Serpent or a bronze colossus of *moi*, but ostriches can run at forty miles an hour. They charged with their metal teeth snapping, their spiked helmets swiping side to side, their barbed-wire legs trampling across the turf like an ugly pink forest of deadly Christmas trees.

I nocked an arrow in my bow, but even if I could match Commodus's skill, I doubted I could decapitate all six birds before they killed us. I wasn't even sure Meg could defeat so many with her formidable blades.

I silently composed a new death haiku right on the spot: *Big birds are evil / They charge me with razor legs / I die and it hurts.*

In my defense, I did not have much time to edit.

The only thing that saved us? Basketballs *ex machina*. Another bag must have opened above us, or perhaps a small batch of balls had gotten stuck in the netting. Twenty or thirty rained down around us, forcing the ostriches to dodge and veer. One less fortunate bird stepped on a ball and took a header, planting his sharpened beak in the turf. Two of his brethren stumbled over him, creating a dangerous pile-up of feathers, legs, and razor wire.

"Come on!" Meg yelled to me. Rather than fighting the birds, she grabbed one's neck and swung onto its back, somehow without dying. She charged away, swinging her blades at monsters and gladiators.

Mildly impressive, but how was I supposed to follow her? Also, she'd just rendered useless my plan of hiding behind her. Such an inconsiderate girl.

I shot my arrow at the nearest threat: a Cyclops charging me and waving his club. Where he'd come from, I had no idea, but I sent him back to Tartarus where he belonged.

I dodged a fire-breathing horse, kicked a basketball into the gut of a gladiator, then sidestepped a lion who was lunging at a tasty-looking ostrich. (All of this, by the way, with a chair strapped to my back.)

Meg aimed her deadly bird at the emperor's box, slashing down anything that got in her way. I understood her plan: kill Commodus. I staggered after her as best I could, but my head throbbed from the pounding country music, the jeering of the crowd, and the whine of the Formula One engines gaining speed around the track.

A pack of wolf-headed warriors loped toward me—too many, at too close range for my bow. I ripped off my bandolier of medical syringes and squirted ammonia in their lupine faces. They screamed, clawing their eyes, and began to crumble to dust. As any Mount Olympian custodian can tell you, ammonia is an excellent cleaning agent for monsters and other blemishes.

I made my way toward the only island of calm on the field: the elephant.

She did not seem interested in attacking anyone. Given her size and formidable chain-mail defenses, none of the other combatants seemed anxious to approach her. Or perhaps, seeing her Colts helmet, they simply didn't want to mess with the home team.

Something about her was so sad, so despondent, I felt drawn to her as a kindred spirit.

I pulled out my combat ukulele and strummed an elephant-friendly song: Primus's "Southbound Pachyderm." The instrumental intro was haunting and sad—perfect for solo ukulele.

"Great elephant," I sang as I approached. "May I ride you?"

Her wet brown eyes blinked at me. She huffed as if to say, *Whatever, Apollo. They got me wearing this stupid helmet. I don't even care anymore.*

A gladiator with a trident rudely interrupted my song. I smashed him in the face with my combat ukulele. Then I used the elephant's foreleg to climb onto her back. I hadn't practiced that technique since the storm god Indra took me on a late-night road trip in search of vindaloo, but I guess riding an elephant is one of those skills you never forget.

I spotted Meg at the twenty-yard line, leaving groaning gladiators and piles of monster ash in her wake as she rode her ostrich toward the emperor.

Commodus clapped with delight. "Well done, Meg! I'd love to fight you, but HOLD THAT THOUGHT!"

The music abruptly shut off. Gladiators stopped in

mid-combat. The race cars slowed to an idle. Even Meg's ostrich paused and looked around as if wondering why it was suddenly so quiet.

Over the speakers came a dramatic drumroll.

"Meg McCaffrey!" Commodus boomed in his best game-show announcer voice. "We've got a special surprise for you—straight from New York, someone you know! Can you save him before he bursts into flames?"

Spotlight beams crossed in midair at a point above the end zone, level with the top of the goalposts. That old post-vindaloo feeling came back to me, burning its way through my intestines. Now I understood what Meg had sensed earlier—that vague *something* that had drawn her into the stadium. Suspended from the rafters by a long chain, snarling and wriggling in a rope cocoon, was the emperor's special surprise: Meg's trusty sidekick, the karpos Peaches.

26

I tip my hat to

The excellent elephant

Let's be besties, 'kay?

I NOCKED AN ARROW and fired at the chain.
In most circumstances, my first instinct was to shoot.
Usually this worked out. (Unless you count the time
Hermes burst into my bathroom without knocking. And,
yes, I always keep my bow handy when I'm on the toilet.
Why would I not?)

This time, my shot was ill-planned. Peaches struggled
and swung so much, my arrow sailed past his chain and
felled a random blemmyae in the stands.

"Stop!" Meg shrieked at me. "You might hit Peaches!"

The emperor laughed. "Yes, that would be a shame
when he's about to burn to death!"

Commodus leaped from his box onto the racetrack. Meg
raised her sword and prepared to charge, but mercenaries
in the stands leveled their rifles. No matter that I was fifty
yards away—the snipers had aim worthy of . . . well, me. A
swarm of red targeting dots floated over my chest.

"Now, now, Meg," the emperor chided, pointing to me.
"My game, my rules. Unless you want to lose *two* friends in
the dress rehearsal."

Meg lifted one sword, then the other, weighing them like options. She was too far away for me to clearly see her expression, but I could sense her agony. How many times had I been caught in such a dilemma? Do I destroy the Trojans or the Greeks? Do I flirt with my sister's Hunters and risk getting slapped, or do I flirt with Britomartis and risk getting blown up? These are the kinds of choices that define us.

As Meg hesitated, a pit crew in togas rolled another Formula One car onto the track—a bright purple machine with a golden number 1 on the hood. Protruding from the roof was a wiry lance about twenty feet tall, topped with a wad of cloth.

My first thought: Why did Commodus need such a big antenna? Then I looked again at the dangling karpos. In the spotlights, Peaches glistened as if he'd been slathered with grease. His feet, usually bare, were covered in rough sandpaper—like the striking surface of a matchbook.

My gut twisted. The race car's antenna wasn't an antenna. It was a giant match, set at just the right height to ignite against Peaches's feet.

"Once I'm in the car," Commodus announced, "my mercenaries will not interfere. Meg, you may try to stop me any way you please! My plan is to complete one circuit, light your friend on fire, then circle back around and hit you and Apollo with my car. I believe they call that a victory lap!"

The crowd roared with approval. Commodus leaped into his car. His pit crew scattered, and the purple racer peeled out in a cloud of smoke.

My blood turned to cold-pressed olive oil, pumping sluggishly through my heart. How long would it take for that race car to get around the track? Seconds, at most. I suspected Commodus's windshield was arrow-proof. He wouldn't leave me such an easy solution. I didn't even have time for a decent ukulele riff.

Meanwhile, Meg guided her ostrich under the swinging karpos. She stood on the bird's back (no easy task) and reached as high as she could, but Peaches was much too far above her.

"Turn into a fruit!" Meg shouted up at him. "Disappear!"

"Peaches!" Peaches wailed, which probably meant: *Don't you think I would if I could?* I guessed that the ropes were somehow magically restricting his shape-shifting, confining him to his present form, much as Zeus had shoehorned my awesome divinity into the miserable body of Lester Papadopoulos. For the first time, I felt a kinship with the diapered demon baby.

Commodus was now halfway around the track. He could have gone faster, but he insisted on swerving and waving to the cameras. The other race cars pulled over to let him pass, making me wonder if they understood the concept of racing.

Meg leaped from the ostrich's back. She caught the goalpost's crossbeam and began to climb, but I knew she wouldn't have time to help the karpos.

The purple car rounded the far end zone. If Commodus accelerated in the straightaway, it would all be over. If only I could block his path with something large and heavy.

Oh, wait, thought my genius brain, *I am sitting on an elephant.*

Engraved across the base of the massive Colts helmet was the name LIVIA. I assumed that was the elephant's.

I leaned forward. "Livia, my friend, do you feel like stomping an emperor?"

She trumpeted—her first real show of enthusiasm. I knew elephants were intelligent, but her willingness to help surprised me. I got the feeling that Commodus had treated her terribly. Now she wanted to kill him. This, at least, we had in common.

Livia charged toward the track, shouldering other animals aside, sweeping her trunk to smack gladiators out of our path.

"Good elephant!" I cried. "Excellent elephant!"

The Throne of Memory bounced precariously on my back. I spent all my arrows (except for the stupid talking one) shooting down combat ostriches, fire-breathing horses, Cyclopes, and cynocephali. Then I snatched up my combat ukulele and played the bugle call for *CHARGE!*

Livia barreled down the center lane, heading for the purple race car. Commodus veered straight toward us, his grinning face reflected on every video monitor around the stadium. He looked delighted by the prospect of a head-on collision.

Me, not so much. Commodus was hard to kill. My elephant and I were not, nor was I sure how much protection Livia's chain mail would give her. I'd been hoping we might force Commodus off the road, but I should've known he would never back down in a game of chicken. Without a helmet, his hair flapped wildly around him, making his golden laurels look like they were on fire.

Without a helmet . . .

I pulled a scalpel from my bandolier. Leaning forward, I sawed through the chin strap off Livia's football helmet. It snapped easily. Thank the gods for cheap plastic merchandise!

"Livia," I said. "Throw it!"

The excellent elephant understood.

Still charging full speed ahead, she curled her trunk around her face guard and flung the helmet like a gentleman tipping his hat . . . if that hat were allowed to hurtle forward as a deadly projectile.

Commodus swerved. The giant white helmet bounced off his windshield, but the real damage had been done. Purple One vaulted onto the field at an impossibly steep angle, canted sideways, and flipped three times, bowling over a herd of ostriches and a couple of unlucky gladiators.

"OHHHHHHH!" The crowd rose to its feet. The music stopped. The remaining gladiators backed toward the edge of the field, eyeing the overturned imperial race car.

Smoke poured from the chassis. The wheels spun, sloughing off shavings of tread.

I wanted to believe the crowd's silence was a hopeful pause. Perhaps, like me, their fondest wish was that Commodus would *not* emerge from the wreckage, that he had been reduced to an imperial smear on the artificial turf at the forty-two-yard line.

Alas, a steaming figure crawled from the wreckage. Commodus's beard smoldered. His face and hands were black with soot. He rose, his smile undimmed, and stretched as if he'd just had a good nap.

"Nice one, Apollo!" He grabbed the chassis of the ruined race car and lifted it over his head. "But it will take more than this to kill me!"

He tossed the car aside, flattening an unfortunate Cyclops.

The audience cheered and stomped.

The emperor called, "CLEAR THE FIELD!"

Immediately dozens of animal handlers, medics, and ball retrievers rushed onto the turf. The surviving gladiators sulked away, as if realizing no fight to the death could compete with what Commodus had just done.

As the emperor ordered his servants around, I glanced toward the end zone. Somehow, Meg had climbed all the way to the top of the goalpost. She leaped toward Peaches and caught his legs, causing a great deal of screeching and cursing from the karpos. For a moment, they swung together from the chain. Then Meg climbed her friend's body, summoned her sword, and slashed the chain. They dropped twenty feet, landing on the track in a heap. Happily, Peaches acted as a cushion for Meg. Given the soft, squishy nature of peach fruit, I imagined Meg would be fine.

"Well!" Commodus strode toward me. He limped slightly on his right ankle, but if it caused him any serious pain, he gave no sign. "That was a good rehearsal! Tomorrow, more deaths—including yours, of course. We'll tweak the combat phase. Perhaps add a few more race cars and basketballs? And, Livia, you naughty old elephant!" He wagged his finger at my pachyderm mount. "*That's* the sort of energy I was looking for! If you'd showed that much enthusiasm in our previous games, I wouldn't have had to kill Claudius."

Livia stomped and trumpeted. I stroked the side of her head, trying to calm her, but I could feel her intense anguish.

"Claudius was your mate," I guessed. "Commodus killed him."

The emperor shrugged. "I *did* warn her: play my games or else. But elephants are so stubborn! They're big and strong and used to getting their way—rather like gods. Still"—he winked at me—"it's amazing what a little punishment can accomplish."

Livia stamped her feet. I knew she wanted to charge, but after seeing Commodus toss a race car, I suspected he would have little trouble hurting Livia.

"We will get him," I murmured to her. "Just wait."

"Yes, until tomorrow!" Commodus agreed. "You'll get another chance to do your worst. But for now—ah, here come my guards to escort you to your cell!"

A squadron of Germani hustled onto the field with Lityerses in the lead.

Across his face, the Cornhusker had an ugly new bruise that looked suspiciously like an ostrich's footprint. That pleased me. He was also bleeding from several new cuts on his arms, and his pant legs were slashed to ribbons. The rips looked like grazes from small-game arrowheads, as if the Hunters had been toying with their target, doing their best to eliminate his trousers. This pleased me even more. I wished I could add a new arrow wound to Lityerses's collection—preferably one right in the middle of his sternum—but my quiver was empty except for the Arrow of Dodona. I'd had enough drama for one day without adding bad Shakespearean dialogue.

Lityerses bowed awkwardly. "My lord."

Commodus and I spoke in unison. "Yes?"

I thought I looked much more lordly sitting atop my chain-mail elephant, but Lityerses just sneered at me.

"My lord, *Commodus*," he clarified, "the invaders have been pushed back from the main gates."

"About time," the emperor muttered.

"They were Hunters of Artemis, sire."

"I see." Commodus didn't sound particularly concerned. "Did you kill them all?"

"We . . ." Lit gulped. "No, my lord. They sniped at us from multiple positions and fell back, leading us into a series of traps. We only lost ten men, but—"

"You lost ten." Commodus examined his soot-stained fingernails. "And how many of these Hunters did you kill?"

Lit edged away. His neck veins pulsed. "I—I am not sure. We found no bodies."

"So you cannot confirm any kills." Commodus glanced at me. "What would you advise, Apollo? Should I take time to reflect? Should I consider the consequences? Should I perhaps tell my prefect, Lityerses, not to worry? He will be fine? He will ALWAYS HAVE MY BLESSINGS?"

This last line he screamed, his voice echoing through the stadium. Even the wild centaurs in the stands fell quiet.

"No," Commodus decided, his tone once again calm. "Alaric, where are you?"

One of the Germani stepped forward. "Sire?"

"Take Apollo and Meg McCaffrey into custody. See that they get nice cells for the night. Put the Throne of Mnemosyne back into storage. Kill the elephant and the karpos. What else? Oh, yes." From the boot of his racing suit, Commodus pulled a hunting knife. "Hold Lityerses's arms for me while I cut his throat. It's time for a new prefect."

Before Alaric could carry out these orders, the stadium's roof exploded.

27

Destroy me a roof
Bring me wenches with winches
We're so out of here

WELL, I SAY *EXPLODED.* More accurately, the roof crumpled inward, as roofs tend to do when a bronze dragon smashes into them. Girders bent. Rivets popped. Sheets of corrugated metal groaned and folded with a sound like colliding aircraft carriers.

Festus plummeted through the gap, his wings unfolding to slow his descent. He seemed no worse for wear from his time in suitcase form, but judging from the way he blow-torched the audience in the stands, I guessed he was feeling a bit cranky.

Wild centaurs stampeded, trampling the mortal mercenaries and Germani. The blemmyae clapped politely, perhaps thinking the dragon was part of the show, until a wave of flames reduced them to dust. Festus flew his own fiery victory lap around the track, torching race cars, as a dozen silvery ropes uncoiled from the roof, lowering the Hunters of Artemis into the arena like a clutter of spiders.

(I've always found spiders fascinating creatures, despite what Athena thinks. If you ask me, she's just jealous of their beautiful faces. BOOM!)

More Hunters remained on the roofline with their bows drawn, laying down suppressing fire as their sisters lowered themselves to the field. As soon as the rappellers hit the turf, they drew bows, swords, and knives and leaped into battle.

Alaric, along with most of the emperor's Germani, charged to meet them.

At the goalpost, Meg McCaffrey worked frantically to cut Peaches free from his ropes. Two Hunters dropped next to her. They had a hurried conversation with lots of pointing, something along the lines of: *Hello, we are your friends. You're going to die. Come with us.*

Clearly agitated, Meg glanced across the field in my direction.

I yelled, "GO!"

Meg allowed the Hunters to grab her and Peaches. Then the Hunters slapped some sort of mechanisms on the sides of their belts and shot back up their ropes as if the laws of gravity were mere recommendations.

Motorized winches, I thought, a very nice accessory. If I live through this, I'm going to recommend that the Hunters of Artemis make T-shirts that read WENCHES WITH WINCHES. I'm sure they'll love that idea.

The closest group of Hunters charged in my direction, meeting the Germani in battle. One of the Hunters looked familiar, with choppy black hair and dazzling blue eyes. Instead of the usual gray camo of Artemis's followers, she wore jeans and a black leather jacket that was held together with safety pins and had patches for the Ramones and Dead Kennedys. A silver tiara glinted on her forehead. On one arm, she brandished a shield imprinted with the gruesome visage of Medusa—not the original, I suspected, since that would've turned me to stone, but a good enough replica to make even the Germani cower and back away.

The girl's name came to me: Thalia Grace. Artemis's lieutenant, the leader of the Hunters, had personally come to rescue me.

"Save Apollo!" she yelled.

My spirits soared.

Yes, thank you! I wanted to yell. *FINALLY someone has their priorities straight!*

I felt, for a moment, as if the world were back in its proper order.

Commodus sighed in exasperation. "I did *not* schedule this for my games." He looked around, apparently just realizing he had only two guards and Lityerses left to command. The rest were already in combat. "Lityerses, get out there!" he snapped. "Slow them down while I go change. I can't fight in a racing outfit. This is ridiculous!"

Lit's eye twitched. "Sire . . . you were about to relieve me of duty. By killing me?"

"Oh, right. Well, then go sacrifice yourself! Prove you're more useful than that idiot father of yours! Honestly, Midas had the golden touch, and he *still* couldn't do anything right. You're no better!"

The skin around Lityerses's ostrich bruise reddened, as if the bird were still standing on his face. "Sire, with respect—"

Commodus's hand shot out like a rattlesnake, clamping around the swordsman's throat.

"*Respect?*" the emperor hissed. "You talk to me of *respect?*"

Arrows sailed toward the emperor's remaining guards. Both Germani fell with lovely new silver-feathered nose piercings.

A third missile hurtled toward Commodus. The emperor yanked Lityerses into its path and the arrow point erupted from the front of Lit's thigh.

The swordsman screamed.

Commodus dropped him in disgust. "Do I have to kill you myself? *Really?*" He raised his knife.

Something inside me, no doubt a character flaw, made me feel pity for the wounded Cornhusker.

"Livia," I said.

The elephant understood. She trunk-smacked Commodus upside the head, knocking him flat on the turf. Lityerses fumbled for the hilt of his sword. Finding it, he jabbed the point into the emperor's exposed neck.

Commodus howled, clamping his hand over the wound. Judging from the amount of blood, I deduced that the cut, sadly, had missed his jugular.

Commodus's eyes blazed. "Oh, Lityerses, you *traitor*. I will kill you *slowly* for that!"

But it was not meant to be.

The closest Germani, seeing their emperor bleeding on the ground, ran to his aid. Livia scooped up Lityerses and backed us away as the barbarians closed ranks around Commodus, forming a shield wall, their bristling polearms pointed at us. The Germani looked ready to counterattack, but before they could, a line of flames rained down between our two groups. Festus the dragon landed next to Livia. The

Germani hastily retreated while Commodus screamed, "Put me down! I need to kill those people!"

Atop Festus, Leo saluted me like a fellow fighter pilot. "What's up, Lesteropoulos? Jo got your emergency signal. She sent us back right away."

Thalia Grace jogged over with two of her Hunters. "We need to evacuate. We'll be overrun in a few minutes." She pointed to the end zone, where the survivors from Festus's fiery victory lap were starting to form ranks: a hundred assorted centaurs, cynocephali, and demigods from the Imperial Household.

I glanced to the sidelines. Leading into the lowest tier of seats was a ramp—possibly wide enough for an elephant. "I'm not leaving Livia behind. Take Lityerses. And take the Throne of Memory." I unslung the chair, thankful again for its light weight, and tossed it across to Leo. "That throne *has* to get back to Georgie. I'll ride Livia out one of the mortal exits."

The elephant dumped Lityerses onto the turf. The Cornhusker groaned and pressed his hands around the arrow in his leg.

Leo frowned. "Uh, Apollo—"

"I will not leave this noble elephant behind to be tortured!" I insisted.

"No, I get that." Leo pointed at Lit. "But why would we take *this* fool? He tried to kill me in Omaha. He threatened Calypso at the zoo. Can't I just let Festus stomp him?"

"No!" I wasn't sure why I felt so strongly about it. Commodus betraying this swordsman made me almost as angry as Nero manipulating Meg, or . . . well, yes, Zeus abandoning me in the mortal world for the *third time*. "He needs healing. He'll behave himself, won't you, Lit?"

Lityerses grimaced in pain, blood soaking through his tattered jeans, but he managed a slight nod.

Leo sighed. "Whatever, man. Festus, we're taking this bleeding idiot with us, okay? But if he gets uppity en route, feel free to chuck him against the side of a skyscraper."

Festus creaked in agreement.

"I'll go with Apollo." Thalia Grace climbed up behind me on the elephant—which fulfilled a daydream I'd once had about the pretty Hunter, though I hadn't imagined it happening quite this way. She nodded at one of her comrades. "Iphigenia, get the rest of the Hunters out of here. Go!"

Leo grinned and slung the Throne of Memory across his back. "See y'all back home. And don't forget to pick up some salsa!"

Festus flapped his metallic wings. The dragon grabbed Lityerses and launched himself skyward. The Hunters activated their winches. They ascended as the first wave of angry spectators arrived on the field, throwing spears and vuvuzelas that fell clattering back to earth.

When the Hunters were gone, the crowd turned their attention to us.

"Livia," I said. "How fast can you run?"

The answer: fast enough to evade an armed mob, especially with Thalia Grace on her back, shooting arrows and brandishing her shield of terror at anyone who got too close.

Livia seemed to know the corridors and ramps of the stadium. They'd been designed for large crowds, which made them equally convenient for elephants. We made a few turns around the souvenir kiosks, barreled through a service tunnel, and finally emerged on a loading dock on South Missouri Street.

I'd forgotten how wonderful sunlight felt! Crisp fresh air on a late winter day! Granted, it wasn't as exhilarating as driving the sun chariot, but it was a darn sight better than the snake-infested sewers of Commode Palace.

Livia lumbered down Missouri Street. She turned into the first blind alley she saw, then stomped and shook. I was pretty sure I understood her message: *Take off this stupid chain mail.*

I translated for Thalia, who shouldered her bow. "I don't blame her. Poor elephant. Women warriors should travel light."

Livia lifted her trunk as if to say thank you.

We spent the next ten minutes de-armoring the elephant.

Once we were done, Livia gave Thalia and me a group hug with her trunk.

My adrenaline rush was fading, leaving me feeling like a deflated inner tube. I sank down with my back against the brick wall and shivered in my damp clothes.

Thalia produced a canteen from her belt. Instead of offering it to me first, as would have been proper, she poured some liquid into her cupped hand and let Livia drink. The elephant slurped down five handfuls, not much for a big animal, but she blinked and grunted in a satisfied way. Thalia took a sip herself, then handed the canteen to me.

"Thanks," I mumbled. I drank, and my vision cleared immediately. I felt as if I'd just had six hours of sleep and a good hot meal.

I stared in amazement at the battered canteen. "What *is* this? Not nectar . . ."

"No," Thalia agreed. "It's moonwater."

I'd dealt with the Hunters of Artemis for millennia, but I had never heard of moonwater. I recalled Josephine's story about bootlegging in the 1920s. "Do you mean moonshine? As in liquor?"

Thalia laughed. "No. It's not alcoholic, but it *is* magic. Lady Artemis never told you about this stuff, eh? It's like an energy drink for Hunters. Men rarely ever get a taste."

I poured a tiny bit into my palm. The stuff looked like regular water, though perhaps more silver, as if it had been blended with a trace amount of liquid mercury.

I considered taking another sip, then decided it might make my brain vibrate to the point of liquefying. I passed back the canteen. "Have you . . . Have you talked to my sister?"

Thalia's expression turned serious. "In a dream, a few weeks ago. Lady Artemis said that Zeus has forbidden her from seeing you. She's not even supposed to give us orders to help you."

I had suspected as much, but having my fears confirmed would have overwhelmed me with despair if not for the moonwater. Its energy burst kept me humming right along over the deeper emotions, like wheels skimming across the top of loose sand.

"You're not supposed to help me," I said. "And yet you're here. Why?"

Thalia gave me a coy smile that would have made Britomartis proud. "We were just in the area. Nobody *ordered* us to help. We've been searching for a particular monster for months now and . . ." She hesitated. "Well, that's another story. The point is, we were passing through. We helped you the way we'd help any demigod in danger."

She didn't mention anything about Britomartis finding the Hunters and urging them to come here. I decided to play her little game of let's-pretend-that-never-happened.

"Can I guess another reason?" I asked. "I think you decided to help me because you *like* me."

The corner of Thalia's mouth twitched. "What makes you say that?"

"Oh, come now. The first time we met, you said I was hot. Don't think I didn't hear that comment."

I was gratified to see her face turn red.

"I was younger then," she said. "I was a different person. I'd just spent several years as a pine tree. My vision and reasoning were impaired from sap damage."

"Ouch," I complained. "That's harsh."

Thalia punched my arm. "You need an occasional dose of humility. Artemis says so all the time."

"My sister is a sneaky, deceptive—"

"Watch it," Thalia warned. "I *am* her lieutenant."

I crossed my arms in a petulant, Meg sort of way.

"Artemis never told me about moonwater. She never told me about the Waystation. It makes me wonder how many other secrets she's hiding."

"Maybe a few." Thalia's tone was carefully nonchalant. "But you've gotten to see more this week than most non-Hunters ever do. You should feel lucky."

I stared down the alley, thinking of that first New York alley I'd fallen into as Lester Papadopoulos. So much had changed since then, yet I was no closer to being a god. In fact, the memory of being a god seemed more distant than ever. "Yes," I grumbled. "Very lucky."

"Come on." Thalia offered me a hand. "Commodus won't wait long before he launches a reprisal. Let's get our elephant friend back to the Waystation."

28

Belching stinky smoke
What gene pool did you come from?
Wait. What? (Insert scream)

AS IT TURNED OUT, getting an elephant into the Waystation was not as hard as I'd imagined.

I'd had visions of trying to cram Livia up a ladder chute, or renting a helicopter to drop her through the roof hatch into the griffin nests. But as soon as we arrived at the side of the building, bricks rumbled and rearranged themselves, creating a wide archway and a gentle downward ramp.

Livia tromped inside without hesitation. At the bottom of the corridor, we found a perfect elephant stable with high ceilings, ample stacks of hay, slatted windows to let in the sunlight, a stream wending through the middle of the room, and a big-screen television turned to Hephaestus-TV's Elephant Channel, showing *The Real Elephants of the African Veld*. (I did not know Hephaestus-TV had such a channel. It must have been included in the premium bundle, which I didn't subscribe to.) Best of all, there was not a gladiator or a set of elephant armor in sight.

Livia huffed in approval.

"I'm glad you like it, my friend." I dismounted, followed

by Thalia. "Now enjoy yourself while we go find our hosts."

Livia waded into the stream and rolled onto her side, giving herself a trunk shower. She looked so content I was tempted to join her, but I had less pleasant matters to attend to.

"Come on," Thalia said. "I know the way."

I didn't see how. The Waystation shifted and changed so much, it shouldn't have been possible for anyone to learn their way around. But true to her word, Thalia led me up several flights of stairs, through a gymnasium I'd never seen, and back to the main hall, where a crowd had gathered.

Josephine and Emmie knelt by the sofa where Georgina lay shaking, crying, and giggling. Emmie tried to get the little girl to drink some water. Jo dabbed Georgie's face with a washcloth. Next to them stood the Throne of Mnemosyne, but I couldn't tell whether they had tried to use it yet. Certainly, Georgie appeared no better.

Over at Josephine's workstation, Leo was inside Festus's chest cavity, using a welding torch. The dragon had curled up as tightly as possible, but he still took up a third of the room. The side of his rib cage was propped open like the hood of a Mack truck. Leo's legs stuck out, sparks showering the floor around him. Festus didn't seem concerned by this invasive surgery. Deep in his throat, he made a low, clattering purr.

Calypso looked fully recovered from yesterday's jaunt to the zoo. She dashed around the room, bringing food, drink, and medical supplies to the rescued prisoners. Some of the folks we'd freed made themselves right at home, helping themselves to the pantry, rummaging through cabinets with such familiarity I suspected they'd been longtime residents at the Waystation before being captured.

The two emaciated boys sat at the dining table, trying to pace themselves as they chewed pieces of fresh bread. Hunter Kowalski, the silver-haired girl, stood in a tight circle with the other Hunters of Artemis as they muttered together and cast suspicious glances at Lityerses. The Cornhusker sat in a recliner in the corner, facing the wall, his wounded leg now properly bandaged.

Sssssarah the dracaena had discovered the kitchen. She stood at the counter, holding a basket of fresh henhouse eggs, swallowing each whole, one after the other.

Tall, Dark & Jamie was up in the griffin roost, making friends with Heloise and Abelard. The griffins allowed him to scratch under their beaks—a sign of great trust, especially since they were guarding an egg in their nest (and no doubt worried that Sssssarah might see it). Sadly, Jamie had put on clothes. He now wore a caramel-brown business suit with an open-collared dress shirt. I didn't know where he'd found such a nice outfit to fit his massive frame. Perhaps the Waystation supplied clothing as easily as it supplied elephant habitats.

The rest of the freed prisoners milled around, nibbling on bread and cheese, staring in awe at the stained-glass ceiling and occasionally flinching at loud noises, which was completely normal for those suffering from Post-Commodus Stress Disorder. Headless Agamethus floated among the newcomers, offering them his Magic 8 Ball, which I suppose was his idea of schmoozing.

Meg McCaffrey had changed into a different green dress and jeans, which completely threw off her usual spotlight color scheme. She walked over to me, punched me in the arm, then stood next to me as if we were waiting for a bus.

"Why did you hit me?" I asked.

"Saying hello."

"Ah . . . Meg, this is Thalia Grace."

I wondered if Meg would hit her hello as well, but Meg simply reached across and shook Thalia's hand. "Hi."

Thalia smiled. "A pleasure, Meg. I've heard you're quite a swordswoman."

Meg squinted through her grimy glasses. "Where'd you hear that?"

"Lady Artemis has been watching you. She keeps an eye on all promising young women warriors."

"Oh, no," I said. "You can tell my beloved sister to back off. Meg is *my* demigod companion."

"*Master*," Meg corrected.

"Same difference."

Thalia laughed. "Well, if you two will excuse me, I'd better go check on my Hunters before they kill Lityerses." The lieutenant marched off.

"Speaking of that . . ." Meg pointed toward the wounded son of Midas. "Why'd you bring him here?"

The Cornhusker hadn't moved. He stared at the wall, facing away from the crowd as if intentionally inviting a knife in the back. Even from across the room, waves of hopelessness and defeat seemed to radiate from him.

"You said it yourself," I told Meg. "Everything living deserves a chance to grow."

"Hmph. Chia seeds don't work for evil emperors. They don't try to kill your friends."

I realized Peaches was nowhere to be seen. "Is your karpos all right?"

"He's okay. Went away for a while . . ." She waved vaguely at the air, indicating that magical land where peach spirits go when they are not devouring their enemies or screaming PEACHES! "You actually *trust* Lit?"

Meg's tone was harsh, but her lower lip trembled. She lifted her chin as if preparing for a punch—the same way Lityerses had looked when the emperor betrayed him, the same way the goddess Demeter had looked, ages ago, standing in front of Zeus's throne, her voice full of pain and disbelief: *Will you actually let Hades get away with kidnapping my daughter Persephone?*

Meg was asking if we could trust Lityerses. But her *real* question was much larger: Could she trust anyone? Was there anyone in the world—family, friend, or Lester—who would ever truly have her back?

"Dear Meg," I said. "I can't be sure about Lityerses. But I think we must try. We only fail when we stop trying."

She studied a callus on her index finger. "Even after somebody tries to kill us?"

I shrugged. "If I gave up on everyone who has tried to kill me, I would have *no* allies left on the Olympian Council."

She pouted. "Families are dumb."

"On that," I said, "we can fully agree."

Josephine glanced over and saw me. "He's here!"

She hustled over, grabbed my wrist, and hauled me

toward the couch. "We've been waiting! What took you so long? We have to use the chair!"

I bit back a retort.

It might have been nice to hear, *Thank you, Apollo, for freeing all these prisoners! Thank you for returning our daughter!* She could at least have decorated the main hall with a few APOLLO IS THE GREATEST banners, or offered to remove the uncomfortable iron manacle on my ankle.

"You didn't have to wait for me," I complained.

"Yes, we did," Josephine said. "Every time we tried to put Georgie in the throne, she flailed around and shrieked your name."

Georgie's head lolled toward me. "Apollo! Death, death, death."

I winced. "I really wish she'd stop making that connection."

Emmie and Josephine lifted her gently and set her on the Throne of Mnemosyne. This time, Georgie did not resist.

Curious Hunters and freed prisoners gathered around, though I noticed Meg stayed in the back of the room, well away from Georgina.

"The notepad on the counter!" Emmie pointed toward the kitchen. "Someone grab it, please!"

Calypso did the honors. She hurried back with a small yellow legal pad and a pen.

Georgina swayed. Suddenly all her muscles seemed to melt. She would have slumped out of the chair if her parents hadn't held her.

Then she sat bolt upright. She gasped. Her eyes flew open, her pupils as wide as quarters. Black smoke belched from her mouth. The rancid smell, like boiling roof tar and rotten eggs, forced everyone back except for the dracaena, Sssssarah, who sniffed the air hungrily.

Georgina tilted her head. Smoke curled through the choppy brown tufts of her hair as if she were an automaton, or a blemmyae with a malfunctioning fake noggin.

"Father!" Her voice pierced my heart—so sharp and painful, I thought my bandolier of scalpels had turned inward. It was the same voice, the same cry I had heard thousands of years ago, when Trophonius had prayed in agony, pleading for me to save Agamethus from the collapsed thieves' tunnel.

Georgina's mouth contorted into a cruel smile. "So have you finally heard my prayer?"

Her voice was still that of Trophonius. Everyone in the room looked at me. Even Agamethus, who had no eyes, seemed to fix me with a withering glare.

Emmie tried to touch Georgina's shoulder. She recoiled as if the little girl's skin were molten hot. "Apollo, what is this?" she demanded. "This isn't prophecy. This has never happened before—"

"You sent this little sister of mine to do your errands?" Georgina tapped her own chest, her eyes wide and dark, still focused on me. "You're no better than the emperor."

I felt as if a chain-mail elephant were standing on my chest. *This little sister?* If he meant that literally, then . . .

"Trophonius." I could barely speak. "I—I didn't send Georgina. She isn't my—"

"Tomorrow morning," Trophonius said. "The cave will only be accessible at first light. Your prophecy will unfold— or the emperor's. Either way, there will be no hiding in your little haven. Come in person. Bring the girl, your master. You will both enter my sacred cavern."

A horrible laugh escaped Georgina's mouth. "Perhaps both of you will survive. Or will you suffer the same fate as my brother and I? I wonder, Father, to whom will you pray?"

With one final belch of blackness, Georgina toppled sideways. Josephine scooped her up before she could hit the floor.

Emmie rushed to help. Together they placed Georgie gently on the couch again, tucking her in with blankets and pillows.

Calypso turned to me. The empty notepad dangled from her hand. "Correct me if I'm wrong," she said, "but that was no prophecy. That was a message to you."

The collective gaze of the crowd made my face itch. It was the same feeling I used to have when an entire Greek village looked to the heavens and called my name, pleading for rain, and I was too embarrassed to explain that rain was actually Zeus's department. The best I could offer them was a catchy new song.

"You're right," I said, though it pained me to agree with the sorceress. "Trophonius did not give the girl a prophecy. He gave her a—a recorded greeting."

Emmie stepped toward me, her fists clenched. "Will she be healed? When a prophecy's expelled on the Throne of Memory, the supplicant usually returns to normal within a few days. Will Georgie—" Her voice broke. "Will she come back to us?"

I wanted to say yes. Back in the old days, the recovery rate for supplicants of Trophonius had been around 75 percent. And that was when the petitioners were properly prepared by the priests, the rituals all done correctly, and the prophecy interpreted on the throne immediately after visiting the cave of terrors. Georgina had sought out the cave on her own with little or no preparation. She'd been trapped with that madness and darkness for weeks.

"I—I don't know," I admitted. "We can hope—"

"We can *hope?*" Emmie demanded.

Josephine took her hand. "Georgie *will* get better. Have faith. That's better than hope."

But her eyes stayed on me a little too long—accusing, questioning. I prayed she would not fetch her submachine gun.

"Ahem," Leo said. His face was lost in the shadow of his raised welding visor, his grin fading in and out of sight à la the Cheshire Cat. "Uh . . . the thing about *little sister?* If Georgie is Trophonius's sister, does that mean . . . ?" He pointed at me.

Never before had I wished I were a blemmyae. Now, I wanted to hide my face inside my shirt. I wanted to pull off my head and throw it across the room. "I don't know!"

"It would explain a lot," Calypso ventured. "Why Georgina felt so attuned to the Oracle, why she was able to survive the experience. If you . . . I mean . . . not Lester, but Apollo is her parent—"

"She *has* parents." Josephine put her arm around Emmie's waist. "We're standing right here."

Calypso raised her hands in apology. "Of course. I just meant—"

"Seven years," Emmie interrupted, stroking her daughter's forehead. "Seven years we've raised her. It never mattered where she came from, or who her biological parents might have been. When Agamethus brought her . . . we checked the news. We checked the police reports. We sent Iris-messages to all our contacts. *No one* had reported a missing baby girl like her. Her birth parents either didn't want her, or couldn't raise her. . . ." She glared at me. "Or maybe they didn't even know she existed."

I tried to remember. Honestly, I did. But if the god Apollo had enjoyed a brief romance with some Midwesterner eight years ago, I had no recollection of it. I was reminded of Wolfgang Amadeus Mozart, who had also come to my attention when he was seven years old. Everyone said, *Oh, surely he is the son of Apollo!* The other gods looked at me for confirmation, and I wanted *so badly* to say, *Yes, that boy's genius was all me!* But I simply could not remember ever having met Wolfgang's mother. Or, for that matter, his father.

"Georgina has excellent parents," I said. "Whether she is a child of—of Apollo . . . I'm sorry, I can't say for sure."

"You can't say," Josephine echoed flatly.

"B-but I do think she will heal. Her mind is strong. She risked her life and her sanity to bring us that message. The best we can do now is follow the Oracle's instructions."

Josephine and Emmie exchanged looks that said, *He's a scoundrel, but we have too much going on right on. We'll kill him later.*

Meg McCaffrey crossed her arms. Even she seemed to sense the wisdom of changing the subject. "So we go at first light?"

Josephine focused on her with difficulty, as if wondering where Meg had suddenly appeared from. (I had this thought often.) "Yes, hon. That's the only time you can enter the Cavern of Prophecy."

I sighed inwardly. First it had been the zoo at first light. Then the Canal Walk at first light. Now the caverns. I really wished dangerous quests could start at a more reasonable time, like perhaps three in the afternoon.

An uneasy silence settled over the room. Georgina breathed raggedly in her sleep. Up in the roost, the griffins ruffled their feathers. Jamie cracked his knuckles pensively.

Finally, Thalia Grace stepped forward. "What about the rest of the message: 'Your prophecy will unfold—or the emperor's. No hiding in your little haven'?"

"I'm not sure," I admitted.

Leo raised his arms. "All hail the god of prophecy!"

"Oh, shut up," I grumbled. "I don't have enough information yet. If we survive the caverns—"

"I can interpret those lines," Lityerses said from his chair in the corner.

The son of Midas turned to face the crowd, his cheeks a patchwork of scars and bruises, his eyes empty and desolate. "Thanks to the tracking devices I put on your griffins, Commodus knows where you are. He'll be here first thing tomorrow morning. And he'll wipe this place off the map."

29

Carrot-peeling god
Tofu stir-fry is good, but
Needs more ìgboyà

LITYERSES HAD A TALENT for making friends.

Half the crowd surged forward to kill him. The other half shouted that they, too, wanted to kill him and the first half should get out of their way.

"You villain!" Hunter Kowalski yanked Lityerses from his chair and shoved him against the wall. She pressed a borrowed screwdriver against his throat.

"Sssssstand asssssside!" Sssssarah yelled. "I will sssssswallow him whole!"

"I should've thrown him against the side of the building," Leo growled.

"STOP!" Josephine waded through the mob. Not surprisingly, folks moved aside. She pulled Hunter Kowalski off her prey, then glared at Lityerses as if he were a chariot with a busted axle. "You put trackers on our griffins?"

Lit rubbed his neck. "Yes. And the plan worked."

"You're *sure* Commodus knows our location?"

Normally, I avoided attracting the attention of an angry mob, but I felt compelled to speak.

"He's telling the truth," I said. "We heard Lityerses

talking to Commodus in the throne room. Leo was sup-posed to tell you about that."

"*Me?*" Leo protested. "Hey, things were chaotic! I thought you—" His welding visor fell shut, making the rest of his sentence unintelligible.

Lityerses spread his arms, which were so scarred they looked like testing logs for hacksaw blades. "Kill me if you want. It'll make no difference. Commodus will level this place and everyone in it."

Thalia Grace drew her hunting knife. Instead of gutting the swordsman, she drove the blade into the nearest cof-fee table. "The Hunters of Artemis won't allow that. We've fought too many impossible battles. We've lost too many of our sisters, but we've never backed down. Last summer, in the Battle of Old San Juan . . ." She hesitated.

It was difficult to imagine Thalia at the edge of tears, but she seemed to be struggling to maintain her punk rock facade. I remembered something Artemis had told me when we were in exile together on Delos . . . how her Hunters and the Amazons had fought the giant Orion in Puerto Rico. An Amazon base had been destroyed. Many had died—Hunters who, if not cut down in battle, might have continued to live for millennia. As Lester Papadopoulos, I found that idea freshly horrifying.

"We will *not* lose the Waystation too," Thalia contin-ued. "We'll stand with Josephine and Emmie. We kicked Commodus's podex today. We'll do it again tomorrow."

The Hunters cheered. I may have cheered also. I always love it when courageous heroes volunteer to fight battles I don't want to fight.

Lityerses shook his head. "What you saw today was only a fraction of Commodus's full strength. He's got . . . *vast* resources."

Josephine grunted. "Our friends gave him a bloody nose today, at least. Maybe he won't attack tomorrow. He'll need time to regroup."

Lit let out a broken laugh. "You don't know Commodus like I do. You just made him mad. He won't wait. He *never* waits. First thing tomorrow, he'll strike *hard*. He'll kill us all."

I wanted to disagree. I wanted to think that the emperor would drag his feet, then decide to leave us alone because we'd been so entertaining at the dress rehearsal, then possibly send us a box of chocolates by way of apology.

But I *did* know Commodus. I remembered the Flavian Amphitheater floor littered with corpses. I remembered the execution lists. I remembered him snarling at me, his lips flecked with blood: *You sound like my father. I'm done thinking about consequences!*

"Lityerses is right," I said. "Commodus received a prophecy from the Dark Oracle. He needs to destroy this place and kill me before he can have his naming ceremony tomorrow afternoon. Which means he'll strike in the morning. He's not a fan of waiting for what he wants."

"We could ssssslither away," suggested Sssssarah. "Move. Hide. Live to fight another day."

At the back of the crowd, the ghost Agamethus pointed empathically to the dracaena, obviously agreeing with her idea. You have to wonder about your chances in combat when even your dead friends are worried about dying.

Josephine shook her head. "I'm not slithering anywhere. This is our home."

Calypso nodded. "And if Emmie and Jo are staying put, so are we. They saved our lives. We'll fight to the death for them. Right, Leo?"

Leo raised his visor. "Absolutely. Though I've already done the whole *dying* thing, so I'd prefer to fight to someone else's death. For instance, Commode Man's—"

"Leo," Calypso warned.

"Yeah, we're in. They'll never get past us."

Jamie slipped to the front through a line of Hunters. Despite his size, he moved as gracefully as Agamethus, almost as if floating.

"I owe you a debt." He inclined his head to the Hunters, to Meg and me, to Josephine and Emmie. "You saved me from the madman's prison. But I hear much talk about *us* and *them*. I am always wary when people speak this way, as if people can be so easily divided into friend and enemy. Most of us here do not even know each other."

The big man swept a hand across the crowd: Hunters, ex-Hunters, an ex-god, an ex-Titaness, demigods, a snake woman, a couple of griffins, a decapitated ghost. And down-stairs, we had an elephant named Livia. Rarely had I seen a more motley collection of defenders.

"Also, this one." Jamie pointed to Lityerses. Jamie's voice remained a sonorous rumble, but I fancied I could hear thunderclaps under the surface, ready to break loose. "Is he now a friend? Am I to fight side by side with my enslaver?"

Hunter Kowalski brandished her screwdriver. "Not likely."

"Wait!" I yelped. "Lityerses can be useful."

Again, I wasn't sure why I spoke up. It seemed counterproductive to my main goal, which was to always keep myself safe and popular. "Lityerses knows Commodus's plans. He knows what sort of forces will attack us. And Lityerses's life is at stake, just like ours are."

I explained how Commodus had ordered Lit's death, and how Lityerses had stabbed his former master in the neck.

"That doesssss not make me trussssst him," Sssssarah hissed.

The crowd grumbled in agreement. A few Hunters reached for their weapons.

"Hold it!" Emmie climbed onto the dining table.

Her long hair had come undone from its braid, strands of silver sweeping the sides of her face. Her hands were splotchy with bread dough. Over her camouflage combat clothes, she wore an apron with a picture of a hamburger and the slogan KEEP YOUR HANDS OFF MY BUNS.

Still, the hard gleam in her eyes reminded me of that young princess of Naxos who had jumped off a cliff with her sister, trusting the gods—the princess who had decided she would rather die than live in fear of her drunken angry father. I had never considered that growing older, grayer, and thicker might make someone more beautiful. Yet that seemed to be the case for Emmie. Standing on the table, she was the room's calm, steady center of gravity.

"For those of you who don't know me," she began,

"my name is Hemithea. Jo and I run the Waystation. We never turn away people who are in trouble, even former enemies." She nodded to Lityerses. "We attract outcasts here—orphans and runaways, folks who've been abused, mistreated, or misled, folks who just don't feel at home anywhere else."

She gestured to the barreled ceiling, where the stained glass fractured sunlight into green and gold geometry. "Britomartis, the Lady of Nets, helped build this place."

"A safety net for your friends," I blurted, remembering what Josephine had told me. "But a trap for your enemies."

Now I was the center of attention. Once again, I didn't like it. (I was *really* starting to worry about myself.) My face burned from the sudden flush of blood to my cheeks. "Sorry," I told Emmie.

She studied me as if wondering where to aim her next arrow. She had, apparently, not quite forgiven me for possibly being Georgina's divine father, even though she'd had that news for at least five minutes. I supposed I could forgive her. Sometimes such a revelation can take an hour or more to process.

At last, she nodded brusquely. "Apollo is right. Tomorrow we may be attacked, but our enemies are going to find out that the Waystation protects its own. Commodus *won't* leave this net alive. Josephine and I will fight to defend this place and anyone who is under our roof. If you want to be part of our family, for a day or forever, you are welcome. *All* of you." She looked directly at Lit.

The Cornhusker's face paled, his scars almost disappearing. He opened his mouth to say something but managed only a choking noise. He slid down against the wall and began to shudder, silently sobbing.

Josephine crouched next to him. She gazed at the crowd as if asking, *Anybody still got a problem with this guy?*

Next to me, Jamie grunted. "I like these women," he said. "They have *ìgboyà.*"

I didn't know what ìgboyà meant. I couldn't even guess what language it was. But I liked the way Jamie said it. I decided I would have to purchase some ìgboyà as soon as possible.

"Well, then." Emmie wiped her hands on her apron. "If anyone wants to leave, now's the time to say so. I'll make you a brown bag lunch to go."

No one replied.

"Right," Emmie said. "In that case, everyone gets an afternoon chore!"

She made me peel carrots.

Honestly, we were facing an imminent invasion, and I—the former god of music—was stuck in the kitchen prepping salad. I should have been strolling around with my ukulele, lifting everyone's spirits with my songs and my shining charisma, not skinning root vegetables!

On the bright side, the Hunters of Artemis had to clean the cow pens, so perhaps there was some justice in the cosmos.

Once dinner was ready, the crowd scattered across the main hall to eat. Josephine sat with Lityerses in his corner, talking to him slowly and calmly, the way one might treat a pit bull rescued from a bad owner. Most of the Hunters sat in the griffin roosts, dangling their legs over the ledge as they surveyed the hall below. From their low voices and grave expressions, I imagined they were talking about how best to kill large numbers of enemies tomorrow.

Hunter Kowalski volunteered to bunk in Georgina's room for the night. The little girl had remained fast asleep since her experience on the Throne of Memory, but Hunter wanted to be there for her just in case she woke up. Emmie gratefully agreed, but not until after shooting me an accusatory look that said, *I don't see you volunteering to sit with your kid all night.* Honestly, as if I was the first god who'd ever forgotten he sired a child who was then carried away by a decapitated ghost to be raised by two women in Indianapolis!

The two half-starved demigods, brothers named Deacon and Stan, who I learned had been residents of the Waystation for over a year, now rested in the infirmary with IV drips of nectar. Sssssarah had taken a basket of eggs and slithered off to the sauna for the night. Jamie ate with some of the other escapees on the sofas, which did not make me feel neglected at all.

This left me at the dining table with Meg (what else is new?), Leo, Calypso, Emmie, and Thalia Grace.

Emmie kept glancing across the room at Josephine and Lityerses. "Our new friend, Lityerses . . ." She sounded remarkably earnest when she said the word *friend.* "I talked with him during chore time. He helped me churn the ice cream. He told me quite a bit about the armies we'll be facing tomorrow."

"There's ice cream?" I asked. I had a natural ability to

focus on the most important details when someone was talking.

"Later," Emmie promised, though her tone told me I might not be getting any. "It's vanilla. We were going to add frozen peaches, but . . ." She looked at Meg. "We thought that might be in poor taste."

Meg was too busy shoveling tofu stir-fry into her mouth to respond.

"At any rate," Emmie continued, "Lityerses estimates a few dozen mortal mercenaries, about the same number of demigods from the Imperial Household, a few hundred assorted cynocephali and other monsters, plus the usual hordes of blemmyae disguised as local police, firefighters, and bulldozer operators."

"Oh, good," said Thalia Grace. "The usual hordes."

Emmie shrugged. "Commodus means to raze Union Station. He'll make it look to the mortals like an emergency evacuation."

"A gas leak," Leo guessed. "It's almost always a gas leak."

Calypso picked the shredded carrots out of her salad, which I took as a personal insult. "So we're outnumbered ten to one? Twenty to one?"

"No sweat," Leo said. "I'll handle the first two hundred or so myself, then if I get tired—"

"Leo, stop." Calypso gave Emmie an apologetic frown. "He jokes more when he's nervous. He also jokes *worse* when he's nervous."

"I have no idea what you're talking about." Leo inserted carrot fangs in his mouth and snarled.

Meg almost choked on her stir-fry.

Thalia let out a long sigh. "Oh, yeah. This is going to be a fun battle. Emmie, how are you stocked for extra arrows? I'm going to need a full quiver just for shooting Leo."

Emmie smiled. "We have plenty of weaponry. And thanks to Leo and Josephine, the Waystation's defenses have never been stronger."

"You're welcome!" Leo spat out his fangs. "Also I should mention the giant bronze dragon in the corner—assuming I can finish his tune-up tonight. He's still not at a hundred percent."

Normally, I would've found that giant bronze dragon quite reassuring, even at 75 percent, but I did not like twenty-to-one odds. The bloodthirsty cries of the arena audience still rang in my ears.

"Calypso," I said, "what about your magic? Has it returned?"

Her look of frustration was quite familiar. It was the same look I got whenever I thought of all the marvelous godly things I could no longer do.

"Only a few bursts," she said. "This morning, I moved a coffee cup across the counter."

"Yeah," Leo said, "but you did that *awesomely*."

Calypso swatted him. "Josephine says it'll take time. Once we . . ." She hesitated. "Once we survive tomorrow."

I got the feeling that wasn't what she'd intended to say. Leo and Emmie exchanged a conspiratorial glance. I didn't press the issue. At the moment, the only conspiracy I'd be interested in would be a clever plan to smuggle me back to Mount Olympus and reinstate me to godhood before breakfast tomorrow.

"We will make do," I decided.

Meg slurped down the last of her stir-fry. Then she demonstrated her usual exquisite manners by belching and wiping her mouth with her forearm. "Not you and me, Lester. We won't be here."

My stomach started tossing its own little salad. "But—"

"Prophecy, dummy. First light, remember?"

"Yes, but if the Waystation is attacked . . . shouldn't we be here to help?"

This was an odd question coming from me. When I was a god, I would have been delighted to leave the mortal heroes to fend for themselves. I would have made popcorn and watched the bloodbath from a distance on Mount Olympus, or simply caught the highlight reel later. But as Lester, I felt obliged to defend these people—my dear old Emmie, gruff Josephine, and no-so-little Georgina, who might or might not be my child. Thalia and the Hunters, Jamie of the Lovely Loincloth, the proud griffin parents upstairs, the excellent elephant downstairs, even the dislikable Lityerses . . . I wanted to be here for them.

It may seem strange to you that I hadn't already considered my conflicting obligation—to seek out the Cave of Trophonius at first light—and that this might prevent me from being at the Waystation. In my defense, gods can split their essence into many different manifestations at once. We don't have a lot of experience with scheduling.

"Meg is right," Emmie said. "Trophonius has summoned you. Getting *your* prophecy may be the only way to prevent the emperor's prophecy from coming true."

I was the god of prophecies, and even *I* was starting

to hate prophecies. I glanced at the spirit of Agamethus, hovering by the ladder to the loft. I thought of the last message he had given me: *We cannot remain.* Did he mean the defenders of the Waystation? Or Meg and me? Or something else entirely? I felt so frustrated I wanted to grab his Magic 8 Ball and bounce it off his nonexistent head.

"Cheer up," Thalia told me. "If Commodus comes at us with his full strength, the Oracle might be guarded with just a skeleton crew. It'll be your best chance to get in."

"Yeah," Leo said. "Besides, maybe you'll make it back in time to fight with us! Or, you know, we'll all die, and it won't matter."

"That makes me feel much better," I grumbled. "What problems could we possibly run into, just Meg and I?"

"Yep," Meg agreed.

She did not sound the least bit worried. This seemed like a failure of imagination to me. I could envision all sorts of horrible fates that might befall two people wandering into the dangerous cavern of a terrifying, hostile spirit. I would rather fight a host of blemmyae on bulldozers. I would even consider peeling more carrots.

As I was cleaning up the dinner plates, Emmie caught my arm.

"Just tell me one thing," she said. "Was it payback?"

I stared at her. "Was . . . what payback?"

"Georgina," she murmured. "For me . . . you know, giving up your gift of immortality. Was she . . ." She pressed her lips into a tight line, as if she didn't trust them to say any more.

I hadn't known I could feel any worse, until I did. I really hate that about the mortal heart. It seems to have an infinite capacity for getting heavier.

"Dear Emmie," I said. "I would *never*. Even on my worst days, when I'm destroying nations with plague arrows or putting together set lists for Kidz Bop compilations, I would *never* take revenge in such a way. I swear to you, I had no idea you were here, or that you had left the Hunters, or that Georgina existed, or . . . Actually, I just had no idea about anything. And I'm so sorry."

To my relief, a faint smile flickered on her face. "That's one thing I can believe, at least."

"That I am sorry?"

"No," she said. "That you had no idea about anything."

"Ah . . . So, we're good?"

She considered. "For now. But when Georgie recovers . . . we should talk further."

I nodded, though I was thinking that my to-do list of unwelcome tasks was already quite full.

"Well, then." I sighed. "I suppose I should get some rest, and perhaps start composing a new death haiku."

30

Lester, slap yourself
Oh, for just one night without
Looking like a fool

I HAD NO LUCK WITH THE HAIKU.

I kept getting stuck on the first line, *I don't want to die,* and couldn't think of anything to add. I hate elaborating when the main idea is so perfectly clear.

The Hunters of Artemis bedded down in the griffin roosts after setting trip wires and motion-sensor alarms. They always did this whenever I camped with them, which I found silly. Sure, when I was a god, I used to flirt with them shamelessly, but I never went further than that. And as Lester? I had no wish to die with a thousand silver arrows in my chest. If nothing else, the Hunters should have trusted my self-interest.

Thalia, Emmie, and Josephine sat together at the kitchen table for a long while, conversing in hushed tones. I hoped they were discussing more Hunter secrets—some deadly weapons they could use against Commodus's armies. Moon–ballistic missiles, perhaps. Or moon-napalm.

Meg hadn't bothered finding a guest room. She'd crashed on the nearest couch and was snoring away.

I stood nearby, not ready to go back to the room I shared with Leo Valdez. I watched the moon rise through the giant rose window above Josephine's workstation.

A voice at my shoulder said, "Not tired?"

It was a good thing I was no longer god of the sun. If someone had startled me that badly in my chariot, I would've charged upward so fast that high noon would've happened at 6:00 A.M.

Jamie stood next to me, a dapper apparition in brown. The moonlight gleamed copper on his scalp. His necklace of red and white beads peeked from beneath the collar of his dress shirt.

"Oh!" I said. "Um . . . Nah." I leaned against the wall, hoping to look casual, attractive, and suave. Unfortunately, I missed the wall.

Jamie was kind enough to pretend not to notice. "You should try to sleep," he rumbled. "The challenge you face tomorrow . . ." Worry lines creased his forehead. "I cannot imagine."

Sleep seemed like an alien concept, especially now, with my heart *chunk-chunk-chunk*ing like a defective pedal boat. "Oh, I don't sleep much. I used to be a god, you know." I wondered if flexing my muscles would help prove this point. I decided it would not. "And you? Are you a demigod?"

Jamie grunted. "An interesting word. I would say I am *elomǐràn*—one of the *others*. I am also a graduate accounting student at Indiana University."

I had no idea what to do with that information. I could think of no topics of conversation that would make me look interesting to a graduate student of accounting. I also hadn't realized how much older Jamie was than me. I mean mortal Lester me, not god me. I was confused.

"But Sssssarah said you worked for Commodus?" I recalled. "You're a gladiator?"

The edges of his mouth tugged downward. "Not a gladiator. I only fight on weekends for money. Mixed martial arts. Gidigbo and Dambe."

"I don't know what those are."

He chuckled. "Most people don't. They are Nigerian martial-art forms. The first, Gidigbo, is a wrestling style of my people, the Yoruba. The other is a Hausa sport, more violent, but I like it."

"I see," I said, though in fact I didn't.

Even in ancient times, I had been woefully ignorant of anything below the Saharan Desert. We Olympians tended to stay in our own neighborhood around the Mediterranean, which was, I agree, terribly cliquish. "You fight for money?"

"To pay my tuition," Jamie agreed. "I did not know what I was getting into with this emperor person."

"And yet you survived," I noted. "You can see that the world is, uh, much stranger than most mortals realize. You, Jamie, must have lots of ìgboyà."

His laughter was deep and rich. "Very good. My name is actually Olujime. For most Americans, Jamie is easier."

I understood. I'd only been a mortal for a few months and I was getting very tired of spelling out *Papadopoulos*.

"Well, Olujime," I said, "I'm pleased to meet you. We are lucky to have such a defender."

"Mmm." Olujime nodded gravely. "If we survive tomorrow, perhaps the Waystation can use an accountant. A piece of real estate so complex . . . there are many tax implications."

"Uh—"

"I am joking," he offered. "My girlfriend says I joke too much."

"*Uh.*" This time I sounded like I'd been kicked in the gut. "Your girlfriend. Yes. Will you excuse me?"

I fled.

Stupid Apollo. Of course Olujime had a girlfriend. I didn't know who or what he was, or why fate had dragged him into our strange little world, but obviously someone so interesting would not be single. Besides, he was much too old for me, or young, depending on how you looked at it. I decided not to look at it at all.

Exhausted but restless, I wandered the shifting corridors until I stumbled upon a small library. When I say *library,* I mean the old-fashioned kind without books, just scrolls stacked in cubbies. Ah, the smell of papyrus brought me back!

I sat at the table in the center of the room and remembered the chats I used to have in Alexandria with the philosopher Hypatia. Now *she* was a smart *melomakarona.* I wished she were here now. I could've used her advice on how to survive the Cave of Trophonius.

Alas, at present, my only advisor was stuck in the quiver on my back. Reluctantly, I pulled out the Arrow of Dodona and set him on the table.

The shaft of the arrow rattled against the table. *LONG HAST THOU KEPT ME QUIVERED. VERILY, THY LEVELS OF STUPID ASTOUND ME.*

"Have you ever wondered," I asked, "why you have no friends?"

UNTRUE, said the arrow. *EACH BRANCH OF DODONA'S SACRED GROVE, EACH TWIG AND ROOT—TO ALL OF THESE, I AM MOST DEAR.*

I doubted that. More likely, when it had come time to choose a branch to carve into an arrow to send on a quest with me, the entire grove had unanimously elected this particularly annoying length of ash. Even sacred Oracles could only stand hearing *forsooth* and *verily* so many times.

"Then tell me," I said, "O, Wise Arrow, most dear to all manner of trees, how do we get to the Cave of Trophonius? And how do Meg and I survive?"

The arrow's fletching rippled. *THOU SHALT TAKE A CAR.*

"That's it?"

LEAVEST THOU WELL BEFORE DAWN. 'TIS A COUNTER-COMMUTE, AYE, BUT THERE SHALL BE CONSTRUCTION ON HIGHWAY THIRTY-SEVEN. EXPECTEST THOU TO TRAVEL ONE HOUR AND FORTY-TWO MINUTES.

I narrowed my eyes. "Are you somehow . . . checking Google Maps?"

A long pause. *OF COURSE NOT. FIE UPON YOU. AS FOR HOW THOU SHALT SURVIVE, ASK ME THIS ANON, WHEN THOU REACHEST THY DESTINATION.*

"Meaning you need time to research the Cave of Trophonius on Wikipedia?"

I SHALL SAY NO MORE TO YOU, BASE VILLAIN! THOU ART NOT WORTHY OF MY SAGE ADVICE!

"*I'm* not worthy?" I picked up the arrow and shook it. "You're no help at all, you useless piece of—!"

"Apollo?" Calypso stood in the doorway.

Next to her, Leo grinned. "We didn't realize you were arguing with your arrow. Should we come back later?"

I sighed. "No, come in."

The two of them sat across from me. Calypso laced her fingers on the table like a teacher at a parent conference.

Leo did his best to impersonate someone capable of being serious. "So, uh, listen, Apollo—"

"I know," I said miserably.

He blinked as if I'd thrown welding sparks in his eyes. "You do?"

"Assuming we live through tomorrow," I said, "you two intend to remain at the Waystation."

They both stared at the table. A little more weeping and pulling of hair might have been nice, some heartfelt sobs of *Please forgive us!* But I guessed that was more apology than Lester Papadopoulos deserved.

"How did you know?" Calypso asked.

"The serious conversations with our hosts?" I said. "The furtive glances?"

"Hey, man," Leo said. "I'm not furtive. I've got zero furtivity."

I turned to Calypso. "Josephine has a wonderful workshop for Leo. And she can teach you to regain your magic. Emmie has gardens worthy of your old home, Ogygia."

"My old *prison*," Calypso corrected, though her voice carried no anger.

Leo fidgeted. "It's just . . . Josephine reminds me so much of my mom. She needs help around here. The Waystation may be a living building, but it's almost as high-maintenance as Festus."

Calypso nodded. "We've been traveling so much, Apollo, in constant danger for months. It's not just the magic and the gardens that appeal to me. Emmie says we could live like normal young people in this city. Even go to the local high school."

If not for the seriousness in her eyes, I might have laughed. "You—a former immortal even older than I—you want to go to high school?"

"Hey, man," Leo said. "Neither of has ever had a chance of a normal life."

"We would like to see," Calypso continued, "what we would be like together, and separately, in the mortal world. Taking things more slowly. Dating. Boyfriend. Girlfriend. Perhaps . . . hanging out with friends."

She spoke these words as if they were infused with an exotic spice—a taste she wished to savor.

"The thing is, Lester Man," Leo said, "we promised to help you. We're worried about leaving you on your own."

Their eyes were so full of concern—concern for *me*— that I had to swallow back a lump in my throat. Six weeks we had been traveling together. Most of that time, I had fervently wished I could be anywhere else, with anyone else. But with the exception of my sister, had I ever shared so many experiences with anyone? I realized, gods help me, that I was going to miss these two.

"I understand." I had to force the words out. "Josephine and Emmie are good people. They can offer you a home. And I won't be alone. I have Meg now. I don't intend to lose her again."

Leo nodded. "Yeah, Meg's a fireball. Takes one to know one."

"Besides," Calypso said, "we won't . . . what's the expression . . . skip off the radar completely."

"Drop," I suggested. "Though skipping sounds more fun."

"Yeah," Leo said. "We've still got a lot of demigodly stuff to do. At some point, I gotta reconnect with my other peeps: Jason, Piper, Hazel, Frank. Lotta people out there still want to punch me."

"And we have to survive tomorrow," Calypso added.

"Right, babe. Good call." Leo tapped the table in front of me. "Point is, *ese*, we're not going to abandon you. If you need us, holler. We'll be there."

I blinked back tears. I was not sad. I was not overwhelmed by their friendship. No, it had just been a very long day and my nerves were frayed.

"I appreciate it," I said. "You are both good friends."

Calypso wiped her eyes. No doubt she was just tired as well. "Let's not get carried away. You are still hugely annoying."

"And you are still a pain in the gloutos, Calypso."

"Okay, then." She smirked. "Now we all really *should* get some rest. Busy morning ahead."

"Ugh." I clawed at my hair. "I don't suppose you could summon a wind spirit for me? I have to drive to the Cave of Trophonius tomorrow, and I have neither a chariot nor a car."

"A car?" Leo grinned evilly. "Oh, I can hook you up with one of those!"

31

Start with a C chord
Not all the keys, Meg. C does
Not stand for Chaos

AT 5:00 A.M. the next morning, in the roundabout outside the Waystation, Meg and I found Leo standing in front of a gleaming red Mercedes XLS. I did not ask him how he had procured the vehicle. He did not volunteer the information. He *did* say that we should return it within twenty-four hours (assuming we lived that long) and try not to get pulled over by the police.

The bad news: just outside the city limits, I got pulled over by the police.

Oh, the miserable luck! The officer stopped us for no good reason that I could see. At first I feared he might be a blemmyae, but he was not nearly polite enough.

He frowned at my license. "This is a junior driver's license from New York, kid. What are you doing driving a car like this? Where are your parents, and where're you taking this little girl?"

I was tempted to explain that I was a four-thousand-year-old deity with plenty of experience driving the sun, my parents were in the celestial realm, and the little girl was my demigod master.

"She is my—"

"Little sister," Meg chimed in. "He's taking me to piano lessons."

"Uh, yes," I agreed.

"And we're late!" Meg waggled her fingers in a way that did not at all resemble playing the piano. "Because my brother is stooo-pid."

The officer frowned. "Wait here."

He walked to his patrol car, perhaps to run my license through his computer or to call for SWAT backup.

"Your brother?" I asked Meg. "Piano lessons?"

"The stupid part was true."

The officer came back with a confused look on his face. "Sorry." He handed me my license. "My mistake. Drive safely."

And that was that.

I wondered what had changed the officer's mind. Perhaps, when Zeus created my license, he had put some sort of spell on the ID that allowed me to pass simple scrutiny such as highway stops. No doubt Zeus had heard that driving while mortal could be dangerous.

We continued on, though the incident left me shaken. On Highway 37, I glanced at every car heading the opposite direction, wondering which were driven by blemmyae, demigods, or mercenaries commuting in to work at Commode Palace, anxious to destroy my friends in time for the naming ceremony.

In the east, the sky lightened from onyx to charcoal. Along the roadside, sodium vapor streetlamps tinted the landscape Agamethus orange—fences and pastures, stands of trees, dry gullies. Occasionally we spotted a gas station or a Starbucks oasis. Every few miles, we passed billboards declaring GOLD: BEST PRICES! with a smiling man who looked suspiciously like King Midas in a cheap suit.

I wondered how Lityerses was doing back at the Waystation. When we'd left, the whole place had been abuzz—everyone pitching in to fix armor, sharpen weapons, and ready traps. Lityerses had stood at Josephine's side, offering advice about Commodus and his various troops, but he'd seemed only half-present, like a man with a terminal disease, explaining to other patients how best they could prolong the inevitable.

Strangely, I trusted him. I believed he would not betray Josephine and Emmie, little Georgina, and the rest of the ragtag impromptu family I cared about. Lit's commitment seemed genuine. He now hated Commodus more than any of us.

Then again, six weeks ago, I never would have suspected Meg McCaffrey of working for Nero. . . .

I glanced over at my small master. She slumped in her seat, her red high-tops on the dashboard above the glove compartment. This scrunched-up position didn't look comfortable to me. It struck me as the sort of habit a child learns, then is reluctant to abandon when they grow too big.

She wriggled her fingers over her knees, still playing air piano.

"You might try putting a few rests in your composition," I told her. "Just for variety."

"I want lessons."

I wasn't sure I'd heard her correctly. "Piano lessons? Now?"

"Not now, dummy. But sometime. Can you teach me?"

What a horrifying idea! I wanted to think I was far enough along in my career as a music god not to give piano lessons to beginners. Then again, I noticed that Meg had *asked* me, not ordered me. I detected something tentative and hopeful in her voice, a fresh green chia shoot emerging. I was reminded of Leo and Calypso last night in the library, talking wistfully of the normal life they might build in Indiana. Strange, how often humans dream about the future. We immortals don't bother. For us, dreaming of the future is like staring at the hour hand of a clock.

"Very well," I said. "Assuming we survive this morning's adventures."

"Deal." Meg banged out a final chord that Beethoven would have loved. Then, from her backpack of supplies, she produced a baggie of carrots (peeled by me, thank you very much) and began munching them loudly while knocking the tips of her shoes together.

Because Meg.

"We should talk strategy," I suggested. "When we get to the caverns, we'll need to find the secret entrance. I doubt it will be as obvious as the regular mortal entrance."

"Mm-kay."

"Once you've dispatched whatever guards we find—"

"Once *we* have dispatched them," she corrected.

"Same difference. We'll need to look for two nearby streams. We'll have to drink from both of them before—"

THE DARK PROPHECY 299

"Don't tell me." Meg held up a carrot like a baton. "No spoilers."

"*Spoilers?* This information might save our lives!"

"I don't like spoilers," she insisted. "I want to be surprised."

"But—"

"No."

I clenched the wheel. It took great effort not to punch the gas and send us hurtling toward the horizon. I wanted to talk about the Cave of Trophonius . . . not just to enlighten Meg, but to see if I myself had the details straight.

I'd stayed up most of the night in the Waystation library. I'd read scrolls, sifted through my imperfect memories, even tried to wrangle more answers from the Arrow of Dodona and Agamethus's Magic 8 Ball. I'd had limited success, but what I'd managed to piece together just made me more nervous.

I liked to talk when I was nervous.

Meg, however, seemed unconcerned by the task ahead of us. She acted as annoying and carefree as she had the first day I'd encountered her in that Manhattan alley.

Was she just putting on a brave act? I didn't think so. I was constantly amazed at how resilient mortals could be in the face of catastrophe. Even the most traumatized, ill-treated, shell-shocked humans could carry on as if things were completely normal. Meals were still prepared. Work was still done. Piano lessons were commenced and carrot sticks munched.

For miles, we rode in silence. I couldn't even play any decent tunes, because the Mercedes did not have satellite radio. Curse Leo Valdez and his free luxury vehicles!

The only FM station I could find featured something called the Morning Zoo. After my experience with Calypso and the griffins, I was in no mood for zoos.

We passed through small towns with run-down motels, secondhand clothing shops, feed stores, and various vehicles for sale on the side of the road. The countryside was flat and monotonous—a landscape that would not have been out of place in the ancient Peloponnese except for the telephone poles and billboards. Well, and the road itself. Greeks were never very good at building roads. That's probably because Hermes was their god of travel. Hermes was always more interested in fascinating, dangerous journeys than he was in quick and easy interstates.

Finally, two hours after leaving Indianapolis, dawn started to break, and I started to panic.

"I'm lost," I admitted.

"Knew it," Meg said.

"It's not my fault! I followed those signs for God's Place!"

Meg squinted at me. "The Christian Bible store we passed? Why'd you do that?"

"Well, honestly! The locals need to be more specific about which gods they're advertising!"

Meg belched into her fist. "Pull over and ask the arrow. I'm getting carsick."

I did not want to ask the arrow. But I also did not want Meg throwing up her carrots all over the leather upholstery. I pulled to the side of the road and dug my prophetic missile weapon from my quiver.

"O, Wise Arrow," I said. "We're lost."

I KNEWST THAT WHEN I MET YOU.

Such a thin shaft the arrow had. How easy it would be to break! I restrained myself. If I destroyed the Grove of Dodona's gift, I worried that its patron, my hippie grandmother, Rhea, might curse me to smell like patchouli for all time.

"What I mean," I said, "is that we need to find the entrance to the Cave of Trophonius. Quickly. Can you direct us there?"

The arrow vibrated, perhaps testing for local Wi-Fi connections. Given our remote location, I feared he might start channeling the Morning Zoo.

THE MORTAL ENTRANCE LIES ONE LEAGUE EAST, he intoned. NEAR A PORTABLE SHED WITH A ROOF OF BLUE.

For a moment, I was too surprised to speak. "That . . . was actually helpful."

BUT THOU CANST NOT USE THE MORTAL ENTRANCE, he added. 'TIS GUARDED TOO WELL, AND 'TWOULD BE DEATH.

"Ah. Less helpful."

"What's he saying?" Meg asked.

I gestured for her to be patient. (Why, I don't know. It was a hopeless wish.) "Great Arrow, I don't suppose you know how we *should* get into the cave?"

GOEST THOU DOWN THIS ROAD TO THE WEST. THOU SHALT SEEST A ROADSIDE STAND WHICH SELLETH FRESH EGGS.

"Yes?"

THIS ROADSIDE STAND IS NOT IMPORTANT. KEEP DRIVING.

"Apollo?" Meg poked me in the ribs. "What's he saying?"

"Something about fresh eggs."

This answer seemed to satisfy her. At least she stopped poking me.

GOEST THOU FARTHER, the arrow advised. TAKEST THE THIRD LEFT. WHEN THOU SEEST THE ROAD SIGN OF THE EMPEROR, THOU SHALT KNOW 'TIS TIME TO STOP.

"What road sign of the emperor?"

THOU SHALT KNOWEST IT WHEN THOU SEEST IT. STOPPEST THERE, JUMPEST THOU THE FENCE, AND PROCEED INLAND TO THE PLACE OF TWO STREAMS.

Cold fingers played an arpeggio down my vertebrae. *The place of two streams*—that, at least, made sense to me. I wished it did not.

"And then?" I asked.

THEN THOU MAYST DRINK AND JUMP INTO THE CHASM OF HORRORS. BUT TO DO SO, THOU MUST FACE THE GUARDIANS THAT CANNOT BE KILLED.

"Fantastic," I said. "I don't supposeth— I don't *suppose* your Wikipedia article has more information about these unkillable guardians?"

THOU DOST JAPE LIKE A JAPING JAPER. BUT NAY. MY PROPHETIC POWERS SEE THIS NOT. AND ONE MORE THING.

"Yes?"

LEAVEST ME IN THE MERCEDES. I WISH NOT TO PLUNGE INTO DEATH AND DARKNESS.

I slid the arrow under the driver's seat. Then I reported the entire conversation to Meg.

She frowned. "Unkillable guardians? What does that mean?"

"At this point, Meg, your guess is as good as mine. Let's go find a chasm of horrors to jump into, shall we?"

32

Pretty fuzzy cow
So cute, so warm and vicious!
Squee! Can I kill him?

THE EMPEROR'S road sign was easy enough to spot:

ADOPT-A-HIGHWAY
NEXT FIVE MILES SPONSORED BY:
TRIUMVIRATE HOLDINGS

Commodus and his colleagues may have been power-hungry murderers bent on world domination, but at least they cared about cleaning up litter.

Along the roadside ran a barbed-wire fence. Beyond this lay more nondescript countryside—a few stands of trees and shrubs, but mostly rolling meadows. In the pre-dawn light, dew exhaled a blanket of vapor over the grass. In the distance, behind a clump of hackberry bushes, two large animals stood grazing. I couldn't make out their exact forms. They looked like cows. I doubted they were cows. I spotted no other guardians, killable or otherwise, which did not reassure me in the slightest.

"Well," I told Meg. "Shall we?"

We shouldered our supplies and left the Mercedes.

Meg removed her jacket and laid it across the barbed wire. Despite the arrow's instructions to *jumpest*, we only managed a wobbly giant *steppeth*. I held down the top wire for Meg, then she failed to do the same for me. This left me with some awkward rips in the seat of my jeans.

We sneaked across the field in the direction of the two grazing beasts.

I was sweating an unreasonable amount. The cold morning air condensed on my skin, making me feel as if I were bathing in a cold soup—Apollo gazpacho. (Hmm, that sounded rather good. I will have to trademark it once I become a god again.)

We crouched behind the hackberries, only twenty or thirty feet from the animals. Dawn tinged the horizon with red.

I didn't know how short our time window would be to enter the cavern. When the spirit of Trophonius said "first light," did he mean nautical twilight? Dawn? The moment when the sun chariot's headlights were first visible, or when the chariot was high enough in the sky that you could actually read my bumper stickers? Whatever the case, we had to hurry.

Meg adjusted her glasses. She started to edge sideways for an unobstructed view around the bushes when one of the creatures lifted its head just enough for me to glimpse its horns.

I stifled a scream. I grabbed Meg's wrist and pulled her back into the cover of the hackberries.

Normally, that might have provoked a bite from her, but I was willing to risk it. It was a little too early in the morning to watch my young friend get killed.

"Stay very still," I whispered. "Those are yales."

She blinked one eye, then the other, as if my warning was slowly making its way from her left brain to her right. "Yales? Isn't that a university?"

"Yes," I murmured. "And one of Yale University's symbols is the yale, but that's not important. These monsters . . ." I swallowed down the aluminum taste of fear. "The Romans knew them as *centicores*. They are absolutely deadly. They're also attracted to sudden movements and loud noises. So *shh*."

In fact, even as a god, I had never been this close to yales before. They were fierce, proud animals, highly territorial and aggressive. I remembered catching a glimpse of them in my vision of Commodus's throne room, but the beasts were so rare I'd half convinced myself they were some other manner of monster. Also, I could not imagine that even Commodus would be crazy enough to keep yales in such proximity to humans.

They looked more like giant yaks than cows. Shaggy brown fur with yellow spots covered their bodies, while the fur on their heads was solid yellow. Horselike manes trailed down their necks. Their fluffy tails were as long as my arm, and their large amber eyes . . . Oh, dear. The way I'm describing them, they sound almost cute. Let me assure you, they were not.

The yales' most prominent features were their horns—two glistening white spears of ridged bone, absurdly long for the creature's head. I had seen those horns in action before. Eons ago, during Dionysus's eastern campaign, the wine god had unleashed a herd of yales into the ranks of an Indian army five thousand strong. I remembered the screams of those warriors.

"What do we do?" Meg whispered. "Kill them? They're kind of pretty."

"The Spartan warriors were kind of pretty, too, until they skewered you. No, we can't kill yales."

"Okay, good." A long pause, then Meg's natural rebellious streak kicked in. "Why not? Is their fur invulnerable to my swords? I hate that."

"No, Meg, I don't think so. The reason we can't kill these creatures is that yales are on the endangered-monster list."

"You're making that up."

"Why would I make up such a thing?" I had to remind myself to keep my voice down. "Artemis is very careful about monitoring the situation. When monsters start to fade from mortals' collective memory, they regenerate less and less often from Tartarus. We have to let them breed and repopulate!"

Meg looked dubious. "Uh-huh."

"Oh, come on. Surely you heard about that proposed temple of Poseidon in Sicily? It had to be relocated simply because the land was found to be the nesting area of a red-bellied hydra."

Meg's blank stare suggested she hadn't heard about that, even though it had been headline news just a few thousand years ago.

"At any rate," I persisted, "yales are *much* rarer than red-bellied hydras. I don't know where Commodus found these, but if we killed them, all the gods would curse us, starting with my sister."

Meg gazed again at the shaggy animals grazing peacefully in the meadow. "Aren't you already cursed by the River Styx or whatever?"

"That's not the point."

"Then what do we do?"

The wind shifted. Suddenly, I remembered another detail about yales. They had an excellent sense of smell.

The pair simultaneously lifted their heads and turned their lovely amber eyes in our direction. The bull yale bellowed—a sound like a foghorn gargling mouthwash. Then both monsters charged.

I remembered more interesting facts about yales. (Had I not been about to die, I could have narrated a documentary.) For such large animals, their speed was impressive.

And those horns! As yales attacked, their horns swiveled like insect antennae—or, perhaps more accurately, the lances of medieval knights, who had been so fond of putting these creatures on their heraldic shields. The horns also spun, their sharp ridges corkscrewing, all the better to pierce our bodies.

I wished I could take a video of these majestic animals. I would've gotten millions of likes on GodTube! But if you have ever been charged by two woolly spotted yaks dual-wielding lances on their heads, you understand that camera work in such circumstances is difficult.

Meg tackled me, pushing me out of the yales' path as they rushed through the hackberries. The bull's left horn grazed my calf, slicing through my jeans. (My jeans were having a bad day.)

"Trees!" Meg yelled.

She grabbed my hand and pulled me toward the nearest stand of oaks. Fortunately, the yales were not as fast turning as they were charging. They galloped in a wide arc as Meg and I took cover.

"They're not so pretty now," Meg noted. "You sure we can't kill them?"

"No!" I ran through my limited repertoire of skills. I could sing and play the ukulele, but yales were notoriously tone-deaf. My bow and arrow would do me no good. I could try to simply wound the animals, but with my luck, I'd end up accidentally killing them. I was fresh out of ammonia syringes, brick walls, elephants, and bursts of godly strength. That left only my natural charisma, which I didn't think the yales would appreciate.

The animals slowed as they approached. Probably, they were confused about how to kill us through the trees. Yales were aggressive, but they weren't hunters. They didn't use fancy maneuvers to corner and defeat prey. If somebody got in their territory, they just charged. The trespassers died or fled. Problem solved. They weren't accustomed to intruders who played keep-away.

We edged around the oaks, doing our best to stay opposite the beasts.

"Nice yales," I sang. "Excellent yales."

The yales did not seem impressed.

As we shifted perspective, I spotted something about thirty yards beyond the animals: a cluster of washing-machine-size boulders in the tall grass. Nothing terribly dramatic, but my keen ears picked up the sound of trickling water.

I pointed out the rocks to Meg. "The cave entrance must be there."

She wrinkled her nose. "So do we run for it and jump in?"

"No!" I yelped. "There should be two streams. We have to stop and drink from them. Then the cave itself . . . I doubt it will be an easy descent. We'll need time to find a safe way down. If we just jump in, we might die."

"These harvards aren't going to give us time."

"Yales," I corrected.

"Same difference," she said, totally stealing my line. "How much do you think those things weigh?"

"A lot."

She seemed to run that through her mental calculator. "Okay. Get ready."

"For what?"

"No spoilers."

"I hate you."

Meg thrust out her hands. All around the yales, the grass went into overdrive, braiding itself into thick green ropes that wrapped around the beasts' legs. The creatures thrashed and bellowed like gargling foghorns, but the grass continued to grow, climbing across their flanks, entangling their massive bodies.

"Go," Meg said.

I ran.

Thirty yards had never seemed so far.

Halfway to the rocks, I glanced back. Meg was stumbling, her face glistening with sweat. It must have been taking all her strength to keep the yales entangled. The beasts strained and spun their horns, slashing at the grass, pulling against the sod with all their might.

I reached the pile of rocks.

As I'd suspected, from side-by-side fissures in the face of one boulder, twin springs gurgled, as if Poseidon had come by and cracked the stone with his trident: *I want hot water here, and cold water here.* One spring bubbled diluted white, the color of nonfat milk. The other was as black as squid ink. They ran together in a mossy streak before splattering against the muddy ground.

Beyond the springs, a crevasse zigzagged between the largest boulders—a ten-foot-wide wound in the earth, leaving no doubt as to the presence of the cavern system below. At the lip of the chasm, a coil of rope was tied to an iron piton.

Meg staggered toward me. "Hurry," she gasped. "Jump in."

Behind her, the yales were slowly ripping through their grassy bonds.

"We have to drink," I told her. "Mnemosyne, the Spring of Memory, is black. Lethe, the Spring of Forgetfulness, is white. If we drink both at the same time, they should counteract each other and prepare our minds—"

"Don't care." Meg's face was now as white as the waters of Lethe. "You go."

"But you have to come with me! The Oracle said so! Besides, you won't be in any shape to defend yourself."

"Fine," she groaned. "Drink!"

I cupped one hand in the water of Mnemosyne, the other hand in the water of Lethe. I gulped them down simultaneously. They had no taste—just intense, numbing cold, the sort that hurts so badly you don't feel the pain until much later.

My brain began to swivel and corkscrew like a yale horn. My feet felt like helium balloons. Meg struggled with the rope, trying to wrap it around my waist. For some reason, I found this hysterical.

"Your turn," I giggled. "Drinkie, drinkie!"

Meg scowled. "And lose my wits? Nuh-uh."

"Silly willy! If you don't prepare yourself for the Oracle—"

In the meadow, the yales ripped themselves free, peeling off several square yards of turf from the ground.

"No time!" Meg lunged forward, tackling me around the waist. Like the good friend she was, she sent me tumbling over the ledge and into the black void below.

33

Feeling groovy, I'm
Drowning, freezing, snake surfing
Life is good, Batman!

MEG AND I PLUMMETED through the dark, our rope unspooling as we bounced off one rock then another, my clothing and skin getting brutally scraped away.

I did the natural thing. I screamed, "WHEEEEEE!"

The rope snapped taut, giving me the Heimlich maneuver so violently I almost coughed up my appendix. Meg grunted with surprise and lost her grip on me. She fell deeper into the darkness. A heartbeat later, a splash echoed from below.

I laughed, dangling in the void. "That was fun! Again!"

The knot unraveled at my waist, and I plunged into frigid water.

My delirious state probably saved me from drowning immediately. I felt no need to struggle, thrash, or gasp for breath. I floated down, vaguely amused by my predicament. The sips I had taken from Lethe and Mnemosyne battled in my mind. I couldn't remember my own name, which I found extremely funny, but I could recall with perfect clarity the yellow flecks in Python's serpentine eyes as he sank his fangs into my immortal biceps millennia ago.

Beneath the dark water, I shouldn't have been able to see anything. Nevertheless, images floated in and out of my vision. Perhaps this was the effect of my eyeballs freezing.

I saw my father, Zeus, sitting in a patio chair by an infinity pool at the edge of a terrace. Beyond the pool, an azure sea stretched to the horizon. The scene would have been more fitting for Poseidon, but I knew this place: my mother's condo in Florida. (Yes, I had one of those immortal moms who retired to Florida; what can you do?)

Leto knelt at Zeus's side, her hands clasped in prayer. Her bronze arms glowed against her white sundress. Her long golden hair zigzagged down her back in an elaborate ladder weave.

"Please, my lord!" she implored. "He is your son. He has learned his lesson!"

"Not yet," Zeus rumbled. "Oh, no. His real test is yet to come."

I laughed and waved. "Hi, Mom! Hi, Dad!"

Since I was underwater and most likely hallucinating, my words should not have been audible. Nevertheless, Zeus glanced over and scowled.

The scene evaporated. I found myself facing a different immortal.

Floating before me was a dark goddess, her ebony hair wafting in the cold current, her dress billowing around her like volcanic smoke. Her face was delicate and sublime, her lipstick, eye shadow, and mascara all expertly done in shades of midnight. Her eyes gleamed with absolute hatred.

I found her presence delightful. "Hi, Styx!"

Her obsidian eyes narrowed. "You. Oath-breaker. Do not think I have forgotten."

"But *I* have!" I said. "Who am I again?"

In that moment, I was absolutely serious. I knew this was Styx, goddess of the Underworld's most important river. I knew she was the most powerful of all water nymphs, eldest daughter of the sea Titan, Oceanus. I knew she hated me, which wasn't surprising, since she was also the goddess of hatred.

But I had no idea who I was or what I'd done to earn her animosity.

"Did you know I'm drowning right now?" This was so hilarious I started to giggle a stream of bubbles.

"I will have my due," Styx snarled. "You will PAY for your broken promises."

"Okay!" I agreed. "How much?"

She hissed in annoyance. "I can't even do this with you right now. Return to your foolish quest!"

The goddess vanished. Someone grabbed me by the scruff of my neck, yanked me out of the water, and dumped me on a hard stone surface.

My rescuer was a young girl of about twelve. Water dripped from her tattered green sheath dress. Bloody scratches covered her arms. Her jeans and red high-tops were shellacked with mud.

Most alarmingly, the rhinestones in the corners of her cat-eye glasses were not just glinting. They emitted their own pale light. I realized those small constellations hovering next to her eyes were the only reason I could see the girl at all.

"I feel like I know you," I croaked. "I want to say Peg. Or Megan?"

She frowned, looking almost as dangerous as the goddess Styx. "You're not kidding, are you?"

"Nope!" I gave her a cheerful smile, despite the fact that I was soaked and shivering. It occurred to me that I was probably going into hypothermic shock. I remembered all the symptoms of that: shivering, dizziness, confusion, rapid heart rate, nausea, fatigue . . . Wow, I was batting a thousand!

Now if only I could remember my name. It occurred to me that I had two of them. Was one of them Lester? Oh, dear. How awful! The other was something that began with an A.

Alfred? Hmm. No. That would make this young girl Batman, and that didn't feel right.

"My name is Meg," she offered.

"Yes! Yes, of course. Thanks. And I'm—"

"An idiot."

"Hmm. No. . . . Oh! That's a joke."

"Not really. But your name is Apollo."

"Right! And we're here for the Oracle of Trophonius."

She tilted her head, sending her left eyeglass frame constellation into a higher astrological house. "You can't remember our names, but you remember *that*?"

"Strange, isn't it?" I struggled to sit up. My fingers had turned blue, which probably wasn't a good sign. "I remember the steps for petitioning the Oracle! First, we drink from the Springs of Lethe and Mnemosyne. I did that already, didn't I? That's why I feel so odd."

"Yeah." Meg wrung the water out of her skirt. "We need to keep moving or we'll freeze to death."

"Okay!" I accepted her help getting me to my feet. "After drinking from the springs, we descend into a cave. Oh! We're here! Then we go farther into the depths. Hmm. That way!"

In fact, there was only one way.

Fifty feet above us, a tiny slash of daylight glowed from the crevice we'd fallen through. The rope dangled well out of reach. We would not be exiting the same way we entered. To our left rose a sheer face of rock. About halfway up the wall, a waterfall gushed from a fissure, spilling into the pool at our feet. To our right, the water formed a dark river and flowed out through a narrow tunnel. The ledge we were standing on wound alongside the river, just wide enough to walk on, assuming we didn't slip, fall in, and drown.

"Well, then!" I led the way, following the stream.

As the tunnel turned, the rock sill narrowed. The ceiling lowered until I was almost crawling. Behind me, Meg breathed in shivering puffs, her exhales so loud they echoed over the babble of the river.

I found it difficult to walk and form rational thoughts at the same time. It was like playing syncopated rhythms on a drum set. My sticks needed to move in a completely different pattern than my feet on the bass and top hat pedals. One small mistake and my edgy jazz beat would turn into a leaden polka.

I stopped and turned to Meg. "Honey cakes?"

In the glowing rhinestone light of her glasses, her

expression was difficult to read. "I hope you're not calling me that."

"No, we need honey cakes. Did you bring them or did I?" I patted my soaking wet pockets. I felt nothing but a set of car keys and a wallet. I had a quiver, a bow, and a uku-lele on my back—Oh, a ukulele! Wonderful!—but I didn't think I would have stored pastries in a stringed instrument.

Meg frowned. "You never said anything about honey cakes."

"But I just remembered! We need them for the snakes!"

"Snakes." Meg developed a facial tic that I did not think was related to hypothermia. "Why would there be snakes?"

"Good question! I just know we're supposed to have honey cakes to appease them. So . . . we forgot the cakes?"

"You never said anything about cakes!"

"Well, that's a shame. Anything we can substitute? Oreos, perhaps?"

Meg shook her head. "No Oreos."

"Hmm. Okay. I guess we'll improvise."

She glanced apprehensively down the tunnel. "You show me how to improvise with snakes. I'll follow."

This sounded like a splendid idea. I strolled merrily onward, except where the tunnel's ceiling was too low. In those places, I squatted merrily onward.

Despite slipping into the river a few times, whacking my head on a few stalactites, and choking on the acrid smell of bat guano, I felt no distress. My legs seemed to float. My brain wobbled around in my skull, constantly rebalancing like a gyroscope.

Things I could remember: I'd had a vision of Leto. She'd been trying to convince Zeus to forgive me. That was *so* sweet! I'd also had a vision of the goddess Styx. She'd been angry—hilarious! And for some reason, I could remember every note Stevie Ray Vaughan played on "Texas Flood." What a great song!

Things I could not remember: Didn't I have a twin sister? Was her name . . . Lesterina? Alfreda? Neither of those sounded right. Also, why was Zeus mad at me? Also, why was Styx mad at me? Also, who was this girl behind me with the glowing rhinestone glasses, and why didn't she have any honey cakes?

My thoughts may have been muddled, but my senses were as sharp as ever. From the tunnel ahead of us, wafts of warmer air brushed against my face. The sounds of the river dissipated, the echoes growing deeper and softer, as if the water were spreading out into a larger cavern. A new smell assaulted my nostrils—a scent drier and sourer than bat guano. Ah, yes . . . reptilian skin and excrement.

I halted. "I know why!"

I grinned at Peggy—Megan—no, *Meg.*

She scowled. "You know why what?"

"Why snakes!" I said. "You asked me why we would find snakes, didn't you? Or was that someone else? Snakes are symbolic! They represent prophetic wisdom from deep in the earth, just as birds symbolize prophetic wisdom from the heavens."

"Uh-huh."

"So snakes are attracted to Oracles! Especially ones in caves!"

"Like that big snake monster we heard in the Labyrinth, Python?"

I found this reference vaguely unsettling. I was pretty sure I'd known who Python was a few minutes ago. Now I was blanking. I flashed on the name Monty Python. Was that correct? I didn't think the monster and I had ever been on a first-name basis.

"Well, yes, I suppose it's like that," I said. "Anyway, the snakes should be right up ahead! That's why we need honey cakes. You have some, you said?"

"No, I—"

"Excellent!" I forged on.

As I'd suspected, the tunnel widened into a large chamber. A lake covered the entire area, perhaps sixty feet in diameter, except for a small island of rock in the center. Above us, the domed ceiling bristled with stalactites like black chandeliers. Covering the island and the surface of the water was a writhing sheet of serpents, like spaghetti left too long in boiling water. Water moccasins. Lovely creatures. Thousands of them.

"Ta-da!" I exclaimed.

Meg did not seem to share my enthusiasm. She edged back into the tunnel. "Apollo . . . you'd need a zillion honey cakes for that many snakes."

"Oh, but you see, we need to get to that little island in the center. That's where we'll receive our prophecy."

"But if we go into that water, won't the snakes kill us?"

"Probably!" I grinned. "Let's find out!"

I jumped into the lake.

34

Meg takes a solo
Scares away her audience
Good job, McCaffrey

"APOLLO, SING!" MEG YELLED.

No words could have stopped me more effectively. I loved being asked to sing!

I was halfway across the lake, up to my waist in reptilian noodle soup, but I turned and looked back at the girl standing at the mouth of the tunnel. I must have agitated the snakes in my wake. They swished back and forth, their cute little heads gliding just above the surface, their white mouths open. (Oh, I get it! That's why they were called cottonmouths!)

Many of the snakes swarmed toward Meg, nosing around her shoes as if deciding whether to join her on the ledge. Meg tiptoed from foot to foot as if she wasn't crazy about this idea.

"Did you say *sing*?" I asked.

"Yes!" Her voice squeaked. "Charm the snakes! Make them go away!"

I didn't understand what she meant. When I sang, my audiences always came *closer*. Who was this girl Meg, anyway? She had apparently confused me with Saint Patrick.

(Nice guy, by the way; terrible singing voice. The legends don't normally mention that he drove the snakes out of Ireland with his hideous version of "Te Deum.")

"Sing that song you did in the ants' nest!" she pleaded.

The Ants' Nest? I remembered singing with the Rat Pack and A Flock of Seagulls, but the Ants' Nest? I didn't recall ever being part of such a group.

However, it did occur to me why Megan/Peg/Meg might be nervous. Water moccasins are poisonous. Much like yales, they can be aggressive when their territory is invaded. But Meg stood at the mouth of the tunnel, not really in the snakes' territory. Why was she nervous?

I looked down. Hundreds of vipers swirled around me, displaying their cute little mouths with their sharp little fangs. They moved sluggishly in the frigid water, or perhaps they were just awestruck to be in my presence—cheerful, charismatic, charming old Whatever-my-name-was!—but they did seem to be hissing a lot.

"Oh!" I laughed as the realization struck me. "You're worried about me! I'm about to die!"

I had a vague impulse to do something. Run? Dance? What was it Meg had suggested?

Before I could decide, Meg began to sing.

Her voice was weak and off-key, but I recognized the melody. I was pretty sure I had composed it.

Whenever someone bursts into song in public, there is a moment of hesitation. Passersby stop to listen, trying to discern what they are hearing and why a random person in their midst has decided to serenade them. As Meg's uneven voice echoed through the cavern, the snakes sensed the vibrations. More thumb-size viper heads popped to the surface. More white mouths opened, as if they were trying to taste the song. Around my waist, the swirling storm of water moccasins lost its cohesion as the snakes turned their attention to Meg.

She sang of loss and regret. Yes . . . I vaguely recalled singing this song. I'd been walking through the tunnels of a myrmekes' nest, pouring out my sadness, baring my heart as I searched for Meg. In the song, I had taken responsibility for the deaths of my greatest loves, Daphne and Hyacinthus. Their names came back to me as sharp as broken window shards.

Meg repeated my performance, but with different words. She was making up her own verses. As the vipers gathered at her feet, her voice grew stronger, more self-assured. She was still off-key, but she sang with heartbreaking conviction—her song every bit as sad and genuine as mine had been.

"It's my fault," she sang. "Your blood on my hands. The crushed rose I couldn't save."

I was stunned she had such poetry in her. Clearly, the snakes were too. They bobbed around her feet in a thick mass, just like the crowd at the Pink Floyd floating concert in Venice in 1989—which, for some reason, I remembered perfectly.

A bit late, I realized it was a miracle I had not yet been bitten to death by water moccasins. What was I doing in the middle of this lake? Only Meg's music was keeping me alive—her discordant voice somehow beautiful and enchanting, holding the attention of thousands of rapt vipers.

Like them, I wanted to stay where I was and listen. But a sense of unease was building up inside me. This cave . . . the Oracle of Trophonius. Something told me this cave was not the right place to bare one's soul.

"Meg," I whispered. "Stop."

She apparently couldn't hear me.

The entire cavern seemed fixated on her voice now. The rock walls glistened. Shadows swayed as if dancing. The glittering stalactites strained toward Meg like compass needles.

She sang of betraying me, of returning to Nero's household, of succumbing to her fear of the Beast. . . .

"No," I said, a little louder. "No, Meg!"

Too late. The cavern's magic caught her song, magnifying her voice a hundredfold. The chamber filled with the sound of pure pain. The lake boiled as panicked serpents submerged and fled, pushing past my legs in a strong riptide.

Perhaps they escaped down some hidden waterway. Perhaps they dissolved. All I knew: the little rock island in the center of the cave was suddenly empty, and I was the only living thing left in the lake.

Still Meg sang. Her voice now sounded forced out of her—as if some giant invisible fist were squeezing her like a squeaky toy. Lights and shadows flickered over the cavern walls, forming ghostly images to illustrate her lyrics.

In one scene, a middle-aged man crouched down and smiled as if looking at a child. He had dark curly hair like mine (I mean Lester's), a broad freckled nose, and soft, kind eyes. He held out a single red rose.

"From your mother," he whispered, a chorus to Meg's song. "This rose will never fade, sweetheart. You will never have to worry about thorns."

The pudgy hand of a child appeared in the vision, reaching for the flower. I suspected this was one of Meg's earliest memories—something just on the edge of consciousness. She took the rose, and the petals unfolded into brilliant full bloom. The stem curled lovingly around Meg's wrist. She squealed with delight.

A different vision: the emperor Nero in his purple three-piece suit, kneeling to look Meg in the eye. He smiled in a way that might have been mistaken for kindly if you didn't know Nero. His double chin puffed out under his helmet-strap beard. His bejeweled rings glittered on his fat fingers.

"You'll be a good girl, won't you?" He gripped Meg's shoulder a little too tightly. "Your daddy had to go away. Perhaps if you're good, you'll see him again. Won't that be nice?"

The younger version of Meg nodded. I sensed, somehow, that she was about five years old. I imagined her thoughts and emotions curling up inside her, forming a thick protective shell.

Another scene flickered into view. Just outside the New York Public Library in Midtown, a man's corpse sprawled on the white marble steps. One hand was splayed on his gut, which was a gruesome battleground of red trenches—perhaps slashes from a knife, or the claws of a large predator.

Police milled around, taking notes, snapping photos,

holding the crowd behind a line of yellow tape. They parted, however, to let two people in—Nero, in a different purple suit but the same ghastly beard and jewelry, and Meg, now maybe six, horrified, pale, reluctant. She saw the body and began to whimper. She tried to turn away, but Nero planted a heavy hand on her shoulder to keep her in place.

"I want you to see this." His voice dripped with false sympathy. "I am so sorry, my dear. The Beast . . ." He sighed as if this tragic scene was unavoidable. "I need you to be more diligent in your studies, do you understand? Whatever the swords-master says, you must do. It would break my heart if something else happened, something even worse than this. Look. Remember."

Tears pooled in Meg's eyes. She edged forward. Clutched in her dead father's other hand was the stem of a rose. The crushed petals were strewn across his stomach, almost invisible against the blood. She wailed, "Daddy! Help me!" The police paid her no attention. The crowd acted as if she didn't exist. Only Nero was there for her.

At last she turned to him, buried her face in his suit vest, and sobbed uncontrollably.

Shadows flickered more rapidly across the cavern walls. Meg's song began to reverberate, breaking into random waves of noise. The lake churned around me. On the small rock island, darkness gathered, swirling upward like a waterspout, forming the shape of a man.

"Meg, stop singing!" I yelled.

With one final sob, she crumpled to her knees, her face streaked with tears. She fell to her side, groaning, her voice like crumpling sandpaper. The rhinestones in her glasses still glowed, but with a faint bluish tint, as if all the warmth had been drained from them.

I wanted more than anything to rush to Meg's side. The sips of Memory and Forgetfulness had mostly burned out of my system. I knew Meg McCaffrey. I wanted to comfort her. But I also knew that the danger to her had not passed.

I faced the island. The apparition was only vaguely humanoid, composed of shadows and fractals of light. Afterimages from Meg's lyrics flashed and faded in his body. He radiated fear even more strongly than Thalia's Aegis shield—waves of terror that threatened to rip my self-control from its moorings.

"Trophonius!" I yelled. "Leave her alone!"

His form came into clearer focus: his lustrous dark hair, his proud face. Around him swarmed a host of phantom bees, his sacred creatures, small smudges of darkness.

"Apollo." His voice resonated deep and harsh, just as it had sounded when expelled from Georgina on the Throne of Memory. "I've waited a long time, Father."

"Please, my son." I clasped my hands. "Meg is not your petitioner. I am!"

Trophonius regarded young McCaffrey, now curled up and shivering on the stone ledge. "If she is not my petitioner, why did she summon me with her song of grief? She has many unanswered questions. I could answer them, for the price of her sanity."

"No! She was— She was trying to protect me." I choked on the words. "She is my friend. She did not drink from the springs. I did. I am the supplicant to your holy Oracle. Take me instead!"

Trophonius's laughter was a horrible sound . . . worthy of a spirit who dwelled in the darkness with thousands of poisonous snakes.

"*Take me instead,*" he repeated. "The very prayer I made when my brother Agamethus was caught in a tunnel, his chest crushed, his life fading. Did you listen to me then, Father?"

My mouth turned dry. "Don't punish the girl for what I did."

Trophonius's ghostly bees swarmed in a wider cloud, buzzing angrily past my face.

"Do you know how long I wandered the mortal world after killing my brother, Apollo?" asked the ghost. "After cutting off his head, my hands still covered in his blood, I staggered through the wilderness for weeks, months. I pleaded to the earth to swallow me up and end my misery. I got half my wish."

He gestured around him. "I dwell in darkness now because I am *your son.* I see the future because I am *your son.* All my pain and madness . . . Why should I not share it with those who seek my help? Does *your* help ever come without a price?"

My legs gave out. I plunged to my knees, the frigid water up to my chin. "Please, Trophonius. I am mortal now. Take your price from me, not her!"

"The girl has already volunteered! She opened her deepest fears and regrets to me."

"No! No, she didn't drink of the two springs. Her mind is not prepared. She will die!"

Images flickered through Trophonius's dark form like

flashes of lightning: Meg encased in goo in the ants' lair; Meg standing between me and Lityerses, his sword stopped cold by her crossed golden blades; Meg hugging me fiercely as we flew our griffin from the Indianapolis Zoo.

"She is precious to you," said the Oracle. "Would you give your life in exchange for hers?"

I had trouble processing that question. Give up my life? At any point in my four thousand years of existence, my answer would've been an emphatic *No! Are you crazy?* One should *never* give up one's life. One's life is important! The whole point of my quests in the mortal world, finding and securing all these ancient Oracles, was to regain immortality so I wouldn't have to ponder such awful questions!

And yet . . . I thought of Emmie and Josephine renouncing immortality for each other. I thought of Calypso giving up her home, her powers, and eternal life for a chance to roam the world, experience love, and possibly enjoy the wonders of high school in Indiana.

"Yes," I found myself saying. "Yes, I would die to save Meg McCaffrey."

Trophonius laughed—a wet, angry sound like the churning of vipers in water. "Very good! Then promise me that you'll grant me a wish. Whatever I ask, you will do."

"Y-your wish?" I wasn't a god anymore. Trophonius knew that. Even if I *could* grant wishes, I seemed to recall a very recent conversation with the goddess Styx about the dangers of making oaths I couldn't keep.

But what choice did I have?

"Yes," I said. "I swear. Whatever you ask. Then we have an agreement? You will take me instead of the girl?"

"Oh, I didn't promise anything in return!" The spirit turned as black as oil smoke. "I just wanted to exact that promise from you. The girl's fate is already decided."

He stretched out his arms, expelling millions of dark ghostly bees.

Meg screamed in terror as the swarm engulfed her.

35

Man, I hate my son
A real arrogant jerkwad
Nothing like his dad

I DID NOT KNOW I could move so fast. Not as Lester Papadopoulos, anyway.

I bounded across the lake until I reached Meg's side. I tried desperately to shoo away the bees, but the wisps of darkness swarmed her, flying into her mouth, nose, and ears—even into her tear ducts. As a god of medicine, I would have found that fascinating if I hadn't been so repulsed.

"Trophonius, stop it!" I pleaded.

"This is not my doing," said the spirit. "Your friend opened her mind to the Dark Oracle. She asked questions. Now she is receiving the answers."

"She asked no questions!"

"Oh, but she did. Mostly about you, Father. What will happen to you? Where must you go? How can she help you? These worries are foremost in her mind. Such misplaced loyalty . . ."

Meg began to thrash. I turned her onto her side, as one should do for someone having a seizure. I wracked my brain. What else? Remove sharp objects from her environment. . . . All the snakes were gone, good. Not much I could do about the bees. Her skin was cold, but I had nothing warm and dry to cover her with. Her usual scent—that faint, inexplicable smell of apples—had turned dank as mildew. The rhinestones in her glasses were completely dark, the lenses white with condensation.

"Meg," I said. "Stay with me. Concentrate on my voice."

She muttered incoherently. With a twinge of panic, I realized that if she gave me a direct order in her delirious state, even something as simple as *Leave me alone* or *Go away*, I would be compelled to obey. I had to find a way to anchor her mind, to shield her from the worst of the dark visions. That was difficult when my own mind was still a little fuzzy and not completely trustworthy.

I muttered some healing chants—old curative tunes I hadn't used in centuries. Before antibiotics, before aspirin, before even sterile bandages, we had songs. I was the god of both music and healing for good reason. One should never underestimate the healing power of music.

Meg's breathing steadied, but the shadowy swarm still enveloped her, attracted to her fears and doubts like . . . well, like bees to pollen.

"Ahem," Trophonius said. "So about this favor you promised—"

"Shut up!" I snapped.

In her fever, Meg murmured, "Shut up."

I chose to take this as an echo, not an order, aimed at Trophonius rather than me. Thankfully, my vocal cords agreed.

I sang to Meg about her mother, Demeter—the goddess who could heal the entire earth after drought, fire, or flood.

I sang of Demeter's mercy and kindness—the way she had made the prince Triptolemus into a god because of his good deeds; the way she had nursed the baby boy Demophon for three nights, attempting to make him immortal; the way she had blessed the cereal makers of modern times, flooding the world with a bounty of Froot Loops, Lucky Charms, and Count Chocula. Truly, she was a goddess of infinite benevolence.

"You know she loves you," I promised, cradling Meg's head in my lap. "She loves all her children. Look at how much she cherished Persephone even though that girl . . . Well, she makes your table manners look positively refined! Er, no offense."

I realized I wasn't even singing anymore. I was rambling, trying to drive off Meg's fears with a friendly voice.

"Once," I continued, "Demeter married this minor harvest god, Karmanor? You've probably never heard of him. No one had. He was this local deity in Crete. Rude, backward, poorly dressed. But, oh, they loved each other. They had this son . . . ugliest boy you ever saw. Had *no* redeeming qualities. He looked like a pig. Everyone said so. He even had a horrible name: Eubouleus. Sounds like Ebola, I know. But Demeter turned everyone's criticisms around. She made Eubouleus the god of swineherds! I only say this because . . . Well, you never know, Meg. Demeter has plans for you, I'm sure. You can't die on me, you see. You have too much to look forward to. Demeter might make you the minor goddess of cute little piglets!"

I couldn't tell if she was hearing me. Her eyes shifted under closed lids as if she'd entered REM sleep. She wasn't twitching and thrashing quite as much. Or was that my imagination? I was shaking from cold and fear so much myself, it was hard to be sure.

Trophonius made a sound like a steam valve opening. "She's just fallen into a deeper trance. That's not necessarily a good sign. She could still die."

I kept my back to him. "Meg, don't listen to Trophonius. He's all about fear and pain. He's just trying to make us lose hope."

"Hope," said the spirit. "Interesting word. I had hope once—that my father might act like *a father*. I got over it after a few centuries of being dead."

"Don't blame me for you robbing the king's treasury!" I snarled. "You are here because *you* messed up."

"I prayed to you!"

"Well, perhaps you didn't pray for the right thing at the right time!" I yelled. "Pray for wisdom before you do something stupid! Don't pray for me to bail you out after you follow your worst instincts!"

The bees swirled around me and buzzed angrily, but they did me no harm. I refused to offer them any fear to feed on. All that mattered now was staying positive, staying anchored for Meg's sake.

"I'm here." I brushed the wet hair from her forehead. "You are not alone."

She whimpered in her trance. "The rose died."

I felt as if a water moccasin had wriggled into my chest and was biting my heart, one artery at a time. "Meg, a flower is only part of the plant. Flowers grow back. You have deep roots. You have strong stems. You have . . . Your face is green."

I turned to Trophonius in alarm. "Why is her face green?"

"Interesting." He sounded anything but interested. "Perhaps she's dying."

He tilted his head as if listening to something in the distance. "Ah. They're here, waiting for you."

"What? Who?"

"The emperor's servants. Blemmyae." Trophonius gestured to the far side of the lake. "An underwater tunnel just there . . . it leads into the rest of the cavern system, the part known to mortals. The blemmyae have learned better than to come into this chamber, but they're waiting for you on the other end. That's the only way you can escape."

"Then we will."

"Doubtful," said Trophonius. "Even if your young friend survives, the blemmyae are preparing explosives."

"WHAT?"

"Oh, Commodus probably told them to use the explosives only as a last resort. He likes having me as his personal fortune-teller. He sends his men in here from time to time, pulls them out half-dead and insane, gets free glimpses of the future. What does he care? But he'd rather destroy this Oracle than allow you to escape alive."

I was too dumbfounded to respond.

Trophonius let loose another harsh peal of laughter. "Don't look so down, Apollo. On the bright side, it won't matter if Meg dies here, because she's going to die anyway! Look, she's frothing at the mouth now. This is always the most interesting part."

Meg was indeed gurgling white foam. In my expert medical opinion, that was rarely a good sign.

I took her face between my hands. "Meg, listen to me." The darkness roiled around her, making my skin tingle. "I'm here. I'm Apollo, god of healing. You will *not* die on me."

Meg didn't take orders well. I knew this. She twitched and foamed, coughing up random words like *horse, crossword, cloven, roots*. Also not a great sign, medically speaking.

My singing had not worked. Stern language had not worked. There was only one other remedy I could think of—an ancient technique for drawing out poison and evil spirits. The practice was no longer endorsed by most medical associations, but I remembered the limerick from the Grove of Dodona, the line I had lost the most sleep over: *Was forced death and madness to swallow.*

Here we were.

I knelt over Meg's face, as I used to do when I taught mouth-to-mouth resuscitation as part of first aid training at Camp Jupiter. (Those silly Roman demigods were *always* drowning.)

"I'm sorry about this." I pinched Meg's nose and clamped my mouth over hers. A slimy, unpleasant sensation—much like what I imagined Poseidon experienced when he realized he was kissing the gorgon Medusa.

I could not be deterred. Instead of exhaling, I inhaled, sucking the darkness from Meg's lungs.

Perhaps, at some point in your life, you've gotten water up your nose? Imagine that feeling, except with bee venom and acid instead of water. The pain almost made me black out, a noxious cloud of horror flooding through my sinuses,

down my throat, and into my chest. I felt ghostly bees rico-
cheting through my respiratory system, trying to sting their
way out.

I held my breath, determined to keep as much of the
darkness away from Meg for as long as I could. I would share
this burden with her, even if it killed me.

My mind slid sideways into Meg's own memories.

I was a frightened little girl, trembling on the steps of
the library, staring down at the body of my murdered father.

The rose he had given me was crushed and dead. Its
petals were scattered across the wounds the Beast had made
in his belly.

The Beast had done this. I had no doubt. Nero had
warned me again and again.

Daddy had promised me the rose would never die. I
would never have to worry about thorns. He said the flower
was a gift from my mother, a lady I had never met.

But the rose was dead. Daddy was dead. My life was
nothing but thorns.

Nero put his hand on my shoulder. "I'm so sorry, Meg."

His eyes were sad, but his voice was tinged with disappointment. This only proved what I already suspected.
Daddy's death was my fault. I should have been a better
daughter. I should have trained harder, minded my manners, not objected when Nero told me to fight the larger
children . . . or the animals I did not want to kill.

I had upset the Beast.

I sobbed, hating myself. Nero hugged me. I buried my
face in his purple clothes, his sickly sweet cologne—not
like flowers, but like old, desiccated potpourri in a nursing

home. I wasn't sure how I even *knew* that smell, but it brought back a half-remembered feeling of helplessness and terror. Nero was all I had. I didn't get real flowers, a real father, a real mother. I wasn't worthy of that. I had to cling to what I had.

Then, our minds comingled, Meg and I plunged into primordial Chaos—the miasma from which the Fates wove the future, making destiny out of randomness.

No one's mind should be exposed to such power. Even as a god, I feared to go too near the boundaries of Chaos.

It was the same sort of danger mortals risked when they asked to see a god's true form—a burning, terrible pyre of pure possibility. Seeing such a thing could vaporize humans, turn them into salt or dust.

I shielded Meg from the miasma as best I could, wrapping my mind around hers in a sort of embrace, but we both heard the piercing voices.

Swift white horse, they whispered. *The crossword speaker. Lands of scorching death.*

And more—lines spoken too fast, overlapping too much to make sense of. My eyes began to bake. The bees consumed my lungs. Still I held my breath. I saw a misty river in the distance—the Styx itself. The dark goddess beckoned me from the shore, inviting me to cross. I would be immortal again, if only in the way human souls were immortal after death. I could pass into the Fields of Punishment. Didn't I deserve to be punished for my many crimes?

Unfortunately, Meg felt the same way. Guilt weighed her down. She did not believe she deserved to survive.

What saved us was a simultaneous thought:

I cannot give up. Apollo/Meg needs me.

I endured for another moment, then two. At last, I could stand it no more.

I exhaled, expelling the poison of the prophecy. Gasping for fresh air, I collapsed next to Meg on the cold, wet stone. Slowly, the world returned to a solid state. The voices were gone. The cloud of ghostly bees had vanished.

I rose to my elbows. I pressed my fingers against Meg's neck. Her pulse pattered, thready and weak, but she was not dead.

"Thank the Three Fates," I murmured.

For once, I actually meant it. If Clotho, Lachesis, and Atropos had been in front of me right then, I would have kissed their warty noses.

On his island, Trophonius sighed. "Oh, well. The girl might still be insane for the rest of her life. That's some consolation."

I glared at my deceased son. "Some *consolation?*"

"Yes." He tilted his ethereal head, listening again. "You'd best hurry. You'll have to carry the girl through the underwater tunnel, so I suppose you might both drown. Or the blemmyae might kill you at the other end. But if not, I want that favor."

I laughed. After my plunge into Chaos, it wasn't a pretty sound. "You expect a *favor?* For attacking a defenseless girl?"

"For giving you your prophecy," Trophonius corrected. "It's yours, assuming you can extract it from the girl on the Throne of Memory. Now my favor, as you promised: Destroy this cave."

I had to admit . . . I'd just come back from the miasma

of pure prophecy, and I *still* didn't see that request coming. "Say what, now?"

"This location is too exposed," said Trophonius. "Your allies at the Waystation will never be able to defend it from the Triumvirate. The emperors will just keep attacking. I do not wish to be used by Commodus anymore. Better that the Oracle is destroyed."

I wondered if Zeus would agree. I had been operating under the assumption that my father wanted me to *restore* all the ancient Oracles before I could regain my godhood. I wasn't sure if destroying the Cavern of Trophonius would be an acceptable plan B. Then again, if Zeus wanted things done in a certain way, he should've given me instructions in writing. "But, Trophonius . . . what will happen to you?"

Trophonius shrugged. "Perhaps my Oracle will reappear somewhere else in a few centuries—under better circumstances, in a more secure location. Maybe that will give you time to become a nicer father."

He was definitely making it easier to consider his request. "How do I destroy this place?"

"I may have mentioned the blemmyae with explosives in the next cave? If they do not use them, you must."

"And Agamethus? Will he disappear as well?"

Dim flashes of light erupted from within the spirit's form—perhaps sadness?

"Eventually," said Trophonius. "Tell Agamethus . . . Tell him I love him, and I'm sorry this has been our fate. That's more than I ever got from you."

His swirling column of darkness began to unspool.

"Wait!" I yelled. "What about Georgina? Where did Agamethus find her? Is she my child?"

The laughter of Trophonius echoed weakly through the cavern. "Ah, yes. Consider that mystery my last gift to you, Father. I hope it drives you insane!"

Then he was gone.

For a moment, I sat on the ledge, stunned and devastated. I didn't feel physically hurt, but I realized it was possible to suffer a thousand bites in this snake pit, even if none of the vipers came near you. There were other kinds of poison.

The cave rumbled, sending ripples across the lake. I didn't know what that meant, but we could not stay here. I lifted Meg in my arms and waded into the water.

36

Mind your p's and q's
When you are arming bombs or—
SPLAT—trample jelly

I MAY HAVE MENTIONED: I am not the god of the sea.

I have many fascinating abilities. In my divine state, I am good at nearly everything I attempt. But as Lester Papadopoulos, I was *not* the master of one-armed swimming underwater while encumbered, nor could I go without oxygen any longer than a normal mortal.

I clawed my way through the passage, hugging Meg close, my lungs burning in outrage.

First you fill us with dark prophetic bees! my lungs screamed at me. *Now you force us to stay underwater! You are a horrible person!*

I could only hope Meg would survive the experience. Since she was still unconscious, I couldn't very well warn her to hold her breath. The best I could do was make our journey as brief as possible.

At least the current was in my favor. The water pushed me in the direction I wanted to go, but after six or seven seconds I was pretty sure we were going to die.

My ears throbbed. I groped blindly for handholds on the

slick rock walls. I was probably destroying my fingertips, but the cold rendered my nervous system useless. The only pain I felt was inside my chest and head.

My mind began to play tricks on me as it sought more oxygen.

You can breathe underwater! it said. *Go ahead. It'll be fine!*

I was about to inhale the river when I noticed a faint green glow above me. Air? Radiation? Limeade? Any of those sounded better than drowning in the dark. I kicked upward.

I expected to be surrounded by enemies when I surfaced, so I tried to emerge with as little gasping and flailing as possible. I made sure Meg's head was above water, then gave her a quick abdominal thrust to expel any fluid from her lungs. (That's what friends are for.)

Doing all this quietly was no easy task, but as soon as I took in our surroundings, I was glad to be such a ninja of soft gasping and flailing.

This cave was not much larger than the one we had left. Electric lamps hung from the ceiling, casting green streaks of light across the water. Along the opposite side of the cave, a boat dock was lined with boxy aluminum barges— for touring the mortally accessible areas of the subterranean river, I assumed. On the dock, three blemmyae crouched over a large object that looked like two scuba tanks duct-taped together, the cracks stuffed with wads of putty and lots of wires.

Had Leo Valdez made such a contraption, it could have been anything from a robotic butler to a jet pack. Given the blemmyae's lack of creativity, I came to the depressing conclusion that they were arming a bomb.

The only reasons they had not noticed and killed us already were 1) they were busy arguing, and 2) they were not looking in our direction. Blemmyae's peripheral vision consists entirely of their own armpits, so they tend to focus straight ahead.

One blemmyae was dressed in dark green slacks and an open green dress shirt—a park ranger's outfit, perhaps? The second wore the blue uniform of an Indiana State Trooper. The third . . . Oh, dear. She wore a very familiar-looking flowery dress.

"No, sirree!" the trooper yelled as politely as possible. "That is *not* where the red wire goes, thank you very much."

"You're welcome," said the ranger. "But I studied the diagram. It does go there, you see, because the blue wire has to go *here*. And if you'll excuse me for saying so, you're an idiot."

"You're excused," the trooper said amiably, "but only because *you're* an idiot."

"Now, boys," said the woman. Her voice was definitely that of Nanette, the woman who had welcomed us on our first day in Indianapolis. It seemed impossible that she should have regenerated from Tartarus so soon after being killed by Josephine's crossbow turret, but I put this down to my usual wretched luck. "Let's not argue. We can just call the customer-support line and—"

Meg took this opportunity to gasp, much louder than I had. We had no place to hide except underwater, and I wasn't in any shape to submerge again.

Nanette spotted us. Her chest-face twisted in a smile, her heavy orange lipstick glistening like mud in the green light.

"Well, lookee here! Visitors!"

The ranger unsheathed a hunting knife. The trooper drew his gun. Even with his species' bad depth perception, he wasn't likely to miss us at such close range.

Helpless in the water, holding a gasping, half-conscious Meg, I did the only thing I could think of. I yelled, "Don't kill us!"

Nanette chuckled. "Now, honey, why shouldn't we kill you?"

I glanced at the scuba-tank bomb. No doubt Leo Valdez would know exactly what to do in a situation like this, but the only advice I could think of was something Calypso had told me at the zoo: *Half of magic is acting like it will work. The other half is picking a superstitious mark.*

"You should not kill me," I announced, "because I know where the red wire goes!"

The blemmyae muttered among themselves. They may have been immune to charm and music, but they shared mortals' reluctance for either reading instructions or calling customer support. Their hesitation gave me a moment to slap Meg (*gently* on the cheek, simply to help her wake up).

She spluttered and twitched, which was an improvement over being passed out cold. I scanned the cave for possible escape routes. To our right, the river wound through a low-ceilinged tunnel. I was not anxious to swim through these caves any longer. To our left, at the edge of the boat dock, a ramp with railings led upward. That would be the exit to the surface, I decided.

Unfortunately, standing in our way were three super-strong humanoids with an explosive device.

The blemmyae concluded their conference.

Nanette faced me again. "Very well! Please tell us where the red wire goes. Then we will kill you as painlessly as possible, and we can all go home happy."

"A generous offer," I said. "But I really need to *show* you. It's too hard to explain from way over here. Permission to come ashore?"

The trooper lowered his gun. A bushy mustache covered the width of his lowest rib. "Well, he asked permission. That was polite."

"Hmm." Nanette stroked her chin, simultaneously scratching her belly. "Permission granted."

Joining three enemies on the dock was only marginally better than freezing in the river, but I was glad to get Meg out of the water.

"Thank you," I told the blemmyae after they hauled us up.

"You're welcome," all three said in unison.

"Just let me put my friend down. . . ." I stumbled toward the ramp, wondering if I could make a break for it.

"That's far enough," Nanette warned, "please and thank you."

There were no ancient Greek words for *I hate you, scary clown-woman*, but I muttered a close approximation under my breath. I propped Meg against the wall. "Can you hear me?" I whispered.

Her lips were the color of blueberries. Her teeth chattered. Her eyes rolled back in her head, showing the bloodshot whites of her eyes.

"Meg, please," I said. "I will distract the blemmyae, but you need to get out of here. Can you walk? Crawl? Anything?"

"Hum-um-um." Meg shivered and gasped. "Shumma-shumma."

This was no language that I knew, but I inferred that Meg would not be going anywhere on her own. I would have to do more than just distract the blemmyae.

"All righty, then!" Nanette said. "Please show us what you know, so we can bring down this cave on top of you!"

I forced a smile. "Of course. Now, let's see. . . ."

I knelt next to the device. It was sadly uncomplicated. There were, in fact, only two wires and two receptors, both color-coded blue and red.

I glanced up. "Ah. Quick question. I am aware that blemmyae are tone-deaf, but—"

"That's not true!" The ranger looked offended. "I don't even know what that means!"

The other two bowed emphatically—the blemmyae equivalent of nodding.

"I enjoy all tones," Nanette agreed.

"Explosions," the trooper said. "Gunshots. Car engines. All tones are good."

"I stand corrected," I said. "But my question was . . . could it be possible that your species is also color-blind?"

They looked dumbfounded. I examined Nanette's makeup, dress, and shoes once again, and it became clear to me why so many blemmyae preferred to disguise themselves in mortal uniforms. *Of course* they were color-blind.

For the record, I am *not* implying that color blindness or tone deafness indicate any lack of creativity or intelligence. Far from it! Some of my favorite creative people, from Mark Twain to Mister Rogers to William Butler Yeats, had these conditions.

In blemmyae, however, sensory limitations and dull thinking seemed to be part of the same depressing package.

"Forget it," I said. "Let's get started. Nanette, would you please pick up the red wire?"

"Well, since you asked so nicely." Nanette leaned in and picked the blue wire.

"The other red wire," I advised.

"Of course. I knew that!"

She took the red wire.

"Now attach it to the red—to *this* receptor." I pointed.

Nanette did as I instructed.

"There you are!" I said.

Clearly still perplexed, the blemmyae stared at the device.

The trooper said, "But there's another wire."

"Yes," I said patiently. "It goes to the second receptor. However"—I grabbed Nanette's hand before she could blow us all up—"once you connect it, you will most likely activate the bomb. Do you see this small screen here? I am no Hephaestus, but I assume this is the timer. Do you happen to know what the default countdown is?"

The trooper and ranger conferred in the guttural,

monotone language of the blemmyae—which sounded like two busted power sanders speaking in Morse code. I glanced over at Meg, who was right where I'd left her, still shivering and muttering *shumma-shumma* under her breath.

The ranger smiled in a self-satisfied way. "Well, sir. Since I'm the only one who read the diagram, I've decided I can safely give you the answer. The default time is five seconds."

"Ah." A few phantom bees crawled up my throat. "So once you connect the wire, there will be virtually no time to exit the cave before the bomb goes off."

"Exactly!" Nanette beamed. "The emperor was very clear. If Apollo and the child make it out of the Oracle chamber, kill them and bring down the cavern in a mighty explosion!"

The trooper frowned. "No, he said to kill them *with* the mighty explosion."

"No, sirree," said the ranger. "He said to use the mighty explosion only if we had to. We could kill these two if they appeared, but if they didn't . . ." He scratched his shoulder hair. "I'm confused now. What was the bomb for?"

I said a silent prayer of thanks that Commodus had sent blemmyae and not Germani to do this job. Of course, that probably meant the Germani were fighting my friends at the Waystation right now, but I could only handle one earth-shattering crisis at a time.

"Friends," I said. "Frenemies, blemmyae. My point is this: if you activate the bomb, the three of you will die, too. Are you prepared for that?"

Nanette's smile melted. "Oh. Hmm . . ."

"I've got it!" The ranger wagged his finger at me enthusiastically. "Why don't *you* connect the wire after the three of us leave?"

"Don't be silly," said the trooper. "He won't kill himself and the girl just because we ask him to." He gave me a cautiously hopeful glance. "Will you?"

"It doesn't matter," Nanette chided. "The emperor told *us* to kill Apollo and the girl. Not to have them do it themselves."

The others mumbled agreement. Following orders to the letter was everything, of course.

"I have an idea!" I said, when in fact I did not.

I had been hoping to come up with some clever plan to overpower the blemmyae and get Meg out of there. So far, no clever plan had materialized. There was also the matter of my promise to Trophonius. I had sworn to destroy his Oracle. I preferred to do that without destroying myself.

The blemmyae waited politely for me to continue. I tried to channel some of Calypso's bravado. (Oh, gods, please never tell her I drew on her for inspiration.)

"It's true you have to kill us yourselves," I began. "And I do understand! But I have a solution that will accomplish all your goals: a mighty explosion, destroying the Oracle, killing us, and getting out alive."

Nanette nodded. "That last one is a bonus, for sure."

"There's an underwater tunnel just here. . . ." I explained how Meg and I had swum through from Trophonius's chamber. "To effectively destroy the Oracle room, you can't set the bomb off here. Someone would have to swim with the device deep inside the tunnel, activate the timer, and swim back out. Now, I am not strong enough, but a blemmyae could do this easily."

The trooper frowned. "But five seconds . . . is that enough time?"

"Ah," I said, "but it's a well-known fact that underwater, timers take twice as long, so you'd actually have ten seconds."

Nanette blinked. "Are you sure about that?"

The ranger elbowed her. "He just *said* it was a well-known fact. Don't be impolite!"

The trooper scratched his mustache with the barrel of his gun, which was probably against department safety protocols. "I'm still not sure why we have to destroy the Oracle. Why can't we just kill you two, say . . . with this gun . . . and leave the Oracle alone?"

I sighed. "If only we could! But, my friend, it's not safe. This girl and I got in and got out with our prophecy, didn't we? That means other trespassers can, too. Surely that's what the emperor meant about the mighty explosion. You don't want to have to come back here with your bomb every time someone breaks in, do you?"

The trooper looked horrified. "Goodness, no!"

"And leaving the Oracle intact, in this place where mortals obviously have guided tours . . . well, that's a safety hazard! Not closing off the Oracle's cave would be *very* discourteous of us."

"Mmmm." All three blemmyae nodded/bowed earnestly.

"But," Nanette said, "if you're trying to trick us somehow . . . and I apologize for raising that possibility . . ."

"No, no," I said. "I fully understand. How about this: Go

set the bomb. If you come back safely and the cave blows up on schedule, then you can do us the courtesy of killing us quickly and painlessly. If something goes wrong—"

"Then we can rip your limbs off!" the trooper suggested.

"And trample your bodies into jelly!" added the ranger.

"That's a marvelous idea. Thank you!"

I tried to keep my queasiness under control. "You're most welcome."

Nanette studied the bomb, perhaps sensing that something was still off about my plan. Thank the gods, she either didn't see it or was too polite to mention her reservations.

"Well," she said at last, "in that case, I'll be back!"

She scooped up the tanks and leaped into the water, which gave me a few luxurious seconds to come up with a plan to avoid getting trampled into jelly. At last, things were looking up!

37

Your favorite fruit?

I hope you didn't say grapes

Or apples, or figs

POOR NANETTE.

I wonder what went through her mind when she realized that a five-second timer underwater still lasted exactly five seconds. As the device exploded, I imagine she bubbled out one last vile curse like, *Oh, gosh darn it.*

I might have felt sorry for her had she not been planning to kill me.

The cave shook. Chunks of wet stalactite dropped into the lake and whanged against the hulls of the barges. A burst of air erupted from the middle of the lake, upheaving the dock and filling the cavern with the scent of tangerine lipstick.

The trooper and the ranger frowned at me. "You blew up Nanette. That was not polite."

"Hold on!" I yelped. "She's probably still swimming back. It's a long tunnel."

This bought me another three or four seconds, during which a clever escape plan still did not present itself. At the very least, I hoped Nanette's death had not been in vain. I hoped the explosion had destroyed the Cave of the Oracle as Trophonius wished, but I could not be certain.

Meg was still only half-conscious, muttering and shivering. I had to get her back to the Waystation and set her on the Throne of Memory quickly, but two blemmyae still stood in my way. My hands were too numb to be any good with a bow or a ukulele. I wished I had some other weapon—even a magical Brazilian handkerchief that I could wave in my enemies' faces! Oh, if only a surge of divine strength would course through my body!

At last the ranger sighed. "All right, Apollo. Would you prefer we stomp or dismember you first? It's only right you get to choose."

"That's very polite," I agreed. Then I gasped. "Oh, my gods! Look over there!"

You must forgive me. I realize that this method of distraction is the oldest trick in the book. In fact, it is a trick so old it predates papyrus scrolls and was first recorded on clay tablets in Mesopotamia. But the blemmyae fell for it.

They were slow at "looking over there." They could not glance. They could not turn their heads without turning their entire bodies, so they executed a full one-hundred-and-eighty-degree waddle.

I had no follow-up trick in mind. I simply knew I had to save Meg and get out of there. Then an aftershock rattled the cavern, unbalancing the blemmyae, and I took advantage. I kicked the ranger into the lake. At precisely the same moment, a portion of the ceiling peeled loose and fell on top of said ranger like a hailstorm of major appliances. The ranger disappeared under churning foam.

I could only stare in amazement. I was fairly sure *I* hadn't caused the ceiling to crack and collapse. Blind luck? Or perhaps the spirit of Trophonius had granted me one last grudging favor for destroying his cave. Crushing someone under a rain of rocks did seem like the sort of favor he would grant.

The trooper missed the whole thing. He turned back to me, a puzzled look on his chest-face. "I don't see any . . . Wait. Where did my friend go?"

"Hmm?" I asked. "What friend?"

His impressive mustache twitched. "Eduardo. The ranger."

I feigned confusion. "A ranger? Here?"

"Yes, he was just here."

"I'm sure I don't know."

The cavern shuddered once again. Sadly, no more obliging chunks of ceiling broke free to crush my last enemy.

"Well," the trooper said, "maybe he had to leave. You'll excuse me if I have to kill you by myself now. Orders."

"Oh, yes, but first . . ."

The trooper was not to be deterred any longer. He grabbed my arm, crushing my ulna and radius together. I screamed. My knees buckled.

"Let the girl go," I whimpered through the pain. "Kill me and let her go."

I surprised myself. These were not the last words I had planned. In the event of my death, I'd been hoping to have time to compose a ballad of my glorious deeds—a very *long* ballad. Yet here I was, at the end of my life, pleading not for myself, but for Meg McCaffrey.

I'd love to take credit for what happened next. I'd like to think my noble gesture of self-sacrifice proved my worthiness and summoned our saviors from the ethereal plane. More likely, though, they were already in the area, searching for Meg, and heard my scream of agony.

With a bloodcurdling battle cry, three karpoi hurtled down the tunnel and flew at the trooper, landing on his face.

The trooper staggered across the dock, the three peach spirits howling, clawing, and biting like a school of winged, fruit-flavored piranhas . . . which, in retrospect, I suppose does not make them sound very piranha-like.

"Please get off!" the trooper wailed. "Please and thank you!"

The karpoi were not concerned with good manners. After twenty more seconds of savage peachery, the trooper was reduced to a pile of monster ash, tattered fabric, and mustache whiskers.

The middle karpos spit out something that might have once been the officer's handgun. He flapped his leafy wings. I deduced that he was our usual friend, the one known as Peaches, because his eyes gleamed a little more viciously, and his diaper sagged a little more dangerously.

I cradled my broken arm. "Thank you, Peaches! I don't know how I can ever—"

He ignored me and flew to Meg's side. He wailed and stroked her hair.

The other two karpoi studied me with a hungry gleam in their eyes.

"Peaches?" I whimpered. "Could you tell them I'm a friend? Please?"

Peaches howled inconsolably. He scraped dirt and rubble around Meg's legs, the way one might plant a sapling.

"Peaches!" I called again. "I can help her, but I need to get her back to the Waystation. The Throne of Memory—"

Nausea made the world tilt and twist. My vision went green.

Once I could focus again, I found Peaches and the other two karpoi standing in a line, all staring at me.

"Peaches?" demanded Peaches.

"Yes," I groaned. "We need to get her to Indianapolis quickly. If you and your friends . . . Um, I don't think we've been properly introduced. I'm Apollo."

Peaches pointed to his friend on the right. "Peaches." Then to the baby demon on his left. "Peaches."

"I see." I tried to think. Agony spiked up my arm into my jaw. "Now, listen, I—I have a car. A red Mercedes, nearby. If I can get to it, I can drive Meg to—to . . ."

I looked down at my broken forearm. It was turning some beautiful shades of purple and orange, like an Aegean sunset. I realized I wasn't going to be driving anywhere.

My mind began sinking into a sea of pain under that lovely sunset.

"Be with you in a minute," I muttered.

Then I passed out.

38

Waystation damaged
Commodus will pay for this
And I don't take cash

I REMEMBER VERY LITTLE about the trip back.

Somehow, Peaches and two his friends carried Meg and me out of the cave and to the Mercedes. More disturbingly, the three karpoi somehow drove us to Indianapolis while Meg sat muttering and shivering in the passenger seat and I lay groaning in the back.

Don't ask me how three karpoi combined forces to drive an automobile. I can't tell you which of them used the wheel, the brake, or the gas pedal. It's not the sort of behavior you expect from edible fruit.

All I know is that by the time I regained more or less full consciousness, we had reached the city limits.

My broken forearm was wrapped in leaves glued together with sap. I had no memory of how this came to pass, but the arm felt better—still sore, but not excruciating. I counted myself lucky the peach spirits had not tried to plant me and water me.

I managed to sit upright just as the peach spirits curbed the Mercedes on Capital Street. Ahead of us, police cars

blocked the road. Large red signs on sawhorses announced:
GAS LEAK EMERGENCY. THANK YOU FOR YOUR PATIENCE!

A gas leak. Leo Valdez had been right again. Assuming
he was still alive, he'd be insufferable about this for weeks.

A few blocks beyond the barricades, a column of
black smoke rose from the approximate location of the
Waystation. My heart fractured more painfully than my
arm. I glanced at the Mercedes's dashboard clock. We had
been gone less than four hours. It felt like a lifetime—a
godly lifetime.

I scanned the sky. I saw no reassuring bronze dragon flying overhead, no helpful griffins defending their nest. If the
Waystation had fallen . . . No, I had to think positive. I
wouldn't let my fears attract any more prophetic bee swarms
today.

"Peaches," I said. "I need you—"

I turned my gaze forward and nearly jumped through
the car ceiling.

Peaches and his two friends were staring at me, their
chins in a line atop the back of the driver's seat like See-
No-Evil, Peel-No-Evil, and Eat-No-Evil.

"Ah . . . yes. Hi," I said. "Please, I need you to stay with
Meg. Protect her at all costs."

Peaches Prime bared his razor-sharp teeth and snarled,
"Peaches."

I took this as agreement.

"I have to check on our friends at the Waystation," I
said. "If I don't come back . . ." The words stuck in my
throat. ". . . then you'll have to search for the Throne of

Memory. Getting Meg into that chair is the only way to heal her mind."

I stared at the three pairs of glowing green eyes. I couldn't tell if the karpoi understood what I was saying, and I didn't know how they could possibly follow my instructions. If the battle was over and the Throne of Memory had been taken or destroyed . . . No. That was bee-pollen thinking!

"Just . . . take care of her," I pleaded.

I stepped out of the car and valiantly threw up on the sidewalk. Pink emojis danced across my eyes. I hobbled down the street, my arm covered in sap and leaves, my damp clothes smelling of bat guano and snake excrement. It was not my most glorious charge into battle.

No one stopped me at the barricades. The officers on duty (regular mortals, I guessed) looked more interested in their smartphone screens than in the smoke rising behind them. Perhaps the Mist concealed the true situation. Perhaps they figured if a ragged street person wanted to stumble toward a gas-leak emergency, they weren't going to stop him. Or perhaps they were engrossed in an epic *Pokémon Go* gym battle.

A block inside the cordoned zone, I saw the first burning bulldozer. I suspected it had driven over a land mine specially modified by Leo Valdez, since along with being half-demolished and in flames it was also splattered with smiley-face stickers and gobs of whipped cream.

I hobbled faster. I spotted more disabled bulldozers, scattered rubble, totaled cars, and piles of monster dust, but no bodies. That raised my spirits a little. Just around the corner from the Union Station roundabout, I heard clanging swords ahead—then a gunshot and something that sounded like thunder.

I had never been so happy to hear a battle in progress. It meant not everyone was dead.

I ran. My weary legs screamed in protest. Every time my shoes hit the pavement, a jarring pain shot up my forearm.

I turned the corner and found myself in combat. Charging toward me with murder in his eyes was a demigod warrior—some teenage boy I'd never seen, wearing Roman-style armor over his street clothes. Fortunately, he'd already been badly beaten up. His eyes were almost swollen shut. His bronze chest plate was dented like a metal roof after a hailstorm. He could barely hold his sword. I wasn't in much better shape, but I was running on anger and desperation. I managed to unsling my ukulele and slam the demigod in the face.

He crumpled at my feet.

I was feeling pretty proud of my heroic act until I looked up. In the middle of the roundabout, on top of the fountain and surrounded by Cyclopes, my favorite graduate accounting student, Olujime, stood like an ancient war god, swinging a bronze weapon that resembled a double-wide hockey stick. Each sweep sent crackling tendrils of electricity through his enemies. Every hit disintegrated a Cyclops.

I liked Jamie even more now. I'd never had much affection for Cyclopes. Still . . . something was strange about his use of lightning. I could always recognize the power of Zeus in action. I'd been zapped by his bolts often enough.

Jamie's electricity was different—a more humid scent of ozone, a darker red hue to the flashes. I wished I could ask him about that, but he looked a little busy.

Smaller fights raged here and there across the round-about. The Waystation's defenders appeared to have the upper hand. Hunter Kowalski leaped from foe to foe, shooting down blemmyae, wolf-headed warriors, and wild centaurs with ease. She had an uncanny ability to fire on the move, avoid counterstrikes, and target her victims' kneecaps. As an archer, I was impressed. If I'd still had my godly powers, I would have blessed her with fabulous prizes like a magic quiver and possibly a signed copy of my greatest-hits anthology on classic vinyl.

In the hotel drive-through, Sssssarah the dracaena sat propped against a mailbox, her snake-tail legs curled around her, her neck swollen to the size of a basketball. I ran to her aid, afraid she might be wounded. Then I realized the lump in her throat was in the shape of a Gallic war helmet. Her chest and belly were also quite bloated.

She smiled at me lazily. "'Sssssup?"

"Sssssarah," I said, "did you swallow a Germanus whole?"

"No." She belched. The smell was definitely barbarian, with a hint of clove. "Well, perhapsssss."

"Where are the others?" I ducked as a silver arrow flew over my head, shattering the windshield of a nearby Subaru. "Where's Commodus?"

Sssssarah pointed toward the Waystation. "In there, I think. He killed a path into the building."

She didn't sound too concerned about this, probably

because she was sated and sleepy. The pillar of dark smoke I'd noticed earlier was pouring from a hole in the roof of the Waystation. Even more distressing, lying across the green shingles like an insect part stuck on flypaper was the detached bronze wing of a dragon.

Rage boiled inside me. Whether the sun chariot or Festus or a school bus, *no one* messes with my ride.

The main doors of the Union Station building had been blown wide open. I charged inside past piles of monster dust and bricks, burning pieces of furniture, and a centaur hanging upside down, kicking and whinnying in a net trap.

In one stairwell, a wounded Hunter of Artemis groaned in pain as a comrade bound her bleeding leg. A few feet farther on, a demigod I didn't recognize lay unmoving on the floor. I knelt next to him—a boy of about sixteen, *my* mortal age. I felt no pulse. I didn't know whose side he had fought on, but that didn't matter. Either way, his death was a terrible waste. I had begun to think that perhaps demigod lives were not as disposable as we gods liked to believe.

I ran through more corridors, trusting the Waystation to send me in the right direction. I burst into the library where I'd sat last night. The scene within hit me like the explosion from one of Britomartis's bouncing mines.

Lying across the table was the body of a griffin. With a sob of horror, I rushed to her side. Heloise's left wing was folded across her body like a shroud. Her head lay bent at an unnatural angle. The floor around her was piled with broken weapons, dented armor, and monster dust. She had died fighting off a host of enemies . . . but she had died.

My eyes burned. I cradled her head, breathing in the clean smell of hay and molting feathers. "Oh, Heloise. You saved me. Why couldn't I save you?"

Where was her mate, Abelard? Was their egg safe? I wasn't sure which thought was more terrible: the whole family of griffins dead, or the father and the griffin chick forced to live with the devastating loss of Heloise.

I kissed her beak. Proper grieving would have to wait. Other friends might still be in need of help.

With newfound energy, I bounded up a staircase two steps at a time.

I stormed through a set of doors into the main hall.

The scene was eerily calm. Smoke flooded out the gaping hole of the roof, billowing from the loft where a smoldering bulldozer chassis was, inexplicably, lodged nose-down. Heloise and Abelard's nest appeared to be intact, but there were no signs of the male griffin or the egg. In Josephine's workshop area, sprawled across the floor, lay the severed head and neck of Festus, his ruby eyes dark and lifeless. The rest of his body was nowhere to be seen.

Sofas had been smashed and overturned. Kitchen appliances were riddled with bullet holes. The scope of damage was heartbreaking.

But the most serious problem was the standoff around the dining table.

On the side nearest me stood Josephine, Calypso, Lityerses, and Thalia Grace. Thalia had her bow drawn. Lit brandished his sword. Calypso raised her bare hands, martial arts–style, and Josephine hefted her submachine gun, Little Bertha.

On the far side of the table stood Commodus himself, smiling brilliantly despite a bleeding diagonal cut across his face. Imperial gold armor gleamed over his purple tunic. He held his blade, a gold *spatha*, casually at his side.

To either side of him stood a Germanus bodyguard. The barbarian on the right had his arm clamped around Emmie's neck, his other hand pressing a pistol crossbow against Emmie's head. Georgina stood with her mother, Emmie hugging the little girl tightly to her chest. Alas, the little girl seemed to have fully recovered her wits only to be faced with this fresh horror.

To Commodus's left, a second Germanus held Leo Valdez in a similar hostage stance.

I clenched my fists. "Villainy! Commodus, let them go!"

"Hello, Lester!" Commodus beamed. "You're just in time for the fun!"

39

During this standoff
No flash photography, please
Oops. My bad. Ha-ha

THALIA'S FINGERS clenched her bowstring. A bead of sweat, silvery as moonwater, traced the side of her ear. "Say the word," she told me, "and I will bore a hole between this moron emperor's eyes."

A tempting offer, but I knew it was bravado. Thalia was just as terrified as I was of losing Leo and Emmie . . . and especially poor Georgie, who'd been through so much. I doubted any of our weapons could kill an immortal like Commodus, much less him and two guards. No matter how quickly we attacked, we would not be able to save our friends.

Josephine shifted her grip on the submachine gun. Her coveralls were splattered with goo, dust, and blood. Her short silver hair glistened with perspiration.

"It's gonna be okay, baby," she muttered. "Stay calm." I wasn't sure if she was talking to Emmie or Georgie or herself.

Next to her, Calypso's hands were frozen in midair as if she were standing in front of her loom, considering what to weave. Her eyes were fixed on Leo. She shook her head ever so slightly, perhaps telling him, *Don't be an idiot.* (She told him that a lot.)

Lityerses stood next to me. His leg wound had started to bleed again, soaking through the bandages. His hair and clothes were scorched as if he'd run through a gauntlet of flamethrowers, leaving his Cornhuskers shirt looking like the surface of a burnt marshmallow. Only the word CORN was still visible.

Judging from the bloody edge of his sword, I guessed he was responsible for the ghastly new slash across Commodus's face.

"No good way to do this," Lit muttered to me. "Somebody's gonna die."

"No," I said. "Thalia, lower your bow."

"Excuse me?"

"Josephine, the gun, too. Please."

Commodus chuckled. "Yes, you all should listen to Lester! And Calypso, dear, if you try to summon one of those wind spirits again, I *will* kill your little friend here."

I glanced at the sorceress. "You summoned a spirit?"

She nodded, distracted, shaken. "A small one."

"But the larger issue," Leo called out, "is that I am *not* little. We are *not* going to make *say hello to my little friend* a thing." He raised his palms, despite his captor tightening his hold around the demigod's neck. "Besides, guys, it's okay. I've got everything under control."

"Leo," I said evenly, "a seven-foot-tall barbarian is holding a crossbow against the side of your head."

"Yeah, I know," he said. "It's all part of the plan!"

On the word *plan*, he winked at me in an exaggerated

way. Either Leo really *did* have a plan (unlikely, since in the weeks I'd known him he mostly relied on bluffs, jokes, and improvisation) or he was expecting *me* to have a plan. That was depressingly likely. As I may have mentioned, people often made that mistake. Just because I'm a god does not mean you should look to me for answers!

Commodus lifted two fingers. "Albatrix, if the demigod speaks again, you have my permission to shoot him."

The barbarian grunted assent. Leo clamped his mouth shut. I could see in his eyes that even under pain of death, he was having trouble holding back a witty retort.

"Now!" Commodus said. "As we were discussing before Lester got here, I require the Throne of Mnemosyne. Where is it?"

Thank the gods. . . . The throne was still hidden, which meant Meg could still use it to heal her mind. This knowledge steeled my resolve.

"Are you telling me," I asked, "that your great army surrounded this place, invaded, and couldn't even find a chair? Is this all you have left—a couple of witless Germani and some hostages? What sort of emperor are you? Now, your father, Marcus Aurelius, *there* was an emperor."

His expression soured. His eyes darkened. I recalled a time in Commodus's campaign tent when a servant carelessly spilled wine on my friend's robes. Commodus had that same dark look in his eyes as he beat the boy almost to death with a lead goblet. Back then, as a god, I found the incident only mildly distasteful. Now I knew something about being on the receiving end of Commodus's cruelty.

"I'm not finished, *Lester*," he snarled. "I'll admit this

cursed building was more trouble than I expected. I blame my former prefect Alaric. He was *woefully* unprepared. I had to kill him."

"Shocking," muttered Lityerses.

"But most of my forces are merely lost," Commodus said. "They'll be back."

"Lost?" I looked at Josephine. "Where did they go?"

Her eyes stayed focused on Emmie and Georgie, but she seemed to take pride in answering. "From what the Waystation is telling me," she said, "about half of his monstrous troops fell into a giant chute marked LAUNDRY. The rest ended up in the furnace room. Nobody ever comes back from the furnace room."

"No matter!" Commodus snapped.

"And his mercenaries," Josephine continued, "wound up at the Indiana Convention Center. Right now, they're trying to navigate their way through the trade-show floor of the Home and Garden Expo."

"Soldiers are expendable!" Commodus shrieked. Blood dripped down his new facial wound, speckling his armor and robes. "Your friends here cannot be so easily replaced. Neither can the Throne of Memory. So let's make a deal! I will take the throne. I will kill the girl and Lester, and raze this building to the ground. That's what the prophecy said for me to do, and I never argue with Oracles! In exchange, the rest of you can go free. I don't need you."

"Jo." Emmie said her name like an order.

Perhaps she meant: *You cannot let him win.* Or: *You cannot let Georgina die.* Whatever it was, in Emmie's face I saw that same disregard for her own mortal life that she'd had as a young princess, flinging herself off the cliff. She didn't mind death, as long as it was on her terms. The determined light in her eyes had not dimmed in three thousand years.

Light . . .

A shiver rolled down my back. I remembered something Marcus Aurelius used to tell his son, a quote that later became famous in his *Meditations* book: *Think of yourself as dead. You have lived your life. Now, take what's left and live it properly. What doesn't transmit light creates its own darkness.*

Commodus *hated* that piece of advice. He found it suffocating, self-righteous, impossible. What was *proper?* Commodus intended to live forever. He would drive away the darkness with the roar of crowds and the glitter of spectacle.

But he generated no light.

Not like the Waystation. Marcus Aurelius would have approved of this place. Emmie and Josephine lived properly with what time they had left, creating light for everyone who came here. No wonder Commodus hated them. No wonder he was so bent on destroying this threat to his power.

And Apollo, above all, was the god of light.

"Commodus." I drew myself up to my full, not-very-impressive height. "This is the only deal. You will let your hostages go. You will leave here empty-handed and never return."

The emperor laughed. "That would sound more intimidating coming from a god, not a zitty adolescent."

His Germani were well-trained to stay impassive, but

they betrayed scornful smirks. They didn't fear me. Right now, that was fine.

"I am still Apollo." I spread my arms. "Last chance to leave of your own accord."

I detected a flicker of doubt in the emperor's eyes. "What will you do—kill me? Unlike you, *Lester*, I am immortal. I cannot die."

"I don't need to kill you." I stepped forward to the edge of the dining table. "Look at me closely. Don't you recognize my divine nature, old friend?"

Commodus hissed. "I recognize the betrayer who strangled me in my bath. I recognize the so-called *god* who promised me blessings and then deserted me!" His voice frayed with pain, which he tried to conceal behind an arrogant sneer. "All I see is a flabby teenager with a bad complexion. You also need a haircut."

"My friends," I told the others, "I want you to avert your eyes. I am about to reveal my true godly form."

Not being fools, Leo and Emmie shut their eyes tight. Emmie covered Georgina's face with her hand. I hoped my friends on my side of the dining table would also listen. I had to believe that they trusted me, despite my failings, despite the way I looked.

Commodus scoffed. "You're damp and speckled with bat poop, Lester. You're a pathetic child who has been dragged through the darkness. That darkness is still in your mind. I see the fear in your eyes. This *is* your true form, Apollo! You're a fraud!"

Apollo. He had called me by my name.

I saw the terror he was trying to hide, and also his sense of awe. I remembered what Trophonius told me: Commodus would send servants into the caverns for answers, but he would never go himself. As much as he needed the Dark Oracle, he feared what it might show him, which of his deepest fears that bee swarm might feed on.

I had survived a journey he would never dare take.

"Behold," I said.

Commodus and his men could have looked away. They didn't. In their pride and contempt, they accepted my challenge.

My body superheated, every particle igniting in a chain reaction. Like the world's most powerful flashbulb, I blasted the room with radiance. I became pure light.

It lasted only a microsecond. Then the screaming began. The Germani reeled backward, their crossbows firing wildly. One bolt zipped past Leo's head and embedded itself in a sofa. The other bolt shattered against the floor, splinters skittering across the tiles.

Melodramatic to the end, Commodus pressed his palms against his eye sockets and screamed, "MY EYES!"

My strength faded. I grabbed the table to keep from falling.

"It's safe," I told my friends.

Leo broke from his captor. He lunged toward Emmie and Georgina, and the three of them scrambled away as Commodus and his men, now quite blind, stumbled and howled, steam pouring from their eye sockets.

Where the captors and hostages had stood, silhouettes were burned across the tile floor. The details on the brick walls now seemed in super–high definition. The nearest sofa covers, once dark red, were now pink. Commodus's purple robes had been bleached a weak shade of mauve.

I turned to my friends. Their clothes had also lightened by several shades. The fronts of their hair had been frosted with highlights, but they had all, wisely, kept their eyes shut.

Thalia studied me in amazement. "What just happened? Why are you toasted?"

I looked down. True enough, my skin was now the color of maple bark. My leaf-and-sap cast had burned away, leaving my arm fully healed. I thought I looked quite nice this way, though I hoped I could become a god again before I discovered what sort of horrible skin cancers I'd just given myself. Belatedly, I realized how much danger I'd been in. I had actually managed to reveal my true divine form. I had become pure light. Stupid Apollo! Amazing, wonderful, stupid Apollo! This mortal body was not meant for channeling such power. I was fortunate I hadn't burned up instantly like an antique flashbulb.

Commodus wailed. He grabbed the nearest thing he could find, which happened to be one of his Germani, and lifted the blind barbarian over his head. "I will destroy you all!"

He threw his barbarian toward the sound of Thalia's voice. Since we could all see, we scattered easily and avoided becoming bowling pins. The Germanus hit the opposite wall with such force, he broke into a starburst of yellow powder and left a beautiful abstract expressionist statement across the bricks.

"I do not need eyes to kill you!" Commodus slashed

upward with his sword, taking a chunk out of the dining table.

"Commodus," I warned, "you will leave this city and never return, or I will take more than your sight."

He charged toward me. I sidestepped. Thalia let loose an arrow, but Commodus was moving too fast. The missile hit the second Germanus, who grunted in surprise, fell to his knees, and crumbled to powder.

Commodus tripped over a chair. He face-planted on the living room rug. Let me be clear: it's *never* okay to take delight in the struggles of someone who can't see, but in this rare instance, I couldn't help myself. If anyone deserved to fall on his face, it was Emperor Commodus.

"You will leave," I told him again. "You will not return. Your reign in Indianapolis is over."

"It's Commodianapolis!" He struggled to his feet. His armor sported some new skid marks. The slash across his face was not getting any prettier. A little figurine made of pipe cleaners—maybe something Georgina had made—clung to the emperor's shaggy beard like a mountain climber.

"You haven't won anything, Apollo," he growled. "You have no idea what's being prepared for your friends in the east and the west! They will die. All of them!"

Leo Valdez sighed. "All right, guys. This has been fun, but I'm gonna melt his face now, 'kay?"

"Wait," said Lityerses.

The swordsman advanced on his former master. "Commodus, go while you still can."

"I *made* you, boy," said the emperor. "I saved you from obscurity. I was a second father to you. I gave you purpose!"

"A second father even worse than the first," Lit said. "And I've found a new purpose."

Commodus charged, swinging his sword wildly.

Lit parried. He stepped toward Josephine's workshop. "Over here, New Hercules."

Commodus took the bait, rushing toward Lit's voice.

Lit ducked. He blade-slapped the emperor's butt. "Wrong way, sire."

The emperor stumbled into Josephine's welding station, then backed into a circular saw, which, fortunately for him, was not running at the time.

Lityerses positioned himself at the base of the giant rose window. I realized his plan as he yelled, "Over here, Commode!"

The emperor howled and charged. Lit stepped out of the way. Commodus barreled straight toward the window. He might have been able to stop himself, but at the last second, Calypso flicked her hands. A gust of wind carried Commodus forward. The New Hercules, the god-emperor of Rome, shattered the glass at the six o'clock mark and tumbled into the void.

40

Shakespeare, don't bring that
Iambic pentameter
Up in my face, yo

WE GATHERED at the window and peered down. The emperor was nowhere to be seen. Some of our friends stood in the roundabout below, gazing up at us with confused expressions.

"A little warning, perhaps?" Jamie called.

He had run out of enemies to electrocute. He and Hunter Kowalski now stood unscathed in the middle of a mosaic of fallen glass shards.

"Where's Commodus?" I asked.

Hunter shrugged. "We didn't see him."

"What do you mean?" I demanded. "He literally just flew out this window."

"No," Leo corrected. "He *Lityerses-ly* flew out the window. Am I right? Those were some sweet moves, man."

Lit nodded. "Thanks."

The two bumped fists as if they hadn't spent the last few days talking about how much they wanted to kill each other. They would have made fine Olympian gods.

"Well," Thalia said. Her new gray highlights from my solar blast looked quite fetching. "I guess we should do a sweep of the neighborhood. If Commodus is still out there . . ." She gazed down South Illinois Street. "Wait, is that *Meg?*"

Rounding the corner were three karpoi, holding Meg McCaffrey aloft as if she were bodysurfing (or peach-surfing). I almost jumped out the window to get to her. Then I remembered I could not fly.

"The Throne of Memory," I told Emmie. "We need it now!"

We met the karpoi in the building's front foyer. One of the Peacheses had retrieved the Arrow of Dodona from under the Mercedes's driver's seat and now carried it in his teeth like a pirate's accessory. He offered it to me. I wasn't sure whether to thank him or curse him, but I slipped the arrow back into my quiver for safekeeping.

Josephine and Leo rushed in from a side room, carrying between them my old backpack—the Throne of Memory. They placed it in the center of a still-smoldering Persian rug.

The peach babies carefully lowered Meg into the seat.

"Calypso," I said. "Notepad?"

"Got it!" She brandished her small legal tablet and pencil. I decided she would make an excellent high school student after all. She actually came to class prepared!

I knelt next to Meg. Her skin was too blue, her breath too ragged. I placed my hands on the sides of her face and checked her eyes. Her pupils were pinpoints. Her conscious-ness seemed to be withdrawing, getting smaller and smaller.

"Stay with me, Meg," I pleaded. "You're among friends now. You're in the Throne of Mnemosyne. Speak your prophecy!"

Meg lurched upright. Her hands gripped the sides of the

chair as if a strong electric current had taken hold of her.

We all backed away, forming a rough circle around her as dark smoke spewed from her mouth and encircled her legs.

When she spoke, it was thankfully not in Trophonius's voice—just a deep neutral monotone worthy of Delphi itself:

> *The words that memory wrought are set to fire,*
> *Ere new moon rises o'er the Devil's Mount.*
> *The changeling lord shall face a challenge dire,*
> *Till bodies fill the Tiber beyond count.*

"Oh, no," I muttered. "No, no, no."

"What?" Leo demanded.

I glanced at Calypso, who was scribbling furiously. "We're going to need a bigger notepad."

"What do you mean?" Josephine asked. "Surely the prophecy's done—"

Meg gasped and continued:

> *Yet southward must the sun now trace its course,*
> *Through mazes dark to lands of scorching death*
> *To find the master of the swift white horse*
> *And wrest from him the crossword speaker's breath.*

It had been centuries since I'd heard a prophecy in this form, yet I knew it well. I wished I could stop this recitation and save Meg the agony, but there was nothing I could do.

She shivered and exhaled the third stanza:

To westward palace must the Lester go;
Demeter's daughter finds her ancient roots.
The cloven guide alone the way does know,
To walk the path in thine own enemy's boots.

Then, the culminating horror, she spewed forth a rhyming couplet:

When three are known and Tiber reached alive,
'Tis only then Apollo starts to jive.

The dark smoke dissipated. I rushed forward as Meg slumped into my arms. Her breathing was already more regular, her skin warmer. Thank the Fates. The prophecy had been exorcised.

Leo was the first to speak. "What *was* that? Buy one prophecy, get three free? That was a lot of lines."

"It was a sonnet," I said, still in disbelief. "May the gods help us; it was a Shakespearean sonnet."

I had thought the limerick of Dodona was bad. But a full Shakespearean sonnet, complete with ABAB rhyme scheme, ending couplet, and iambic pentameter? Such a horror could only have come from Trophonius's cave.

I recalled my many arguments with William Shakespeare.

Bill, I said. *No one will accept this poetry! Du-DUH, du-DUH, du-DUH, du-DUH, du-DUH. What sort of beat is that?*

I mean, in real life, no one talks like that!

Hmm . . . actually the line I just wrote *was* in iambic pentameter. The stuff is infectious. Gah!

Thalia shouldered her bow. "That was all one poem? But it had four different sections."

"Yes," I said. "The sonnet conveys only the most elaborate prophecies, with multiple moving parts. None of them good, I fear."

Meg began to snore.

"We will parse our doom later," I said. "We should let Meg rest—"

My body chose that moment to give out. I had asked too much of it. Now it rebelled. I crumpled sideways, Meg spilling over on top of me. Our friends rushed forward. I felt myself being gently lifted, wondering hazily if I was peach-surfing or if Zeus had recalled me to the heavens.

Then I saw Josephine's face looming over me like a Mount Rushmore president as she carried me through the corridor.

"Infirmary for this one," she said to someone next to her. "And then . . . pee-yoo. He definitely needs a bath."

A few hours of dreamless sleep, followed by a bubble bath.

It was not Mount Olympus, my friends, but it was close.

By late afternoon, I was freshly dressed in clothes that weren't freezing and did not smell of cave excrement. My belly was full of honey and just-baked bread. I roamed the Waystation, helping out where I could. It was good to stay busy. It kept me from thinking too much about the lines of the Dark Prophecy.

Meg rested comfortably in a guest room, guarded vigilantly by Peaches, Peaches, and Other Peaches.

The Hunters of Artemis tended the wounded, who were

so numerous the Waystation had to double the size of its infirmary. Outside, Livia the elephant helped with cleanup, moving broken vehicles and wreckage from the roundabout. Leo and Josie spent the afternoon collecting pieces of Festus the dragon, who had been torn apart bare-handed, they told me, by Commodus himself. Fortunately, Leo seemed to find this more of an annoyance than a tragedy.

"Nah, man," he said when I offered my condolences. "I can put him back together easy enough. I redesigned him so he's like a Lego kit, built for quick assembly!"

He went back to helping Josephine, who was using a crane to extract Festus's left hind leg from the Union Station bell tower.

Calypso, in a burst of aerial magic, summoned enough wind spirits to reassemble the glass shards of the rose window, then promptly collapsed from the effort.

Sssssarah, Jamie, and Thalia Grace swept the surrounding streets, looking for any sign of Commodus, but the emperor had simply disappeared. I thought of how I'd saved Hemithea and Parthenos when they jumped off that cliff long ago, dissolving them into light. Could a quasi-deity such as Commodus do something like that to himself? Whatever the case, I had a suspicion that we hadn't seen the last of good old New Hercules.

At sunset I was asked to join a small family memorial for Heloise the griffin. The entire population of the Waystation would have come to honor her sacrifice, but Emmie explained that a large crowd would upset Abelard even worse than he already was. While Hunter Kowalski sat on egg duty in the henhouse (where Heloise's egg had been moved for safekeeping before the battle) I joined Emmie, Josephine, Georgie, and Calypso on the roof. Abelard, the grieving widower, watched in silence as Calypso and I— honorary relatives since our rescue mission to the zoo—laid the body of Heloise gently across a fallow bed of soil in the garden.

After death, griffins become surprisingly light. Their bodies desiccate when their spirits pass on, leaving only fur, feathers, and hollow bones. We stepped back as Abelard prowled toward the body of his mate. He ruffled his wings, then gently buried his beak in Heloise's neck plumage one last time. He threw back his head and let out a piercing cry—a call that said, *I am here. Where are you?*

Then he launched himself into the sky and disappeared in the low gray clouds. Heloise's body crumbled to dust.

"We'll plant catnip in this bed." Emmie wiped a tear from her cheek. "Heloise loved catnip."

Calypso dried her eyes on her sleeve. "That sounds lovely. Where did Abelard go?"

Josephine scanned the clouds. "He'll be back. He needs time. It'll be several more weeks before the egg hatches. We'll keep watch over it for him."

The idea of father and egg, alone in the world, made me unspeakably sad, yet I knew they had the most loving extended family they could hope for here at the Waystation.

During the brief ceremony, Georgina had been eyeing me warily, fiddling with something in her hands. A doll? I hadn't really been paying attention. Now Josephine patted her daughter's back.

"It's all right, baby," Josephine assured her. "Go ahead."

Georgina shuffled toward me. She was wearing a clean set of coveralls, which looked much better on her than they did on Leo. Newly washed, her brown hair was fluffier, her face pinker.

"My moms told me you might be my dad," she murmured, not meeting my eyes.

I gulped. Over the ages, I'd been through scenarios like this countless times, but as Lester Papadopoulos, I felt even more awkward than usual. "I—I might be, Georgina. I don't know."

"'Kay." She held up the thing she was holding—a figure made of pipe cleaners—and pressed it into my hands. "Made this for you. You can take it with you when you go away."

I examined the doll. It wasn't much, a sort of gingerbread-man silhouette of wire and rainbow fuzz, with a few beard whiskers stuck in the joints. . . . Wait. Oh, dear. This was the same little doll that had been smashed against Commodus's face. I supposed it must have fallen out when he charged toward the window.

"Thank you," I said. "Georgina, if you ever need me, if you ever want to talk—"

"No, I'm good." She turned and ran back to Josephine's arms.

Josephine kissed the top of her head. "You did fine, baby."

They turned and headed for the stairs. Calypso smirked at me, then followed, leaving me alone with Emmie.

For a few moments, we stood together in silence at the garden bed.

Emmie pulled her old silver Hunter's coat around her. "Heloise and Abelard were our first friends here, when we took over the Waystation."

"I'm so sorry."

Her gray hair glinted like steel in the sunset. Her wrinkles looked deeper, her face more worn and weary. How much longer would she live in this mortal life . . . another twenty years? The blink of an eye to an immortal. Yet I could no longer feel annoyed with her for giving up my gift of divinity. Artemis obviously had understood her choice. Artemis, who shunned all sorts of romantic love, saw that Emmie and Josephine deserved to grow old together. I had to accept that, too.

"You've built something good here, Hemithea," I said. "Commodus could not destroy it. You'll restore what you've lost. I envy you."

She managed a faint smile. "I never thought I'd hear those words from you, Lord Apollo."

Lord Apollo. The title did not fit me. It felt like a hat I'd worn centuries ago . . . something large and impractical and top-heavy like those Elizabethan chapeaus Bill Shakespeare used to hide his bald pate.

"What of the Dark Prophecy?" Emmie asked. "Do you know what it means?"

I watched a stray griffin feather tumble across the dirt. "Some. Not all. Perhaps enough to make a plan."

Emmie nodded. "Then we'd best gather our friends. We can talk at dinner. Besides"—she punched my arm gently— "those carrots aren't going to peel themselves."

41

Prophecies don't mix
With Tofurky and biscuits
Just give me dessert

MAY THE FATES consign all root vegetables to the depths of Tartarus.

That is all I will say on the matter.

By dinnertime, the main hall had been mostly put back together.

Even Festus, amazingly, had been more or less reconstructed. He was now parked on the roof, enjoying a large tub of motor oil and Tabasco sauce. Leo looked pleased with his efforts, though he was still searching for a few last missing parts. He'd spent the afternoon walking around the Waystation, shouting, "If anyone sees a bronze spleen about yea big, please let me know!"

The Hunters sat in groups around the hall, as was their habit, but they had integrated the newcomers we'd freed from Commodus's cells. Fighting side by side had created bonds of friendship.

Emmie presided at the head of the dining table. Georgina lay asleep in her lap, a stack of coloring books and markers in front of her. Thalia Grace sat at the other end, twirling her dagger on its point like a top. Josephine and Calypso were shoulder to shoulder, studying Calypso's notes and dis-cussing various interpretations of the prophetic lines.

I sat next to Meg. What else is new? She seemed fully recovered, thanks to Emmie's healing. (At my suggestion, Emmie had removed her enclosure of curative snakes from the infirmary while treating Meg. I feared if McCaffrey woke up and saw serpents, she might panic and turn them into chia pets.) Her three peach-spirit attendants had gone off, for now, to the extra-dimensional plane of fruit.

My young friend's appetite was even more voracious than usual. She shoveled in her Tofurky and dressing, her movements as furtive as if she'd gone back to being a half-feral alley child. I kept my hands well away from her.

At last, Josephine and Calypso looked up from the yel-low legal pad.

"Okay." Calypso let out a deep sigh. "We've interpreted some of these lines, but we need your help, Apollo. Maybe you could start by telling us what happened at the Cave of Trophonius."

I glanced at Meg. I was afraid if I recounted our horrible adventures, she might crawl under the table with her plate and snarl at us if we tried to get her out.

She merely belched. "Don't remember much. Go ahead."

I explained how I had collapsed the Cave of the Oracle at Trophonius's request. Josephine and Emmie did not look pleased, but they didn't yell or scream, either. Josephine's submachine gun stayed safely in its gun cabinet in the kitchen. I could only hope my father, Zeus, would react as calmly when he learned I'd destroyed the Oracle.

Emmie scanned the main hall. "Now that I think of

it, I haven't seen Agamethus since before the battle. Has anyone?"

No one reported sighting a headless orange ghost.

Emmie stroked her daughter's hair. "I don't mind the Oracle being destroyed, but I worry about Georgie. She's always felt connected to that place. And Agamethus . . . she likes him a lot."

I looked at the sleeping girl. I tried, for the millionth time, to see some resemblance to godly me, but it would have been easier to believe she was related to Lester Papadopoulos.

"The last thing I want," I said, "is to cause more pain to Georgina. I think, though, the destruction of the cave was necessary. Not just for us. But for her. It may free her to move forward."

I remembered the dark crayon drawings on the girl's wall, made in the throes of her prophetic lunacy. I hoped, perhaps, that by sending me away with that ugly pipe cleaner man, Georgie was attempting to send away her entire experience. With a few cans of pastel paint, Josephine and Emmie could now give her a fresh canvas of bedroom walls.

Emmie and Josephine exchanged a look. They seemed to come to silent agreement.

"All right, then," Josephine said. "About the prophecy . . ."

Calypso read the sonnet aloud. It sounded no more cheerful than it had before.

Thalia spun her knife. "The first stanza mentions the new moon."

"Time limit," Leo guessed. "Always a dang time limit."

"But the next new moon is in only five nights," Thalia said.

Trust a Hunter of Artemis to keep track of the phases of the moon.

No one jumped up and down in glee. No one shouted, *Hooray! Another catastrophe to stop in just five days!*

"*Bodies filling up the Tiber.*" Emmie hugged her daughter closer. "I assume the Tiber refers to the Little Tiber, the barrier of Camp Jupiter in California."

Leo frowned. "Yeah. The changeling lord . . . that's gotta be my homeboy Frank Zhang. And the Devil's Mount, that's Mount Diablo, right near the camp. I hate Mount Diablo. I fought Enchiladas there once."

Josephine looked like she wanted to ask what he meant, then wisely decided not to. "So the demigods of New Rome are about to be attacked."

I shivered, partly because of the words of the prophecy, partly because of the Tofurky gravy dribbling down Meg's chin. "I believe the first stanza is all of a piece. It mentions *the words that memory wrought.* Ella the harpy is at Camp Jupiter, using her photographic memory to reconstruct the lost books of the Cumaean Sybil."

Meg wiped her chin. "Huh?"

"The details aren't important right now." I gestured for her to continue eating. "My guess is that the Triumvirate means to eliminate the threat by burning down the camp. *The words that memory wrought are set to fire.*"

Calypso frowned. "Five days. How do we warn them in time? All our means of communication are down."

I found this irritating in the extreme. As a god, I could

have snapped my fingers and instantly sent a message across the world using the winds, or dreams, or a manifestation of my glorious self. Now, we were crippled. The only gods who had shown me any sort of favor were Artemis and Britomartis, but I couldn't expect them to do more—not without them incurring punishment as bad as what Zeus had done to me. I wouldn't wish that even on Britomartis.

As for mortal technology, it was useless to us. In our hands, phones malfunctioned and blew up (I mean, even more than they did for mortals). Computers melted down. I had considered pulling a random mortal off the street and saying, *Hey, make a call for me.* But who would they call? Another random person in California? How would the message get through to Camp Jupiter when most mortals couldn't *find* Camp Jupiter? Besides, even attempting this would put innocent mortals at risk of monster attacks, death by lightning bolt, and exorbitant data-plan overage fees.

I glanced at Thalia. "Can the Hunters cover that much ground?"

"In five days?" She frowned. "If we broke all the speed limits, perhaps. If we suffered no attacks along the way—"

"Which never happens," Emmie said.

Thalia laid her knife on the table. "The bigger problem is that the Hunters must continue their own quest. We have to find the Teumessian Fox."

I stared at her. I was tempted to ask Meg to order me to slap myself, just to make sure I wasn't stuck in a nightmare. "The Teumessian Fox? *That's* the monster you've been hunting?"

"Afraid so."

"But that's impossible! Also horrible!"

"Foxes are cute," Meg offered. "What's the problem?"

I was tempted to explain how many cities the Teumessian Fox had leveled in ancient times, how it gorged on the blood of its victims and ripped apart armies of Greek warriors, but I didn't want to ruin anyone's Tofurky dinner.

"The point is," I said, "Thalia's right. We cannot ask the Hunters to help us any more than they already have. They've got their own problem to solve."

"That's copacetic," Leo said. "You've done enough for us, T."

Thalia inclined her head. "All in a day's work, Valdez. But you do owe me a bottle of the Texas hot sauce you were telling me about."

"That can be arranged," Leo promised.

Josephine crossed her arms. "Well and good, but we're left with the same dilemma. How do we get a message to California in five days?"

"Me," Leo said.

We all stared at him.

"Leo," Calypso said. "It took us six weeks just to get here from New York."

"Yeah, but with three passengers," he said. "And . . . no offense, one of them was a former god who was attracting us all kinds of negative attention."

I could not argue with that. Most of the enemies who had attacked us on our journey had introduced themselves by screaming, *There's Apollo! Kill him!*

"I travel fast and light," Leo said. "I've covered that much distance before by myself. I can do it."

Calypso did not look pleased. Her complexion turned just a shade lighter than her yellow legal pad.

"Hey, *mamacita*, I'll come back," he promised. "I'll just enroll late for the spring semester! You can help me catch up on my homework."

"I hate you," she grumbled.

Leo squeezed her hand. "Besides, it'll be good to see Hazel and Frank again. And Reyna, too, though that girl still scares me."

I assumed Calypso was not *too* upset by this plan, since aerial spirits did not pick up Leo and hurl him through the rose window.

Thalia Grace gestured to the notepad. "So we've got one stanza figured out. Yippee. What about the rest?"

"I'm afraid," I said, "the rest is about Meg and me."

"Yep," Meg agreed. "Pass the biscuits?"

Josephine handed her the basket, then watched in awe as Meg stuffed her mouth with one fluffy biscuit after another.

"So the line about the sun going southward," Josephine said. "That's you, Apollo."

"Obviously," I agreed. "The third emperor must be somewhere in the American Southwest, in a *land of scorching death*. We get there through mazes—"

"The Labyrinth," Meg said.

I shuddered. Our last trip through the Labyrinth was still fresh in my mind—winding up in the caverns of Delphi, listening to my old enemy Python slithering and hissing right above our heads. I hoped this time, at least, Meg and I would not be bound together for a three-legged race.

"Somewhere in the Southwest," I continued, "we must find the crossword speaker. I believe that refers to the Erythraean Sybil, another ancient Oracle. I . . . I don't remember much about her—"

"Surprise," Meg grumbled.

"But she was known to issue her prophecies in acrostics— word puzzles."

Thalia winced. "Sounds bad. Annabeth told me how she met the Sphinx in the Labyrinth once. Riddles, mazes, puzzles . . . No thanks. Give me something I can shoot."

Georgina whimpered in her sleep.

Emmie kissed the girl's forehead. "And the third emperor?" she asked. "Do you know who it is?"

I turned over phrases of the prophecy in my mind— *master of the swift white horse.* That didn't narrow it down. Most Roman emperors liked to portray themselves as victorious generals riding their steeds through Rome. Something unsettled me about that third stanza: *to westward palace, in thine own enemy's boots.* I could not wrap my mental fingers around the answer.

"Meg," I said, "what about the line *Demeter's daughter finds her ancient roots?* Do you have any family in the Southwest? Do you remember ever going there before?"

She gave me a guarded look. "Nah."

Then she shoved another biscuit in her mouth like an act of rebellion: *Make me talk now, sucker.*

"Hey, though." Leo snapped his fingers. "That next line, *The cloven guide alone the way does know.* That means you get a satyr? They're guides, aren't they, like Coach Hedge was? That's, like, their thing."

"True," Josephine said. "But we haven't seen a satyr in these parts since—"

"Decades," Emmie finished.

Meg gulped down her wad o' carbs. "I'll find us one."

I scowled. "How?"

"Just will."

Meg McCaffrey, a girl of few words and much belching.

Calypso flipped to the next page of her notepad. "That just leaves the closing couplet: *When three are known and Tiber reached alive, / 'Tis only then Apollo starts to jive.*"

Leo snapped his fingers and began dancing in his seat. "About time, man. Lester needs more jive."

"Hmph." I did not feel like getting into that topic. I was still sore that Earth, Wind & Fire had rejected my audition in 1973 because I was jive-deficient. "I believe those lines mean we will soon know the identity of all three emperors. Once our next quest is complete in the Southwest, Meg and I can travel to Camp Jupiter, reaching the Tiber alive. Then, I hope, I can find the path back to my former glory."

"By . . . *jive talkin'*," Leo sang.

"Shut up," I grumbled.

No one offered any further interpretations of the sonnet. No one volunteered to take on my perilous quest duties for me.

"Well!" Josephine patted the dining table. "Who wants carrot cake with blowtorched meringue for dessert?"

The Hunters of Artemis left that night at moonrise.

As tired as I was, I felt the need to see them off. I found Thalia Grace in the roundabout, overseeing her Hunters as they saddled a herd of liberated combat ostriches.

"You trust them to ride?" I had thought only Meg McCaffrey was that crazy.

Thalia arched her eyebrows. "It's not their fault they were trained for combat. We'll ride them for a while, recondition them, then find a safe place to release them where they can live in peace. We're used to dealing with wild animals."

Already the Hunters had freed the ostriches from their helmets and razor wire. The steel fang implants had been removed from their beaks, making the birds look much more comfortable and (slightly) less murderous.

Jamie moved among the herd, stroking their necks and speaking to them in soothing tones. He was immaculate in his brown suit, completely unscathed from the morning's battle. His strange bronze hockey-stick weapon was nowhere to be seen. So the mysterious Olujime was a pit fighter, an accountant, a magical warrior, and an ostrich whisperer. Somehow I was not surprised.

"Is he going with you?" I asked.

Thalia laughed. "No. Just helping us get ready. Seems like a good guy, but I don't think he's Hunter material. He's not even, uh . . . a Greek-Roman type, is he? I mean, he's not a legacy of you guys, the Olympians."

"No," I agreed. "He is from a different tradition and parentage entirely."

Thalia's short spiky hair rippled in the wind, as if reacting to her uneasiness. "You mean from other gods."

"Of course. He mentioned the Yoruba, though I admit I know very little about their ways."

"How is that possible? Other pantheons of gods, side by side?"

I shrugged. I was often surprised by mortals' limited imaginations, as if the world was an *either/or* proposition. Sometimes humans seemed as stuck in their thinking as they were in their meat-sack bodies. Not, mind you, that gods were much better.

"How could it *not* be possible?" I countered. "In ancient times, this was common sense. Each country, sometimes each city, had its own pantheon of gods. We Olympians have always been used to living in close proximity to, ah . . . the competition."

"So you're the sun god," Thalia said. "But some other deity from some other culture is *also* the sun god?"

"Exactly. Different manifestations of the same truth."

"I don't get it."

I spread my hands. "Honestly, Thalia Grace, I don't know how to explain it any better. But surely you've been a demigod long enough to know: the longer you live, the weirder the world gets."

Thalia nodded. No demigod could argue with that statement.

"So listen," she said. "When you're out west, if you get to L.A., my brother Jason is there. He's going to school with his girlfriend, Piper McLean."

"I will check on them," I promised. "And send your love."

Her shoulder muscles unknotted. "Thanks. And if I talk to Lady Artemis . . ."

"Yes." I tried to swallow down the sob in my throat. Oh, how I missed my sister. "Give her my best."

She extended her hand. "Good luck, Apollo."

"To you as well. Happy foxhunting."

Thalia laughed bitterly. "I doubt it will be happy, but thanks."

The last I saw the Hunters of Artemis, they were trotting down South Illinois Street on a herd of ostriches, heading west as if chasing the crescent moon.

42

Pancakes for the road
Need a guide for your journey?
Check the tomatoes

THE NEXT MORNING, Meg kicked me awake. "Time to get going."

My eyelids fluttered open. I sat up, groaning. When you are the sun god, it's a rare treat to be able to sleep late. Now here I was, a mere mortal, and people kept waking me up at the crack of dawn. I'd spent millennia *being* the crack of dawn. I was tired of it.

Meg stood at my bedside in her pajamas and red high-tops (good gods, did she *sleep* in them?), her nose running as always, and a half-eaten green apple in her hand.

"I don't suppose you brought me breakfast?" I asked.

"I can throw this apple at you."

"Never mind. I'll get up."

Meg went off to take a shower. Yes, sometimes she actually did that. I dressed and packed as best I could, then headed to the kitchen.

While I ate my pancakes (yum), Emmie hummed and banged around in the kitchen. Georgina sat across from me coloring pictures, her heels kicking against her chair legs. Josephine stood at her welding station, happily fusing plates of sheet metal. Calypso and Leo—who refused to say good-bye to me on the assumption that we would all see each other soon—stood at the kitchen counter, arguing about what Leo should pack for his trip to Camp Jupiter and throwing bacon at each other. It all felt so cozy and homey, I wanted to volunteer to wash dishes if it meant getting to stay another day.

Lityerses sat down next to me with a large cup of coffee. His battle wounds had been mostly patched up, though his face still looked like the runway system at Heathrow Airport.

"I'll watch after them." He gestured at Georgina and her mothers.

I doubted Josephine or Emmie wanted to be "watched after," but I did not point that out to Lityerses. He would have to learn on his own how to adapt to this environment. Even I, the glorious Apollo, sometimes had to discover new things.

"I'm sure you'll do well here," I said. "I trust you."

He laughed bitterly. "I don't see why."

"We share common ground—we're both sons of overbearing fathers, and we've been misled and burdened by bad choices, but we're talented in our chosen ways."

"And good-looking?" He gave me a twisted smile.

"Naturally that. Yes."

He cupped his hands around his coffee. "Thank you. For the second chance."

"I believe in them. And third and fourth chances. But I only forgive each person once a millennium, so don't mess up for the next thousand years."

"I will keep that in mind."

Behind him, in the nearest hallway, I saw a flicker of ghostly orange light. I excused myself and went to say another difficult good-bye.

Agamethus hovered in front of a window overlooking the roundabout. His glowing tunic rippled in an ethereal wind. He pressed one hand against the windowsill as if holding himself in place. His other hand held the Magic 8 Ball.

"I'm glad you're still here," I said.

He had no face to read, but his posture seemed sad and resigned.

"You know what happened at the Cave of Trophonius," I guessed. "You know he is gone."

He bowed in acknowledgement.

"Your brother asked me to tell you he loves you," I said. "He is sorry about your fate.

"I want to apologize, too. When you died, I did not listen to Trophonius's prayer to save you. I felt you two deserved to face the consequences of that robbery. But this . . . this has been a very long punishment. Perhaps too long."

The ghost did not respond. His form flickered as if the ethereal wind was strengthening, pulling him away.

"If you wish," I said, "when I attain my godhood again, I will personally visit the Underworld. I will petition Hades to let your soul pass on to Elysium."

Agamethus offered me his 8 Ball.

"Ah." I took the sphere and shook it one last time. "What is your wish, Agamethus?"

The answer floated up through the water, a dense block

of words on the small white die face: I WILL GO WHERE I
MUST. I WILL FIND TROPHONIUS. TAKE CARE OF EACH OTHER, AS
MY BROTHER AND I COULD NOT.

He released his grip on the windowsill. The wind took
him, and Agamethus dissolved into motes in the sunlight.

The sun had risen by the time I joined Meg McCaffrey on
the roof of the Waystation.

She wore the green dress Sally Jackson had given her,
as well as her yellow leggings, now mended and clean. All
the mud and guano had been scrubbed from her high-tops.
On either side of her face, rainbow-colored pipe cleaners
twisted through her hair—no doubt a parting fashion gift
from Georgina.

"How do you feel?" I asked.

Meg crossed her arms and stared at Hemithea's tomato
patch. "Yeah. Okay."

By which I think she meant: *I just went insane and spewed
prophecies and almost died. How are you asking me this question and expecting me not to punch you?*

"So . . . what is your plan?" I asked. "Why the roof? If we
are seeking the Labyrinth, shouldn't we be on the ground
floor?"

"We need a satyr."

"Yes, but . . ." I looked around. I saw no goat men growing
in any of Emmie's planting beds. "How do you intend—?"

"Shhh."

She crouched next to the tomato plants and pressed her
hand against the dirt. The soil rumbled and began to heave
upward. For a moment, I feared a new karpos might burst

forth with glowing red eyes and a vocabulary that consisted entirely of *Tomatoes!*

Instead, the plants parted. The dirt rolled away, revealing the form of a young man sleeping on his side. He looked about seventeen, perhaps younger. He wore a black collarless jacket over a green shirt, and jeans much too baggy for his legs. Over his curly hair flopped a red knit cap. A scruffy goatee clung to his chin. At the tops of his sneakers, his ankles were covered in thick brown fur. Either this young man enjoyed shag-carpet socks, or he was a satyr passing for human.

He looked vaguely familiar. Then I noticed what he cradled in his arms—a white paper food bag from Enchiladas del Rey. Ah, yes. The satyr who enjoyed enchiladas. It had been a few years, but I remembered him now.

I turned to Meg in amazement. "This is one of the more *important* satyrs, a Lord of the Wild, in fact. How did you find him?"

She shrugged. "I just searched for the right satyr. Guess that's him."

The satyr woke with a start. "I didn't eat them!" he yelped. "I was just . . ." He blinked and sat up, a stream of potting soil trickling from his cap. "Wait . . . this isn't Palm Springs. Where am I?"

I smiled. "Hello, Grover Underwood. I am Apollo. This is Meg. And you, my lucky friend, have been summoned to lead us through the Labyrinth."

GUIDE TO APOLLO-SPEAK

Aegis   a shield used by Thalia Grace that has a fear-inducing image of Medusa on its front; it turns into a silver bracelet when she isn't using it

Aethiopian Bull   a giant, aggressive African bull whose red hide is impervious to all metal weapons

Agamethus   son of King Erginus; half brother of Trophonius, who decapitated him to avoid discovery after their raid on King Hyrieus's treasury

Amazon   a member of a tribe of warrior women

amphitheater   an oval or circular open-air space used for performances or sporting events, with spectator seating built in a semicircle around the stage

amphora   ceramic jar used to hold wine

Ares   the Greek god of war; the son of Zeus and Hera, and half brother to Athena

Artemis   the Greek goddess of the hunt and the moon; the daughter of Zeus and Leto, and the twin of Apollo

Asclepius   the god of medicine; son of Apollo; his temple was the healing center of ancient Greece

Athena   the Greek goddess of wisdom

Athenian   of the city of Athens, Greece

Atlas   a Titan; father of Calypso and Zoë Nightshade; he was condemned to hold up the sky for eternity after the war between the Titans and the Olympians; he tried unsuccessfully to trick Hercules into taking his place forever, but Hercules tricked him in return

blemmyae   a tribe of headless people with faces in their chests

Britomartis   the Greek goddess of hunting and fishing nets; her sacred animal is the griffin

Bruttia Crispina   a Roman Empress from 178 to 191 CE; she was married to future Roman Emperor Commodus when she was sixteen years old; after ten years of marriage, she was banished to Capri for adultery and later killed

Byzantium   an ancient Greek colony that later became Constantinople (now Istanbul)

caduceus   the traditional symbol of Hermes, featuring two snakes winding around an often winged staff

Calliope   the muse of epic poetry; mother of several sons, including Orpheus

Calypso   the goddess nymph of the mythical island of Ogygia; a daughter of the Titan Atlas; she detained the hero Odysseus for many years

Camp Half-Blood   the training ground for Greek demigods, located in Long Island, New York

Camp Jupiter   the training ground for Roman demigods, located between the Oakland Hills and the Berkeley Hills, in California

Carthaginian Serpent   a 120-foot snake that emerged

from the River Bagrada in North Africa to confront
Roman General Marcus Atilius Regulus and his troops
during the First Punic War

Cave of Trophonius   a deep chasm, home to the Oracle
Trophonius

centaur   a race of creatures that is half-human, half-horse

centicore (*see also* **yale**)   a fierce antelope-like creature
with large horns that can swivel in any direction

Chiron   a centaur; the camp activities director at Camp
Half-Blood

chiton   a Greek garment; a sleeveless piece of linen or
wool secured at the shoulders by brooches and at the
waist by a belt

Cloacina   goddess of the Roman sewer system

Colosseum   an elliptical amphitheater in the center of
Rome, Italy, capable of seating fifty thousand spectators;
used for gladiatorial contests and public spectacles; also
called the Flavian Amphitheater

Colossus Neronis (Colossus of Nero)   a gigantic bronze
statue of the Emperor Nero; was later transformed into
the sun god with the addition of a sunray crown

Commodus   Lucius Aurelius Commodus was the son of
Roman Emperor Marcus Aurelius; he became co-emperor
when he was sixteen and emperor at eighteen, when his
father died; he ruled from 177 to 192 CE and was mega-
lomaniacal and corrupt; he considered himself the New
Hercules and enjoyed killing animals and fighting gladiators at the Colosseum

Cretan   of the island of Crete

Cyclops (Cyclopes, pl.)   a member of a primordial race of giants, each with a single eye in the middle of his or her forehead

Daedalus   a skilled craftsman who created the Labyrinth on Crete in which the Minotaur (part man, part bull) was kept

daimon   Greek for *demon*; an intermediary spirit between mortals and the gods

Dambe   a centuries-old form of boxing associated with the Hausa people of West Africa

Danubian   bordering the Danube river in Europe

Daphne   a beautiful naiad who attracted Apollo's attention; she was transformed into a laurel tree in order to escape him

Delos   a Greek island in the Aegean Sea near Mykonos; birthplace of Apollo

Demeter   the Greek goddess of agriculture; a daughter of the Titans Rhea and Kronos

Demophon   the baby son of King Celeus, whom Demeter nursed and tried to make immortal as an act of kindness; brother of Triptolemus

Dionysus   the Greek god of wine and revelry; the son of Zeus

Dionysus Festival   a celebration held in Athens, Greece, to honor the god Dionysus, the central events of which were theatrical performances

Doors of Death   the doorway to the House of Hades, located in Tartarus; doors have two sides—one in the mortal world, and one in the Underworld

elomìíràn   the Yoruba word for *others*

Elysium   the paradise to which Greek heroes were sent when the gods gave them immortality

Erythaea   an island where the Cumaean Sibyl, a love interest of Apollo, originally lived before he convinced her to leave it by promising her a long life

Eubouleus   son of Demeter and Karmanor; the Greek god of swineherds

Fields of Punishment   the section of the Underworld where people who were evil during their lives are sent to face eternal punishment for their crimes after death

Flavian   the Flavians were an imperial dynasty that ruled the Roman Empire between 69 and 96 CE

Gaea   the Greek earth goddess; wife of Ouranos; mother of Titans, giants, Cyclopes, and other monsters

Ganymede   a divine hero from Troy whom Zeus abducted to serve as his cupbearer in Olympus

Germani (**Germanus**, sing.)   tribal people who settled to the west of the Rhine river

Gidigbo   a form of wrestling that involves head-butting, from the Yoruba of Nigeria, Africa

gloutos   Greek for *buttocks*

Gorgons   three monstrous sisters (Stheno, Euryale, and Medusa) who have hair of living, venomous snakes; Medusa's eyes can turn the beholder to stone

Greek fire   an incendiary weapon used in naval battles because it can continue burning in water

griffin   a winged creature with the head of an eagle and the body of a lion; the sacred animal of Britomartis

Grove of Dodona   the site of the oldest Greek Oracle, second only to Delphi in importance; the rustling of trees in the grove provided answers to priests and priestesses who journeyed to the site

Hades   the Greek god of death and riches; ruler of the Underworld

harpy   a winged female creature that snatches things

Hausa   a language spoken in northern Nigeria and Niger; also the name of a people

Hecate   goddess of magic and crossroads

Hemithea   teenage daughter of King Staphylus of Naxos; sister of Parthenos; Apollo made her and her sister divine to save them when they jumped off a cliff to escape their father's rage

Hephaestus   the Greek god of fire and crafts and of blacksmiths; the son of Zeus and Hera, and married to Aphrodite

Hera   the Greek goddess of marriage; Zeus's wife and sister; Apollo's stepmother

Heracles   the Greek equivalent of Hercules; the son of Zeus and Alcmene; the strongest of all mortals

Hercules   the Roman equivalent of Heracles; the son of Jupiter and Alcmene, who was born with great strength

Hermes   Greek god of travelers; guide to spirits of the dead; god of communication

Hessian mercenaries   the approximately thirty thousand German troops hired by the British to help fight during the American Revolution when they found it too difficult to recruit their own soldiers

hippocampi (**hippocampus**, sing.) half-horse, half-fish creatures

Hunters of Artemis a group of maidens loyal to Artemis and gifted with hunting skills and eternal youth as long as they reject men for life

Hyacinthus a Greek hero and Apollo's lover, who died while trying to impress Apollo with his discus skills

ichor the golden fluid that is the blood of gods and immortals

ìgboyà the Yoruba word for *confidence, boldness,* and *bravery*

Imperial gold a rare metal deadly to monsters, consecrated at the Pantheon; its existence was a closely guarded secret of the emperors

Iris the Greek goddess of the rainbow, and a messenger of the gods

Julius Caesar a Roman politician and general who became a dictator of Rome, turning it from a republic into the Roman Empire

Karmanor a minor Greek harvest god; a local deity in Crete who married Demeter; together they had a son, Eubouleus, who became the god of swineherds

karpoi (**karpos**, sing.) grain spirits

Kronos the youngest of the twelve Titans; the son of Ouranos and Gaea; the father of Zeus; he killed his father at his mother's bidding; Titan lord of fate, harvest, justice, and time

Labyrinth an underground maze originally built on the island of Crete by the craftsman Daedalus to hold the Minotaur

Lethe the Greek word for *forgetfulness*; the name of a river in the Underworld whose waters caused forgetfulness; the name of a Greek spirit of oblivion

Leto   mother of Artemis and Apollo with Zeus; goddess of motherhood

Little Tiber   the barrier of Camp Jupiter

Lityerses   the son of King Midas; he challenged people to harvesting contests and beheaded those he beat, earning him the nickname "Reaper of Men"

Marcus Aurelius   Roman Emperor from 161 to 180 CE; father of Commodus; considered the last of the "Five Good Emperors"

Marsyas   a satyr who lost to Apollo after challenging him in a musical contest, which led to Marsyas being flayed alive

melomakarona   Greek Christmas honey cookies

Midas   a king with the power to transform anything he touched to gold; Lityerses's father; he selected Marsyas as the winner in the musical contest between Apollo and Marsyas, resulting in Apollo giving Midas the ears of a donkey

Minotaur   the half-man, half-bull son of King Minos of Crete; the Minotaur was kept in the Labyrinth, where he killed people who were sent in; he was finally defeated by Theseus

Mnemosyne   Titan goddess of memory; daughter of Ouranos and Gaea

Mount Olympus   home of the Twelve Olympians

Mount Othrys   a mountain in central Greece; the Titans' base during the ten-year war between the Titans and the Olympians

myrmeke   a large antlike creature that poisons and para-
lyzes its prey before eating it; known for protecting
various metals, particularly gold

Narcissus   a hunter known for his beauty; the son of the
river god Cephissus and the nymph Liriope; he was
vain, arrogant, and disdainful of admirers; he fell in love
with his own reflection; Narcissus was also the name
of Commodus's personal trainer and wrestling partner,
who drowned the emperor in his bathtub—these were
two different Narcissuses

Nemean Lion   a large, vicious lion that plagued Nemea in
Greece; its pelt was impervious to all human weapons;
Hercules strangled it with his bare hands

Nero   ruled as Roman Emperor from 54 to 58 CE; he had his
mother and his first wife put to death; many believe he
was responsible for setting a fire that gutted Rome, but
he blamed the Christians, whom he burned on crosses;
he built an extravagant new palace on the cleared land
and lost support when construction expenses forced
him to raise taxes; he committed suicide

Nine Muses   Greek goddesses of literature, science, and the
arts, who have inspired artists and writers for centuries

nymph   a female nature deity who animates nature

Oceanus   the eldest son of Ouranos and Gaea; the Titan
god of the sea

Ogygia   the island home—and prison—of the nymph
Calypso

Oracle of Delphi   a speaker of the prophecies of Apollo

Oracle of Trophonius   a Greek who was transformed

into an Oracle after his death; located at the Cave of Trophonius; known for terrifying those who seek him

Orion a giant huntsman who was the most loyal and valued of Artemis's attendants until he was slain by a scorpion

Ouranos the Greek personification of the sky; husband of Gaea; father of the Titans

Pan the Greek god of the wild; the son of Hermes

Parthenos teenage daughter of King Staphylus of Naxos; sister of Hemithea; Apollo made her and her sister divine to save them when they jumped off a cliff to escape their father's rage

Peloponnese a large peninsula and geographic region in southern Greece, separated from the northern part of the country by the Gulf of Corinth

Persephone the Greek queen of the Underworld; wife of Hades; daughter of Zeus and Demeter

podex Latin for *anus*

Poseidon the Greek god of the sea; son of the Titans Kronos and Rhea, and brother of Zeus and Hades

Potina a Roman goddess of children, who watches over what they are drinking

praetor an elected Roman magistrate and commander of the army

Primordial Chaos the first thing ever to exist; the miasma from which the Fates wove the future; a void from which the first gods were produced

princeps prince of Rome; the early emperors used this title for themselves

Python a monstrous serpent that Gaea appointed to guard the Oracle at Delphi

River Styx the river that forms the boundary between earth and the Underworld

satyr a Greek forest god, part goat and part man

Sibyl a prophetess

Sibylline Books a collection of prophecies in rhyme written in Greek

Sparta a city-state in ancient Greece with military dominance

spatha a long sword used by Roman cavalry units

Staphylus king of Naxos, Greece; a demigod son of Dionysus; father of Hemithea and Parthenos

Styx a powerful water nymph; the eldest daughter of the sea Titan, Oceanus; goddess of the Underworld's most important river; goddess of hatred; the River Styx is named after her

Suburra an area of the city of Rome that was crowded and lower-class

Tantalus a king who fed the gods a stew made of his own sons; he was sent to the Underworld, where his curse was to be stuck in a pool of water under a fruit tree but never be able to drink or eat

Tartarus husband of Gaea; spirit of the abyss; father of the giants; the lowest part of the Underworld

Teumessian Fox a giant fox sent by the gods to ravage the city of Thebes in punishment for a crime; the beast was destined never to be caught

Three Fates Even before there were gods there were the Fates: Clotho, who spins the thread of life; Lachesis, the measurer, who determines how long a life will be; and Atropos, who cuts the thread of life with her shears

Three Mile Island   a nuclear power plant near Harrisburg, Pennsylvania, where, on March 28, 1979, there was a partial meltdown in reactor number 2, causing public concern

Throne of Memory   Mnemosyne carved this chair, in which a petitioner would sit after visiting the Cave of Trophonius and receiving bits of verse from the Oracle; once seated in the chair, the petitioner would recount the verses, the priests would write them down, and they would become a prophecy

Tiber River   the third-longest river in Italy; Rome was founded on its banks; in ancient Rome, executed criminals were thrown into the river

Titan War   the epic ten-year battle between the Titans and the Olympians that resulted in the Olympians taking the throne

Titans   a race of powerful Greek deities, descendants of Gaea and Ouranos, that ruled during the Golden Age and were overthrown by a race of younger gods, the Olympians

Triptolemus   son of King Celeus and brother of Demophon; a favorite of Demeter; he became the inventor of the plow and agriculture

trireme   a Greek warship, having three tiers of oars on each side

triumvirate   a political alliance formed by three parties

Trojan War   According to legend, the Trojan War was waged against the city of Troy by the Achaeans

(Greeks) after Paris of Troy took Helen from her husband, Menelaus, king of Sparta

Trophonius   demigod son of Apollo, designer of Apollo's temple at Delphi, and spirit of the Dark Oracle; he decapitated his half brother Agamethus to avoid discovery after their raid on King Hyrieus's treasury

Troy   a Roman city situated in modern-day Turkey; site of the Trojan War

Underworld   the kingdom of the dead, where souls go for eternity; ruled by Hades

Via Appia   the Appian Way, one of the first and most important roads of the ancient Roman republic; after the Roman army subdued the revolt led by Spartacus in 73 BC, they crucified more than six thousand slaves and lined the road for 130 miles with their bodies

yale   (*see also* **centicore**) a fierce antelope-like creature with large horns that can swivel in any direction

Yoruba   one of the three largest ethnic groups in Nigeria, Africa; also a language and a religion of the Yoruba people

Zeus   the Greek god of the sky and the king of the gods

Zoë Nightshade   a daughter of Atlas who was exiled and later joined the Hunters of Artemis, becoming the loyal lieutenant of Artemis

PRAISE FOR RICK RIORDAN

Percy Jackson and the Olympians

The Lightning Thief
"Perfectly paced, with electrifying moments
chasing each other like heartbeats."
—*The New York Times Book Review*

The Sea of Monsters
★ "In a feat worthy of his heroic subjects, Riordan crafts
a sequel stronger than his compelling debut."
—*Publishers Weekly* (starred review)

The Titan's Curse
"All in all, a winner of Olympic proportions."
—*School Library Journal*

The Battle of the Labyrinth
★ "Look no further for the next Harry Potter; meet
Percy Jackson, as legions of fans already have."
—*Kirkus Reviews* (starred review)

The Last Olympian
"The hordes of young readers who have devoured Rick Riordan's
books ... will no doubt gulp down this concluding volume as
greedily as they would a plateful of ambrosia, or maybe pizza."
—*The Wall Street Journal*

The Heroes of Olympus

Book One: The Lost Hero

"Percy Jackson fans can rest easy: this first book in Riordan's Heroes of Olympus spin-off series is a fast-paced adventure with enough familiar elements to immediately hook those eager to revisit his modern world of mythological mayhem. Rotating among his three protagonists, Riordan's storytelling is as polished as ever, brimming with wit, action, and heart—his devotees won't be disappointed."

—*Publishers Weekly*

"With appealing new characters within a familiar framework, this spin-off will satisfy the demand for more."

—*Booklist*

"Riordan excels at clever plot devices and at creating an urgent sense of cliff-hanging danger. His interjection of humor by incongruous juxtaposition . . . provides some welcome relief. The young heroes deal with issues familiar to teens today: Who am I? Can I live up to the expectations of others? Having read the first series is helpful but not essential, and the complex plot is made for sequels."

—*School Library Journal*

"Riordan extends the franchise in a logical direction while maximizing the elements that made the first series so popular: irreverent heroes, plenty of tension-filled moments fighting monsters, and authentic classical mythology mixed in with modern life. Completely in control of pacing and tone, he balances a faultless comic banter against deeper notes that reveal the characters' vulnerabilities. With Percy Jackson slated to make an appearance in later volumes, fans nostalgic for the old books should find in this new series everything they've been pining for."

—*Horn Book*

Percy Jackson's Greek Gods

"Percy's gift, which is no great secret, is to breathe new life into the gods. Closest attention is paid to the Olympians, but Riordan has a sure touch when it comes to fitting much into a small space—as does Rocco's artwork, which smokes and writhes on the page as if hit by lightning. . . . The inevitable go-to for Percy's legions of fans who want the stories behind his stories."
—*Kirkus Reviews*

"The age-old stories are endlessly strong, resonant, and surprising, while the telling here is fresh, irreverent, and amusing. A must-have for the Percy Jackson canon."
—*Booklist*

Percy Jackson's Greek Heroes

". . . the most voluble of Poseidon's many sons dishes on a dozen more ancient relatives and fellow demigods. Riordan leavens full, refreshingly tart accounts of the ups and downs of such higher-profile heroes as Theseus, Orpheus, Hercules, and Jason with the lesser-known but often equally awesome exploits of such butt-kicking ladies as Atalanta, Otrera (the first Amazon), and lion-wrestling Cyrene. The breezy treatment effectively blows off . . . the dust obscuring the timeless themes in each hero's career."
—*Kirkus Reviews*

"Written in the voice of Percy Jackson, these ancient stories sound fresh and vital. Like its predecessor, this large, handsome tome . . . will fly off library shelves."
—*Booklist*

The Kane Chronicles

Book One: The Red Pyramid

★ "The first volume in the Kane Chronicles, this fantasy adventure delivers what fans loved about the Percy Jackson and the Olympians series: young protagonists with previously unsuspected magical powers, a riveting story marked by headlong adventure, a complex background rooted in ancient mythology, and wry, witty twenty-first-century narration."

—*Booklist* (starred review)

"This tale explodes into action from chapter one. . . . Readers pining for Percy Jackson will find new heroes in Carter and Sadie Kane."

—*Kirkus Reviews*

★ "A truly original take on Egyptian mythology . . .
A must-have book."

—*School Library Journal* (starred review)

"Once again, Riordan masterfully meshes modern life with mythology and history, reinvigorating dusty artifacts such as the Rosetta stone and revitalizing ancient Egyptian story lines."

—*The Los Angeles Times*

Magnus Chase and the Gods of Asgard

Book One: The Sword of Summer

"Rick Riordan's new series is simply brilliant—maybe his best yet! I thought I knew Norse mythology, but now that I've read the gripping and hilarious *Sword of Summer*, I'll never see Thor the same way again. Get ready to stay up all night reading!"

—*New York Times* #1 best-selling author Harlan Coben

"*The Sword of Summer* is a propulsive, kinetic, witty rebooting of Norse mythology with all the charm of the Percy Jackson novels. Instantly likeable heroes! Insane action! Cool villains! A twisting, turning, always exciting story! Rick Riordan does it again, even better."

—*New York Times* best-selling author Michael Grant

"*The Sword of Summer* combines the glory of Norse myth with the joy of Rick Riordan's effervescent world-building. One of Riordan's funniest books—everything from the chapter titles to the wry humor of Magnus Chase will have you chuckling; even as the plot races along at breakneck speed. Check me into the Hotel Valhalla, please. I'll be staying."

—*New York Times* #1 best-selling author Cassandra Clare

"With an epic plot, engaging (and diverse) characters, and tones of wisecracking humor, Riordan's latest is a page-turner. Those new to the author's past series can jump right in; fans of his previous works will be happy to see clever nods and references to the other in-universe books."

—*School Library Journal*

"[A] whirlwind of myth, action, and wry sarcasm, perfect for readers hungry for a new hit of that Percy Jackson–type magic."

—*Horn Book*

"Riordan offers a terrific cast that is effortlessly diverse—all of the allies stand as independent, well-constructed characters who each bring entirely different skills, histories, interests, and personalities to the group. Riordan fans will be thrilled, and Norse mythology buffs will be pleased to see that his focus has shifted to their faves."

—*Bulletin of the Center for Children's Books*

ABOUT THE AUTHOR

RICK RIORDAN, dubbed "storyteller of the gods" by *Publishers Weekly*, is the author of five *New York Times* #1 best-selling series. He is best known for his Percy Jackson and the Olympians books, which bring Greek mythology to life for contemporary readers. He expanded on that series with two more: the Heroes of Olympus and the Trials of Apollo, which cleverly combine Greek and Roman gods and heroes with his beloved modern characters. Rick also tackled the ancient Egyptian gods in the magic-filled Kane Chronicles trilogy, and Norse mythology in the otherworldly Magnus Chase and the Gods of Asgard series. Millions of fans across the globe have enjoyed his fast-paced and funny quest adventures as well as his two #1 best-selling myth collections, *Percy Jackson's Greek Gods* and *Percy Jackson's Greek Heroes*. Rick lives in Boston, Massachusetts, with his wife and two sons. For more information, go to www.rickriordan.com, or follow him on Twitter @camphalfblood.

COMING IN SPRING 2018

THE TRIALS OF APOLLO

◄ 3 ►

THE BURNING MAZE